THE

Aeneid
Vergil

TRANSLATED BY SARAH RUDEN

YALE UNIVERSITY PRESS / NEW HAVEN & LONDON

WARMEST THANKS TO THE CLASSICS DEPARTMENTS OF SWARTHMORE
COLLEGE AND THE UNIVERSITY OF PENNSYLVANIA

Designed by Nancy Ovedovitz and set
in Galliard Oldstyle by The Composing
Room of Michigan, Inc.

The Library of Congress has cataloged
the hardcover edition as follows:

Virgil.
[Aeneis. English]
The Aeneid / Vergil ; translated by
Sarah Ruden.

p. cm.

ISBN 978-0-300-11904-6 (alk. paper)
1. Epic poetry, Latin—Translations
into English. 2. Aeneas (Legendary
character)—Poetry. 3. Legends—
Rome—Poetry. I. Ruden, Sarah.
II. Title.

PA6807.A5R83 2008
873'.01—dc22

2008001328

ISBN 978-0-300-15141-1 (pbk.)

A catalogue record for this book is
available from the British Library.

10   9   8   7   6   5   4

THE AENEID

CONTENTS

I am in awe of scholars who can expertly debate Vergil's political purpose and attitude; I find him difficult just to read. In part, I blame the half-finished state of his epic: only twelve out of the projected twenty-four books exist, and many lines are two- or three-word fragments. Some full lines (the translations of which I bracket) were obviously misplaced, either by Vergil or by a scribe struggling with the text. We have a reliable report that Vergil was unhappy with the draft, and I am grouchily convinced that this was not only on aesthetic grounds but also on those of clarity. There is certainly enough learned help, starting with the commentator Servius in the fourth century, for exploring the probable meanings of phrases. But a typical translator (like me) has neither the time nor the expertise to satisfy herself on every point and works with only one edition and a few commentaries: I concentrated on R. D. Williams' well-respected text with basic notes.

Yet line-by-line interpretation is, I think, the least of the challenges. The greatest is Vergil's particular, culminating version of Roman epic style. He relentlessly repeats certain strong words: *fatum* (fate), *numen* (divine power/will), *caelum* (heaven/sky), *flamma* (flame), *dextra* (the right hand, given in pledge), *genus* (family/birth), *ferox* (fierce), *furor* (frenzy), *ruere* (to rush headlong), and *agmen* (battle line), to name a few that I have given up trying to get out of my head. One of his favorite words is *ingens* (immense/boundless), often giving a sense of the surroundings—sometimes of the whole universe—uncontrollably swooping in: at sea, on the battlefield, and even in the boundlessly ambitious creations of civilizations at peace.

Whereas the vocabulary is plain and powerful, the word order is extremely artful yet manages to enhance the power of the words. When the target language is English, with its strict word-order rules, to approach Vergil's effects is beyond fantasy, but monotony is well within reach. I could have rendered each Latin word with the same English word again and again (sometimes a Latin word is repeated within three lines!), but this would have yielded dull and lazy-looking English. I had to vary the vocabulary; the only question was how. A basic policy of mine was to choose—as far as meter allowed—the strongest words for my variations: Anglo-Saxon rather than Latinate, short and hard-sounding and sometimes colloquial. I favored *huge,* for example, over *immense,* and *hard* over *difficult.*

I also had to vary the word order as much as possible, within some approximation of Vergil's alien hexameter (a six-foot and up to seventeen-syllable verse line). In Classical Latin meter was based on the length of syllables, not on stress accents, as in English. That is, a syllable with a long vowel, or ending in two consonants, was drawn out, and the differing amount of time spent on long and short syllables created the metrical pattern. But at the same time the Latin language was stress-accented, as English is. One result in Latin verse is a frequent contrast between the length of the syllables and their stress. The impression—strikingly so in Vergil—is one of struggle and conflict. For a translator trying to get this across in English, there seems to be no hope aside from a pounding traditional meter. But pound too hard, and you get doggerel, as in Edgar Allan Poe: "Quaff, oh quaff this kind nepenthe and forget this lost Lenore!" Pervert word order too, and you can get super-doggerel, as in William McGonagall: "For the stronger we our houses do build, / The less chance we have of being killed." Given these demands and dangers, I chose iambic pentameter for its archetypal literary character, its flexibility, and its friendliness to natural English sentence rhythms. But it was hardly an original choice; I have lots of company among Vergil translators.

In the number and the violence of his enjambments, Vergil offers his translators another difficulty. Perhaps it is not pure critical pretension to ask whether the common and commonly startling spillovers of sentences from one line to the next correspond to the burgeoning emotions of the characters, or whether perhaps they are a stylistic representation of the amazing amount of boundary crossing in the narrative. I have reproduced enjambments wherever I could, but Anglo-American poetic taste in this connection is fairly stringent. Though making exceptions for emergencies, I took as a ready reminder of what is allowed two lines of A. E. Housman's that I particularly like: "It looked like a toad, and it looked so because / A toad was the actual object it was." I sensed that I could go as far as ending a line with a subordinating conjunction, but that I needed to think hard before—for example—splitting between two lines a noun and adjective that would be adjacent in prose, as Vergil does at 2.213–14: there the serpent is eating Laocoön's two sons and *small* and *bodies* appear in separate lines.

At the same time, it was necessary to keep in mind what those lines exemplify—that Vergil's enjambments can be quite blunt in their significance, forming part of the narrative. In 1.114–16, to take another instance, he writes, "excutitur pronusque magister / volvitur in caput," which means (more or less) "is thrown out and forward the helmsman / is whirled onto his head." This is one place where enjambment works in English: "and whirled the helmsman out / head first."

My greatest fear, while I sorted through my various options, was of cheating the reader of content, especially in the roiling masses of images, emotions, thoughts, and identities that are Vergil's battle scenes. But depicting the role of culture and institutions faithfully is the toughest thing of all in a metrical translation, as here the corresponding words may not even exist in English. The Latin *fas,* for example, has a strong religious tinge, but "right," which is perhaps the best brief English equivalent, has a more civic color for us. I could have made the difference clear to the reader had I always used a whole line to translate the one word. But sometimes I had only a couple of syllables to work with because my translation is line for line.

Many metrical translations of Vergil simply take as much space as they need, using hundreds more lines than Vergil did. Not mine. (But I could not achieve a precise overlay; I sometimes had to swap the content of entire successive lines to avoid bizarre sentence structure in English.) Why? Classical Latin isn't friendly to such an approach, and not just because of the cultural distance, which makes brevity a challenge. Latin is an inflected language, packing bulky collections of concepts into few words by shoving these words into different shapes. For example, in the Twelve Tables of early Roman law, the sentence "Si in ius vocat, ito" is hard to translate more succinctly than "If a man is summoned to court, he must go." To use, in translating, twice as many words as appear in the original is typical; in poetry translated line for line, the pressure for parity in number of words can lead either to torturous decisions about which details to let go or—as I prefer—to attempts at compression on the scale of those little foam-rubber pellets that you can buy in museum gift shops: put them in water, and they turn into respectable-sized toy dinosaurs.

Some translators choose to skip over the entire set of verse problems and work in prose, using as many long phrases as needed to translate each line. But I think that correspondence in form is vital to authentic rendering, especially of Greek and Roman poetry. Nonmetrical poetry would have been inconceivable to the ancients. Their metrical rules were strict and complex. Lyric poetry was actually sung, the epic hexameter probably semi-musically chanted. In prose, I would have been tempted, in the typical way of a modern thinker, to squeeze out all the plausible meanings of Vergil's juicy lines, dilute them with my own explanatory verbiage, and offer a watery drink without much actual flavor of the *Aeneid* left.

I also believe that it is useful for the translating to be hard, for a translator to go through a little of the kind of technical struggle that the author went through in composing the original—especially in the case of Vergil, who is said to have written only a couple of lines a day. In writing fiction you should work to get into your characters' minds; in translating you should work to get into your author's, and an attempt to keep as close as possible to his style is one way to do this.

In creating a line-by-line, metrical translation, I reached a sort of lowland view of the great controversy about Vergil's "real" attitude toward Roman imperialism. I think it was somewhat like his attitude toward poetry. Conquest, settlement, and composition, done in ways that make the results last, are alike in taking a great deal out of you (not to mention others). Before the end, you will be sick of it all—as Vergil on his deathbed clamored for his manuscript to be burned, and as Aeneas during a storm yearns to be a corpse among the others in the Simois River outside Troy rather than an aspiring colonist. But the question of whether the task is ultimately "worth it" feels rather empty. Have human beings ever had a choice about struggling for land, livelihood, and security for the next generation? We would be an extinct species if we didn't do this, by proxy if not directly. It is particularly strange for present-day Americans to offer pious criticisms of Vergil's praise of imperialism, praise which is blended with forthright sorrow over necessity, and not to see that the tragedies and failures he depicts come mainly from characters being alive and belonging to society. There is no divine pontification, as in Homer, about mortals willfully making life worse for themselves. In Vergil, hardly any person behaves that way, but nearly everybody is still in for it. Several miscalculate, several are instruments or victims of divine rage or intrigue, but the only crudely, independently, steadily evil human I find is Ulysses— who is more of a reputation, a bogeyman in the background, than a character in the story. A few idiots like Misenus and boastful warriors flash on the screen, signals that someone whose plight a Greek tragedy might mull over for a thousand lines or more is a mere nonstarter in the endurance contest for control of the future of Italy.

Similarly, human beings appear to have no choice but to strive for beautiful, orderly explanations of the ugly things we do. These explanations may also represent a basic drive—and in one way a more painful one. We have chances to get land, livelihood, and security for the next generation, pretty much in the forms we imagined or even better, though the cost will be high. We cannot match in reality our vision of what we need to create from our minds. Vergil couldn't, and I certainly couldn't in my efforts to translate his glorious poem.

I

Arms and a man I sing, the first from Troy, *   *Ilium*
A fated exile to Lavinian shores
In Italy. On land and sea, divine will—
And Juno's unforgetting rage—harassed him.   *Queen of Gods*
War racked him too, until he set his city   5
And gods in Latium. There his Latin race rose,   *Latium's Kingdom*
With Alban patriarchs, and Rome's high walls.   *pre-Roman*   *Italy*
Muse, tell me why. What stung the queen of heaven,   *Trojans in Italy.*
What insult to her power made her drive
This righteous hero through so many upsets   10
And hardships? Can divine hearts know such anger?
Carthage, an ancient Tyrian settlement,   *Dido's city   N. Africa*
Faces the Tiber's mouth in far-off Italy;   *Phoenocian Island*
Rich, and experienced and fierce in war.   *City/Dido*
They say that it was Juno's favorite, second   15
Even to Samos. Carthage held her weapons,   *Aegeon Island*
Her chariot. From the start she planned that Carthage
Would rule the world—if only fate allowed!

But she had heard that one day Troy's descendants
Would pull her Tyrian towers to the ground. 20
A war-proud race with broad domains would come
To cut down Africa. The Fates ordained it.
Saturn's child feared this. She recalled the war   *Juno*
That she had fought at Troy for her dear Greeks—
And also what had caused her savage anger. 25
Deep in her heart remained the verdict given
By Paris, and his insult to her beauty,   *Trojan prince / adultery*
And the rape and privileges of Ganymede—   *w/ Helen / caused*
Trojan Prince / Trojan War
A Trojan. In her rage, she kept from Italy
Those spared by cruel Achilles and the Greeks.   *Greatest Greek warrior* 30
@ Troy / Killed Hector
They tossed on endless seas, went wandering,
Fate-driven, year on year around the world's seas.
$+$ It cost so much to found the Roman nation.

Sicily fell from sight. They sailed with joy
Into the open, bronze prows churning foam. 35
But Juno, with her deep, unhealing heart-wound,
Muttered, "Will I give up? Have I been beaten
In keeping Italy from the Trojan king?
Fate blocks me. But then why could Pallas burn   *Minerva*
The Argive fleet and drown the men it carried,   *Greeks* 40
Only to punish Ajax' frenzied crime?   *Warrior for Greece*
Iraped Cassandra
Out of the clouds she hurled Jove's hungry fire,   *Jupiter*
Scattered the ships and overturned the sea.
Ajax, panting his life out, pierced with flame,
She whirled away and pinioned on a sharp rock. 45
But I, parading as the queen of heaven,
Jupiters Jove's wife and sister, fight a single people
For years. Will anybody now beseech me,
Bow to me, and put presents on my altar?"
Her heart aflame with all of this, the goddess 50
Went to Aeolia, land of storm clouds, teeming
With wild winds. There King Aeolus rules a vast cave   *Master of winds*

That struggling winds and howling tempests fill.
He disciplines them, chains them in their prison.
They shriek with rage around the bolted doors;   55
The mountain echoes. Seated on a pinnacle,
Aeolus holds a scepter, checks their anger—
Without him, they would seize land, sea, and deep sky
To carry with them in their breakneck flight.
Fearing this, the almighty father shut them   60
In that black cave and heaped high mountains on it,
And set a ruler over them to slacken
Or pull the reins in, strict in his control.
Juno approached him now and made this plea:
"The king of men and father of the gods   65
Gives you the right to rouse and soothe the waves.
A race I hate sails the Tyrrhenian sea,
Bringing Troy's beaten gods to Italy.
Goad your winds into fury, swamp the ships,
Or scatter them, strew bodies on the water.   70
Fourteen voluptuous nymphs belong to me,
And the most beautiful is Deiopea.
Her I will make your own, in steadfast union,
If you will help me. She will spend her life
With you—the lovely children that you'll father!"   75
Aeolus said, "You merely must decide,
My sovereign. I must hurry to obey.
My power, my modest kingdom, and Jove's favor
You brought me. I recline at the gods' banquets,
I rule the stormy clouds because of you."   80
With his upended spear he struck a flank
Of the hollow mountain. Like a battle charge,
The winds pour out. They spiral through the world—
The East and South gales, and the mass of whirlwinds
From Africa swoop down, uproot the sea,   85
And send enormous billows rolling shoreward.
The men begin to shout, the ropes to squeal.

Sudden clouds snatch away the daylight sky
From Trojan sight. Black night roosts on the sea.
Heaven resounds, and fires dance in its heights.   90
The world becomes a threat of instant death.
A swift and icy terror numbed Aeneas.
He moaned and held his hands up to the stars
And gave a cry: "Three times and four times blessed
Are those who perished in their fathers' sight   95
Beneath Troy's walls. You, Diomedes, boldest *Greek hero*
Of Greeks, could you not spill my soul and let me *@ Troy*
Fall on the fields of Troy, like raging Hector
Slain by Achilles' spear, or tall Sarpedon, *Son of Jupiter, Ally of Troy*
Where the Simois River churns beneath her ripples   100
Shields, helmets, bodies of so many strong men?"
A screaming northern gale flew past his wild words
And slammed the sails, and pulled a wave toward heaven.
The oars broke, the prow swerved and set the ship
Against a looming precipice of water.   105
Crews dangled on the crest, or glimpsed the seabed
Between the waves. Sand poured through seething water.
Three times the South Wind hurled them at rocks lurking
Midway across—Italians call them Altars;
Their massive spine protrudes—three times the East Wind   110
Drove them toward sandy shallows—awful sight—
And rammed them tight, and ringed them with a sand wall.
Before Aeneas' eyes a towering wave tipped,
To strike head-on the ship of staunch Orontes
And the Lycians, and whirled the helmsman out   115
Head first. The boat was whipped in three tight circles,
And then the hungry whirlpool swallowed it.
The endless sea showed scatterings of swimmers.
Planks, gear, and Trojan treasure strewed the waves.
The storm subdued the strong ships carrying   120
Ilioneus, Abas, brave Achates, *Aeneas' retainer*
And old Aletes. Deadly water pushed
name of friend of Aeneas

Through the hulls' weakened joints, and fissures started
To gape. Now Neptune felt, with some alarm,
The roaring havoc that the storm let loose.   125
Even the still depths spurted up. He raised
His calm face from the surface and looked down.
He saw Aeneas' ships thrown everywhere,
Trojans crushed under waves, the plunging sky.
Juno's own brother knew her guile and anger.   130
He called the East and South Winds and addressed them:
"Is this the arrogance of noble birth?
Without my holy sanction, you have dared
To churn up land and sea and raise these mountains?
Which I—but first I'll calm these waves you've roused.   135
Later I'll punish you with more than words.
Get out now, fast, and tell this to your ruler:
I was allotted kingship of the sea,
And the harsh trident. In his massive stone hall—
Your home, East Wind, and all the rest—we let him   140
Swagger, but he must keep that dungeon locked."
Faster than words, he calmed the swollen sea,
Chased off the mass of clouds, brought back the sun.
Cymothoe and Triton heaved the ships   *sea god*
Off jagged boulders. Neptune with his trident   145
Helped them. He freed vast sandbanks, smoothed the surface,
His weightless chariot grazing the waves' peaks;
As often in a crowded gathering
Crude commoners in rage begin to riot,
Torches and stones fly, frenzy finds its weapons—   150
But if they see a stern and blameless statesman,
They all fall silent, keen for him to speak.
Then he will tame their hearts and guide their passions:
Like this, the roar of the broad sea grew quiet
Under the lord's gaze. Now beneath a clear sky,   155
He slacked the reins and flew on with the breeze.
Aeneas' worn-out group now fought to reach

The nearest shore, turning toward Libya.
A bay runs inland, and an island makes
A harbor with its sides; waves from the deep   160
Break there and flutter out their separate ways.
Mammoth cliffs flank the place, and twin stone spires
Loom to the sky. Beneath them, smooth and safe
The water hushes. Forests as a backdrop
Quiver, a grove with its black shadows rises.   165
At the bay's head, rocks dip to form a cavern
With a clear spring and seats of natural rock.
Nymphs live there. At the shore no rope is needed
To hold worn ships, no hooked and biting anchor.
Aeneas landed seven ships, regrouped   170
From the whole fleet. The Trojans went ashore
In great and yearning love of that dry sand.
Still dripping with salt water, they lay down.
To start, Achates struck a spark from flint *Aeneas' return.*
And caught the flame in leaves and fed it dry twigs   175
From all sides, till it blazed up through the tinder.
Downheartedly they got out instruments
Of Ceres, and the soaking grain they'd rescued; *goddess of agriculture*
They had to sear it dry before they ground it.
Meanwhile Aeneas climbed a crag to view   180
The great expanse of sea. Where did the wind toss
Antheus, Capys, Caicus' lofty prow
Hung with his arms—or any Trojan vessel?
There was no ship in sight; but three stags wandered
The shore. Entire herds came after them,   185
And grazed in a long column through the valley.
Taking a stand, he snatched the bow and arrows
That his devoted friend Achates carried.
He brought the strutting, branching-antlered leaders
To the ground first, and then his arrows chased   190
The mass in havoc through the leafy groves.
Exulting, he continued till he brought down

Seven large bodies for his seven ships,
Then went to share the meat out at the harbor,
And with it casks of wine that good Acestes   *Trojan hero who hosted*   195
Had stashed with them when they left Sicily—   *Aeneas in Sicily*
A noble gift. Aeneas spoke this comfort:
"Friends, we are all at home with suffering—
Some worse than this—but god will end this too.
You came near Scylla's frenzy, and the deep roar   *Sea monster*   200
At the cliffs, you saw the rocks the Cyclops threw.   *one-eyed giants of Sicily*
Revive your hearts, shake off your gloomy fear.
Sometime you may recall today with pleasure.
We fight through perils and catastrophes
To Latium, where divine fate promises   205
A peaceful homeland, a new Trojan kingdom.
Endure and live until our fortunes change."
Sick with colossal burdens, he shammed hope
On his face, and buried grief deep in his heart.
Trojans around his prey prepared their feast,   210
Ripped the hide off the ribs and bared the guts.
Some of them pierced the quivering chunks with spits,
Some set out cauldrons, others tended flames.
The food restored and filled them—the old wine,
The rich game—as they stretched out on the grass.   215
After the feast, their hunger put away,
They dwelt in longing on their missing friends.
They hoped, they feared: were these men still alive,
Or past the end and deaf to any summons?
Loyal Aeneas, most of all, was groaning   220
Softly for keen Orontes, Amycus, Lycus,
For Gyas and Cloanthus—brave men, hard deaths.   *2/11/19*

The day was over. Jove looked down from heaven   *Jupiter (Zeus) ruler of gods*
At the sail-flying waters, outstretched lands
And shores, and far-flung nations. At the sky's peak,   225
He fixed his gaze on Libyan territory.

His mind was anxious, busy. And now Venus   *Aeneas's mother*
Spoke these sad words to him, her shining eyes
Filling with tears, "You, everlasting ruler
Of gods and men and fearful lightning-thrower,   230
What great crime did Aeneas and the Trojans
Commit against you? They have died and died,
But in the whole world found no Italy.
You promised that the circling years would draw
Teucer's new lineage from them, Romans, chieftains, *original ancestory of Troys Royal house* 235
To rule an empire on the land and sea.
Father, what new thought turns you from this purpose?
When Troy calamitously fell, I weighed it
Against the fate to come, to my great comfort.
And yet the pummeling fortunes of these heroes   240
Don't change. When will you end their trials, great ruler?
Antenor could escape the swarm of Greeks;
Into Illyrian coves, into Liburnia,
He safely voyaged, to the Timavus' source,
Where the sea breaks through nine mouths, and the mountain   245
Roars, and the echoing waves oppress the fields.
And here he founded Padua, a homeland
For Trojans, with a Trojan name, its gateway
Displaying Trojan arms. He has his rest there.
But we, your children, promised heirs to heaven,   250
Have lost our ships—obscene!—through Someone's anger
And treachery. We are kept from Italy.
Is this our new realm, won through righteousness?"
The gods' and mortals' father gave his daughter
The smile that clears the sky of storms and kissed her   255
Lightly, and this was how he answered her:
"Take heart—no one will touch the destiny
Of your people. You will see Lavinium
In its promised walls, and raise your brave Aeneas
To the stars. No new thoughts change my purposes.   260
But since you suffer, I will tell the future,

Opening to the light fate's secret book.
In Italy your son will crush a fierce race
In a great war. With the Rutulians beaten,
Three winters and three summers he'll shape walls   265
And warrior customs, as he reigns in Latium.
But his son Ascanius, now called Iulus too   *Aeneas's father*
(He was named Ilus during Ilium's empire),
Will rule while thirty spacious years encircle
Their circling months, and he will move the kingdom   270
To Alba Longa, heaving up strong ramparts.
Three centuries the dynasty of Hector
Will govern, until Ilia, royal priestess,
Conceives twin boys by Mars and gives them birth.
And the wolf's nursling (glad to wear brown wolfskin),   275
Romulus, will then lead the race and found
The walls of Mars for Romans—named for him.
For them I will not limit time or space.
Their rule will have no end. Even hard Juno,
Who terrorizes land and sea and sky,   280
Will change her mind and join me as I foster
The Romans in their togas, the world's masters.
I have decreed it. The swift years will bring
Anchises' clan as rulers into Phthia,
And once-renowned Mycenae, and beaten Argos.   285
The noble Trojan line will give us Caesar—
A Julian name passed down from the great Iulus—
With worldwide empire, glory heaven-high.
At ease you will receive him with his burden
Of Eastern plunder. Mortals will send him prayers here.   290
Then wars will end, cruel history grow gentle.   *Goddess of Hearth*
Vesta, old Faith, and Quirinus, with Remus   *Romulus*
His twin, will make the laws. Tight locks of iron
Will close War's grim gates. Inside, godless Furor,
Drooling blood on a heap of brutal weapons,   295
Will roar against the chains that pinion him."

Concluding, he dispatched the son of Maia
To have the Trojans welcomed down in Carthage
With its new fort. Dido, who was not privy *Aeneas's lover who*
To fate, might keep them out. The god's wings rowed him *killed herself when he* 300
Through the vast air, to stand on Libya's shore. *deserted*
Since it was heaven's will, the fierce Phoenicians
Peacefully yielded; most of all their queen
Turned a calm, gentle face to meet the Trojans.

Steadfast Aeneas had a worried night, 305
But at the light of nurturing dawn decided
To go and find out where the wind had brought them
And who or what—the land looked wild—lived here,
And bring what he could learn to his companions.
The fleet lay hidden in a tree-lined inlet, 310
Under a rocky overhang enclosed
By bristling shade. He set off with Achates, *Aeneas's retainer*
Holding two quivering pikes with iron blades.
Deep in the woods his mother came to him,
A girl in face and clothes—armed, as in Sparta, 315
Or like Harpalyce in Thrace, outracing
The breakneck Hebrus with her harried horses—
A huntress with a bow slung, quick to hand,
From her shoulders, and the wind in her free hair,
And a loosely tied-up tunic over bare knees: 320
She greeted them and asked, "Please, have you met
One of my sisters wandering here, or shouting,
Chasing a foam-mouthed boar? She has a quiver,
And wears a spotted lynx skin and a belt."
Venus stopped speaking, and her son began. 325
"Young girl, I haven't seen or heard your sister.
But I should call you—what? There's nothing mortal
In your face or voice. No, you must be a goddess:
Apollo's sister? Daughter of a nymph clan?
No matter: have compassion, ease our hardship. 330
On which of the world's shores have we been thrown?

Beneath which tract of sky? The wind and huge waves
Drove us to this strange land in which we wander.
I'll slaughter many victims at your altar."
She answered, "That would surely not be right.   335
These quivers are what Tyrian girls all carry;
We all wear purple boots, laced on our calves.
This is the Punic realm and Agenor's city.
Unconquerable Africans surround us.
Dido is queen; she came here out of Tyre,   340
Escaping from her brother's persecution.
It's quite a story; I'll just tell the main parts.
Her husband was Sychaeus, the Phoenician
Richest in land—and she, poor thing, adored him.
Her father gave her as a virgin to him   345
In marriage. But Pygmalion her brother *Dido's broth*
Is king, and there is no one more depraved.
Hate rose between them. In blind lust for gold,
And indifferent to his sister's love, Pygmalion
Wickedly caught Sychaeus at an altar   350
And murdered him. He dodged and made up stories,
Cynically drawing out her anxious hope.
But in her dreams there came to her the vision
Of her unburied husband's strange, pale face.
He bared his stabbed chest, told of that cruel altar,   355
Stripped bare the monstrous crime the house had hidden.
He urged a quick escape. To aid her journey
Out of her country, he revealed where treasure,
A mass of gold and silver, lay long buried.
Alarmed, she made her plans, alerted friends—   360
All those who also hated the cruel tyrant
Or lived in sharp fear. Seizing ready ships,
They loaded them with gold. The ocean carried
Greedy Pygmalion's wealth. A woman led.
They came here, where you now see giant walls   365
And the rising citadel of newborn Carthage.

They purchased land, 'as much as one bull's hide
Could reach around,' and called the place 'the Bull's Hide.'
But who are you? What country are you from?
Where are you going?" Answering, Aeneas   370
Sighed and drew words out of the depths of feeling.
"Goddess, our whole sad story, from its start,
Would keep you here until the Evening Star
Closed off Olympus, bringing this day rest.
Through endless seas, we come from ancient Troy—   375
Perhaps you've heard that name. A storm has thrust us,
By its whim, onto these shores of Africa.
I am devout Aeneas, known in heaven.
I saved my household gods and now transport them
To a home in Italy. I descend from high Jove.   380
My goddess mother and the fates have led me.
Of twenty ships launched on the Phrygian sea,
Seven remain—torn by the waves and east wind.
Europe and Asia banished me, to wander
In empty Africa, a needy stranger."   385
Venus cut short this grief, these grievances.
"Whoever you might be, it's by the favor
Of the gods, I think, that you're alive to reach
This Tyrian city. Go straight to the queen's house.
I have good news. Your friends and ships are safe.   390
The north wind turned and brought them back. My parents
Taught me to read the sky—I hope correctly.
Look at that cheerful squadron of twelve swans.
Jove's eagle swooped from heaven through the clear sky
And routed them. But the long row regrouped—   395
Those still aloft look down on those who've landed.
Their joyful rushing wings on their return,
Their cries, and their tight circles through the sky
Are like the ships that carry all your people:
Come into port or heading in with full sails.   400
Go on, then, make your way along the road."

She turned away. Her rosy neck now shone.
Her hair's ambrosia breathed a holy fragrance.
Her belt fell loose, her robe now swept her feet.
Like a true god she walked. He recognized   *Venus*   405
His mother, and called after her retreat:
"I am your child—must you keep torturing me
With these illusions? Let me take your hand—
Let there be words between us, as we are!"
Bitterly he approached the city walls,   410
But Venus hid the group in murky air,
In a thick cloud draped over them like clothing.
This way no one could see or touch them. No one
Could ask why they were there or hold them back.
She soared to Paphos in a glad return home   415
To her temple's hundred altars, warm with incense
From Arabia, and fragrant with fresh garlands.
Meanwhile they hurried, following the path.
They climbed a lofty hill above the city,
And looked down at the fortress straight ahead.   420
Aeneas was amazed at those great structures
Where huts had been: the gates, paved roads—the hubbub!
Some Tyrians feverishly laid out long walls
Or rolled rocks in to raise the citadel;
Others chose sites and bordered them with trenches.   425
Laws, offices, a sacred senate formed.
A port was being dug, the high foundations
Of a theater laid, great columns carved from cliffs
To ornament the stage that would be built there:
Like bees in spring across the blossoming land,   430
Busy beneath the sun, leading their offspring,
Full grown now, from the hive, or loading cells
Until they swell with honey and sweet nectar,
Or taking shipments in, or lining up
To guard the fodder from the lazy drones;   435
The teeming work breathes thyme and fragrant honey.

"What luck they have—their walls grow high already!"
Aeneas cried, his eyes on those great roofs.
Still covered by the cloud—a miracle—
He went in through the crowds, and no one saw him.   440
Deep in the city is the verdant shade
Where the Phoenicians, tired from stormy waves,
Dug up the sign that Juno said would be there:
A horse's head, foretelling martial glory
And easy livelihood through future ages.   445
Dido was building Juno a vast shrine here,
Filled with rich offerings and holy power.
The stairs soared to a threshold made of bronze;
Bronze joined the beams; the doors had shrill bronze hinges.
Here a strange sight relieved Aeneas' fear   450
For the first time, and lured him into hope
Of better things to follow all his torments.
While waiting for the queen and looking over
The whole huge temple, marveling at the wealth
It showed, the work, the varied artistry,   455
He saw Troy's battles painted in their sequence—
A worldwide story now: the sons of Atreus,
And Priam, and Achilles, cruel to both.   *King of Troy, Father of Paris + Hector*
He halted, weeping: "What land isn't full
Of what we suffered in that war, Achates?   460
There's Priam! Even here is praise for valor,
And tears of pity for a mortal world.
Don't be afraid. Somehow our fame will save us."
With steady sobbing and a tear-soaked face,
He fed his heart on shallow images.   465
He saw men fight around the citadel—
Trojan troops routing Greeks, crested Achilles
Driving his chariot at the Trojans' backs.
He wept to recognize, close by, the white tents
Of Rhesus: savage Diomedes stormed   470
And massacred the camp on its first night,

And seized the ardent horses there before
They tasted Trojan grass or drank the Xanthus. *river @ Troy*
Here Troilus, wretched boy who'd lost his armor,
And no match for Achilles, sprawled behind   475
His empty chariot and its panicked horses—
Holding the reins. His neck and long hair skidded
Over the ground. His spear point scored the dust.
The Trojan women, hair unbound, went begging
To the temple of implacable Athena.   480
They took a robe for her and beat their breasts.
She would not raise her eyes and look at them.
Three times Achilles dragged the corpse of Hector
Around Troy's walls, then traded it for gold.
Aeneas gave a soulful groan to see   485
His comrade's armor, chariot, and body,
And Priam stretching out defenseless hands.
He saw himself among Greek chieftains, fighting;
He saw black Memnon and the ranks of Dawn. *King Ethiopia*
Penthesilea, leader of the Amazons   490
With their crescent shields, was storming through the throng,
Her gold belt tied beneath her naked breast—
This virgin warrior dared to fight with men.
Dardanian Aeneas gazed in wonder, *Trojan's my king*
Transfixed and mesmerized—but while he stood,   495
Dido the lovely queen came to the temple,
Surrounded by a copious troop of soldiers.
Diana on the banks of the Eurotas *Goddess Hunt*
Or high on Cynthus, leading dances, followed
By a thousand clustering, trailing nymphs but taller   500
Than all of them, and shouldering her quiver
(Latona in her silent heart rejoices)— *Mother of Apollo, Diana/Nymph*
Dido was like her, striding happily
Through her people, planning, urging on her kingdom.
Beneath the vault, before the goddess' doors,   505
She sat on her high throne, hemmed in by soldiers,

Made laws, gave judgments, and assigned the work
In fair proportions or by drawing lots.
But now Aeneas saw, among a crowd,
Antheus, Sergestus, spirited Cloanthus,   510
And other Trojans whom the pitch-black whirlwind
Had scattered, driving them to distant shores.
He and Achates both were riveted
With fear and joy. They yearned to clasp their friends' hands,
But didn't—they were startled and bewildered.   515
They hung back, watching from the hollow cloud.
What was the news, where were they moored, and why
Had they come here? Spokesmen from every ship
Came clamoring to the shrine with their petition.
When they had entered and had leave to speak,   520
The eldest, Ilioneus, calmly started:
"Your highness, we poor Trojans plead with you:
Jove let you found a city and bring justice
To lawless tribes. We are sea-wandering,
Wind-harried: save our ships from evil fires.   525
Spare decent people—think of what we've been through.
We have not come to plunder Libyan homes
Or drive your herds away onto the shore.
Arrogant crime is not for beaten men.
There is a place Greeks call Hesperia,   *I taly*   530
An ancient land—rich-loamed and strong in war.
Oenotrians lived there, whose descendants called it
Italy, from king Italus, as we're told.
On our way there,
Stormy Orion heaved the surge against us,   535
Cruel south winds drove us far into the shallows,
Scattered us under conquering waves and over
Rock barriers. We few rowed here to your shores.
What race is this? What nation would permit
Such outrage? They have thrust us from the beach   540
With war and yield no stopping place on land.

You scorn the human race and human weapons?
Be sure the gods remember good and evil.
Aeneas was our leader—none more just
Or faithful ever was, no better warrior.   545
If fate still lets him breathe instead of sleeping
Among the shades of death, we'd have no fear,
And you would not be sorry for competing
With him in kindness. We have towns and troops, though,
In Sicily. We are kin of great Acestes. *Trojan Heno who has* 550 *ed*
Please let us beach the fleet the winds have ruined,   *Aeneas in Italy*
And saw new planks, shape new oars in your woods.
Perhaps our friends and leader will return—
Then we can sail with joy to Italy.
If that won't save us, and our loving father   555
Lies in this sea, and there's no hope of Iulus,
We'll sail to Sicily—a king, Acestes,
A home is there for us across the strait."
So Ilioneus spoke, and all the Trojans
Instantly roared approval.   560
Dido looked down and gave this brief reply:
"Ease your hearts, Trojans, put away your fears.
The threats to my new kingdom here have forced me
To carefully place guards on all the borders.
Who hasn't heard about Aeneas' family,   565
Or Troy—those brave men and the flames of war?
Phoenicians know the world! This town's not set
Beyond where the Sun harnesses his horses.
To Saturn's fields, the great lands of the West,
Or the kingdom of Acestes next to Eryx,   570
I'll send you off secure and well-supplied.
Or would you settle here and share my kingdom?
This town I found is yours too. Land your ships.
To me, you will be equal to my own.
I wish the storm had brought your king Aeneas   575
Himself. But I will send some trusted men

Along the shore as far as Libya reaches—
He might be cast up, wandering woods or towns."
Heartened now, staunch Achates and Aeneas
The patriarch were burning to break free   580
From their cloud. But first Achates asked his leader:
"Goddess' son, what new thoughts rise up in you?
Your fleet and followers are in safe havens.
Save for one man our own eyes saw the waves
Take under, it is as your mother said."   585
He'd scarcely finished when the cloud that veiled them
Ripped apart and dissolved in open air.
Aeneas stood, his godlike face and shoulders
Flashing in clear light, since his mother breathed
Graceful long hair, the blushing glow of youth,   590
And happy, shining eyes onto her son—
Like ivory beautifully carved, like silver
Or marble that is edged with tawny gold.
The queen, the crowd were startled. He addressed them,
Unhesitating: "Here I am, you see—   595
Trojan Aeneas, saved from Libyan waters.
You are the first to pity Troy's disasters.
We are the scraps the Greeks left. We have nothing.
Disasters pelted us on land and sea.
It is not in the power of all our people—   600
Who are world-scattered now—to thank you, Dido,
For making us the sharers of this place.
The gods and your own conscience must reward you.
Surely divine powers honor selflessness,
And justice does exist. What happy era   605
And what outstanding parents gave you birth?
While streams run seaward, while the shadows move
On mountain slopes, and the stars graze in heaven,
Your name will have unceasing praise and honor—
Whatever country calls me." He clasped hands   610
With Ilioneus and Serestus, right and left,

Then others, brave Cloanthus and brave Gyas.
Phoenician Dido was amazed to see him,
And shocked by all his suffering. She spoke:
"What fate has hounded you through endless dangers?   615
What force has brought you to our savage shores?
Are you the one born by the river Simois—
Trojan Anchises' and kind Venus' son?   *Aeneas' father*
Teucer in exile came to Sidon, looking   *original ancestors*
For a new kingdom, I recall, and seeking   *of Trojan house*   620
My father Belus' help, who was away
Ravaging wealthy, newly conquered Cyprus.
Since then I've known the tragedy of Troy,
And the Greek kings who fought there, and your name.
Your enemy himself admired Trojans,   625
And claimed the ancient "Teucrian" line as his too.
So come now, warriors, join me in my house.
Fate dragged me through much suffering myself   *) DIDO*
Until it let me settle in this land.
My own experience has taught compassion."   630
She spoke, and led Aeneas to her palace,
Proclaiming sacrifices in the temples.
She sent his shore-bound comrades twenty bulls,
A hundred giant boars with bristling backs,
And a hundred fat lambs, and their mothers too,   635
Gifts for a joyful day.
Her house was now prepared luxuriously
And regally, with a feast laid in the middle,
With embroidered covers and imperial ivory,
Dishes of massive silver, gold-embossed   640
With heroism through the generations—
The whole long story of her ancient race.
Aeneas, with an anxious father's love,
Dispatched Achates swiftly to the ships,
To give Ascanius news and bring him here.   645
To his fond father, he was everything.

Aeneas ordered gifts brought in—the salvage
Of Troy: a mantle stiff with gold-stitched figures,
A veil trimmed yellow with acanthus flowers—
Greek Helen's finery, taken from Mycenae   650
When she set off for Troy and lawless marriage,
Glorious presents from her mother, Leda—
And the scepter that was held by Ilione,
Eldest of Priam's daughters; a pearl necklace;
And a crown's double bands of gold and gems.   655
Achates rushed to fetch them from the ships.
But a new strategy was in the mind
Of Venus. She sent Cupid in disguise,
Looking like sweet Ascanius, with the gifts,
To twist a frenzied flame around the queen's bones.   660
She feared this lying race, this doubtful refuge.
At evening, too, came thoughts of ruthless Juno
To trouble her, so she approached winged Love:
"My son, you are my strength, I rule through you.
You even scorn the patriarch's lightning bolts.   665
Humbly I come to seek your holy aid.
Your know your brother's tortuous worldwide voyage,
How Juno's spite will never let him rest.
You've shared my grief about this many times.
Phoenician Dido flatters and detains him.   670
Juno has sanctioned this; but for what purpose?
She won't hang back at this decisive time.
So I'll move quickly, shrewdly, trap the queen
In fire—and then no heavenly will can change her.
She will be mine, through passion for Aeneas.   675
Now listen while I tell you how to do it.
My darling prince, at his dear father's call,
Is setting out to the Phoenician city
With gifts saved from the sea and Trojan flames.
I'll put the boy to sleep and hide him high   680
On Cythera or Idalium, in my shrine.

He won't know, he won't stumble on the scheme.
You are a boy too: for a single night
Impersonate the features Trojans know.
Amid the royal banquet's flowing wine,   685
Dido will be enchanted with you, hold you
In her lap, with doting kisses. That's your chance:
Stealthily breathe on her your flame of poison."
Love stripped his wings, obeying his dear mother,
And strutted in a gleeful imitation.   690
Venus poured deep sleep through the prince's body
And took him in her arms to the high groves
Of Idalium. Soft marjoram wrapped its flowers,
Its breath of aromatic shade around him.
Now with delight and deference Cupid went   695
After Achates, with the royal gifts.
He found the queen among her splendid hangings,
Posed in the middle, on a golden couch.
Father Aeneas and the ranks of Trojans
Assembled and lay down on purple covers.   700
Servants poured water on their hands, provided
Baskets of bread and fine-spun napkins. Inside,
Fifty maids honored household gods with hearth fires
And made the long feast ready course by course.
Two hundred men and women of the same age   705
Served wine and weighed the tables down with good things.
Phoenician guests flocked in the festive doorway
And took their places on embroidered couches,
Admiring Aeneas' gifts, admiring Iulus
(Or the god's bright face and masquerading words)   710
And the cloak and the embroidered yellow flowers.
The Punic queen—cursed and disaster-bound—
Was looking on with hunger in her heart,
Enchanted by the presents and the boy.
He put his arms around Aeneas' neck—   715
Which gratified the duped and loving father—

Then sought the queen. Her eyes and mind were fixed
On him. Poor thing, she held him on her lap,
The powerful hidden god. He thought of Venus,
His mother, and began to ease Sychaeus   720
Out of her mind and try a living love
Against a heart long quiet and disused.
An interval; the tables are removed.
They set out massive wine bowls crowned with flowers.
A clamor rises, and their voices roll   725
Through the wide hall. Lamps hang from golden panels,
Blazing, and waxed-rope torches rout the darkness.
The queen called for a bowl—massed gems and gold—
To hold unwatered wine. From Belus onward,
The dynasty had drunk from it. Now, silence.   730
"Jove, your laws govern visits, as they say.
Make this a glad day for our Trojan guests
And us, a day our children all remember.
Come, Bacchus, giver of joy, and kindly Juno;
Join in this gathering with good will, Tyrians."   735
She poured a sacrifice onto the table
And made a start—her lips just brushed the rim—
And passed the bowl to Bitias with a challenge.
He wallowed in the full, foam-brimming gold.
The other leaders drank. Long-haired Iopas,   740
Great Atlas' pupil, struck his golden lyre.
He sang the wandering moon, the sun's eclipses,
Fire and rain, how men and beasts were made,
The Keeper of the Bear, the Twins, the Rain Stars;
Why winter suns dive in the sea so quickly,   745
What obstacle makes winter nights so slow.
Repeated cheers rose, led by Tyrians.
Unlucky Dido spoke of various things,
Drawing the night out, deep in love already.
She asked so many questions: Priam, Hector,   750
The armor of the son of Dawn, how good

Diomedes' horses were, how tall Achilles.
"Tell it from the beginning, friend—the ambush
By the Greeks, your city's fall, your wanderings.
This is the seventh summer now that sends you   755
Drifting across the wide world's lands and seas."

2

All faces now were fixed on him in silence.
Father Aeneas spoke from his high couch:
"Must I renew a grief beyond description,
Telling how Greeks destroyed the power of Troy,
That tear-stained kingdom—since I saw the worst,   5
And played a leading role? Telling the story,
A Myrmidon, a Dolopian, a soldier   *a Greek Hero@Troy*
Of cruel Ulysses would shed tears. The moist night
Falls to its end, the setting stars urge sleep.
But if you are so passionate to hear—   10
Briefly—of the death agony of Troy,
I will begin, although my heart shrinks back
From memory. The years of war had broken
The Greek kings; destiny had pushed them back.
They built a mountainous horse, with woven ribs   15
Of fir—Athena's genius aided them.
'An offering for a safe voyage home!' The news spread.
They picked the bravest men. With stealth they shut them

Into the darkness of the flanks: an armed squad
Filling the vast, deep cavern of the belly.   20
Tenedos shows offshore, the famous island—
Wealthy while Priam's empire still existed,   *King of Troy*
Now just an inlet with its treacherous mooring.
They sailed there. On the lonely beach they lurked.
We thought they'd made off windward to Mycenae.   25
The whole of Troy broke free of its long mourning.
We poured out through the open gates, delighted
To tour the Greek camp on the empty shore.
Achilles' tent was here, there the Dolopians.   *Greatest Greek warrior*
The fleet moored there, here was the battleground.   *@ Troy*   30
Some ogled the huge horse, gift of the virgin
Minerva for our ruin. Thymoetes
Was first to want it taken to our stronghold—
His own guile or the fate of Troy inspired him.
Capys and those who shared his good sense urged us   35
To hurl the treacherous present of the Greeks
Into the sea or set a fire beneath it,
Or drill into the secrets of its womb.
The fickle mob took opposite positions.
Now leading his attendants in a crowd,   40
Laocoön rushed raging from the town's heights.
'Poor Trojans, have you lost your minds?' he called.
'You think they're gone? With no deceit, the Greeks
Give presents? Don't you know Ulysses better?
The Greeks are hiding in this wooden thing,   45
Or else this is a siege machine they've built
For spying—or alighting—on our homes,
Or some such trick. Don't trust the horse, my people.
Even when they bring gifts, I fear the Greeks.'
He hurled a massive spear with all his great strength   50
Into the creature's round and riveted belly.
The shaft stuck, trembling, and that cave, that wound
Gave out an echoing, a groaning noise.

Had heaven willed it, had we all been sane,
We would have followed, shattering that Greek lair;   55
Priam's high citadel would still be standing.   Τroy
Shepherds approached the king now, clamoring,
Dragging a youth whose hands were tied behind him,
A stranger they had come across just now—
But he had plotted it, to open Troy   60
To the Greeks. He was tough-minded and quite ready
To weave his lies or meet unyielding death.
Trojan boys rushed to see the captive, crowding
Around him, seeing who could taunt him hardest.
Hear how the Greek plot worked: this single crime   65
Shows them for what they all are.
In the center of those stares, unarmed and harried,
He stood and swept his eyes around our ranks.
'Is there some sea, is there some soil to take me?'
He cried. 'I'm finished—what do I have left?   70
No place among the Greeks, and now the Trojans
As well are shouting for my blood in payment.'
At this our rage was calmed, our onslaught stifled.
But still we had to know—who were his people?
What was the news he brought? Why should we spare him?   75
He finally put his 'fear' aside and said,
'All that I'm going to say, my king, is true,
Whatever happens. First, I am a Greek,
Sinon. If fate has made me miserable,
She will not make me lie, cruel as she is.   80
Perhaps you've heard the name of Palamedes,
The glorious son of Belus, whom the Greeks
Falsely and quite outrageously accused
Of treason when he stood against the war.
They drained his body of light but mourn him now.   85
My father, who was poor, sent me in boyhood
To be his page—we were his relatives.
While he still safely ruled, strong in the councils

Of kings, I had my share of reputation
And honor. But when sly Ulysses' envy—   90
You know it—thrust him from this upper world,
I lived in mourning darkness, persecuted
And furious at my blameless patron's death.
I was in fact a fool, and pledged revenge
If chance allowed, if I came home in triumph   95
To Argos. Hatred rose against my words.
This tipped me toward disaster. Now Ulysses
Kept threatening, accusing, scattering rumors,
Recruiting helpers in his plot against me.
He didn't rest until the seer Calchas—   100
But no, it's useless—you don't want to hear it.
I'm wasting time. If Greeks are all the same,
Then kill me, I'm a Greek. The sons of Atreus
Would pay to see; Ulysses would be pleased.'
That only made us burn to hear it all.   105
We didn't know the evil guile of Greeks.
Shaking with false emotion, he went on:
'The Greeks were often yearning, often trying
To leave; the endless war had worn them out.
I wish they'd gone. The stormy winter sea   110
Or south wind often turned them from the journey.
The maple horse was standing here already,
When the sky rang with even louder storms.
In doubt, we sent Eurypylus to query
Apollo's oracle, and we got bad news: 115
"You Greeks appeased the winds with virgin blood
When you first traveled to the shores of Troy.
Now you must make an offering of a Greek life
For your return." The common soldiers heard this
With horror. Icy trembling seized their marrow: 120
Whose death was it Apollo asked of them?
Ulysses dragged old Calchas in, demanding,
With noisy bustle, what the god decreed.

Many foresaw the schemer's brutal crime:
They saw what was to come but held their peace.   125
The seer in his tent refused for ten days
To give a name and send a man to death.
Finally, driven by Ulysses' clamor,
He spoke. They'd planned it: I would be the gift.
They all agreed. Each, fearing death, was happy   130
To see it land on my pathetic self.
The ghastly day had come: the salted grain,
Fillets around my head—the ritual.
From chains, from death I broke free—I confess it.
In the swamp, among the reeds I hid all night,   135
Breathlessly waiting for the fleet to sail.
I can't return again to see my homeland,
Sweet children, and the father that I yearn for—
Perhaps they now may pay for my escape;
It may be that my weakness costs their poor lives.   140
I beg you by those powers that know the truth,
By any pure trust placed in anything
Among us mortals, pity my affliction—
Pity the violation of a good heart.'
We spared his life; we even pitied him.   145
First, Priam had the manacles and tight chains   Troy's King
Removed, and spoke these kind words to the captive:
'Stranger, forget the Greeks, now lost to you.
You will be ours. But speak the truth to me:
Who had the giant horse set up, and why?   150
Is it for worship or for making war?'
Greek cunning and conspiracy now caused him
To raise his hands—unfettered—to the stars.
'By these eternal fires and sacred Troy,
By the altar and the evil blade I fled,   155
And the god's ribbons that this victim wore:
It's right to break my sworn bond to the Greeks,
To hate them and make public everything

They hide. My nation's laws don't hold me now.
But keep your promises, since Troy is saved—   160
If this true news pays richly for my safety.
All that the Greeks could hope for in this war
Was in the power of Pallas. Since the plotter   *Minerva*
Ulysses and the godless Diomedes   *Greek heros*
Slaughtered the keepers of the towering fortress,   165
And tore away that fateful effigy,
The Palladium, from its shrine, and even pawed
Her virgin ribbons with their bloody fingers,
The tide is turned, the Greek cause slipping backward.
Their strength is broken by her stubborn anger.   170
She gave us signs, clear and miraculous:
We'd scarcely set her image in the camp
When its eyes flashed and burned, and salty sweat
Ran down it. From its base, it leaped three times
And shook its shield and spear—strange sight, strange story.   175
Calchas' divine advice: escape by sea;
The Greeks would not raze Troy till they returned
To Argos for new omens and brought back
The deity they'd taken in their curved ships.
They've sailed home to Mycenae, to rearm   180
And gather gods as allies. They will cross
Back here and strike. So Calchas read the omens.
This statue pays for the Palladium,
An offering to violated godhead.
Calchas commanded that it be immense,   185
A mass of joined logs that would reach the sky,
And never pass the gates into your city
And save you, as the cult of Pallas did.   *Minerva*
Handle Minerva's gift impiously,
Then ruin—may the gods turn back the omen   190
Against the seer—will meet the realm of Priam.
If your hands help it climb into your city,
Asia can hurl itself in war against

The walls of Pelops, in our grandsons' time.'
Sinon's false oaths and trickery convinced us.   195
The tears that he contrived did what Achilles
And Diomedes and ten years of war
And a thousand ships could not: they brought us down.
Poor Trojans! Something still more horrible
Sprang up to fill our spirits with confusion.   200
Laocoön, the chosen priest of Neptune,
Was at the altar, slaughtering a large bull,
When over the calm sea from Tenedos
Came two huge, coiled snakes—even now I shake.
Breasting the waters, paired, they sought the beach.   205
They reared among the waves, their blood-red crests
Towering, while their bellies trailed the surface.
Their backs were flowing in enormous spirals.
The salt foam roared. But now they reached dry land.
Fire and blood were brimming from their eyes.   210
Their quivering tongues were licking hissing mouths—
And white with fear, we ran. As if marched forward,
They headed for Laocoön; but first
Each clasped one of his tiny sons, entangling
The body, feeding on its pitiful limbs.   215
Their father snatched a spear and ran to help.
Both serpents caught him in their giant whorls.
Their scaly length went twice around his waist
And throat; above him reared their heads and necks.
He fought to rip apart the knotted forms.   220
Their slime and poison-black drool soaked his fillets.
His shrieks of agony rose to the sky,
As when a bull escapes the altar, shedding
The ax that was half-buried in his neck.
The snakes now ducked away, made for the temple   225
Of Triton's savage daughter in its high place.
At the statue's feet they hid, beneath the round shield.
Now a fresh terror twisted through our hearts:

We all quaked, and some murmured that Laocoön
Deserved this for the hideous crime of striking   230
The sacred wooden image with his spear.
'Take it where it belongs. Beseech the power
Of the goddess.'
We cut the walls and opened up the city.
Bare-legged work put rollers underneath   235
Its feet, and tightened ropes around its neck.
The great catastrophe climbed to the fortress,
Pregnant with arms. Young boys and girls around it
Sang hymns and touched the cables in their joy.
It loomed into the middle of the town.   240
Heroic walls of Ilium, the gods' home,
My country! Four times in the gate itself
It halted—weapons clattered in its belly.
We pushed on, blind with passion and distracted,
And set the monster in our sacred stronghold.   245
Cassandra spoke then, echoing the future. Trojan princess
But by the god's will Troy would never listen.
We wretches on our last day garlanded
The temples of the gods all through the city.
The heavens swung round, night leaped from the ocean   250
To wrap the earth and sky—and Greek deceit—
In its great shadow. On the walls the Trojans
Sprawled, muffled in a deep, exhausted sleep.
Already the Greek fleet came in formation
From Tenedos, through the moon's friendly silence   255
To the familiar shore; and now the king's ship
Signaled with flame, and Sinon, in the shelter
Of heaven's brutal edicts, slipped the pine bolts
And birthed the Greeks. The horse gaped to the sky;
From its wooden cave the eager chieftains slid   260
Down the rope: Machaon first, Thessandrus, Sthenelus,
Cruel Ulysses, Acamas, Thoas, Neoptolemus
(Grandson of Peleus), and Menelaus,

And Epeos, who had built this artifice.
They swarmed a city sunk in wine and sleep, 265
Slaughtered the guards, opened the gates, and let
Their comrades in, uniting ranks as planned.
It was the time when that first, sweetest sleep,
A gift from gods, slips into weary mortals.
I saw a desolate Hector in my dreams, 270
Streaming with tears and black with dust and blood.
His feet were swollen with the thongs that pierced them
When he was dragged behind the chariot.
How different from that Hector who returned
Wearing the plundered armor of Achilles 275
Or hurled our Trojan torches onto Greek ships!
His beard was dirty; dried blood caked his hair.
He had the many wounds he got defending
His city's walls. And in that dream I wept
And greeted that brave man with mournful words: 280
'Light of our country, truest hope of Troy,
Why were you gone so long? What shore has sent us
This longed-for sight of you? So many died.
Your city and its people are worn out
With all their griefs. What undeserved disaster 285
Marred your calm face? What are these wounds I see?'
He took no notice of my empty questions,
But sighing from his heart's depths only said,
'Child of the goddess, run, escape these flames.
The walls are seized. Troy falls from its great height. 290
Our king and land are gone now. If this right hand
Could have defended Troy, you would be safe.
Troy hands its rites, its household gods to you.
Take them to share your fate, and find the place
For their high walls across the seas you'll wander.' 295
Then from the inmost shrine he brought the fillets,
And powerful Vesta and her ceaseless fire. *Goddess of Hearth*
Confusion and distress spread through the fortress.

My father's house was set far back and sheltered
By trees, and yet the din kept growing clearer;   300
The horror of the war was pushing forward.
Startled from sleep, I scrambled to the rooftop
And stood there, motionless and listening:
It was like fire the raging south wind sends
Into the wheat, or torrents from a mountain,   305
Flattening crops—the flourishing work of oxen—
And dragging forests headlong; on a high rock
The shepherd stands and stares in bafflement.
Here was plain evidence of the Greek plot.
The fire topped the broad house of Deiphobus   310
And brought it down. Ucalegon's beside it
Had caught. Sigeum's wide strait shone with red.
The shouts of men, the ring of trumpets rose.
Blindly I seized my weapons—senselessly,
But my heart burned to gather friends and rush   315
To some high place. Rage, furor pitched my mind
Ahead: how beautiful to die in battle!
Now Panthus, son of Othrys, priest of Phoebus
Of the citadel, dodged Greek spears, running panicked
To my door with holy emblems and our gods   320
In their defeat, and with his little grandson.
'Where is the hardest fight?' I asked. 'Our strong point?'
Quickly he answered me, but with a groan:
'This is the last day, inescapable
For our nation—Troy, the Trojans, and our glory   325
Are gone. Fierce Jupiter has given all this
To Argos. Greeks are masters of these flames.
Among us looms the horse and pours out soldiers.
Sinon in mocking triumph sweeps a torch
Everywhere, and as many thousand others   330
Crowd at the gates as great Mycenae sent.
In alleyways the spears are poised for ambush.
A flashing line of sword points is prepared

To murder us. Guards at the entrances
Scarcely put up an early, blind resistance.'   335
The priest's words and the gods' power, which I felt,
Drove me to burning battle. The grim Furies,
The roars and shouts that rose to heaven called me.
I drew in comrades: Rhipeus, Epytus—
Great warrior—emerged by moonlight; Dymas,   340
Hypanis and Coroebus, Mygdon's son,
Strode with me—this young man had come to Troy
In burning and deranged love for Cassandra,
To fight, as Priam's son-in-law, for Troy—
Poor man, his promised bride had raved and warned him: 345
He had not heard.
And when I saw them come together ready
For war, I urged them on. 'Come, are you burning
To waste your courage, fighters, following me
Into a final clash? You see our fortune.   350
All of the gods who kept this kingdom standing
Have left their shrines and altars. These are flames
You fight for. Hurry, die in the dense combat.
The beaten have one hope: to lose all hope.'
The young men's frenzy grew. Like plundering wolves   355
Whose ravening stomachs drive them through black fog
On a blind hunt, whose cubs with dry throats wait
Back in the lair, we kept on pressing forward
Through our armed enemies, straight through the city
To certain death. The blackness swirled around us.   360
Who could describe that night's catastrophes?
What tears could show our agony in full?
An empire, generations old, was falling.
We saw unmoving bodies sprawled and scattered
In houses, on the roads, on holy thresholds   365
Of gods' homes. But not only Trojans paid
The price in blood. New courage seized our hearts.
Greeks in their victory fell. Ferocious grief,

Terror, and every kind of death enclosed us.
Androgeus with his large troop was the first Greek   370
To meet us. He mistook us for his allies
And shouted out in this congenial way:
'Hurry, men! What's this dragging of your feet?
Why hold back? All the rest are plundering
Troy's flames. Did you just come from your tall ships?'   375
No reassuring answers came to him.
Right then he knew he'd fallen among enemies.
Stunned, he retreated from his words and us.
Like someone on a brambly path who treads
On a hidden snake and backs away in terror   380
From the blue swollen neck, erect in rage,
Androgeus backed up, trembling, when he saw us.
We swarmed around them with our weapons, scattered
And killed them—they were panicked in that strange place.
So Fortune blessed our very first endeavor.   385
Coroebus was exuberant and shouted,
'Friends, we should take the road that Fortune's favored
At the beginning: there we'll find our safety.
Let's put on this Greek armor, take these shields.
A trick's as good as courage in a war.   390
And here's our chance!' He took the long-plumed helmet
And shield with its fine blazon from Androgeus
And put them on, and belted on the Greek sword.
Then Rhipeus too, and Dymas, and the others
Eagerly armed themselves with that fresh plunder.   395
We went among the Greeks, beneath their gods' power.
In the thick dark we skirmished many times
With Greeks, and we sent many down to Orcus.
Many ran to their ships and the safe beaches.
A truly craven few climbed back and hid   400
In the familiar belly of the huge horse.
No one should trust the gods against their will:
Her hair down loose, the virgin daughter of Priam

Was dragged out of Minerva's shrine. She lifted
Her burning eyes to heaven, uselessly—   405
Her eyes, because her tender hands were tied.
Seeing this put Coroebus in a frenzy.
He hurled his doomed self straight against her captors;
We followed, rushing where the clash was densest.
But now, from the high rooftop of the temple,   410
Trojan spears overwhelmed us—pitiful slaughter:
Our plumes, our emblems turned us into Greeks.
Roaring frustration at the young girl's rescue,
The gathered Greeks attacked—ferocious Ajax,
Atreus' two sons, Pyrrhus with his army—   415
As when a whirlwind breaks and sets the West Wind
Against the South and the East that relishes
Driving Dawn's horses. Woods roar, frothy Nereus
Rages, rousing the sea clear from its floor.
Even the men we'd ambushed in night's shadows,   420
Routing them, chasing them all through the city,
Emerged now, first to see through our disguise—
And they could hear our language wasn't Greek.
They swarmed us instantly. Coroebus fell first,
At the altar of the goddess strong in warfare.   425
Peneleus killed him. Rhipeus fell too—
It was the gods' will, though no other Trojan
Served justice better. Hypanis and Dymas
Died on their country's spears. Apollo's emblem
That reverent Panthus wore was no protection.   430
By Troy's ashes, by the flames that took my people,
I swear: in that collapse I shirked no fighting
Or other hazard. If my fate had been
To fall, I would have earned it. I was stranded
With Iphitus (heavy with old age) and Pelias   435
(Lame from a wound Ulysses had inflicted).
We now heard shouts and ran to Priam's palace,
Where what we saw drove all the other battles

And massacres in Troy to nothingness.
Implacably the Greeks attacked the building,   440
Crowding the door, their shields above their heads.
Ladders gripped walls right at the doors; feet struggled
Toward higher rungs, left hands held shields in front
For shelter, right hands reached to seize the roof.
The Trojans ripped up parapets and whole roofs   445
For weapons of defense. They knew the end
Was coming: they would fight until it came.
They rolled down gilded beams, the ornaments
Of generations. Others drew their swords
And in a dense rank blocked the doors below.   450
So now we burned to bring the palace help,
To bring relief and new strength to the beaten.
There was a hidden door that linked the two parts
Of Priam's house, remote and at the back.
Andromache—poor thing—while Troy survived,   Wife of Troy   455
Went through there unattended to her in-laws,   champion, Hecto
Taking Astyanax to see his grandsire.
This way I reached the rooftops, where the Trojans
Uselessly, pitiably hurled their weapons.
A tower reached skyward, near a steep drop down;   460
It was our lookout onto all of Troy,
The Achaean camp, and all the ships of Greece.
We battered it around its upper stories,
Where the joints were loose, and ripped it from its high perch,
Shoving it over. In a swift collapse   465
And roar it skidded down. Over the Greek ranks
It smashed—but others came. There was no pause
Of stones or other missiles.
Pyrrhus stood in the gateway to the courtyard,
Exultant, glittering in his bronze armor—   470
Just as a serpent, fed on poison weeds,
Emerges swollen from its winter burrow
And sheds its skin and gleams, its youth renewed,

And swirls its glossy length and rears its head
Straight toward the sun, and darts its three-forked tongue.   475
Huge Periphas and Achilles' squire and driver,
Automedon, with the Scyrian contingent
Pressed up and hurtled torches to the roof.
Pyrrhus was at the front: he took an ax
To smash the bronze-bound doors and tear their hinges,   480
First hacking out a panel for a hole
In the hard oak—a wide and gaping window.
There was the house inside, with its long courtyard—
The ancient kings' and Priam's sanctuary—
And on the threshold stood its armed defenders.   485
Sounds of disaster and confusion echoed
Throughout the place, with howls and lamentation
Of women. Shouting struck the golden stars.
Terrified mothers roamed all through the mansion,
And clung to doorposts, pressing kisses on them.   490
Strong as his father, Pyrrhus came on. Latches,
Guards couldn't hold him back. The battering ram
Made the door sway, unhinged, and topple forward.
The Greeks broke murderously through. They killed
The first defenders, swarmed in all the rooms.   495
A foaming, storming river is far gentler,
Which roars out past its heaped-up banks' resistance.
It hurtles swollen through broad fields, sweeps herds
And barns along. There I saw Atreus' sons
At the door, and Neoptolemus in blood-frenzy—   500
And Hecuba, her hundred daughters, and Priam,
Whose blood fouled altar flames that he had blessed.
Fifty bedrooms (for a rich supply of grandsons),
Pillars that flaunted gold barbarian spoil—
Everything fell. Where flames failed, Greeks laid hold.   505
Perhaps you want to know how Priam died.
He saw his city fallen, taken, gates
Torn open, and the enemy deep inside.

On shaking shoulders he set armor, last worn
Decades ago, strapped on a useless sword,   510
And rushed to die in crowds of hostile soldiers.
Beneath high, open heaven in his courtyard
Was a great altar. A primeval laurel
Leaned to embrace the household gods with shade.
There Hecuba and the princes' wives were huddling—   515
Like doves that rush for refuge from a black storm—
Futilely, and embracing effigies.
The queen saw Priam in his youthful armor
And said, 'Poor husband, what insanity
Dressed you for war? Where are you hurrying?   520
No such defenders, no such help is called for
Today—not even if my Hector lived.
Retreat here, let this altar keep us all safe—
Or die with us.' She took the old king's hand
And in that sacred place she sat him down.   525
But look! The Trojan prince Polites ran
From Pyrrhus' carnage, ducked through hostile spears.
Down the long porch, across the empty courtyard,
Wounded, he fled. Pyrrhus in bloodlust followed,
Thrusting his spear, grasping beyond his reach.   530
Before his father's face at last, Polites
Was brought down. Blood and life gushed out of him.
Now Priam, though encircled by the slaughter,
Did not hold back from shouting in his fury:
'If there is sight and conscience up in heaven,   535
The gods will give you your deserved reward,
Their thanks for this outrageous crime, for letting
Me see with my own eyes my own son's murder.
You have defiled a father's sight with death.
Achilles was your father? It's a lie.   540
This isn't how he fought. He had respect
For a trusting suppliant's rights. He sent me back
To my throne, with Hector's corpse for burial.'

The old man threw a weak, unwarlike spear.
All it could do was clang across the bronze shield   545
And hang there, by the leather of the boss.
Pyrrhus replied: 'Then go tell Peleus' son,
My father, how far short of him I fall.
Be sure he knows what hateful things I did.
Now die.' The king was dragged up to the altar,   550
Shaking and slipping in his own son's blood.
A left hand gripped his hair. A right hand lifted
A flashing sword and sank it to the hilt.
As Priam watched Troy burn, its fortress topple,
Death took him, and his destiny reached its end.   555
But he had once been haughty lord of Asia,
Its lands, its peoples. On the shore a tall corpse
Lies nameless, with its head ripped from its shoulders.
That was the moment savage horror gripped me.
I froze; I seemed to see my darling father   560
In the brutally stabbed king—he was the same age—
Panting his life out. What about Creusa,
Alone—my house torn open—little Iulus?
I looked around to find some troops to help me.
Deserters! In their terror and exhaustion,   565
They'd jumped from walls or dashed into the flames.
Now I was all alone there—no, I saw
Through Vesta's doorway, quiet, skulking, hidden,
Tyndareus' daughter in the glare that flames
Shed for my ranging feet and searching eyes.   570
She feared the Trojans' vengeance for their city,
Justice from Greeks, and her deserted husband
In his outrage—for both lands, she was a Fury.
A loathsome thing, she crouched behind the altar.
My heart caught fire: I had to punish her   575
For crimes that had destroyed my fatherland.
'She'll safely gaze on Sparta and Mycenae,
Where she was born? She'll triumph as the queen?

She'll see her father's home, her husband, children—
Slaves will escort her, Trojan boys and ladies? 580
Priam is butchered. Troy burns. All those times,
Our shore has sweated blood. No—not for this.
To execute a woman brings no glory—
It is no triumph trailing praise behind it.
Yet I'll destroy this evil, bring it justice— 585
I will be praised—I'll satisfy my heart
With flames of vengeance for my own who're dying.'
My ranting fury carried me along,
When, in pure brightness, through the night appeared
My gentle mother, never clearer to me, 590
Revealing her divinity, the form
She had in heaven. Her right hand restrained me.
Out of her rosy mouth there came these words:
'My child, what pain could bring on such wild anger?
Why rave this way? Where is your love for us? 595
Where have you left Anchises, your poor father,
Broken with age? Ascanius, Creusa—
Are they still living? Everywhere around them
Greek forces mill. If not for my protection,
The weapons and the flames would have consumed them. 600
Give up your hatred of the lovely Helen
And wicked Paris, since it is the gods
Who are so cruel and topple wealthy Troy.
Look! I will take away the whole black cloud
That wraps around you mistily and dims 605
Your mortal sight. But have no fear and do
As I command. Have faith in me, your mother.
Here where you see a giant mass of rock
Shattered and strewn in rippling, dusty smoke,
Neptune has smashed the walls with his great trident, 610
And shaken and uprooted the whole city.
Bloodthirsty Juno, girded with a sword,
Has gained the Scaean Gate and wildly calls

Her army from the ships.
There—on the citadel Athena flashes   615
Her ruthless Gorgon shield through burning cloud.
Our father fills the Greeks with winning courage
Himself—he rouses gods against your troops.
Stop struggling and lay hold of your escape.
I'll take you safely to your household door.'   620
She hid away then in the night's thick mist.
Before me stood grim shapes, great deities
Hostile to Troy.
Truly, I saw the whole of Troy collapsing
In flames, and Neptune's city overthrown,   625
Like an ancient mountain ash that several farmers
Hack with unresting axes in a contest
To tear it loose. It menaces, its leaves
Tremble and dip when its high top is shaken.
Wounds slowly weaken it. It gives a last groan,   630
Rips loose, drags devastation down the hillside.
Some god then led me from the roof, released me
From flames and weapons—all of these gave way.
When I arrived at my ancestral house,
Seeking my father first, and keen to take him   635
Into the towering hills before the others,
He said he could not live past Troy's extinction,
Would not bear exile. 'You, with youth unbroken,
And hearty blood in staunch and solid bodies,
Hurry, escape.   640
If those above had wanted me to live,
They would have saved my city. I've survived
One captured, fallen Troy—it is enough.
Say your farewell: this is my funeral.
Some plunderer will show me mercy, ending   645
My life. To lie unburied is a small loss.
Uselessly, hated by the gods, I linger
Since heaven's father and the king of men

Blasted me with his fire and windy thunder.'
These were his stubborn words. He would not move.   650
In tears we begged him—I, my wife Creusa,
My son, and all our house—not to bring down
Everything with him, making our fate harder.
But he refused, fixed in his plans and place.
My wretched urge was war again, and death.   655
Nothing in life remained to me but these.
'Father, you thought that I would leave you here
And run? Such outrage from a father's mouth?
If out of towering Troy the gods leave nothing,
If you're resolved to give this dying city   660
Yourself and us, the door to that stands open—
To Pyrrhus, soaked with Priam's blood, who kills
The son and then the father at the altar.
Sweet mother, did you save me from the flames
Of war for this? The enemy in my home,   665
My son, my father, and Creusa lying   *Aeneas*
Streaked in each other's blood, like slaughtered cattle?
My armor—bring it: we are not quite beaten.
Let me go back to battle with the Greeks.
Today we won't all die without revenge.'   670
Buckling my sword on, readying my shield
In my left hand, I was about to go.
But my wife, on the threshold, grasped my feet
And thrust our son, our little Iulus, toward me.   *Aeneas' son*
'If you go out to die, then take us with you.   675
But if you think you have some hope in weapons,
Then guard this house. To whom do you leave Iulus,
Your father, and me—your wife but soon your widow?'
Her words, her groans, her wails rang through the house—
But an amazing portent intervened.   680
With Iulus in our arms, near our sad faces,
We saw a filmy, radiant tongue of flame
Rise from his head; it licked his baby locks

And browsed around his temples harmlessly.
In our alarm we tried to slap the fire out   685
And soak the sacred burning of his hair.
But Father Anchises gazed up toward the stars
In joy, stretched out his hands, and spoke these words:
'Almighty Jupiter, father, if prayer moves you,
Merely look down on us; for our devotion   690
Grant us a sky sign to affirm this omen.'
A sudden, crashing roar rose on the left hand
While the old man still spoke, and through the dark sky
A comet hurtled with a dazzling tail.
We saw it glide above the towering rooftops   695
And hide its brilliance in the woods of Ida.
Its tail still glowed, a long, light-brimming furrow.
Its sulfur smoldered over all that country.
My father rose up, conquered by the truth.
In reverence for that sacred star he prayed: 700
'No more delay! Gods of my fathers, lead me:
I'll follow. Save my family, save my grandson.
This was your sign, and Troy is in your power—
And I will yield and go with you, my son.'
Now through the walls the fire's roar grew louder.   705
The blasts of heat were rolling closer to us.
'Dear father, let them set you on my shoulders.
I'll carry you—you will not weigh me down.
Whatever happens, it will be one peril
Or rescue for us both. Our little Iulus   710
Will walk with me, my wife will follow, far back.
Servants, pay close attention to my orders.
A barrow and an old deserted temple
Of Ceres lies outside the fort. Our fathers
Have long revered an ancient cypress near it.   715
All of us will go separate ways and meet there.
Father, you take our gods, these holy statues.
Smeared with the fresh gore of a terrible battle,

I must not touch them but must first be cleansed
In running water.'   720
And now I pulled a tawny lionskin
Over my bending neck and brawny shoulders
And took my load. My little Iulus' fingers
Were twined in mine; he trotted by my long steps.
Behind me came my wife. We went our dark way.   725
Before I hadn't minded the Greeks' spears
Hurled at me, or the Greeks in crowds, attacking.
Now every gust and rustle panicked me
Because of whom I led and whom I carried.
Now I approached the gates. The journey seemed   730
Finished, when suddenly a massive tramping
Sounded. My father, spying through the shadows,
Shouted, 'Run—run, my boy! They're coming close!
I see shields flashing and the glint of bronze.'
Some enemy god then seized me in my terror   735
And stole my reason. Byways led me running
Beyond the streets of the familiar city.
And there my wife, Creusa—no!—was stolen
By fate, or strayed, or else collapsed, exhausted.
Who knows? We never saw her anymore.   740
I did not think of her or note her absence
Before we reached the mound and ancient shrine
Of Ceres. When we gathered there, we found
Her gone—her husband, child, friends cheated of her.
I spared no god or man in my wild curses.   745
Nothing in that whole city's fall was crueler.
I left my son, my father, and my gods
In a twisted gully in the care of comrades.
Bright in my weapons, I went back again,
Determined to run all those risks again,   750
To risk my life in searching all of Troy.
I now approached the walls, the gates' dim threshold
That I had fled from, searching out my footprints

Keenly in darkness, following them back.
The very silence filled my heart with terror.   755
I set out homeward—maybe she had gone there—
Maybe. The Greeks infested that whole building.
It was all over. Flames, rolled by the wind,
Consumed the rooftop, shot insane heat skyward.
I passed to Priam's palace and the fort.   760
In the empty porch of Juno's sanctuary
Phoenix and grim Ulysses stood, assigned
To guard the spoils: a heap of Trojan treasure
Torn from the flaming shrines: wine bowls of pure gold,
The tables and the clothing of the gods   765
Were captured now. Mothers and children stood
In long lines, terrified.
I even dared to shout across the shadows,
Uselessly filling up the roads with grief,
Ceaselessly calling out Creusa's name.   Aeneas' wife   770
I went on, in my race to search the buildings,
But the sad apparition of Creusa
Came to me, taller than the living woman.
Shock choked my voice and stood my hair on end,
But what she said was soothing to my soul: 775
'Why do you rave and revel in this sorrow,
Sweet husband? It was by the will of heaven
This came about. It is not right to take me.
The king of high Olympus will not let you.
In your long exile you will plow a wide sea   780
Clear to the West, where Tiber's Lydian water
Sweeps smoothly through rich fields of warriors.
A prosperous kingdom and a royal wife
Are yours. So weep no longer, though you love me.
I am a Trojan—Venus is your mother: 785
I will not serve Greek matrons in the cities
Of arrogant Myrmidons and Dolopians.
The gods' great mother keeps me on these shores.

Farewell. Cherish the child that we created.'
She left me, cutting short my words and weeping—   790
I had so much to say—and faded off.
Three times I threw my arms around her neck.
Three times her image fled my useless hands,
Like weightless wind and dreams that flit away.
When I rejoined my friends, the night was gone.   795
It startled me to find how many more
Had streamed there—mothers, men in their best years,
Young men, gathered pathetically for exile.
They came from everywhere, supplied, resolved
To sail with me to any land I chose.   800
The Dawn Star rose past Ida's highest slopes
And brought the day. The Greeks held every gate
To the city. There was nothing left to help us.
I picked my father up and sought the mountains."

BOOK 3

"When the gods' decree threw down the Asian empire,
With Priam's innocent race, and noble Ilium;   *Trojan King*
And Neptune's Troy lay smoking on the ground,
Prophecy drove us into empty lands
And far-off exile. Toiling to build our fleet   5
In Phrygian Ida's foothills near Antandros,
We did not know where fate would let us settle,
But mustered men. At summer's start my father
Urged us to spread our sails to destiny.
Weeping, I set out from my country's shores,   10
The plains where Troy had been. I swept to exile
With my friends, my child, my clan's gods, and the great gods.

Far off is Mars' land with its spacious fields
That Thracians till—once cruel Lycurgus reigned there;
Family and ritual bound the place to Troy   15
While our luck held. I landed, set my first walls
On the curving shore, and shaped a name from mine,

'Aeneas' Town'—but fate was hostile here.
I prepared offerings for my mother, Venus,
And the gods who bless new works; I planned to slaughter   20
A fine bull on the beach for heaven's king.
Nearby, a mound was topped with clumps of cornel
And myrtle bristling like a mass of spears.
I tried to wrench that greenwood from the ground,
To roof the altar with the leaves and branches.   25
Then—hideous sight, almost unspeakable—
The first plant pulled away oozed drops of blood
From its torn roots, a filthy gore that tainted
The ground. A freezing tremor shot through me;
My blood ceased flowing, icy with my fear.   30
I didn't stop but pulled a second stem,
To find whatever cause lay deep inside.
Again black blood came dripping from the bark.
I prayed, confounded, to the rustic nymphs
And Father Mars, lord of the Getic fields,   35
To come and take away this omen's curse.
At the third shaft, I made a harder try,
Struggling, with both knees planted on the sand.
Do I dare say this? From the barrow's depths
I heard somebody sob and call to me: 40
'Aeneas, no—don't maul a buried corpse,
Polluting your clean hands. Troy gave me life,
You know me—me, not wood that oozes blood.
Run from this cruel land, from its greedy shore,
Since I am Polydorus, and a woodland   45
Of iron pierced me—and the sharp spears grow here.'
Confused and terrified, I stood unmoving,
My hair on end, words clotted in my throat.
Poor Priam secretly sent Polydorus
And a great treasure to the Thracian king   50
Years ago, in his fear of weapons failing
To save our city from the siege that ringed it.

But when the luckless Trojan power was broken,
The Thracian joined in Agamemnon's victory:
He broke with honor, killing Polydorus   55
To loot the gold. What will that hellish hunger
Not drive a man to do? When I'd stopped quaking,
I told our leaders—first of all my father—
About the omen here and sought advice.
They said that we must sail with the south wind   60
And leave this evil land where guests were outraged.
We gave fresh rites to Polydorus, raising
A huge tomb on the mound. His spirits got
Their altar, grim with dusky bands and cypress.
The Trojan women stood with loosened hair.   65
We brought him cups of warm and frothing milk
And plates of sacred blood. We roused his spirit
With one last shout, then laid it in the tomb.
When we could trust the sea, and the wind called us
With gentle rustling to the placid deep,   70
My men massed on the shore and launched the ships.
The port, the land, the cities dipped behind.
A sacred land lies in the sea, the favorite
Of the Nereids' mother and Aegean Neptune.
It floated loose until the thankful Archer   75
Tied it to Myconos and Gyarus' heights
As a wind-defying place where men could live.
Here I now sailed. The bay serenely welcomed
Our weary crews. We hailed Apollo's town.
King Anius, who was the god's priest too,   80
With ribbons and laurel on his sacred head,
Hurried to meet Anchises, his old friend.
He clasped our hands and took us to his house.

The shrine was built of ancient rock. I prayed,
'Give us a home, Apollo—we're exhausted.   85
Give refugees from Greeks, from cruel Achilles,

A city with secure walls, and descendants.
Where must we go and settle? Under what guide?
Give us an omen, father! Fill our hearts!'
Suddenly, everything appeared to shake: 90
The door, the laurels, the entire hill.
The secret place lay bare; the tripod roared.
We fell and hid our faces. Now a voice came:
'Enduring Trojans, where your race was born,
A fertile, loving land will take you back   95
As nurslings. Seek out your primeval mother.
Aeneas' sons will rule in every country—
His children's children through the generations.'
These were the god's words. Jubilant, wild shouting
Broke out. Where was the town, we asked, that Phoebus (Apollo-shining) 100
Was summoning us back to as we wandered?
My father then considered the traditions.
'Noblemen, hear what we can hope for now.
Great Jupiter's island, Crete, lies in mid-ocean.
There, in Mount Ida's land, our race arose.   105
Crete has a hundred cities, wealthy empires,
And Teucrus, our progenitor, set sail
From there—if I remember what they tell—
And found a place to reign. Troy's citadel
Was not yet built; its people lived in deep vales.   110
From Crete came Mother Cybele, the Corybants
With cymbals, faithful silence for her rites
In Ida's woods, and chariot-yoked tame lions.
We need to hurry where the gods direct us.
Give offerings to the winds and sail for Knossos. Crete   115
It is not far. If Jupiter will help us,
The fleet will moor there when the third dawn breaks.'
And then he slaughtered what he owed the gods:
A bull for Neptune, one for bright Apollo,
The good West Wind's white sheep, the Storm god's black one.   120
The rumor came: Idomeneus banished

From his ancestral kingdom, Crete deserted,
Empty of enemies, homes for the taking.
We left the Delian port and skimmed the sea
Past Naxos' Bacchic ridges, green Reed Island,   125
Olive Island, snow-white Paros, and the scatter
Of the Cyclades. We threaded shallow, roiled straits.
Each sailor fought to do the most. They shouted
For speed to Crete, the country of our fathers.
A fair wind rose behind us, finally wafting   130
Our vessels to the Curetes' ancient shores.
Greedy for work on yearned-for Pergama—
A welcome name—I urged my race to love
The homes and fill the citadel with rooftops.
The ships were on the shore and almost dry,   135
Marriage and farming occupied the young,
Laws and allotments me; when suddenly
That sky rained wretched, rotting sickness on us.
The trees and fields grew only death that year.
We gave our sweet breath up or dragged our lives out.   140
And then the sterile Dog Star scorched the fields.
Shoots withered, and the sick crops gave no food.
My father urged a crossing back to plead
Once more at Phoebus' oracle and ask him
When he would grant an end to our exhaustion,   145
Where we should look for help, where we should go.

Night had brought sleep to all who live on earth.
The sacred forms of Trojan household gods,
Which I had rescued from the city's flames,
Appeared before my eyes as I was lying   150
Asleep. They stood out plainly in the bright light
The moon was pouring through my open window.
They seemed to speak to me and soothe my worry.
'What the god would have told you at his shrine,
He kindly sends with us, right to your threshold.   155

When Troy had burned, we soldiered after you.
We crossed the swelling water with your fleet,
And we will raise your children to the stars
And give the wide earth to your city. High walls
For your high gods you'll need there. Do not shirk   160
Hard travel to a new home, since Apollo
Did not intend your settling here in Crete.
There is a place Greeks call Hesperia,
An old land, strong in war and rich in loam.
Oenotrians lived there, whose descendents take   165
Their name, it's said, from Italus the king.
This is our own home. Dardanus was born here,   *Founder of Troy*
And Father Iasius, founder of our clan.
Wake! Hurry! Go with joy to your old father,
There is no question this time: he must go   170
To Italy. Jove denies you land in Crete.'
The sight and sound of gods dumbfounded me.
(It was no dream, you see. I recognized
Expressions, garlands, faces there before me,
And my whole body dripped with chilly sweat.)   175
I leapt from bed and raised a suppliant's hands
And voice to heaven, and poured unwatered wine
On the hearth. When these heart-easing rites were finished,
I told Anchises all that had transpired.   *Aeneas' father*
He saw we had a double origin;   180
He'd made a fresh mistake about old places.
'Child, how the destiny of Troy torments you!
Only Cassandra gave us such predictions.
Now I recall she often said our race
Was meant to have "the West" or "Italy."   185
But who'd imagine Trojans going there?
And who believed Cassandra in those days?
Have faith in Phoebus—now he sets us right.'   *Apollo*
With shouts of triumph all of us obeyed.
We left another home, but some remained.   190

Now sails unfurled. Light hulls skimmed on the vast sea.
A long way out, with nothing in our sight
Anywhere but the ocean and the sky,
A blue-black mass of rain and stormy midnight
Loomed in; the water bristled in the dark wind.   195
All that colossal surface rose in arcs,
Flinging and strewing us across itself.
The storm clouds muffled day, the sky was hidden
In soaking night, fire shattered on and on.
Slammed off our course, we groped through blinding waves.   200
The sky could not show even Palinurus *Aeneas' helmsman*
The time; he said he'd lost his way in mid-sea.
For three long days (we thought—the gloom confused us)
We wandered, and as many starless nights.
On the fourth day at last we saw land rising: 205
Some distant mountains and a curl of smoke.
We lowered sails. The sailors' plunging rowing
Raised curls of foam and swept us on the blue.
So I was saved, and reached the Turning Islands,
As the Greeks named them. In the wide Ionian   210
They are now fixed, and home to grim Celaeno
And the other Harpies, who have all been banished *"Snatchers," monstrous birds*
From Phineus' palace, routed from his banquet.
The fury of the gods has raised no horror,
No plague more cruel out of the streams of Styx. *river in Hades* 215
They have girls' faces, but their stomachs drip
Revolting filth, their hands have claws, their faces
Are always pale with hunger.
We put to land there. Just beyond the harbor,
We saw a sleek herd scattered in a meadow—   220
Cattle and goats with no one guarding them.
We swarmed in with our swords and called on Jove
And other gods to share our spoils. The curved shore
Filled with our couches as we cooked a great feast.
A terrifying swoop out of the mountains: 225

The Harpies with their clattering wings came screeching
To loot the food. All that they touched they smeared
With filth. We caught their nauseating stench.
In a deep hollow underneath a cliff
Enclosed by trees with bristling shade, we set   230
Fresh tables and restored our altar fires.
From other lairs and corners of the sky—
A circling, screaming, taloned, snatching horde,
Spreading their dirty drool. I called my friends
To arms, to meet that fiendish breed in war.   235
Just as I ordered them, they stashed their swords
In grass clumps all around, and hid their shields.
Now when the birds plunged, shrieking, down the shore's arc,
Misenus gave the signal from his lookout
With his bronze horn. My men rushed in to maim   240
These hideous seabirds with their swords—strange battle.
No one was strong enough to strike a wound
Through those hard plumes. Stampeded to the sky,
They left half-eaten loot and sickening slime.
Celaeno, though, sat on a towering cliff—   245
Ill-omened prophet—shouting out these words:
'Trojans, on top of slaughtering our cattle,
You take up war against the innocent Harpies,
Trying to drive us from our rightful kingdom?
Store in your hearts the prophecy that Phoebus   _Apollo_   250
Gave me. It came from the almighty father;
I, greatest of the Furies, now reveal it.
You'll call the wind to sail to Italy.
When you arrive you'll find an open harbor,
But walls will never ring your promised city   255
Until this crime against us and your hunger
Drive you to grind your tables in your jaws.'
She now took wing and fled into the woods.
My comrades' blood froze. Overcome with fear,
They urged me to abandon arms and plead,   260

With prayers and promises, to be let go—
Whether these things were gods or loathsome birds.
On the shore my father stretched his hands out, calling
The high powers and announcing their due rites.
'Gods, block their threats! Hold this disaster back!   265
We serve you—save us!' He had mooring ropes
Torn free, and sheets let out. Wind from the south
Bellied the sails. On foaming waves we made
The escape the pilot and the winds directed.
Wooded Zacynthus rose amid the waves,   270
Then Dulichium, Same, and steep, rocky Neritos.
We passed the cliffs of Ithaca, where Laertes
Once ruled; we cursed Ulysses' motherland.
The misty peak of Leucate appeared,
With Apollo's shrine, which sailors hold in awe.   275
We dropped our anchors at the little town,
Exhausted. All along the beach our ships stood.
Beyond hope, we had gained a place on dry land.
We cleansed ourselves for Jove, burned promised gifts,
Held Trojan ritual games on Actium's shore. *Headland in*   280
My comrades stripped and wrestled, dripping oil *Greece*
In the old way, relieved at their escape
Through all those cities of the enemy Greeks.
Meanwhile the sun passed through the great year's circuit;
The waves grew sharp in icy winter north winds.   285
The curved bronze shield great Abas' arm once held *Friends*
I nailed outside the gate above this verse: *of Aeneas*
'Aeneas won these arms from conquering Greeks.'
My orders: man the oars and leave the harbor.
With zeal they lashed the sea and swept across it.   290
The Phaeacians' cloud-high fortress sank behind.
We sailed around Epirus and then docked
At the Chaonian port of high Buthrotum.
A rumor—unbelievable—possessed us:
Helenus, Priam's son, reigned in the Greek towns,   295

Succeeding Pyrrhus, even in his marriage
To Andromache—her second Trojan husband.
I was amazed and eager in my heart
To question him about this strange occurrence.
My fleet was in the harbor; I went inland.   300
By chance Andromache was in the woods
Beside the river 'Simois,' offering
The ritual food and gifts to Hector's ashes,
To call his spirit at the hollow green mound
And the two altars sacred to her tears.   305
She saw me coming in my Trojan armor—
Uncanny—and she froze, beside herself.
As she stood gazing, all warmth left her body.
She fainted. Finally, she could speak, and said,
'Goddess' son, is it you I see—alive?   310
You're really here, with news? But if you've lost
The kind light, where is Hector?' Now her tears gushed,
Her wailing filled that place; I was distressed,
And as she raved, I struggled for a few words:
'I am alive, through all of my ordeals.   315
Do not doubt what you see.
Andromache, you were the wife of Hector.
How far you fell! But has some worthy fate
Now caught you? Or is Pyrrhus still your husband?'
She bent her head and whispered this to me: 320
'Lucky beyond us all was Priam's daughter,
Compelled to die beneath Troy's looming walls
At an enemy's grave. No one drew lots for her.
She was no prisoner of a conqueror's bed.
Hauled past remote seas, once my homeland burned,   325
I bore the insults of Achilles' son.
I had a child in slavery. Pyrrhus, chasing
A Spartan bride, Hermione, Leto's grandchild,
Gave me to Helenus, another slave.
Orestes, chased by Furies for his own crime,   330

And full of rage when Pyrrhus stole his bride,
Caught him and killed him at his father's altar.
And at his death a portion of his kingdom
Passed rightfully to Helenus, who named
This land Chaonian, after Trojan Chaon,   335
And put a tower, "Ilium," on that ridge. Troy
What was the wind or fate that set your course here?
Did some god make you stumble on our country?
Your son Ascanius lives and drinks the air?
He was at Troy with you—   340
And does he miss his mother, who is gone?
And do his father and his uncle Hector
Inspire him for his legacy of courage?'
She poured this out, with tears and useless wailing—
Then Priam's son, heroic Helenus,   345
Came to us from the town with a large escort.
He knew us, and with joy he led us homeward,
And every word he spoke was bathed with tears.
Now I approached a little Troy, a tower
Shaped like the great one, and a dry stream, 'Xanthus.' River @ Troy 350
I kissed the threshold of a 'Scaean Gate.'
My Trojans too enjoyed their kindred city.
The king in his broad vestibule received them,
And in his central hall they poured libations,
Holding the wine bowls. Food was set on gold plates.   355

A day passed, then another. Breezes called
Our sails. The canvas puffed out in the south wind,
And I approached our prophet-host and asked,
'Trojan-born spokesman of the gods, you know
Phoebus' power, his Clarian bay trees and his tripod,   360
And omens in the stars, birdcalls, and bird flight.
Tell me (since ritual signs predict a good voyage,
And the gods in all their power urged me on
To make for the far land of Italy—

Except Celaeno spoke of some strange evil 365
To come—a fearful anger that would bring
A hideous hunger), what are my chief dangers?
What can I do to overcome my trials?'
Helenus slaughtered sacramental heifers,
Begged the gods' favor, freed his sacred head 370
Of wreaths and led me into Phoebus' house—
I was so fearful of the godhead there—
And from his priestly mouth came this foretelling:
'Son of the goddess, certainly gods guide you
Across the sea. The king of them allotted 375
This fate, this turning wheel of incident.
These words will help you cross the unknown seas
In safety, clear to an Italian haven.
The Fates have hidden some things I could say;
Some Juno, Saturn's daughter, holds inside me. 380
First, you think Italy's close. You plan to gain
Its harbors easily—but you know nothing.
The formless path there lies beside long coasts.
You'll bend your oars in the Sicilian waves
And cross the salty plain near Italy 385
By Circe's island and the lakes of hell,
Before a safe land lets you found a city.
Keep carefully in mind the signs I speak of:
Troubled at heart, you'll find a huge sow lying
With thirty piglets by a distant river 390
Under the holm oaks. On her bed of dark ground
She will be white, the youngsters at her teats white.
Your city will be there, and your sure respite.
And as for eating tables, calm your terror.
Follow fate's path and ask Apollo's help. 395
Avoid the nearer coast of Italy,
The beaches that are washed by tides we share,
Since evil Greeks inhabit every fort:
The Locrians' walled Narycium, Cretan armies

Of Idomeneus on Sallentian flatlands,   400
And small Petelia set in her safe walls
By Philoctetes, chieftain from Meliboea.
When you have crossed the sea and moored, and give
Your promised gifts at new-built shoreline altars,
Hide your head, drape it in your purple clothing,   405
So that amid the flames of sacred ritual,
You see no enemy and spoil the omens.
Let your companions hold to this—and you too,
And your son's sons: keep pure in this observance.
From here the wind will take you on to Sicily;   410
Pelorus will disclose its narrow gap.
Aim for the left shore, circle in from far out;
Avoid the land and water on the right.
They say some cataclysm split these places.
(Time holds within it such tremendous changes.)   415
It was a single place once, but the waves
Exploded through the middle, splitting Italy
From Sicily, to sever farms and cities
By new-made shores and narrow, sweeping tides.
Scylla lurks on the right, vicious Charybdis   420
On the left; its vortex sucks down vast cascades
Sheer to the bottom three times every day
And spouts them back, striking the stars with froth.
Scylla, down in her secret, murky cave,
Thrusts out her mouths and pulls ships onto rocks.   425
She's human—she's a girl with lovely breasts—
Down to the waist, but then a gruesome sea beast,
With dolphin tails, and wolves massed at her stomach.
Better to double back and make your slow way
Around Pachynum, Sicily's far headland,   430
Than glimpse disgusting Scylla in her huge lair
And hear her blue dogs make the boulders echo.
And if I can be trusted as a prophet,
And know my art, and if the god inspires me,

Then above all hear this, child of the goddess,   435
An urgency I can't repeat enough times:
Plead with and pray to mighty Juno's godhead.
Win the queen over with your suppliant gifts
And cheerful promises: she'll let you triumph
At last, by leaving Sicily for Italy.   440
When you reach Cumae, near the sacred lakes
And the deep-sighing forest of Avernus,
You'll see the raving Sibyl in a deep cave.   *Keeper of gate to Hades*
She chants the future, and with special signs
Marks it on leaves. The virgin puts these verses   445
In sequence and then locks them in her cave.
They stay there motionless, in perfect order.
But when a hinge turns, and a tender breeze
Falls on that flimsy foliage and disturbs it,
She will not chase those flutterings through her cavern,   450
Nor link the lines back in their proper order.
Disgusted, people leave, forgoing counsel.
You must not brood about the time you spend there,
Though your friends grumble, though your goal insists
On canvas bellying across the deep.   455
Approach the seer, beg to know your future
From her own chanting mouth, by her goodwill:
She'll tell of tribes that live there, wars to come,
And hardships to endure or to avoid.
Revere her, and she'll grant a good voyage back.   460
But this is all that I'm allowed to tell you.
Go then, raise Troy to heaven with your strivings.'
After the augur spoke these loving words,
He had his massive presents of carved ivory
And gold brought to our ships. He packed our hulls   465
With silver bars and cauldrons from Dodona. *Oracular Shrine of Jupiter*
A corselet, triple-layered in gold chain mail,
And a splendid helmet, topped with flowing plumes,
Had belonged to Pyrrhus. There were special gifts, too, *Greek hero @ Troy / son of Achilles*

For my father. He provided pilots, horses,   470
Fresh rowers, and new armor for my comrades.
Meanwhile Anchises had the sails refitted— *Aeneas' father*
Nothing must keep us when the wind was right.
Helenus spoke to him with great respect: *Trojan Prince*
'Anchises, fit to marry lofty Venus,   475
Both times Troy fell the gods who love you saved you.
There is your Italy. Run it down with full sails.
Take care: coast past the near side, since the far side
Alone is opened for you by Apollo.
Go now! You're lucky in your son's devotion.   480
I must not waste the rising south wind's time.'
Andromache was as gracious as her husband; *Hector's wife*
In grief to see us go, she heaped on gifts
Of clothing she'd embroidered with gold yarn
And gave Ascanius a Trojan cloak: *Iulus / Aeneas' line*   485
'Take what my hands made and remember me.
Andromache, the wife of Hector, pledges
Her love this way. Receive your family's last gifts.
You are the only image of Astyanax *Infant son of Hector & Andromache killed*
Left to me—with his hands and his expressions   490
And eyes; he'd be at boyhood's end, like you.'
As I was leaving, tears rose to my eyes:
'Be happy, since your destiny is finished.
We are called on to one and then another.
You have your peace: no ocean field to plow,   495
No land to seek that falls away from you
Forever. You've made images of Xanthus *river @ Troy*
And Troy with your own hands—with better omens,
I hope, than Troy, and out of reach of Greeks.
And if I ever come to Tiber's country   500
And see the ramparts granted to my people,
We'll make Epirus and its neighbor Italy,
Which share a history and a founder too—
Dardanus—brothers in their souls: we'll make *Founder of Troy*

A single Troy. Our heirs must see to this.'   505
We sailed out. Skirting the Ceraunian headland
Was the quickest way to Italy by sea.
The sun plunged down. The mountains shadowed over.
On the dry beach—warm, yearned-for earth—we scattered,
After allotting rowing for the next day,   510
And sprawled and took our rest. Sleep filled our drained limbs.
Now Night had driven the Hours halfway round,
When zealous Palinurus rose, his ears
Sifting the air, testing for any wind.
He traced the still sky's gliding constellations: 515
Arcturus, the rainy Hyades, the Ox Yoke,
And in the South, Orion with gold armor.
And seeing the right signs in the clear heavens,
He blared a signal from the stern. We broke camp
And spread our wings of sails and ventured out.   520
Now blushing Dawn had chased the stars away;
We glimpsed dim hills—there, just above the sea,
Was Italy. Achates gave the first shout,   *Aeneas' retaining*
Then the whole company cheered, 'Italy!'
Father Anchises wreathed a giant bowl,   525
Filled it with wine, and stood high on the helm,
Calling the gods:
'Deities who rule land and sea and storms:
Be gracious, send a wind, make our way easy.'
The breezes strengthened, and a harbor opened;   530
Then on the heights we saw Minerva's shrine.   */Athena/*
They furled the sails and turned the prows toward shore.
Waves from the east have made the beach a bow.
In front, sharp rocks foam with the briny water;
On either side stone spires with their low arms   535
Form twin walls, and the shrine is safely inland.
Four snow-white horses, the first omen seen,
Ranged browsing on the plain. My father spoke:
'New land, you'll bring us war, since horses go

To war in armor—these beasts threaten war.   540
But sometimes they are trained to draw a chariot
In harmony, in yokes and reins and bridles:
So peace may come.' Cheering, we disembarked.
We called on Pallas first, shield-clanging godhead.   *Minerva / Athena*
Trojan clothes hooded us before her altars.   545
As Helenus had urged this most of all,   *Trojan prince*
We honored Argive Juno with burnt offerings.
With our promises to gods fulfilled, we hurried
To point the sail-draped yardarms out to sea.
This was a land of Greeks, which made us leery.   550
Tarentum's gulf! (Did Hercules really go there?)   *Hero & Son of Jupiter*
The Lacinian temple and the fort at Caulon,
And Scylaceum, wrecker of ships, rose up to face it.
Above the far sea loomed Sicilian Etna.
We heard the vast groans of the wave-struck rocks   555
Already, and the shattered voice of breakers.
The shallows leapt, and sand ran through their seething.
My father shouted, 'That must be Charybdis—
The crags, the grim rocks Helenus foretold.
Friends, save us! All together at the oars!'   560
The men obeyed, and Palinurus led,   *Aeneas' helmsman*
Wrenching his creaking prow out toward the sea.
The whole fleet rowed and turned their sails to follow.
The arching billow heaved us to the sky,
Then hollowed out: we sank as deep as hell.   565
Three times the caverns at the cliff's base thundered.
Three times the foam shot out and soaked the stars.
Sun and wind left us now. We were exhausted
And lost, and drifted to the Cyclopes' shore.   *one-eyed giants of Sicily*
The harbor, blocked from wind, is broad and peaceful,   570
But Etna's gales of rubble roar beside it.   *Volcano*
Sometimes a dark cloud blasts clear up to heaven,
A pitch-black smoky whirlwind ringed with white ash.
Its swarms of hurtling fire flick the stars.

Sometimes it vomits crags and mountain entrails   575
Into the air, or masses melted stone
From its deep roots and, with a groan, boils over.
They say that huge Enceladus, scorched with lightning,
Is lying pinned beneath enormous Etna,
Which breathes its fires out of shattered forges,   580
And when he turns, exhausted, the whole island
Trembles and roars, and thick smoke masks the sky.
Cowering all night in the woods, we suffered
Inhuman horrors, noises out of nowhere.
Neither the stars' fire nor the moon was showing.   585
The heights of heaven lost all incandescence,
And the hours of night were buried in dark cloud.
The day was rising, and the dawn appeared.
Aurora drove the shadows from the damp sky— *Goddess of Dawn*
When a strange form burst on us from the forest: 590
A pitiful, starved heap of dirt and rags.
He approached us as a suppliant, with his hands out.
We stared. His long beard straggled, he was filthy,
Thorns pinned his clothes. But he was Greek, we saw:
A past invader, in his country's armor.   595
He'd seen our Trojan clothes and arms already
And halted for a little while in terror—
Then he came rushing forward to the shore,
Weeping and pleading: 'By the stars, the gods,
This sky that gives us shining air to breathe,   600
Take me on board, to any country, Trojans.
That is enough. I sailed in that Greek fleet,
And I attacked your homes—yes, I admit it.
Either forgive my crime or throw the pieces
Of my body on the vast sea—let it take me.   605
Give me the joy of death at human hands!'
He clutched my knees in an unyielding grovel.
I strove to draw from him his name and lineage,
And then the story of his misery.

Anchises quickly gave the youth his right hand,   610
A ready sign of friendship, lending courage.
At last he let his terror go and spoke:
'Luckless Ulysses took me—Achaemenides—
To Troy, because my father, Adamastus
Was poor—I wish I'd stayed in poverty.   615
My friends forgot me in their fear and left me
In the Cyclops' desolate cavern when they stole
Out of his savage door. That huge, dark house
Is fouled with gory food. He towers, striking
The stars. (Gods, rid the world of such a plague!)   620
Who'd want to speak to him or look at him?
He eats poor human entrails and black blood.
In the middle of his cave I saw him lying:
He put his giant hand on two of us
And smashed them on a rock; the entranceway   625
Ran with sprayed blood. I saw him chewing bodies
Black with their own gore, while their limbs still quivered.
He paid. Ulysses acted like the hero
He was, and took a great, defiant risk.
The Cyclops, stuffed with food and sunk in wine,   630
Stretched his great length across the cave and laid down
His lolling head, and vomited in his sleep
Blood, wine, and gory fragments. We beseeched
The holy powers, drew lots for tasks, and swarmed
Around him. With a sharpened pike we pierced   635
The single eye beneath his brutal brow—
Sun-big, big as a shield an Argive carries.
The joy, when we avenged our comrades' ghosts!
But run, poor people! Slash your mooring cable
And go.   640
As huge as Polyphemus in his cavern,
Shutting his woolly herds in pens for milking,
A hundred Cyclopes are on the loose

On this curved shore and wander in these mountains.
And now the third moon fills its horns with light,   645
Tally of time endured deep in these woods
Among beasts' dens. From cliffs I see the monsters.
I tremble when I hear their steps and voices.
Trees give me miserable fodder: berries,
And rocky cornels, and I pull at roots.   650
Yours are the first ships I have known to land here
In all my watching. I surrender to them
To escape this savage race, no matter what.
Grant any death you like, and take my spirit.'
Just as he finished, we saw Polyphemus   655
Himself, high on a hill among his herd,
His great bulk moving toward the shore he knew—
A massive, hideous monster, but now blinded.
A pine log led his hand and braced his steps.
The woolly ewes, his sole delight and comfort,   660
Followed him.
He waded to the deep and level water
To wash the scooped-out socket's running gore,
Grinding his teeth and groaning. Now he strode
Far out, but no waves wet his towering flanks.   665
We scrambled to escape, and took the suppliant,
Poor man. With stealth, we cut the rope and rowed
Flat out, and churned the surface frantically.
He wrenched his footsteps toward the sounds we made,
But couldn't get his grasping hands on us—   670
We were too fast on the Ionian currents.
His roar shook every wave on that wide sea;
It sent its terror inland, into Italy,
And bellowed in the arching caves of Etna.
The noise roused the entire Cyclops tribe,   675
Who ran from woods and hills to fill the beach.
We saw the clan of Etna standing there,

Each with a cloud-high head and one wild eye—
Grim council—like the oaks that reach the ether,
Or cone-hung cypresses, their tops exalted,   680
Groves for Diana's hunting and Jove's oracles.
Our terror drove us headlong—anywhere.
We let the sails out for the wind to take.
But Helenus had told us not to travel   *Trojan prince*
By Scylla and Charybdis: death crowds both sides. *Sea monster* 685
We chose to set the canvas for retreat,
But a north wind from Pelorus' narrow cape
Drove us around Pantagias' rocky gates,
The Bay of Megara, and low-lying Thapsus.
Hapless Ulysses' Achaemenides *Greek stranded on Cyclops by Ulysses* 690
Pointed out shores he'd skirted coming there.
Plemyrium, washed with waves, confronts an island
Stretched across a Sicilian bay. The ancients
Called it Ortygia, land of Arethusa,
The spring to which the Alpheus River tunneled   695
From Elis, as they say, to blend in this sea.
We prayed to local gods, as we'd been told to,
And sailed on past Helorus' fertile wetlands.
We grazed Pachynus' high and jutting rocks.
Far off rose Camerina—fate forbade   700
Moving it—and the fields outlying Gela,
A city named for roaring 'Laughter' River;
And then steep Acragas showed its far-off, huge walls—
Once, long ago, it bred high-hearted horses.
With a good wind we passed palm-filled Selinus,   705
And picked through Lilybaeum's vicious shallows.
Then I reached Drepanum's haven, to my grief.
There I lost my comforter in every mishap
And fear, Anchises, whom so many storms   *Aeneas' father*
Had hounded. Best of fathers, you were tired   710
And left me, after all I saved you from.
Among the hateful things foretold by Helenus

And grim Celaeno, this one grief was missing,
And this I suffered last in my long travels.
It was from there god brought me to your shore."   715
With everyone engrossed, Father Aeneas
Told of the fate the gods sent, and his travels.
At last he reached the end and sat in silence.

BOOK 4

Now the queen's lifeblood fed her grievous love wound—
An unseen flame gnawed at her hour on hour.
His bravery, the glory of his family
Came back to her—his face, his words were rooted
In her mind, and new love kept sweet rest away.   5
Dawn raised the torch of Phoebus, which is earth's light,
And pushed the drizzling shadows from the sky,
And stricken Dido told her loving sister:
"Anna, half-waking dreams have terrified me.
This stranger who has come here as our guest—   10
His face, his walk, his heart's and weapons' strength—
I think—it must be true—this is a god's child.
Fear marks plebeian spirits. How I pity
His hard fate and the long, grim war he told of!
If ever my mind moved from where I fixed it—   15
I set myself against the ties of marriage
After my first love cheated me by dying
And made me hate all wedding ceremony—

I might relent, this single time, and falter.
Anna, I must confess, since poor Sychaeus
Fell, since my brother stained our home with murder,   20
This one alone has moved me; now I waver.
I recognize the remnants of that flame.
But let the earth first gape to its foundation,
Or the all-powerful father's lightning drive me   25
To the pale shades in Erebus and deep night,
Before I shamefully break Honor's laws.
The man who first was part of me has taken
My love. He ought to keep it where he's buried."
The tears she now shed left her bosom wet.   30
Anna replied, "You're more to me than life.
Will you let lonely grief devour your whole youth,
Without sweet children and the gifts of Venus?
Do you think ashes care, or ghosts in graveyards?
Both here in Libya and back in Tyre   35
No suitors tamed your grief. Iarbas and others
Reared by this rich, victorious Africa
Are scorned—and now you fight a love that suits you?
Recall whose land this is you've made your home in:
The cities of Gaetulians, never conquered,   40
The wild Numidians and treacherous Syrtis,
Bare desert and marauding Barcaei
Encircle you, and conflict looms from Tyre—
Your brother threatens.
It was the provident gods and Juno's favor   45
That steered the Trojan ships here on the wind.
The city that you'll see, the rising empire
Out of this marriage! Trojan allied arms
Will bring this Punic town to soaring glory.
Seek the gods' sanction. Make propitious offerings.   50
Weave pretexts for delaying as you fête him:
Seas raging through the days of wet Orion,
Ships damaged, and a hard and stubborn sky."

This appeal made the spark of passion blaze,
Lent hope to hesitation, melted shame.   55
First they approached each temple and each altar
With pleas and slaughtered chosen sheep in ritual
For Phoebus, law-giving Ceres, Father Bacchus—
But Juno first, who joins the bonds of marriage.
In her right hand lovely Dido held the bowl   60
And tipped it on a snow-white heifer's forehead;
Paraded past gods' statues to rich altars,
Opened each day with gifts, searched for the meaning
Cut open in the steaming guts of beasts.
Oh, empty-minded prophets! In her madness,   65
What use were prayers and temples? Flame devoured
Her tender marrow. Her heart's wound throbbed in hiding;
Soon Dido burned and raved all through the city,
As when a deer is wounded from far off
By a shepherd who is not aware his arrow   70
Has found its mark; through Dicte's woods the quarry
Runs, with the death reed buried in her side.
Now Dido leads Aeneas through the fortress,
Shows him Sidonian wealth, the rising city,
Begins to speak but leaves her words half-said.   75
At fall of daylight, she repeats her banquet
And asks to hear again of Trojan suffering.
Again, she fixates on the teller's words.
Her guests go, and the moon puts out its dim light,
And falling constellations counsel sleep;   80
She sorrows in the empty house, reclining
On the couch he left. She sees and hears his absence.
She holds Ascanius—so like his father!— *Aeneas' son*
In her lap, and cheats her real and shameful love.
The towers she started do not rise. The young men   85
No longer drill or build defending ramparts
Or ports. The work stalls, halfway done—the menace
Of high walls, and the cranes as tall as heaven.

So sickness gripped the queen, who let her folly   90
Outrun her good name. Juno, Jove's dear wife
And Saturn's daughter, saw and went to Venus.
"Truly, your son and you have won such glory,
Such huge spoils. Power worth eternal praise
Shows in two gods who dupe a mortal woman.   95
I know that you've been wary of our walls here,
Distrustful when you saw high Carthage settled.
Where will this end? Where will this fierce fight take us?
Why not a lasting treaty and a contract
Of marriage? What your heart desired, you have.   100
Dido's love burns. Her bones draw in its fury.
Why not make these one people? We can rule them
Together. As a Phrygian husband's slave,
She'll hand you all these Tyrians as a dowry."
But Venus felt the trick in this, the effort   105
To steer Italian power into Libya.
She countered: "To agree is merely sane.
Who would prefer to take up arms against you?
If only what you plan succeeds in practice . . .
Fate—to me—sways, uncertain. Is Jove's plan   110
One town for Trojan refugees and Tyrians,
An alliance, or a blended population?
You, as his wife, could rightly probe his thinking.
Ask him, then I'll be with you." Juno answered,
"Leave me to do that. Briefly now I'll say—   115
So listen—how we finish what's at hand.
Poor Dido and Aeneas are preparing
A woodland hunting trip at dawn tomorrow,
When the Sun's rising rays reveal the curved earth.
While horsemen rush to cordon off the passes,   120
I'll mingle rain and hail in a black storm cloud
And pour it down and shake the sky with thunder.
Their retinue will scatter in the dark.
The same cave will receive the Trojan leader

And Dido. I'll be there and—with your sanction—   125
Join her to him and make her his in marriage
On firm ground. These will be the rites." Then Venus
Agreed, and laughed to see the guile behind this.

Aurora now rose up, away from Ocean.
In her fresh rays the gates let chosen troops out   130
Who carried various nets and hunting spears.
Massylian horsemen, keen-nosed dogs rushed forward.
At the bedroom door the Tyrian leaders waited
For the queen, whose horse stood, bright in gold and purple,
And fiercely stamped, and gnawed a foaming bit.   135
At last, with a great retinue, she came.
Her Punic cloak was edged with rich embroidery,
Her quiver gold, her hair bound in a gold clasp,
And a gold brooch secured her purple robe.
The Trojan troops and an excited Iulus   140
Came up. Finest of all these was Aeneas,
Who as her escort joined his ranks with hers.
Apollo, coming to his mother's Delos
From winter Lycia and the Xanthus River,
Renews the dance. Around the altar shout   145
Cretans, Dryopians, tattooed Agathyrsans.
He walks the slope of Cynthus with his long hair
Braided and bound with tender leaves and gold.
On his shoulders arrows rattle. Just as lively,
As beautiful, as noble strode Aeneas.   150
They came into the hills and trackless woods.
Wild goats they started from a stony summit
Ran down the slope. Deer from another refuge
Sped off in crowding ranks across the bare plain,
In dusty panic to escape the mountain.   155
The boy Ascanius, keen-horsed, keen rider,
Kept racing past them on the valley floor,
Wanting a tawny lion from the mountain

Or a foam-mouthed boar among so many tame things.
But a racket and a tumult now erupted   160
From the sky; a storm cloud shot in, full of hail,
Scattering Trojans and their Tyrian escorts
And Venus' Trojan grandson through the fields
Toward urgent shelter. Streams rushed from the hillsides.
The Trojan lord and Dido found the same cave.   *Aeneas*   165
Primeval Earth and Juno, giver of brides,
Signaled, and in collusion lightning flashed
At the union. On the mountaintops nymphs howled.
From this day came catastrophe and death.
No thought of public scandal or of hiding   170
Her passion troubled Dido any longer.
She called it marriage, to conceal her shame.

Rumor, the swiftest plague there is, went straight out
To all the settlements of Libya.
She thrives on motion, drawing strength from travel;   175
Tiny and timid first, then shooting upward
To hide her head in clouds yet walk the ground.
Mother Earth, they say, in anger at the gods,
Bore this child last, quick-footed, quick-winged sister
Of Titan Enceladus and giant Coeus.   180
Beneath each feather of the hideous monster—
This is the startling legend—is a wide eye,
A tongue, a blaring mouth, a pricked-up ear.
Between the earth and sky, in shadow, shrieking,
She flies at night. No sweet sleep shuts her eyes.   185
By day she sits as lookout on a rooftop
Or a high tower, and alarms great cities.
Her claws hold both true news and evil lies.
She filled the realms now with her tangled talk,
Chanting in glee a mix of fact and fiction: 190
"Aeneas, from a Trojan family, came here.
Beautiful Dido chose him as her lover.

What kind of rulers spend the whole long winter
Sunk deep in luxury and sordid passion?"
The hideous goddess spread these stories widely, *Rumor*   195
Then, without pausing, flew off to King Iarbas,
And with her words piled high and lit his rage.
A Garamantian nymph and Ammon's violence
Created him. His broad lands raised to Jove
A hundred huge shrines. Priests and altar flames   200
Kept constant vigils for the gods, while herds' blood
Slathered the floor, and bright wreaths decked the doorways.
Stung with the rumor now, beside himself,
He stood in the gods' presence, at their altars,
Raised suppliant hands and prayed insistently: 205
"Almighty Jove, to whom the race of Moors
On embroidered banquet couches pour libations—
Do you see this? When you hurl your thunder, Father,
Is terror needless? Is that fire, that noise
Up in the clouds without an aim or meaning?   210
A woman straying on my borders rented
A scrap of shore for building on and farming
On *my* conditions. She refused me marriage
But lets Aeneas rule with her—no, rule her.
That Paris with his mincing retinue, *Trojan prince caused Trojan*   215
His perfumed hair tied in an Asian headdress, *war / adultery w/ Helen*
Lords it over his loot. So empty legend
Alone has made us fill your shrines with gifts?"
This was the king's prayer as he grasped the altar.
The almighty heard. His eyes turned toward the palace   220
And the lovers who'd forgotten all decorum.
He spoke to Mercury and gave this order: *messenger of god*
"Call the west wind, my son, glide on your wings;
Speak to the Trojan leader, who is loitering
At Tyrian Carthage with no thought for cities   225
Granted by fate. Go, hurry my words landward.
This wasn't what his lovely mother promised,

Or why—both times—she saved him from the Greeks,
But to rule Italy, beget an empire
That roars with war, to give us noble Teucer's   230
Descendants, who will bring the whole world laws.
If this majestic future cannot rouse him
To shoulder his own glory in this labor,
Does he begrudge his son the Roman citadel?
What can he gain here in a hostile nation?   235
Ausonian progeny? Lavinian fields?
The sum of what I want him told: Set sail!"
He spoke. So on his mighty father's orders,
The son prepared, first tying golden sandals
Onto his feet, to take him swift as wind   240
High over land and ocean on their wings.
He took the wand that calls pale souls from Orcus
And sends them into gloomy Tartarus, wakens
And puts to sleep, and opens perished eyes.
With this he drove the winds and skimmed through chaos   245
Of clouds. He saw the brow and the steep flanks
Of rocky Atlas, prop of the high heavens—
Atlas, with black clouds always at his head,
Where the pines grow, and wind and rain blast hard.
The snow spreads down his shoulders. Off the chin   250
Of the old man torrents pour. Ice locks his sharp beard.
Here Mercury halted, poised on balanced wings,
Then hurled his whole weight headlong toward the waves.
There are some birds that skim the shoreline waters
Or round the base of crags where fish are teeming.   255
Like them Cyllene's native sliced the winds,
Left his mother's father, passed from sky to earth,
And landed on the sandy shore of Libya.
He set his feathered feet among the shanties
And saw Aeneas laying out the towers   260
And building houses. Tawny jasper flecked
His sword. His shoulders trailed the glowing richness

Of a purple cloak with thin gold stripes, a present
Woven by wealthy Dido. The god scolded:
"Your wife must like you placing the foundations   265
For lofty Carthage, such a splendid city—
Forgetting your own kingdom that awaits you.
The ruler of the gods, whose strength bends heaven
And earth, has sent me down from bright Olympus,
Commanding that I fly here with this message: 270
What will this loitering in Libya bring you?
If you're unmoved by all the coming splendor
Which is a weight you do not wish to shoulder,
Think of your hopes as Iulus grows, your heir,
Owed an Italian realm and Roman soil."   275
These were the words from the Cyllenian's mouth.
Still speaking, he passed out of human vision
And trailed away until the thin air hid him.
This apparition left Aeneas stunned.
His hair stood up, and words stuck in his throat.   280
He burned to run—however sweet this land was.
The gods' august command had terrified him.
But how? What would he dare say to the queen
In her passion? What beginning could he make?
His mind kept darting and his thoughts dividing   285
Through the whole matter and each baffling question.
After much wavering, this seemed the best plan:
He called Mnestheus and brave Serestus
And Sergestus: they must get the men together
Quietly, rig the fleet, and hide the reason   290
For the stirring. Meanwhile the good lady Dido
Would not expect such strong love could be broken.
He would approach her, seeking out the best words
At the kindest time. With great alacrity,
These men obeyed in everything he ordered.   295
But who can fool a lover? Soon the queen—
Even in safety anxious—sensed the trick,

Though no ship moved yet. Evil Rumor told her
The fleet was being fitted for a journey.
She raved all through the town in helpless passion,   300
Like a Bacchant the biennial mysteries rouse
With shrieks of ritual and brandished emblems
And shouts that summon her to dark Cithaeron.
She faced off with Aeneas and accused him:
"You traitor, did you think that you could hide   305
Such a great crime, that you could sneak away?
The pledge you made, our passion for each other,
Even your Dido's brutal death won't keep you?
Monster, you toil beneath these winter skies
And rush to cross the deep through northern blasts,   310
For a strange home on someone else's land?
If ancient Troy still stood today to sail to,
Would you make off across that surging plain?
You run from me? By your pledged hand, my tears
(Since I am stripped of everything but these),   315
Our union, and the wedding we embarked on—
If I have ever earned it through my kindness,
Have pity on my tottering house and me.
If pleading has a chance still, change your mind.
The Libyan clans and Nomad rulers hate me;   320
So do the Tyrians, because of you.
You ruined me and my good name—my one path
To heaven. My guest leaves me here to die.
Now I must call you guest instead of husband.
Pygmalion my brother will raze my walls,   Dido's brother   325
Gaetulian Iarbas lead me off, a captive.
If only, though deserting me, you gave me
A child—if I could see a small Aeneas
Play in my palace, with a face like yours—
I wouldn't feel so cheated and abandoned."   330
She spoke; he kept his eyes down, at Jove's orders,
Struggling to force his feelings from his heart.

Finally, briefly: "Name your favors, list them.
There isn't one I ever could deny.
Never will I regret Elissa's memory *Another name for* 335
While I *have* memory, while I breathe and move. *Dido.*
A little on the facts, though: don't imagine
I meant to sneak away, and as for 'husband,'
I never made a pact of marriage with you.
If fate would let me live the life I chose, 340
If I had power over my decisions,
I would have stayed at Troy, where I could tend
Belovèd graves; Priam's high citadel
Would stand; I would restore Troy for the conquered.
But Grynean Apollo and the edicts 345
Of Lycia drive me into Italy.
My love, my home are there. You are Phoenician,
But love to see your towers in Libya.
How can you then resent us Trojans settling
In Italy—*our* lawful foreign kingdom? 350
When the night covers earth with drizzling shadows,
When fiery stars rise, then the troubled ghost
Of my father, dear Anchises, hounds my dreams. *father Aeneas*
I know I cheat my darling son Ascanius
Of fields fate gave him in his western realm. 355
From Jove himself a heavenly emissary
(On both our heads, I swear it) brought me orders
Down through the air. In the clear day I saw him
Come through the gate, and these ears heard his voice.
Don't goad me—and yourself—with these complaints. 360
Italy is against my will."
Although her back was turned, she still surveyed
The speaker blankly and distractedly
Over her shoulder. Then her fury broke out.
"Traitor—there is no goddess in your family, 365
No Dardanus. The sharp-rocked Caucasus
Gave birth to you, Hyrcanian tigers nursed you.

Why pretend now? Is something worse in store?
Was there a sigh for tears of mine? A glance?
Did he give in to tears himself, or pity?   370
Injustice overwhelms me, which concerns
Great Juno and our father, Saturn's son.
What bond can hold? I helped a castaway,
I shared my kingdom with him, like a fool.
The ships you lost—I saved your friends from death—   375
Hot madness drives me. *Now* the fortune-teller
Apollo, Lycian lotteries, Jove dispatching
Dire orders earthward through the gods' own mouthpiece—
As if such cares disturbed the gods' calm heaven!
I will not cling to you or contradict you.   380
Ride windy waves to chase Italian kingdoms.
I hope that heaven's conscience has the power
To trap you in the rocks and force your penance
Down your throat, as you call my name. I'll send
My black flames there. When cold death draws my soul out,   385
My ghost will hound you. Even among dead souls
In hell, I'll know when you are finally paying."
In torment, she broke off and turned away,
And ran out of his sight into the palace.
And there he froze—with much he would have said.   390
She fainted and was lifted by her maids,
And the bed inside the marble walls received her.
Now the right-thinking hero, though he wished
To give some comfort for so great a grief,
Obeyed the gods, returning to his ships,   395
While he continued groaning, deeply lovesick.
The Trojans fell to work and pulled the vessels
Down from the beach in one long line. Tarred hulls
Floated. The busy crews brought leafy oars
And logs with bark still on.   400
That rush from everywhere in town resembled
Ants plundering a giant heap of spelt

To store at home in readiness for winter.
Over the grass the thin black phalanx goes,
Loaded with booty. Some are heaving huge grains 405
Forward, and some are marshaling and prodding,
So the entire pathway hums with work.
What did you feel then, Dido, when you saw?
How did you sob when all that shoreline seethed?
You looked out from your tower, and the sea 410
Was an industrious uproar and commotion.
Reprobate Love, wrencher of mortal hearts!
He drives her now to tears, and now to beg
And cravenly submit her pride to love—
Whatever leaves her with a hope of life. 415
"Anna, you see the whole shore in a tumult. *Dido's Sister*
They come from everywhere. Sails draw the breeze.
Sailors in joy hang garlands on the sterns.
As surely as I saw this great grief coming,
So surely I'll endure. But do one favor 420
In pity, since the traitor was your friend—
Yours only: you were trusted with his secrets;
You know how to approach him when he's weak.
Go, sister, kneel to my proud enemy.
I was no Greek at Aulis when they swore 425
To smash his race. I sent no fleet to Troy,
Nor made his father's ghost and ashes homeless.
How can he block his ears against my words?
Where is he running? As a last sad love gift,
He ought to wait for winds that make it easy. 430
I do not plead the marriage he betrayed.
Let the man go be king in charming Latium.
I just want time, a pause to heal my mind
And teach myself to mourn in my defeat.
I ask this final wretched favor, sister— 435
A loan—and I will give my death as interest."
Weeping, she made this plea. Her grieving sister

Delivered it repeatedly. No tears
Could move him; no words found his sympathy.
His fate and Jove were barriers to his ears;   440
As in the Alps, the North Wind's blasts assault
A solid, tough, and venerable oak,
Competing to uproot it; with a creak
At the blows, it strews its high leaves on the ground
But clasps the cliff with roots that go as far   445
Toward hell as its top reaches into heaven:
Just as relentless were the words that battered
The hero. In his noble heart he suffered,
But tears did nothing. His resolve endured.
Appalled now by her fate, poor Dido prayed   450
For death; she wished to see the sky no longer.
Other things also drove her from the daylight:
Her gifts on incense-burning altars rotted,
Horrible to describe: wine turned to black
And filthy gore the second that she poured it.   455
No one was told. Her sister did not know it.
There stood inside her home a marble shrine
To her late husband: there she worshiped him,
Spreading white fleece and hanging holy wreaths.
She thought she heard his voice there, echoing, calling.   460
When the night's darkness covered all the earth,
She listened to a lone owl on the rooftree
Whose song of death kept trailing into sobs.
Many grim warnings of the long-dead seers
Panicked her too. In dreams a fierce Aeneas   465
Chased her. She raved in fear or was abandoned,
Friendless, forever walking a long road,
Seeking her Tyrians in a lifeless land. *Phoenician Land /*
It was like Pentheus seeing bands of Furies,   *Carthage founded*
And a pair of Thebes, and a sun split in two;   470
As in a play the son of Agamemnon *murdered by Clytemnestra*
Runs from his mother's torches and black snakes

While vengeful demons lurk outside the door.
Madness and grief filled her defeated heart,
And she chose death. She had a time and method,   475
But hid her plan behind a face of peace
And hope, in speaking to her wretched sister.
"Anna, I've found a way—congratulate me!—
To bring him back or set me free from love.
Next to the setting sun and Ocean's boundary,   480
In Ethiopia, where giant Atlas
Turns the star-blazing heavens on his shoulder,
Lived a Massylian priestess I've now found,
Who guarded the Hesperides' temple there,
Nourished the snake, preserved the sacred branches,   485
And strewed sleep-bringing poppy and moist honey.
She says her spells soothe any minds she wishes
Or else bring grueling troubles into others,
Stop rivers and turn stars back in their courses,
And call out ghosts at night. The earth will roar   490
Beneath your feet, ash trees will rush down mountains.
Sister, I swear it by your darling life
And by the gods—I would not choose such weapons.
Build me a pyre in secret in the courtyard.
The arms that evil man hung in our bedroom—   495
The clothes I stripped from him, our bed of union,
My death—put it all there. I want the leavings
Of the criminal destroyed. She's shown me how."
Now she was silent, and her face went pale.
But Anna did not guess her sister's funeral   500
Hid in these strange rites, or suspect such frenzy—
What could be worse than when Sychaeus died?   *Dido's husband,*
She did as she was told.   *her brother, Pygmalion*
Deep in the house, beneath the sky, a pyre   *murdered him!*
Now towered high with logs of pine and oak.   505
The queen festooned the walls with funeral garlands.
Conscious of what must be, she put his picture

On the bed, above his sword and cast-off clothes.
Altars encircled her. The loose-haired priestess
Shouted three hundred gods' names—Erebus, Chaos,   510
Three-faced Diana, who is triple Hecate.
She sprinkled drops she said were from Avernus.
Herbs appeared, cut with bronze knives at the full moon,
Swollen and oozing coal-black milk of poison;
A love charm too, torn from a new foal's forehead   515
Before the mare could get it.
Dido, with sacred meal in clean hands, robes loose,
One sandal off, now stood at the high altar,
Called gods, called fate-wise stars as witnesses.
She prayed to anything in heaven that sees   520
And punishes a broken bond of love.

Now it was night, and all earth's weary creatures
Slept peacefully. The woods and savage waters
Were still. The stars were halfway through their journeys
Above the tranquil fields. Cattle and bright birds   525
Of the broad lakes and brambly wilderness
All lay asleep beneath the noiseless sky,
Their troubles soothed, their sufferings forgotten—
But not the desolate Phoenician queen.
Her heart and eyes shunned darkness and the ease   530
Of sleep. Her torments thronged, her love ran wild—
They came and went on seething tides of madness.
Her heart was churning with unceasing questions:
"What should I do? Go back where I'll be laughed at,
And beg to marry a Numidian prince   535
After I turned those suitors all away?
Follow the Trojan ships and do whatever
The Trojans order? Surely they'll recall
The help I gave and, for the past's sake, help me.
But then again, would they allow the outcast   540
On their proud ships? Poor fool, you're not familiar

With the treachery of Laomedon's descendants?
Would I trail those cheering sailors all alone,
A deserter? Would I take my Tyrian ranks
As escorts? Would those barely torn from Sidon   545
Endure another sea voyage on my orders?
No, die—you've earned it. Give the sword your sorrow.
But you, my sister, weakened by my tears,
Turned folly to disaster and defeat.
I could not live a blameless life, unmarried,   550
Like a wild thing, and be spared this agony:
I broke my promise to the dead Sychaeus."
Out of her heart these words of sorrow broke.
Aeneas was asleep on the high stern,
In confidence that everything was ready—   555
When in a dream he saw the god again:
The form had Mercury's face and his complexion,
His yellow hair and handsome young man's body,
And it renewed the warning from before:
"You sleep, child of the goddess, while disaster   560
Teeters above, and perils lurk around?
Fool, can't you hear your guide, the West Wind, breathing?
The woman, who now knows that she will die,
Is tossed in scheming, heaving tides of rage.
While you still can, you need to run for it,   565
Or you'll see storms of wreckage and the glare
Of brutal torches. Flames will fill the beach
If the dawn finds you loitering in this land.
Be quick and go! A woman is a changing
And fitful thing." The form ebbed into black night.   570
The sudden vision of this chilling shade
Ripped him from sleep. He shook his comrades too.
"Wake—now!—and take your places on the benches.
Hurry! Unfurl the sails. Once more from heaven
A god's come, driving our escape: start cutting   575
The twisted ropes! We follow you, whichever

God you might be—again we cheer your orders.
Be with us, guide us graciously, and bring us
Favoring stars." He drew his flashing sword
And struck the mooring line. A single passion   580
Seized all of them. They ran and snatched their gear up
And quit the beach. The blue plain now was hidden
By skimming ships. The oars raised twists of foam.
Dawn, risen from her husband's saffron bed,
Was scattering her light across the world.   585
The sky grew white above the queen's high tower.
Below, the sails went forward in a row.
The port, the shore were bare, the sailors gone.
Repeatedly she struck her lovely breast
And tore her gold hair. "Jupiter! He's leaving?   590
A stranger comes—and goes—and mocks my power?
Why doesn't the whole city arm and follow
On ships torn madly from their moorings? Hurry!
Bring torches, pass out arms, ram the oars forward!
What? Where is this new madness taking me?   595
Poor thing. Your crimes—you feel them only now?
Not when you made him king? This is his pledged word!
They say he brought his household gods with him,
And hauled his frail old father on his shoulders.
I could have scattered the torn pieces of him   600
Across the waves. I could have killed his friends—
His son—and made a banquet for the father—
A struggle I might not have won—no matter:
I still would die. My torches should have swarmed
His camp and gangways till they made a pyre   605
For father and son, the whole race, and myself.
Come, Sun, the blazing lamp of all creation—
Juno, the witness and the go-between—
And Hecate, a name shrieked at the crossroads— *Goddess Th + witchcraft*
Avenging Furies—and my own death demons: *underworld*   610
Turn heaven's justice where it should be turned.

This is my prayer now: if that living curse
Must skim his way to harbor in that country,
If Jove and fate require this to happen,
Then let a bold and warlike people drive him   615
Out of his realm and tear his Iulus from him. (Ascanius - Aeneas' son
Make him a suppliant, let him see the death
Of blameless friends. Humiliating peace terms
Will bring no happy old age in his kingdom.
He'll fall and lie unburied in the sand.   620
And now my last plea, gushing with my blood:
Tyrians, hound with hatred for all time
The race he founds. My ashes call from you
This service. Let there be no pacts of friendship.
Out of my grave let an avenger rise,   625
With fire and iron for Dardanian settlers—
Now—someday—when the power is there to strike.
Our shores will clash, weapons and seas collide.
My curse is war for Trojans and their children."
She finished. Now her thoughts went everywhere,   630
Seeking the fastest way to leave the light.
She told the old nurse of Sychaeus, Barce
(Her own had died back in the fatherland),
"Darling, please bring my sister Anna—hurry!
Have her splash river water on her body   635
And bring the beasts and other offerings.
Cover your own brow with a pious fillet.
I'll now round off the ritual I began
For Jove below the earth, to end my pain,
Putting to flame this pyre—the Trojan's life."   640
Quickly the fond old woman hobbled off.
Now Dido's own grim plans had made her frantic.
Her red eyes darted, and her cheeks were blotched
And shook—but she grew pale in facing death.
She burst into the center of the house,   645
Frenzied, and climbed the pyre and drew the sword

From Troy—she hadn't asked for it for this.
Here she surveyed the bed she knew so well,
And the Trojan clothes. In tearful contemplation
She lay a little while, and spoke these last words: 650
"Sweet spoils—while fate and god still kept you sweet—
Receive my breath and free me from this pain.
I lived, I ran the race that fate allotted.
I'll send the underworld a noble ghost.
I saw the walls of my great city standing,   *Pygmalion*   655
Avenged my husband, made my brother pay.
A happy—no, a more than happy life,
If Trojan ships had never touched these shores."
She kissed the bed. "I die without revenge—
But let me die. I like this path to darkness.   660
Let the cruel Trojan's eyes take in these flames.
The omen of my death will go with him."   *✝ ✝ ✝*
Her maids now saw her falling on her sword,
Still speaking, saw her blood foam down the blade
And fleck her hands. A shout rose to the rooftop,   665
And through the shaken city Rumor raged.
Long-drawn-out shrieks of grief and women's keening
Brimmed from the buildings. Anguish filled the sky,
As if invading troops brought Carthage down—
Or ancient Tyre were sacked—and flames were scaling   670
The rooftops of the houses and the temples.
Her sister heard and ran to her in panic,
Clawing her cheeks, bruising her breast with blows.
As she plunged through the crowd, she called that doomed name.
"This was your purpose, sister—to deceive me?   675
The pyre, the flames, the altars bring me this?
How could you leave me like a cast-off thing
And go alone? You should have called me with you:
One sword, one hour, one agony for both!
I piled this wood, I called our fathers' gods   680
To let you lie alone here, heartless monster?

You killed yourself and me, your city's people,
And the Phoenician lords. Come, give me water
To wash these wounds—and if a last breath hovers,
My mouth will take it." She had climbed the pyre,   685
And held her sister now, that fading life,
And moaned and mopped the black blood with her clothes.
Dido now strained to lift her heavy eyes
But failed. Around the sword, her breast's wound hissed.
Three times she rose a little, on her elbow,   690
Collapsed each time, and with her wandering vision
Searched for the bright, high sky and sighed to find it.
Queen Juno cut this torture short, in pity,
Dispatching Iris earthward from Olympus
To free the struggling spirit from its bonds.   695
There was no fate or justice in her death.
Her madness brought a wretched, early end.
Proserpina had cut no lock of blond hair
To dedicate this life to Stygian Orcus.
So dewy Iris soared on saffron wings,   700
Trailing a thousand sun-reflecting colors,
And floated near her head. "I am to take
This gift to Dis and free you from your body."
Her right hand made the stroke. All living heat
Vanished, and life dissolved into the wind.   705

5

Aeneas resolutely voyaged far out
Through billows driven black by the north wind.
He saw behind him poor Elissa's fire,   Dido
A huge glow in the fort—but what had caused it
The Trojans could not tell. Yet what they knew   5
Of woman's rage in ruined love's hard grief
Gave them a grim foreboding in their hearts.
They sailed the open water; no land met them,
But everywhere was sea and sky alone.
But then a bluish-black light-stifling storm   10
Came swooping down. Night bristled on the water.
Even the pilot Palinurus shouted
From his high stern, "What is this, Father Neptune?
Why do you wrap the sky in such huge storm clouds?"
They must row hard and pull the tackle in.   15
He sloped the sails against the wind and added,
"There is no hope for Italy in this weather,
Not even if Jove promised, brave Aeneas.

The rising western dark sends roaring winds
Into our side. Air thickens into cloud.   20
We do not have the strength to fight against it.
Fortune has triumphed, and we must submit,
Turning our course her way. We're near the havens
Of Sicily and your loyal brother Eryx,   *Mountain*
If I recall the stars I traced in coming."   25
Steadfast Aeneas answered, "I have watched you
Struggling against insistent winds and losing.
Shift the sails, turn. There's no land I prefer
To send these tired ships to than the one
That keeps for me Dardanian Acestes   *Trojan hero who hosted*   30
And holds my father's bones in its embrace."   *Aeneas*
They sought the ports now. Favorable south winds
Hurried the fleet's stretched sails across the deep.
They steered toward welcome and familiar beaches.
Startled to see them from a far-off peak,   35
Acestes rushed to greet the kindred ships.
Child of a Trojan mother and the river
Crinisus, he now wore rough Libyan bearskin
And carried sharp spears. Mindful of his lineage,
He happily received his weary friends   40
As guests again, in rustic luxury.
The stars were routed by the brightening dawn.
From the long beach Aeneas called his comrades
Together and addressed them from a raised mound:
"Descendants of the high gods, glorious Trojans,   45
One circling year is full, its months completed,
From when we laid my honored father's bones
In the ground and consecrated his sad altar.
This seems to be the bitter day the gods
Decreed that I commemorate forever.   50
If I were exiled in Gaetulian Syrtes,
Or caught by storms and captive in Mycenae,
I still would carry out these solemn rites

And pile the altar with the proper gifts.
But here we are now, at a friendly port,   55
In the presence of my father's bones and ashes.
It must have been the gods' will that achieved this.
So let us all be glad in this observance,
Ask for good winds and pray he'll grant this rite
Each year in his own shrine in our new city.   60
Acestes, who was born at Troy, will give you
Two oxen for each ship. Invite our home gods,
Our country's, and our host's to share the feast.
But when the ninth dawn brings the nurturing day
To mortals, and its beams light up the globe,   65
I'll hold a race for speedy Trojan ships.
Then any powerful runners, anyone
Challenging with a javelin or arrows,
Any bold boxers with their rawhide thongs,
Can step up. Victory will bring you prizes.   70
Place garlands on your heads, in holy silence."
He hid his forehead in his mother's myrtle.
Helymus did the same, and old Acestes,
And also young Ascanius and his agemates.   Aeneas'sn
With a great crowd of soldiers for an escort,   75
Aeneas left the gathering for the grave mound.
On the ground there he poured two ritual goblets
Each of pure wine, fresh milk, and holy blood
And scattered purple flowers. "Hallowed father,
I call unceasingly to your poor spirit,   80
Your ghost: the body that I saved is ashes.
I could not seek with you our fated lands
In Italy or a river called the Tiber."
Then from beneath that holy place there slipped
A giant snake, who drew his seven coils   85
Gently around the barrow and the altar.
His back was blue-emblazoned. Gold-flecked scales
Kindled and glowed, as when a rainbow catches

The sun and strikes clouds with a thousand colors.
Aeneas was amazed. It stretched its great length   90
Among the bowls and polished cups. It tasted
The dishes and slid back beneath the tomb
Harmlessly from the banquet on the altar.
The son resumed the rites with greater fervor.
Was this the place's genius, or the spirit   95
Of his father? Now he sacrificed two sheep,
Two sows, and two black bullocks; poured out wine;
And called upon the soul of great Anchises, *Aeneas' father*
The ghost that Acheron had now released. *river in Hades*
With a good will each comrade brought the gifts   100
That he could spare, killed bulls, and heaped the altar.
Others lined cauldrons up and then lay down
On the grass to roast the spitted meat on coals.
The long-awaited ninth day came. The horses
Of Phaeton brought the dawn in pleasant weather. *Child of Sun*   105
The fame of glorious Acestes drew *Trojan hero/host*
The eager neighboring tribes. They filled the shore
To see Aeneas' men—or challenge them.
At the start, the center of the field displayed
The prizes for the winners: sacred tripods,   110
Garlands, palm branches, clothing dyed with purple,
Along with massive bars of gold and silver.
From a mound, a trumpet's blare began the games.
Four evenly matched ships with heavy oars
Were chosen from the fleet for the first contest. *Aeneas' Lieutenant* 115
Mnestheus took the *Whale*, with its keen rowers
(In Italy, the Memmian clan is his),
And Gyas the enormous ship *Chimera*,
Big as a town, rising in triple oar banks,
And driven forward by the youth of Troy.   120
Sergestus, father of the Sergian house,
Rode the vast *Centaur;* on the sky-blue *Scylla* *Sea Monster*
Was Cloanthus, founder of Cluentus' clan.

On the open sea, far from the foaming shore,
A rock lies, sometimes sunk in swollen waves   125
When the northeastern storms conceal the stars.
Now it rose quiet from the tranquil water;
Its flat top was a place for sunning gulls.
Father Aeneas set a leafy oak branch
Out there to show the sailors where to turn   130
And bend their lengthy courses back again.
They drew for starting places, and the captains
Stood on the sterns in radiant gold and purple.
The young men of the crews wore poplar garlands.
Their shoulders glistened with the oil rubbed on.   135
They sat and took a tight grip on the oars,
Keen for the signal; throbbing trepidation
And greed for praise clutched at their leaping hearts.
The trumpet blared, and instantly they sprang
Over the line. Their shouting struck the sky.   140
Their arms drew back, they whipped the sea to foam.
The ships cut trenches in a row. The surface
Split with the force of oars and trident beaks.
Never at such a breakneck pace have chariots
Poured from the gates and torn along the course,   145
Their drivers shaking free the waving reins
And bending forward to apply the whip.
Then the whole forest roared with the applause
Of partisans. The deep-set bay sent voices
Rolling, and shouts sprang off the stricken hills.   150
First Gyas slipped ahead across the waves,
Beyond the crowded clatter. Then Cloanthus
Pursued him, but the heavy pine hull hampered
His better crew. The *Centaur* and the *Whale*,
An equal space behind, struggled for third place.   155
Now the *Whale* has it, now the giant *Centaur*
Passes him, now the two prows shoot in tandem,
With long salt furrows trailing from the hulls.

Now they approached the rock, their turning post.
Gyas was leading still, the halfway victor.   160
He shouted to Menoetes at the helm:
"Why are you headed so far right? Turn this way!
Keep to the shore. Your oars should graze the rocks.
The rest can sail the sea." But still Menoetes
Feared hidden rocks and swerved out to the deep.   165
"Where are you going? Toward the rocks, I said!"
Yelled Gyas. Looking back, he saw Cloanthus
Gaining—and circling closer to the shore,
Between his own ship and the sounding cliffs.
He scraped his way through, quickly passed the leader—   170
Beyond the turning post he reached safe waters.
Fury flamed in the other captain's young bones.
Tears on his cheeks, forgetting dignity
And safety, he threw circumspect Menoetes
Out of the lofty stern into the sea.   175
He himself took the helm now, as the pilot,
Urged on the men and swung the rudder shoreward.
Menoetes (in a while) escaped the sea floor,
Old as he was and hampered by his wet clothes.
He climbed the rock and settled on a dry ledge.   180
Trojans had laughed to see him fall and swim,
And now they laughed to see him spewing brine.
Sergestus and Mnestheus, who were last,
Were thrilled—they might pass Gyas as he lingered.
Sergestus pulled ahead—but it was only   185
By half a length—as he approached the rock.
Alongside skimmed the *Whale*'s competing prow.
Mnestheus paced amidships, rallying
His crew. "Heave! Throw your whole strength into it!
Comrades of Hector, allies whom I chose   190
In Troy's last crisis: show the strength and courage
That served you on the sandbanks of the Syrtes,
The Ionian seas, and savage Malean waves.

I don't demand the glory of first place.
(And yet—no, Neptune, you must choose the winner.)   195
But last—! Humiliation! That at least
We must avoid." They made a flat-out effort.
The bronze-beaked ship was trembling with the blows.
The surface slipped away, their panting shook
Arms, legs, and dry mouths. Sweat flowed down in streams.   200
It was mere chance that brought the men their triumph.
Sergestus in his fervor drove his prow
Close to the rock—an inside, risky passage—
And caught disastrously on jutting outcrops.
His oars struck those rough edges with a crunch.   205
The prow was rammed and hung above the water.
With shouts, the crew sprang up and steadied her,
And took out pointed rods and poles enforced
With iron to fish back their broken oars.
Mnestheus, even keener in his good luck,   210
With a swift sweep of oars and prayers to the winds,
Sped to the shore across the open water,
Like a dove startled from her darling nestlings
Hidden among the crannies of the cave
That is her home. She bursts out with a clatter   215
And makes for the fields. But soon she glides through air
That's calm and clear, and stills her rapid wings.
Like her the *Whale* flew, on its own momentum,
And sliced the surface at the course's end,
Leaving Sergestus struggling on a sharp rock   220
At first, then in the shallows as he yelled
For help and learned to make his way with split oars.
Still, he reached Gyas and the huge *Chimera*—
Robbed of its pilot, this one fell behind.
Only Cloanthus needed overtaking.   225
Mnestheus, with all his power, chased him.
The noise swelled on the shore—everyone clamored
For the ship in second place. The high air echoed.

The leader's crew would have been mortified
To lose their victory, glory worth their lives!   230
The others' strength was growing as they gained:
Now neck in neck, they might have won the prize,
Had not Cloanthus, reaching toward the sea,
Poured out this prayer and made the gods this promise:
"Hear, ocean's rulers, on whose plain I move: 235
To pay my vow as victor on the shore,
I'll set a snow-white bull before your altar,
And give your salt waves flowing wine and entrails."
In the deep currents all the troupe of Phorcus
And the Nereids, and virgin Panopea,   240
Heard, and the Father of Ports, with his huge hand,
Pushed the ship past the speed of wind or arrows.
It bolted to the deep and screening harbor.
Anchises' son then duly had the herald
Summon the people and announce Cloanthus   245
The winner. A wreath of fresh bay hid his temples.
Aeneas let each crew divide its prizes:
Three heifers, wine, a hundredweight of silver.
Particular awards were for the captains:
The winner got a gold cloak, with two waves   250
Of Meliboean purple on the border,
And a woven Ganymede on leafy Ida, *Trojan Prince raped by Jupiter*
A fierce-speared runner down of speedy stags,
Panting like life—then caught up in the air
In the hooked claws of Jove's swift armor bearer.   255
His agèd minders reached up helplessly
To the stars, and dogs barked savagely at air.
The one whose skill had gained him second place
Got a gold breastplate, triple-meshed and polished:
Aeneas himself had stripped it from Demoleos,   260
By the swift Simois under lofty Ilium—
And gave it now, a glorious battle refuge.
Two servants, Sagaris and Phegeus, barely

Could lift its layered weight, and yet Demoleos
Had worn it running after Trojan stragglers.   265
The third prize was a pair of matched bronze cauldrons,
And silver cups, rugged with choice relief.
Now, while the victors swaggered in the thrill
Of rich rewards, red ribbons on their heads,
Sergestus reached the shore. He'd worked his hull free   270
Of the cruel rock, lost his oars, and bashed a row
Of oarlocks useless. He won only laughter.
His ship was like a snake caught on the road's edge,
Cut across by a bronze wheel or left mangled
And half-dead by a traveler's heavy stone.   275
It tries to whip away, but this is hopeless—
The hissing, arching head and burning eyes
Are held back by the crippled part that knots
The struggling creature back upon itself.
Like this the ship moved, with its ruined oars: 280
And yet it reached the port with full-spread sails.
Aeneas, happy that the ship and crew
Were safe, still gave Sergestus what he'd promised:
A Cretan slave girl, Pholoe, quite skilled
At Minerva's work, and mother of twin babies.   285
Righteous Aeneas, at this contest's breakup,
Strode toward a grassy field that was surrounded
By wooded hills, a natural stadium
For a racetrack. Thousands went there with the hero.
He sat down in a raised seat in the center   290
And offered prizes to entice the daring
Of anyone considering the footrace.
Competitors converged—Trojans, Sicilians—
First Nisus and Euryalus:
Euryalus was a handsome, blooming youth   295
Whom Nisus loved devotedly. Diores
Came next, a royal boy from Priam's high house;
Then Salius, an Acarnanian,

And Patron, an Arcadian Tegean;
Then followers of old Acestes, Helymus 300
And Panopes, from the Sicilian woodlands;
And many more, obscure, unknowable.
Aeneas, in the center of them, spoke:
"I know you'll be delighted when you hear this:
No one will leave without a gift from me. 305
Two spearheads of bright iron, worked in Crete,
And a two-headed ax embossed in silver
Will honor everyone. But olive leaves
Of tawny green will crown the fastest three.
The winner gets a horse with handsome trappings, 310
The next an Amazonian quiver full
Of Thracian arrows, bound to a wide belt
Of gold, which has a clasp carved from a gem.
This Argive helmet must content the third."
The runners took their places. At the signal, 315
They sprang across the line and down the course,
Pouring like clouds. Now with the goal in sight,
Nisus flashed out ahead of them to first place
As swiftly as the wind or wings of thunder.
The next, though only after a long gap, 320
Was Salius; Euryalus came third,
Some distance back.
Helymus followed him, and after that
Diores sped—his foot brushed on a heel,
His shoulder loomed. And had the track been longer, 325
He would have slipped ahead or tied for fourth.
But as they came exhausted to the last stretch,
Poor Nisus skidded in some slippery blood
Which had poured down and wet the grassy ground
When—as it happened—steers were slaughtered there. 330
Already thrilled with victory, the young man
Did a short dance against the fall but fell
Face-first in filthy dung and sacred blood.

But with his dear Euryalus in mind,
He staggered up, a stumbling block for Salius,   335
Whom a quick somersault laid on the hard sand.
Euryalus flashed by and flew in first   *Nisis partnered in Trojan*
Through his friend's help, with roaring cheers to greet him.   *war*
Helymus came in next, Diores third.
But through that whole vast stadium, where the elders   340
Watched from the front, the yells of Salius rang,
Demanding the award a foul had stolen.
But the crowd backed Euryalus' shy weeping—
And the great beauty of his ripening manhood.
Diores helped him with loud interjections: 345
He had achieved third prize, but it was void
If Salius was now to have the first.
Father Aeneas answered, "All your prizes
Are safe, boys: nobody will change the order.
But I can soothe a friend who's been unlucky."   350
He gave to Salius a lion's pelt
From Libya: huge and heavy-maned and gold-clawed.
But Nisus said, "If that's what losers get,
And accidents win pity, what's for me?
I deserved first prize, and I would have got it,   355
But for the same bad luck that Salius had."
He gestured to the wet dung on his face
And body. The good father of the Trojans
Laughed and had fetched a shield that Didymaon
Had made—Greek spoil from Neptune's holy door.   360
He gave the excellent youth this splendid gift.
When all of this was done, Aeneas said:
"Whoever has brave, ready manhood in him,
Let him step up and bind and raise his fists."
He set out two more prizes: for the winner,   365
A bull with gilded horns and hanging ribbons;
And a sword and splendid helmet, loser's solace.
Unhesitating, Dares thrust his jaw out

And rose in his vast strength. The whole crowd murmured.
He alone had been used to fighting Paris;   370
He'd crushed the massive champion Butes (boasting
Lineage from Bebrycian Amycus)
And laid him out to die on tawny sand
Beside the tomb where matchless Hector rested.
Such a man reared his towering head to fight,   375
Showed his wide shoulders, shot out first one arm
And then the other, hammering the air.
The second boxer? Out of that whole crowd
Nobody dared to wrap on thongs and face him.
Thinking they were conceding him the prize,   380
He took a happy stand below Aeneas,
Grasped the bull's horn in his left hand and spoke:
"So, goddess' son, if no one dares to fight me, *Venus is Aeneas'*
How long exactly should I be kept standing?   *mother*
Tell me to take my prize." All of the Trojans   385
Roared for the man to have the promised trophy.
Acestes was disgruntled with Entellus,
Who sat beside him on a bench of green turf:
"You were the strongest once—but that's no use
If you look on now, letting go this fine prize   390
Without a fight. What good's the godlike Eryx
You claim as teacher? What about your fame
Throughout this land, and the prizes on your walls?"
Entellus shot back: "It's not fear defeating
My lust for fame, but the slow, freezing blood   395
Of old age, and my cold, depleted strength.
If I were in my prime still, like that fellow—
So insolent, so gleefully cocksure—
I'd take my place, but not to win the fine bull:
Prizes don't draw me." Into the arena   400
He threw the pair of hugely heavy gauntlets
Whose hard hide savage Eryx used to wrap
Around his hands for every boxing battle.

The crowd was stunned: there, sewn with lead and iron
To stiffen them, were seven massive bull's hides.   405
Dares backed well away in stupefaction;
Anchises' brave son turned them over, testing
The weight of those immense loops in his hands.
The veteran boxer spoke then, from his heart:
"What if we saw what Hercules himself wore   410
In the hard contest on this very beach?
Your brother Eryx had these on his hands once
(Look at the caked brains, and the spattered blood)
And faced that hero, and I used to wear them
In my strong-blooded years, when jealous old age   415
Had not yet sowed the white hairs on my temples.
If Dares turns them down, and good Aeneas
Chooses, and if Acestes my supporter
Agrees, we'll make it fair and take away
Eryx' straps and your Trojan ones—don't worry."   420
He let his double cloak drop from his shoulders,
Stripping his heavy-boned, strong-jointed body,
And took his stand, huge-armed and towering.
Anchises' lordly son brought out matched thongs   _Aeneas' fathe_
And bound the hands of both with equal weapons.   425
They didn't pause but faced off, on their toes,
Fearless, alert, their hands up in the air.
Their heads were reared far back and out of range.
Now their fists tangled, sparring for an opening.
The one was younger, quicker on his feet,   430
The other stronger, larger, but his knees
Faltered, and weary panting shook his bulk.
Often they missed in swinging at each other,
But often loudly thumped against a chest
Or curved side; fists were darting around temples   435
And ears, jaws crackled under stony blows.
Entellus' feet were rooted in position—
But sharp eyes kept his body swaying, dodging.

Dares, as if he stormed a city's bulwarks
Or kept a mountain fortress under siege,   440
Scanned thoroughly and shrewdly for a gap,
And drove assaults from everywhere—for nothing.
Entellus sprang and thrust his right arm up,
Then down. His quick opponent saw it falling,
Instantly slipped aside and wasn't there.   445
Entellus spilled his strength into the air.
The force of his own vast weight sent him crashing,
Like a hollow pine tree torn up by the roots
On Erymanthus or the heights of Ida.
Both Trojans and Sicilians stood up, yelling   450
In rivalry. Acestes ran up first—*Trojan hero who hosted Aeneas*
His agemate—and in pity lifted him.
But the fall didn't slow or cow the hero,
Who came back more relentlessly, in anger
And burning shame and knowledge of his own skill.   455
Over the whole arena he pitched Dares.
He battered with his right hand, then his left,
Not letting up. Like clouds that pound the rooftops
With hail, the hero pummeled his opponent
Ceaselessly with both fists and sent him spinning.   460
Father Aeneas now was moved to check
The savage anger of Entellus, ending
The fight—a rescue for exhausted Dares—
And did it with these sympathetic words:
"Poor friend, where has your mind gone? Don't you sense   465
Some strength here more than his? Gods are against you:
Relent." He caused the boxers to be parted.
Faithful companions helped one to the ships.
His head lolled, and he dragged his crippled knees.
He spat out broken teeth and clotted blood.   470
Others were called to claim his sword and helmet,
Leaving the bull and garland for Entellus.
The victor, full of heady pride, proclaimed:

"Son of the goddess, and you other Trojans:
Think of the strength I had when I was young—   475
Think of the death from which you just saved Dares."
He stood before the face of the young bull
That waited as the prize. He rose up, aiming
Between the horns with his hard-bound right hand,
Then shattered the beast's skull and splashed its brains out.   480
Shaking in death, it crumpled and collapsed,
And over it he spoke these fervent words:
"Eryx, I give to you this better soul
Than Dares'—and unbind my hands forever."
Right after this, Aeneas sought contestants   485
For flying archery, and set out prizes.
He planted, with his brawny hand, the mast
From Serestus' ship, and threaded through a rope
At the top, and tied a dove there as a target.
Contestants tossed their lots in a bronze helmet.   490
Hippocoön, the son of Hyrtacus,
Was picked—to warm applause—to take the first shot.
Next was Mnestheus, who had won the ship race
Just now—green olive branches crowned him still;
Eurytion third, brother of famous Pandarus,   495
The one who broke the truce, on heavenly orders,
And took the first shot into the Greek army.
Acestes' was the last lot in the helmet—   *Trojan hero,*
He dared to try the work of younger men.
Now each one took an arrow from his quiver   500
And bent his curving bow with brawny arms.
An arrow first soared off the twanging string
Of Hyrtacus' son and sliced the air in two,
And hit the wooden mast straight on and lodged.
The pole shook, and the terrified dove flapped,   505
And the whole valley echoed with applause.
Now fierce Mnestheus stood and drew his bow
And aimed high, with his eyes and bow both straining.

Too bad! The steel tip failed to reach the bird,
But broke the knotted linen string that tethered   510
The creature by the foot atop the mast.
She sped off toward the storm clouds in the south.
Eurytion had his bow already drawn;
He quickly aimed, while praying to his brother.
With joy and clapping wings, she'd reached the open   515
Beneath the clouded darkness, when he shot her.
She fell and left her life among the stars,
But brought to earth again the piercing arrow.
Acestes' chance was gone—he still let fly
An arrow to the upper air, which showed   520
His bow-resounding skill, though he was old.
Then an omen flashed, whose meaning the great outcome
Proved in the time to come, when fearsome prophets
Chanted of signs that lagged in their fulfillment.
The arrow soared in flame through flowing clouds,   525
Burning a path that faded out and tattered
In the wind—as when a star has been dislodged,
Crosses the sky, and trails its hair behind it.
Both Trojans and Sicilians were astonished
And begged the gods to keep them safe. Aeneas   530
The great revered the omen and embraced
Happy Acestes, heaped on gifts, and spoke:
"Accept these, father, for Olympus' great king
Has marked you out for some supreme distinction.
Venerable Anchises, my own father,   535
Owned this embossed bowl, precious gift from Cisseus,
Keepsake and token of that loving friendship."
He ringed Acestes' head with verdant laurel
And named him winner over all the others.
Eurytion—fine boy—did not resent it,   540
Though he had brought the bird down from the sky.
The breaker of the rope received the next gifts,
Then the one whose flying dart had pierced the mast.

Father Aeneas did not end the contests
Till he had called Epytides, dear tutor   545
Of little Iulus. To this trusty man
He whispered, "Go and tell Ascanius,   *aeneas's son* Iulus
If he has got the squad of boys on horses
Drawn up, to lead it to his grandsire's tomb
And show himself maneuvering with arms."   550
He had the field in its long circuit cleared,
Since people had been pouring onto it.
Before their fathers' eyes, the boys filed in,
Gleaming on bridled horses. Both Sicilians
And Trojans buzzed approval at their coming.   555
A ritual trimmed garland bound each boy's hair;
Each had a pair of steel-tipped cornel spears;
Some had smooth quivers. From their necks hung rings
Of pliant gold that twisted at their throats.
Three troops of riders, each one with its leader,   560
Wove their way; twelve boys in each double file
Followed their captains in a neat division.
One young, glad line was led by little Priam,   *King of Troy's son?*
Polites' son, bright bearer of a great name
One father back—and fated to bless Italy.   565
His Thracian horse was dappled, with white pasterns;
The forehead that it reared was splashed with white.
Iulus' belovèd agemate Atys, founder
Of the Latin clan of Atii, led the next squad;
Iulus, best-looking of the boys, the last.   570
His mount was Tyrian; shining Dido gave it
To be his own in loving memory of her.
The other boys were on Sicilian horses,
The gifts of old Acestes.
The Trojans cheered their shy sons and were happy   575
To see ancestral faces replicated.
In joy they passed the crowd, their families watching.
The line paused. From the side, Epytides

Signaled, first with a shout and then a whip crack.
Now the three squads, each in two columns, wheeled   580
Apart to right and left. Another signal:
They turned back, aiming weapons at each other.
Then they made other moves and countermoves,
Faced off at distances, or overlapped
In circles, or staged battles with their weapons.   585
They fled, their backs defenseless, turned their spears
For an attack, then rode together, peaceful.
Like the fabled labyrinth in lofty Crete
That weaves its blind and baffling passages,
Its thousand tricks to keep its captives lost,   590
Confusing any sequence that might lead them—
So the Trojans' children wove a running pattern,
A net of mock attacks and mock retreats;
Or like the dolphins playing in the waves,
Who cut the Libyan or Carpathian straits.   595
When he was building Alba Longa's walls,
Ascanius revived this battle pageant
And taught the ancient Latins to perform it,
As he had done with other Trojan youngsters.
The Albans passed it down. Rome in her glory   600
Is heir to this ancestral ritual.
The boys are "Troy" and their formation "Trojan."
With this, the sainted father's games concluded.

Now for the first time Fortune changed allegiance.
During these rites in honor of the tomb,   605
Juno the child of Saturn sent down Iris
To the Trojan fleet, and sped the wind behind her,
Plotting to satisfy her ancient rancor.
Over the thousand colors of the rainbow
The goddess swiftly went, and no one saw her.   610
Beyond the crowd, she passed along the shore
And saw the fleet left in an unmanned port.

The Trojan women stood and mourned Anchises, _Aeneas' father_
On a lonely beach. They gazed out at the deep
In tears, and all deplored how many seas   615
Were yet to cross—how it exhausted them!
A city! Not the sufferings of voyages!
Iris, that expert meddler, slipped among   _Goddess of Rainbow / Divine Messenger_
The Trojan mothers, shed the face and clothing
Of a goddess, and put on the form of Beroe,   620
The ancient wife of Doryclus of Tmaros,
Well known and nobly born; she'd been a mother.
"Poor things!" she cried. "Not dragged away to die
By warring Greeks beneath your city's walls!
What doom does Fortune hold for our poor people?   625
The seventh summer since Troy's fall is passing.
We're driven from star to star across the seas,
The whole world's lands and wrecking rocks. We're wave-tossed
On the great gulf. Italy retreats from us.
Our brother Eryx' land, our host Acestes   _Sicilian hero_   630
Must let us found a city of our own.
Fatherland! Gods we saved from war for nothing!
What walls will have Troy's name? Where will I see
A Simois and Xanthus—Hector's rivers?
So come, let's burn these ships that brought such sorrow.   635
In a dream, I saw the prophetess Cassandra;   _Trojan Princess_
She gave me burning torches: 'Seek your Troy here—
This is your home.' Now is the time to act—
Quickly, on such great signs. Here are four altars
Of Neptune. He will give us fire and courage."   640
She was the first to seize destroying flame.
She raised a torch and waved it. Then she strained
And threw it as the Trojan women watched
In horror. But the oldest of then, Pyrgo,
The nurse of Priam's many children, shouted   _(50 sons)_   645
"Mothers, this isn't Beroe of Rhoeteum,
Doryclus' wife! Just look at the divine grace

Shown in her burning eyes, her haughtiness,
Her face, the way her voice sounds, and her gait.
And I myself have just left Beroe   650
Sick, and upset that she alone was missing
Her portion in these honors for Anchises." *Aeneas' mother*
She said this.
The matrons did not know what they should do.
They glared down at the boats, in bitter yearning   655
To stay, yet thinking of the fated kingdom.
Iris But as she fled on even wings, the goddess
Cut a great rainbow underneath the clouds.
This apparition made the women shriek,
Beside themselves. Some pillaged campsite fires,   660
While others snatched up kindling, leaves, and torches
From the altars. Over painted sterns and benches
And oars the god of fire ran amok.
Eumelus brought the news to the arena
Next to Anchises' tomb; but on their own   665
They saw a cloud of ashes surging skyward.
Ascanius capered at his squadron's head—
But now his panting trainers could not stop him
As he turned and galloped to the camp in riot.
"What are you doing? Have you lost your minds?   670
Poor Trojan women! It's no enemy Greek camp
You're burning, but your future. This is me,
Your own Ascanius!" At their feet he dashed   *Aeneas' son*
The helmet he'd been wearing for staged battle.
Aeneas rushed in, with a host of Trojans.   675
The women scattered, panicked, on the shore
And skulked away to trees and rocky hollows.
Shame drove them to the darkness; they awoke
To know their own and free their hearts from Juno.
And yet their raging fire didn't slacken.   680
The caulking was alive beneath the wet wood,
Vomiting steady waves of smoke. Unyielding,

The flame of ruin ate the hulls, the whole ships;
The floods strong heroes hauled there couldn't stop it.
Loyal Aeneas tore his clothes away   685
From his shoulders, stretched his hands out, asked the gods' help:
"Almighty Jove, unless you hate us Trojans
To the last man, and human suffering
Moves you no longer, let our fleet escape!
Save our exhausted race from ruin, Father!   690
Or hurl your thunderbolt of devastation
At what remains of us—if I deserve it."
He'd scarcely finished when a monstrous black storm
Broke in a rage of pouring rain and thunder.
The plains and mountains shook. The whole wild sky   695
Slid blackly down through whirlings of the south winds—
The decks filled up, the half-burned wood was soaked—
Until the fire was completely out,
And all the ships but four were saved from ruin.
A hard blow for the patriarch Aeneas!   700
He was pulled back and forth tormentingly,
Uncertain whether he should stay in Sicily,
Shirking his fate, or reach for Italy.
But then old Nautes spoke, the chosen pupil
Of Tritonian Athena; he was famous   705
For prophecies of what the powerful anger
Of gods would bring—he knew the links in fate's chain.
He comforted Aeneas: "Venus' son,
Staying or going, we must follow fate.
Whatever comes, endurance conquers fortune.   710
You have Acestes, Trojan child of heaven. *Trojan hero who hosted Aeneas in Sicily*
Make plans with him—he'll be a willing partner.
Leave him the lost ships' orphans and the travelers
Defeated by the hardships of your great task.
Spare the old men and ocean-weary mothers,   715
And anybody weak or shy of danger,
And let them rest and have their city here,

Named for Acestes, if he will allow it."
The words of his old friend excited him,
But he was torn between anxieties.   720
The chariot of black Night had reached its zenith.
It was from there that Father Anchises' form
Descended suddenly and poured these words out:
"Son, you were precious beyond life to me
While I was living. How Troy's fate torments you!   725
Jove sent me—it was Jove who drove the fire
From your ships. The high god pities you at last.
Take Nautes' good advice—his age and wisdom
Support it. Choose the heartiest men to voyage
To Italy. The race you must defeat there   730
Is rough and hardy. First, though, you must enter
The house of Dis below, cross deep Avernus,
And meet me—not in Tartarus' cruel prison:
Lovely Elysium is now my home,
Where the guiltless gather. Slaughter many black sheep,   735
And you will have a guide there, the chaste Sibyl.
There you will see your city and descendants.
Good-bye. The dewy Night is at her turning.
Ah, the fierce breath of Dawn's pursuing horses!"
He disappeared, like thin smoke in the air.   740
"Where have you gone so fast?" Aeneas cried.
"Whom do you fear? Who keeps us from embracing?"
He roused the dozing fire from ash, beseeching
Troy's Guardian and old Vesta in her shrine
With ritual flour and a full box of incense.   745
He quickly called Acestes, then his comrades,
And told what Jove enjoined, what his dear father
Counseled, and what he now himself resolved.
The islander complied, with no discussion.
The matrons were enrolled, the city settled   750
With volunteers who had no urge for glory.
Crews small in number but alive with valor

Mended the benches and replaced the wood
The flame had gnawed. New oars and ropes were fitted.
Aeneas plowed out borders, made allotments,   755
Named the town "Ilium," the country "Troy."
Trojan Acestes, pleased to rule, ordained
A forum and made rules for his new senate.
A shrine was laid out on the height of Eryx
For Idalian Venus. A broad sacred grove   760
And a priest were given to Anchises' tomb.
Now the whole tribe had sacrificed and feasted
For nine days. Peaceful winds smoothed out the sea;
The south wind rose and called them to the deep.
Along the winding shore rose noisy weeping.   765
Daylong, nightlong, they clung in last embraces.
Even the mothers, even those disgusted
At the word "sea" and at the sight of it,
Were keen for all the suffering of exile.
Kindly Aeneas soothed his friends. He wept,   770
Trusting them to Acestes, his relation.
He ordered three calves sacrificed to Eryx,
And one lamb to the Storms, before unmooring.
He wore an olive wreath and stood apart
In the prow to hold the bowl and pour clear wine   775
And offer entrails to the salty waves.
A following wind surged up against the stern.
Eager crews beat the sea and skimmed above it.
But meanwhile Venus, in her anguished worry,
Poured out these passionate complaints to Neptune: 780
"Juno's hard anger and her ruthless heart
Force me to make humiliating pleas.
She yields to neither time nor reverence.
Fate and Jove's orders cannot break or halt her.
It did not satisfy her evil hatred   785
To tear Troy from its people and devour it,
Or drag the bones and ashes of the city

Through all this—*she* must know why she's so livid.
You witnessed recently the mountainous storm
She raised off Africa. With Aeolus' whirlwinds,   790
She plunged the world's seas and the sky together,
Meddled in your realm—for nothing!
And see how wickedly she drove the mothers
Of Troy to burn the fleet, like criminals,
To strand the Trojans in this alien place.   795
Let the remainder spread their sails in safety
And cross to reach the Tiber at Laurentum—
If this can be, if the fates grant a city."
Saturn's son, tamer of the deep sea, spoke:
"Lady of Cythera, you rightly trust   800
My realm, where you were born, and I've been steadfast,
Crushing great rages of the sea and sky.
Even on dry land I protect Aeneas—
I call to witness Simois and Xanthus:
Achilles drove the panicked Trojan ranks   805
Against the walls. The river groaned with thousands
Of corpses—Xanthus couldn't reach the sea.
Peleus' fierce son was the brawny favorite *Achilles' father*
Of the gods. To save Aeneas, I concealed him
In a cloud, although I longed to ruin Troy: 810
I built it, but it broke its promises.
Don't be afraid—I feel the same as then.
He'll reach your chosen port beside Avernus.   *Lake in Italy*
The sea will take just one for him to grieve for,   *near Hades*
A single life for many."   815
When he had cheered and comforted the goddess,
The patriarch yoked his team in a gold harness,
Bitted their foaming mouths and gave them rein.
He skimmed across the sea in his blue chariot.
Beneath his rumbling axle swelling waves   820
Spread even, and the savage clouds dispersed.
His suite, in all its forms, came with him: monsters,

Glaucus' old troop, Palaemon son of Ino,
The Tritons, all the army of swift Phorcus;   *Sea gds*
To the left were Thetis, Melite, young Panopea   825
Nesaee, Spio, Thalia, and Cymodoce.
Sweet joy now overwhelmed the anxious thoughts
Of Father Aeneas, who had all the masts
Raised quickly and the yardarms hung with sails.
The crew lined up to set the sheets, released   830
The folds, first left, then right, and then maneuvered
The yardarms. Now a good breeze took the fleet.
Palinurus headed up that crowded column: *Helmsman of Aeneas*
The others were to set their course by him.
The dewy night was near its turning point   835
In the sky, and sailors sprawled, relaxed and peaceful,
Under the oars and on the rigid benches,
When Sleep slipped gently down from starry heaven,
Parting the dusky air and scattering shadows,
To bring grim dreams to guiltless Palinurus.   840
High on the stern Sleep sat, disguised as Phorbas,
And let these words come flowing from his mouth:
"Iasus' son, the sea itself transports us.
The wind breathes evenly; it's time to rest.
Lay down your head, steal shut your weary eyes,   845
And I myself will see your tasks are done."
But Palinurus scarcely raised his eyes:
"You're telling me to trust the sea's calm face
And peaceful waves? I know that it's a monster.
It's fooled me many times—should I turn over   850
Aeneas to the double-dealing winds?"
He spoke, and gripped the helm unyieldingly,
Unwavering in gazing at the stars.
But the god shook a branch, which dripped with dew
Of Lethe and the lulling power of Styx,   855
On his temples, forcing shut his swimming eyes.
The stealthy doze sank in, and he relaxed.

Sleep bent to pitch him into limpid waves,
With the rudder and the piece of helm he clung to.
His comrades didn't hear the cries he gave.   860
Winged Sleep rose through the insubstantial air.
The fleet ran on in safety, undisturbed
And free of fear, as Father Neptune promised.
But now it drifted toward the Sirens' cliffs—
A menace once, once white with heaps of bones—   865
From which rock-pounding water sounded far off.
The father noticed that the ship was drifting
Without its guide. He steered it through the night waves
Himself, with groans of anguish for his friend:
"Oh, trusting victim of calm sea and sky,   870
Unburied on some strange shore, Palinurus!"

6

He spoke in tears, and gave the fleet free rein,
And landed finally at Euboean Cumae.
With biting anchors they secured the ships
Prows seaward, and the curved sterns hemmed the beach.
A band of young men eagerly leaped out   5
On the Hesperian shore. Some searched for seeds
Of flame in veins of flint, some sacked the dense woods,
Home of wild beasts, and brought back news of rivers.
Steadfast Aeneas sought the lofty stronghold
Of Apollo and, beyond it, the huge cave   10
Of the Sibyl, where the Delian prophet breathed
His great will into her and showed the future.
They reached the house of gold in Hecate's woods.
Daedalus, in the story, fled King Minos,   "the Cunning One" built Crete
Venturing to the sky on speedy wings.   the labyrinth in Crete   15
By a new route, he swam into the cold North,
And hung at last above the heights at Cumae.
This land first took him in. He offered Phoebus   Apollo

His wings—like oars—and built him a vast temple,
With Androgeos' death carved on the door, and Athens   20
Paying—how pitiful!—her yearly fine:
Seven sons' lives. The urn is there, the lots drawn.
Beside this scene, Crete looms above the sea:
The brutal passion for the bull; Pasiphae, *Queen of Crete*
His mate by stealth; their human-bovine offspring, *Loved Bull* 25/
The Minotaur, memorial of depraved lust; *Had Minotaur*
And the hopeless, wearying maze beneath the palace.
But pitying the deep love of the princess,
Daedalus solved his own entrapping riddle,
With a thread to guide the lost. You, Icarus, *Son of Daedalus* 30
But for your father's grief, would play a large role
In that great artwork. Twice his hands failed, trying
To show your fall in gold. Now, with Achates *Aeneas' retain.*
Gone in, the Trojans would have scanned each image;
But he came quickly back, with Glaucus' daughter,   35
Deiphobe, Phoebus and Diana's priestess,
Who told the king, "This is no time for gawking.
Come, offer seven calves out of a fresh herd,
And seven ewes as well, correctly chosen."
The Trojans quickly carried out her orders,   40
And then she called them into the high temple.
A cave cuts deep into the cliff at Cumae.
There are a hundred mouths that lead inside;
From all these swarm the answers of the Sibyl. *Keep/Gate of Hades*
"It's time," the virgin shouted at the threshold,   45
"To ask what fate will bring you. Look, the god!"
Just as she spoke before the doors, her color
And expression changed, her hair blew wild; she panted,
Heart full of frenzy, and she seemed to tower
And echo a divine voice, since the god   50
Was near. "Are you so slack, Trojan Aeneas,
In prayers and vows? Such thunder-words alone
Can stun these great gates open." She fell silent.

A trembling chill ran through the Trojans' hard bones.
From deep within his heart, their leader pleaded,   55
"Phoebus, you always pitied Trojan anguish.
You guided Paris' hand to pierce the son
Of Aeacus with his arrow. You have led me
On a daring voyage between the continents,
Clear to Massylian land, along the Syrtes.   60
At last we clutch elusive Italy.
Troy's fortunes must not dog us any farther.
All of you, gods and goddesses, who balked
At Ilium and the splendor of our reign,
Can spare us now, at heaven's will, and you,   65
Most holy seer, since I only seek
That realm fate owes me, let the Trojans settle
In Latium with their wandering, harried gods.   _Italy_
I'll ordain a solid marble shrine for Phoebus
And Diana of the crossroads, and a festival   70
Named for Apollo. And for you, my kind guide,
I'll raise a great shrine in my land, and put there
Your lots and secret forecasts for my people,
And appoint priests. But do not trust your verses
To leaves that gusts can play with and confuse.   75
Chant them yourself, please." There he finished speaking.
Inside, the priestess ran amok, resisting
Phoebus and trying hard to shake that great god
Out of her soul. He drove her harder, twisting
Her face, curbing her heart, pinioning, shaping.   80
On their own, the hundred giant doors broke open
And poured outside the answers of the prophet:
"Your perils on the seas are finally over,
Though worse will come on land. But be assured:
The Trojans will arrive. Lavinium's land, though,   85
Will make them wish they hadn't. I see war,
Grisly war, and the Tiber frothing blood.
You'll have another Simois and Xanthus,

A Greek camp, and a Latin-born Achilles,
Himself a goddess' son. Juno will cling   90
To hounding you, while desperately you plead
With every tribe and town in Italy.
Again a foreign wife, an alien marriage
Will bring the Teucrians ruin.
Do not give in, but where your fortune lets you,   95
Go on more bravely still. The path to safety—
Yes, it is true—will open through a Greek town."
So the Sibyl in her shrine at Cumae chanted.
Her fearsome, truth-entangling riddles boomed
Out of the cave. Apollo lashed his reins   100
Against her, drove his goads into her heart.
But then her frenzy lulled, her rabid mouth
Grew quiet, and the hero spoke. "Pure virgin!
No unfamiliar form of hardship threatens:
My soul has grasped and probed all this before.   105
But grant one thing. They say this is the doorway
To the king below, to Acheron's welling dark swamp.   *Hades*
Let me go see my father, face to face.
Tell me the way, open the holy gates.
From fire and a thousand hostile spears,   110
From the enemies' midst I saved him, on these shoulders.
He was my comrade over all the seas,
Enduring every threat of sky and ocean;
His weak old age deserved another fate.
He begged me, trusted me to come implore you   115
Here at your door. Pity the son, the father.
Your kindness has the power: Hecate   *Goddess of Underworld*
Put in your charge the forest of Avernus.   *Lake in Hades now*
If Orpheus brought out his dead wife's spirit   *Entered   entrance*
With melting sounds strummed on his Thracian lyre,   *Hades to retrieve*   120
If Pollux buys his brother's life, and both   *Euridice*
Go back and forth to death—? And the great Theseus?
And Hercules? I descend from Jove our king, too."

He made this plea while clinging to the altar.
The seer began: "You, Trojan of the gods' line,   125
Anchises' son, the road down to Avernus   *Aeneas' son*
Is easy. Black Dis' door gapes night and day.
The work, the effort, is to walk back up
Into the open air. A few could: godborn,
Favored by just Jove, or transported skyward   130
By burning righteousness. Woods fill the center,
And Cocytus flows in black curves all around.
And yet if the desire overwhelms you
To twice skim Stygian pools, twice see black Tartarus,
And plunge in this demented undertaking,   135
Hear what to do first. In a tree's dense foliage
Hides a pliant gold-leaved gold branch, dedicated
To Juno of the underworld. The whole woods,
The dim and shady valley shelters it.
No one may come within earth's hidden places   140
Before he plucks away this gold-haired offspring.
Lovely Proserpina appointed this   *Queen of Hades*
Her offering. Another will replace it,
And other leaves of gold grow from its stem.
Look high up, and when you have duly found it,   145
Pluck it. It should fall gladly in your hand,
If fate has summoned you. If not, your whole strength
Will fail—you will not tear it off with hard steel.
But—you don't know!—a friend lies dead, defiling
The whole fleet with his corpse, while in my doorway   150
You dawdle, asking for my prophecies.
First, lay him in a tomb, his proper home,
And kill black sheep—the first appeasing rite;
Then only will you see the Stygian groves,
The land that's closed to life." Her lips shut, silent.   155
Aeneas, grim-faced, eyes fixed on the ground,
Walked from the cave and in his mind turned over
What the descent might bring. Faithful Achates,   *Aeneas' retainer*

In stride with him, shared his anxieties.
They spoke in trust and spent a long time guessing   160
Which man was dead and waiting to be buried.
But when they reached the arid shore again,
They saw Misenus dead—he had not earned it.
No one was better than the son of Aeolus
At kindling valor with a bronze horn's song.   165
He'd gone to battles in great Hector's suite:
You knew him by his trumpet and his spear.
But when Achilles won, and Hector's life
Became his plunder, brave Misenus followed
Aeneas, just as great a Trojan leader.   170
But then, the fool, he blared a hollow conch shell
Over the sea and challenged gods at music.
Triton, who envied him—or that's the story—
Caught him among foam-pouring rocks and drowned him.
So howls of mourning rang from all his comrades,   175
Especially good Aeneas. Then they hurried,
In tears, to raise the altar of a tomb,
Heaping wood skyward, as the Sibyl ordered.
They went into the old woods, deep beast shelter.
Pines toppled, holm oaks echoed to the ax.   180
Wedges split beams of ash and fissile oak,
And giant mountain ash rolled down the slope.
Aeneas, with the same tools as the others,
Set an example, urged the workers on.
Scanning the vast woods, pondering his tasks   185
In his sad heart, he happened on this prayer:
"What if that gold branch were revealed to me
In this huge forest! Everything is true
The seer said of you, Misenus—too true."
He'd scarcely finished when two doves came flying   190
Out of the sky and passed before his eyes
To land on the green ground. The matchless hero,
Knowing his mother's birds, now prayed with joy.

"Guide me, if there's a way; direct your flight
Into the grove where that rich branch is shading   195
The fertile ground. And you, immortal mother,
Be with me in this trial." He checked his steps
To see what signs the birds brought, where they flew now.
Browsing, they fluttered just the length ahead
That let a follower keep them in his sight.   200
But when they reached Avernus' reeking throat,
They shot up, then soared down through limpid air,
Then perched on what Aeneas sought, the contrast
Of flashing gold among the tree's green branches;
Just as the mistletoe in dead of winter   205
Grows a fresh leaf, its own and not its host's,
And rings the smooth trunk with its yellow shoot;
So the gold leaves stood out against the darkness
Of the oak. Their foil was jangling in the light wind.
He grasped—it clung: he keenly wrenched it off   210
And took it to the prophet Sibyl's home.
Back on the beach, the Trojans still were weeping
In last rites for Misenus' thankless ashes.
They built a massive pyre first, fueled with pitch pine
And oak logs. On the sides they wove dark leaves,   215
Set funeral cypresses in front, and laid on it
The splendid beauty of his flashing armor.
Some heated pots to make the water swell,
And washed the cold corpse and anointed it.
A groan rose; they now laid out what they wept for,   220
Beneath its own familiar purple cloak.
Now some took on that sad task, shouldering
The giant bier, and in the ancient rite
Applied the torch. Heaped gifts of food and incense
And bowls of olive oil were burned together.   225
After the flame died and the ash collapsed,
Wine washed the thirsty cinders. Corynaeus
Gathered the bones and laid them in a bronze jar.

Three times he walked around his comrades, sprinkling
A clear dew from a fertile olive branch   230
To purify them, and he spoke the last words.
On the ashes good Aeneas raised a high mound,
And placed the hero's horn and armor there
Beneath a lofty mountain called Misenus
To keep his name alive through all the ages.   235

With haste, he now performed the Sibyl's orders.
There was a cave—monstrously gaping, jagged,
Deep. A dark woods, a black lake sheltered it.
Birds at their peril made their winging way
Above, in poison that the black throat breathed,   240
Pouring it upward to the dome of heaven.
The Birdless Place is what the Greeks have named it.
First the priest had four young black bullocks brought
To stand there. He poured wine between their horns
And clipped the bristling tufts that stood up highest,   245
As the first offering for the sacred fire,
And called on Hecate, strong in hell and heaven.
Others applied their knives and caught the warm blood
In bowls. Aeneas slaughtered with his sword
A black-fleeced lamb for Night, the Furies' mother,   250
And Earth, their sister; for Proserpina
A sterile cow; and started the night rituals
Of the Stygian king with whole bulls on the flames
And a rich oil poured on the burning entrails.
Now, right before the rising sun's light broke,   255
The ground beneath their feet roared. Wooded slopes
Shifted. Dogs seemed to howl among the shadows.
It was the goddess. "Get out!" yelled the priestess,
"Get clear out of the grove, if you're not pure.
But *you* go forward boldly. Pull your sword free.   260
It's now you need your fearless heart, Aeneas."
Into the open cave she bolted, maddened.

And he kept pace with her, his guide, with brave steps.   *Sibyl (guide)*
You gods who rule dead souls, you silent shades,
And Phlegethon and Chaos, spread with still night,   265
Give holy sanction, let me pass this tale on
And open what deep earth and darkness cover.
They walked on, in the dark and lonely night,
Through empty shadows in the court of Dis,   *Hades*
As by the stingy moon's cloud-crowded light   270
People walk in the woods when Jove has shadowed
The sky, and color hides beneath black night.
Before the entrance hall, the mouth of Orcus, *(Hades)*
Sorrow and stinging Guilt have made their beds.
Here are pale Sickness, bleak Old Age, and Fear,   275
Crime-urging Hunger, shameful Poverty—
Horrible sights—and Drudgery and Death;
Death's brother Sleep as well; exuberant Evil;
And War, the slaughterer, right on the threshold,
Near the Furies' iron rooms; crazed Discord lives there,   280
Her hair of snakes tied up with bloodstained ribbons.
A huge, dense elm tree in the middle spreads
Its ancient arms. They say it is the roost
Of false dreams, that they cling beneath each leaf.
A great array of monsters has its stables   285
At the entrance: centaurs and half-human Scyllas,
The Lernaean horror-hissing beast, the hundred
Arms of Briareus, the Chimera's flames,
Gorgons and Harpies, Geryon's three-formed ghost.
Aeneas snatched his sword in sudden terror,   290
And held it up against the shapes approaching.
Had not his shrewd guide said these flitting things
Were flimsy forms, illusions without bodies,
He would have rushed to stab them, to no purpose.
The road leads to the river Acheron,   295
Where a whirlpool's endless chasm seethes with thick mud,
And Cocytus drinks the vomit of the sand.   *River in Hades*

Charon, the ghastly boatman, guards these waters
In his grim squalidness. A mass of white beard
Lies in a snarl, his eyes are fixed and fiery,   300
His dirty cloak hangs from a shoulder knot.
He poles his boat along and sets the sails,
Conveying corpses in his rust-red vessel.
Old age in him—a god—is fresh and strong.
All of the mob comes pouring to the shore: 305
Mothers and grown men and the lifeless bodies
Of daring heroes; boys, unmarried girls,
Young men their parents saw placed on the pyre;
As many as the woodland leaves that fall
At the first frost, or birds that flock to land   310
From the high seas when freezing winter drives them
Across that great gulf into sunny lands.
Ghosts stand and beg to be the first to cross,
Stretching their hands out, yearning for the far shore.
But the grim boatman makes his choice among them   315
And shoves the rest far back across the beach.
Aeneas, awed and saddened by this chaos,
Asked, "Tell me why they rush down to the river.
What do these souls want? Why do some retreat
Up the banks, while others row the gloomy water?"   320
The ancient priestess made a brief reply.
"Son of Anchises, heaven's child for certain,   *Aeneas*
Deep Cocytus' pools are here, and the swamp of Styx.
Gods swear by it and keep their word, in terror.
This helpless crowd you see has not been buried.   325
The boatman, Charon there, transports the others.
He may not bring them past the grisly banks
And roaring stream until their bones find rest.
They flit a hundred years around this shore,
Then are let through, home to the pools they long for."   330
Anchises' son now halted in his footsteps,
Brooding in pity on that desolate fate.

He saw there wretched souls deprived of death rites,
Leucaspis and the Lycian fleet's commander,
Orontes. On the stormy way from Troy   335
A southern gale engulfed them with their ship.
And there the helmsman Palinurus paced,
Who in mid-voyage from Africa had fallen
Overboard from the stern while tracking stars.
Aeneas barely recognized his sad form   340
In so much darkness. "Palinurus! Which god
Tore you from us and plunged you in mid-ocean?
Tell me! When did Apollo ever cheat me—
Except about yourself—in prophesying?
He said that you would reach the shore of Italy   345
Uninjured. Is this how he keeps his promise?"
He answered, "No, Anchises' son, my leader,
The oracle was truthful. No god drowned me.
The rudder that I clutched and steered the ship by
Was simply ripped away, and I, its keeper,   350
Fell, dragging it along. I swear by rough seas,
I feared less for myself than for your ship,
Robbed of its tackle, with its pilot toppled;
Would it now falter under these huge waves?
Three stormy nights a violent south wind drove me   355
Over unending sea, and on the fourth day,
From a wave's crest I just glimpsed Italy.
I struggled on and would have landed safely
Had not a cruel tribe come at me with swords—
Stupid: I was no prize. Weighed down by wet clothes,   360
I clutched the jagged cliff top where I landed.
The windy breakers hold me, roll me now.
I beg you by the sky's sweet light and air,
Your father, and your hopes as Iulus grows,
Save me, unconquered hero. Either go back   365
To the port at Velia and bury me
Or, if your deathless mother knows a way

(For I believe the power of gods has brought you
To these great rivers and the Stygian swamp),
Have pity, take my hand, ship me across.   370
Give me at least a place of peace in death."
These were his pleas; the prophetess retorted:
"This wish of yours is monstrous, Palinurus—
To see cold-blooded Styx, the Furies' river,
To go down there, unburied and unsummoned?   375
Don't try to plead away the gods' decrees.
But hear and keep this comfort for your hard fate.
The cities all around your tomb, obeying
Signs from the high gods, will appease your bones.
They'll raise a tomb and give it sacrifices;   380
That district will be named for you forever."
This eased the anguish of his heart a short time:
A place named after him—it made him glad.
They pressed ahead from there and neared the river.
But now from streaming Styx the boatman saw them   385
Walk through the quiet woods and toward the bank.
He was the first to speak, with this rebuke:
"Who are you, marching down here with your weapons?
Stay where you are and, quick, explain yourself.
This is the place of ghosts, sleep, drowsy night: 390
This boat of Styx may not take living bodies.
I regretted taking even Hercules
Across the lake with me, and Theseus,
And Pirithous, unconquered sons of gods.
The first one came to chain the guardian hell hound,   395
And dragged him trembling from beneath the king's throne;
The others tried to take our lady captive—
From the bed of Dis!" Apollo's seer spoke briefly:
"Don't be afraid—we have no plotting purpose;
These arms are peaceful. In his cave, that huge guard   400
May turn ghosts pale forever with his baying,
And the girl stay chaste inside her uncle's house.

Renowned Aeneas, upright, fierce in battle,
Goes to the shades below to find his father.
The sight of such devotion doesn't move you?   405
You know this, then"—the branch, which she drew out
From her clothes' folds. His swelling rage subsided,
And neither spoke. The hallowed gift amazed him,
The branch of fate—so long since he had seen it!
He turned the dark ship to approach the bank,   410
Then shoved souls from their seats along the benches
And cleared the gangways. Towering Aeneas
Entered the hollow leather boat. Its stitching
Groaned at his weight, the swamp poured through the gaps.
But the boat set the prophetess and hero   415
Safe on the muck, among gray reeds, at last.
Enormous Cerberus sprawled there in his cave.
The baying of his three throats filled that country.
The snakes rose on his neck, but then the seer
Threw him a cake of drug-soaked grain and honey.   420
With his three gaping mouths, in savage hunger,
He seized it, and his monstrous arch of spine
Melted, to stretch his huge form through the grotto.
Aeneas passed the guard, now sunk in sleep,
And hurried from the hopeless river's banks.   425
Now a loud howling struck them from the spirits
Of babies: they were crying in the entrance.
They had no share in sweet life. At the breast,
An early death—black day!—had swallowed them.
Next were those executed on false charges.   430
Jurors, assigned by lot, appoint the homes here.
Minos the judge draws names for voiceless panels
And hears what every life now stands accused of.
Beyond this, dismal suicides are lodged.
Though innocent, they threw away their breath   435
In hatred of the light. But now they'd cherish
Hardships and poverty, beneath the sky!

Divine law and the hateful, grim swamp trap them.
Around them the nine loops of Styx are tied.
She pointed out the nearby Fields of Mourning,   440
As they are called, that stretch in all directions.
There hidden tracks, with myrtle trees around them,
Shelter the victims of cruel, wasting love.
Even in death their passions do not leave them.
Phaedra was here, Procris, sad Eriphyle   *Queen of Athens*   445
Displaying wounds her cruel child had inflicted,
And Euadne and Pasiphae. Laodamia
Walked with them, Caeneus too, a young man once,
A woman now, for fate had changed her back.
Phoenician Dido wandered in that broad wood,   450
Her wound still fresh; and when the Trojan hero
Encountered her and recognized her dim form
Through shadows, as a person sees the new moon
Through clouds—or thinks he sees it—as it rises,
He wept and spoke to her in tender love: 455
"Poor Dido, then the messenger was right—
You stabbed yourself and brought about your own end?
And it was my fault? By the stars, the high gods,
And any truth below the earth: my queen,
It was against my will I left your country,   460
And by the orders of the gods, who now
Compel me to pass through this shadowed squalor,
These depths of night. No, I did not believe
That I would bring you so much pain by leaving.
Stay here—don't back away, but let me see you.   465
Who are you running from? Fate gives this last chance
To speak to you." She only glared in fury
While he was pleading, while he called up tears.
Her eyes stayed on the ground, her face averted,
As changeless in expression, while he spoke,   470
As granite or a jagged marble outcrop.
At last she darted bitterly away

To the dark forest, where her spouse Sychaeus
Felt for her sorrow and returned her love.
Aeneas too was shaken by her hard fate.   475
His long gaze and his pitying tears pursued her.
On the appointed path he struggled forward.
They reached the distant fields for famous warriors.
Tydeus met them, and Parthenopaeus,
Glorious in warfare, and Adrastus' pale form.   480
Here were dead Trojans, wept for terribly
In the world above. Aeneas groaned to see
Their long ranks: Glaucus, Medon, and Thersilochus;
Antenor's three sons, Ceres' priest Polyboetes,
And Idaeus, clinging to his arms and chariot.   485
The souls were crowding at his right and left.
Not happy with a look, they held him back
To walk with him and learn why he had come.
But the Greek lords and Agamemnon's cohorts
Were terrified to see the hero's weapons   490
Flash through the shadows; some were turning, running,
As once they'd scampered to their ships; some squeaking—
Their open mouths were thwarted: no shouts came.
He saw Deiphobus, the son of Priam,
All mangled, with cruel slashes on his face   495
And both his hands, his ears stripped from his head,
His nose grotesquely lopped. He shrank back, trying
To hide these awful wounds. Aeneas spoke
As a friend, though he could barely recognize him:
"Strong warrior, from the noble blood of Teucer,   500
Who would have punished you so hideously?
Who had such power? That last night they told me
The slaughtering Greeks had used up all your strength—
You'd fallen on a heap of muddled carnage.
On the Troad's shore I raised an empty tomb,   505
And sent three shouts to the spirits. There your weapons
And name remain, but friend, I never saw you.

I could not set you in our country's earth."
Priam's son answered: "You neglected nothing.
You did your duty by my ghost and me.   510
Fate and the Spartan woman's fatal sin
Have plunged me in this torment—her memorial.
You know how we were duped, and celebrated
That last night?—no, there's no way to forget it.
The fatal horse, pregnant with infantry,   515
Leaped to our citadel, steep Pergama,
And Helen led around our Trojan women
In a sham of Bacchic rites and held a great torch
Herself: our tower signaled to the Greeks.
Anxiety had worn me into dull sleep   520
In my unlucky bed. A sweet, deep rest,
Peaceful as death, muffled me as I lay there.
Meanwhile my prize wife cleared the house of weapons—
Even the trusted sword beneath my pillow.
She opened up our door to Menelaus—   525
Hoping, I guess, this favor for her old flame
Would kill the stink of all her crimes before.
I'll make it brief: they burst in, with Ulysses,
Who's behind every crime. Gods, pay the Greeks back!
The mouth I ask this with does not speak evil.   530
But come—now you: what brought you here still living?
Off course in voyaging, were you driven down?
Did gods direct you? What tormenting fortune
Shows you this sunless town, this sea of darkness?"
Aurora's rosy chariot in the ether   535
Soared past the zenith while the two were talking.
They might have used up all the time permitted,
But Aeneas' guide, the Sibyl, curtly warned him.
"Night rushes in, and tears take up the hours.
The road divides here. This branch on the right,   540
Which stretches to the walls of powerful Dis,
Will take us to Elysium. The left one

for virtuous in Hades

Sends criminals to their due in Tartarus.
"Great priestess, don't be angry," said Deiphobus.
"I'll take my place again in that dark gathering.   545
Go on, Troy's glory—may your fate be better."
He turned his steps back as he finished speaking.
Aeneas turned, and right there, to his left,
Stood a fortress with three walls beneath a cliff.
A raging stream of flame called Phlegethon, ~~River of LAVA~~   550
With crashing, whirling stones, encircled it.
This faced a massive gate and pure steel columns.
No human power, no power of gods at war
Themselves could tear it up. An iron tower soars.
Tisiphone, sleepless guard, sits in the entrance   555
Day and night in her hitched-up, bloody robe.
From this place echo savage blows and groans,
The shriek of iron and the drag of chains.
Terror transfixed Aeneas at the din.
"What crimes did they commit? Tell me, pure virgin!   560
And the punishments? Such howls go toward the sky!"
"Great leader of the Trojans," she began,
"No righteous man may cross this wicked threshold.
Yet Hecate, when she placed Avernus' woods
In my charge, showed the ways gods punish mortals.   565
Here Cretan Rhadamanthus rules, unyielding,
He puts each lie on trial, extracts confessions
Of sins not expiated there above,
Hidden with stupid relish, till it's too late.
Vengeful Tisiphone, ready with her whip,   570
Swoops, lashing. With the fierce snakes in her left hand,
She threatens, and calls the band of her cruel sisters.
Finally, with a grisly scream of hinges,
The holy doors fall open. Do you see
Her form that sits and guards the entranceway?   575
A fiercer monster lives inside, the Hydra,
With fifty black throats. Tartarus itself

Then plunges, twice as far beneath the shades
As the view up toward heavenly Olympus.
Titans, an ancient Earth-born race, struck down   580
By lightning long ago, writhe at the bottom.
Aloeus' giant twins are there—I've seen them.
They tried to wrench away the towering sky,
Attack the gods, and thrust Jove from his kingdom.
And there I saw Salmoneus cruelly punished—   585
He aped Jove's flames and the Olympian thunder.
Shaking a torch, he drove his chariot
In triumph through Greek nations, through his city
Of Elis, claiming honors that the gods have—
Fool: the inimitable thundercloud   590
Shammed by the beat of hooves on a bronze bridge!
Then the almighty father hurled his weapon—
Which was no guttering pine torch—through the cloudbanks
And drove him headlong in a monstrous whirlwind.
Tityon, reared by all-begetting Earth,   595
Was there to see, stretched over nine whole acres.
A giant vulture with its hooked beak browses
On his deathless liver. Through his pain-rich innards
It burrows, feeding—living in his torso;
And with no rest, his viscera grow back.   600
What about the Lapiths, Ixion, Pirithous?
A flint crag hangs above them, set to topple—
It seems—at any second. Banquet couches
Rear high, with shining gold posts. Splendid food
Is spread before their eyes. But the chief Fury,   605
The guest beside them, will not let them touch it.
She leaps up, thrusts her torch at them, and roars.
Those who while living hated brothers, struck
Their fathers, or wove fraud around dependents;
And those who crouched alone on newfound riches   610
(The largest crowd), not sharing with their families;
Adulterers killed when caught, and rebel warriors,

Bold criminals, betrayers of their lords:
Locked up, all wait for sentencing. Don't query
The kinds of torments Fortune's plunged them in.   615
Some roll immense rocks, some are splayed on wheel spokes.
Poor Theseus sits there, and will sit forever.
Phlegyas in his torture shrieks a warning
To everyone—his voice rings through the shadows:
"Learn justice from my fate—and fear the gods."   620
One sold his country and imposed a tyrant;
One, for a price, made laws and then remade them.
One stormed his daughter's room—a lawless marriage.
All of them dared great evil and succeeded.
A hundred tongues and mouths, a voice of iron   625
Would not allow me to describe the crimes
In all their forms, or list the punishments."
The ancient priestess of Apollo added,
"Come, hurry on. Finish the task you started.
Faster! I see the walls the Cyclopes   630
Have forged. There are the doors beneath the archway,
Where we must place our gifts, as we were told to."
They stepped along the dark route, side by side,
Crossed the gap quickly and approached the doors.
Aeneas shook fresh water on himself,   635
And faced the sill, and set the branch there, upright.
Their duty to the goddess done at last,
They came into a glad land: pleasant grounds
In forests of good fortune, blessèd home.
A richer, shimmering air arrays these fields,   640
Which have their own familiar sun and stars.
Men exercised on grassy fields, competed
In games or wrestled in the tawny sand.
Some stamped their dancing feet and chanted songs.
And there the Thracian singer, in his long robe,   645
Played to the beat, through seven intervals,
Changing between his ivory pick and fingers.

Here was the ancient dynasty of Teucer,
Handsome, courageous, born in better years:
Ilus, Assaracus, Dardanus, Troy's founder.   650
Far off, Aeneas marveled at ghost chariots
And armor, planted spears, and scattered horses
Grazing untethered. The delight the living
Take in their arms and chariots, the appeal
Of pasturing shining beasts survives the tomb.   655
Aeneas looked from side to side: some heroes
Feasted and sang a joyous hymn of praise
On fields near fragrant laurel stands. Through these rolled
Mighty Eridanus to the world above.
This group was wounded fighting for their country;   660
These, while they lived, had been pure priests; these prophets
In their righteousness deserved to speak for Phoebus.
Some had enriched our life with their inventions,
Or left the memory of some great service.
All of them had white bands around their foreheads.   665
They poured around the Sibyl, and she spoke—
To Musaeus chiefly (all that huge crowd gazed up
As he towered, massive-shouldered, in the center):
"Tell me, you happy souls, and you, great singer,
Where can we find Anchises, in which region?   670
For him we sailed through Erebus' wide rivers."
With a few words the hero answered her:
"We have no houses. Dim woods are our homes,
Stream banks our couches, verdant flowing meadows
Our settlements. But if you speak your heart's will,   675
Come up this easy path to climb the ridge."
He stepped ahead and showed the shining plains
That stretched below, but soon they left the high ground.
Father Anchises, deep in a green valley,
Cherishingly surveyed the souls confined there   680
Before emerging to the light. He happened
Now to be tallying his dear descendants—

Lives, destinies, achievements, characters—
And when he saw Aeneas making toward him
Over the grass, he stretched his hands out, blissful.   685
The tears poured down his cheeks, and he exclaimed,
"You've come at last?—love made you take this hard road,
Just as I thought?—and can I see your face,
My child, hear your beloved voice, and answer?
Really, I counted on this, calculated   690
The time, and anxious hope did not deceive me.
Welcome! How many lands and wide seas sent you,
My son, and on what giant waves of danger!
And how I feared the Libyan realm would hurt you."
Aeneas answered, "Father, your sad image,   695
Which often meets me, called me to this realm.
My ships stand in the Tuscan sea. My hand—
Clasp it and don't retreat from my embrace."
The tears poured down his face. Three times he tried
To throw his arms around his father's neck,   700
Three times the form slid from his useless hands,
Like weightless wind or dreams that fly away.
The hero now saw, at the valley's end,
A sheltered woods. Wind murmured in its branches.
The river Lethe drifted past the still homes.   705
Above the water, souls from countless nations
Flitted, like bees in tranquil summer meadows
Who move from bud to vivid bud and stream
Around white lilies—the whole field whirs loudly.
The unexpected sight enthralled Aeneas.   710
He wished to learn about it—what the stream was,
And what men filled the banks in that great phalanx.
Father Anchises answered, "These are souls
Fate owes new bodies. Here at Lethe's river
They drink up long oblivion and peace.   715
All of this time, I've yearned to tell of them
And let you see them, counting my descendants,

To share my joy that you've reached Italy."
"Father, do some souls really soar back skyward
From here, returning into sluggish bodies?   720
What dreadful longing sends them toward the light?"
"I'll free you from suspense, my child," he answered,
And told it all, in detail and in order.
"Now first, the earth and sky and plains of water,
The moon's bright globe, the sun and stars are nurtured   725
By a spirit in them. Mind infuses each part
And animates the universe's whole mass.
So arise men and grazing beasts and creatures
That fly and monsters in the glittering ocean.
Their seeds have fiery force; they come from heaven.   730
And yet the noxious body slows them somewhat.
The earthly parts that perish make them numb.
Those parts bring fear, desire, joy, and sorrow.
Souls in dark dungeons cannot see the sky.
But when, on the last day, a life departs,   735
Not every evil sickness of the body
Wholly withdraws from that poor spirit—many
Are long grown in, mysteriously ingrained.
So souls are disciplined and pay the price
Of old wrongdoing. Some are splayed, exposed   740
To hollow winds; a flood submerges some,
Washing out wickedness; fire scorches some pure.
Each bears his own ghosts, then a few are sent
To live in broad Elysium's happy fields,
Till time's great circle is completed, freeing   745
The hardened stain so the ethereal mind,
The fire of pure air, is left unsullied.
When they have circled through a thousand years,
God calls them all in one long rank to Lethe,
To send them back forgetful to the sky's vault,   750
With a desire to go back into bodies."
Anchises finished, and he drew the two guests

Into the middle of the murmuring crowd.
He climbed a ridge that showed him every man
In the long line. He knew each face approaching.   755
"Come, hear your destiny, and the future glory
Of the stock of Dardanus, all the descendants
That we will have from the Italian race—
Great souls who will be born into our family.
That young man leaning on a headless spear   760
Will take the next turn in the airy light:
Your posthumous son Silvius (a name
From Alba), first of Troy's Italian bloodline.
Lavinia will raise him in the forest,
And he will be a king and father kings: 765
Our family that will reign at Alba Longa.
By him stands Procas, glory of Troy's race,
Then Capys, Numitor, and Aeneas Silvius,
Your namesake, irreproachable, high-hearted—
If ever he succeeds to Alba's kingship.   770
What fine young men! You see the strength in them.
Oak leaves of civic honor shade their temples.
They'll found Nomentum, Gabii, Fidena,
The fortress of Collatia on the mountains,
Pometii, Castrum Inui, Bola, Cora—   775
The famous names of places nameless now.
Romulus, child of Mars, and through his mother
A Trojan, will become her father's ally.
You see the twin crests? They're a special emblem
The father of the gods already gives him.   780
Under the omens this man saw, renowned Rome
Will rule the world and raise her heart to heaven—
Blessed in her sons, with seven citadels
In one wall: like the tower-crowned Great Mother
Driving her chariot through Phrygian cities,   785
Holding in blissful arms her hundred grandsons
From gods—all gods themselves, who live in heaven.

Now turn your eyes here, see this clan—your Romans:
Caesar, and all of Iulus' offspring, destined
To make their way to heaven's splendid heights.   790
Here is the man so often promised you,
Augustus Caesar, a god's son, and bringer
Of a new age of gold to Saturn's old realm
Of Latium. He will take our rule past India,
Past Garamantia, past the solar pathway   795
That marks the year, where Atlas hefts the sky
And turns the high vault set with burning stars.
The Caspian realm, the land around Maeotis
Already quake at prophecies—he's coming!
All the Nile's seven mouths are in confusion.   800
Hercules didn't travel through so much land
To pierce the bronze-hooved deer or tame the woods
Of Erymanthus, or make Lerna tremble
With his bow; nor Bacchus, flexing vine reins, drawn
In triumph from high Nysa by his tigers.   805
Shall we hang back and not exert our courage,
Fearing to stake our claim in Italy?
Who is that, far off, olive-crowned, and bringing
A sacrifice? White hair, white beard—I know him:
This Roman king will found the new-built city   810
On laws. From little Cures with its poor soil
He'll rise to great dominion. But that next one,
Tullus, will break the country's peace and rouse
Its men, who've grown unused to victories.
Next is the boaster Ancus, even now   815
Drunk on the breezes of the people's favor.
Do you want to see the Tarquin kings and Brutus,
The proud avenger, winning back the fasces—
First consul, with that office's harsh axes?
For splendid freedom's sake, he'll have his own sons   820
Put to death, when they stir up war again—
Poor man, though ages after him applaud.

Love for his country, greed for praise will triumph.
Look—Torquatus with his savage ax, the Decii,
The Drusi, and Camillus, who'll bring home   825
Our standards. See those two in bright matched armor,
Souls in accord while Night imprisons them.
But once they reach the light, how great a war
They'll rouse, what ranks of slaughter, father-in-law
Come down the bouldered Alps from high Monoecus,   830
And son-in-law deploying all the East.
Children, don't lose your horror of such warfare.
Don't turn your massive strength against your country.
You of the gods' stock: take the lead, have mercy!
My son, throw down your weapons!   835
There's Mummius, who'll drive up the Capitol
In triumph over Corinth's slaughtered Greeks;
Paulus will root out Agamemnon's town,
And Argos: Perseus, Achilles' heir,
Will pay for Troy, for Minerva's sullied temple.   840
Great Cato and Cossus, who could pass you over?
Or the Gracchi, or the Scipios, two thunderbolts
Of war, who'll bring down Libya; or Fabricius
The resourceful; or Serranus, sowing the furrow?
Fabius, stop—I can't keep up; your Greatness   845
In stalling will be all that saves our country.
Others, I know, will beat out softer-breathing
Bronze shapes, or draw from marble living faces,
Excel in pleading cases, chart the sky's paths,
Predict the rising of the constellations.   850
But Romans, don't forget that world dominion
Is your great craft: peace, and then peaceful customs;
Sparing the conquered, striking down the haughty."
They were amazed. Father Anchises added,
"See how Marcellus marches in the glory   855
Of the Rich Spoils, an overtowering victor.
This knight will save a Rome in chaos, crushing

Carthage and rebel Gaul; he'll make our third gift
Of captured arms to Father Quirinus."
Aeneas saw a splendid young man walking   860
With Marcellus in bright armor—but his face
Was overcast, his eyes fixed on the ground.
"Father, who's the companion of the hero?
A son, perhaps, or grandson of that great stock?
What a fine presence, what loud praise around him!   865
But black Night wraps his head with its sad shadow."
Father Anchises then began to sob:
"My son, don't ask about your clan's great sorrow.
Fate will give just a glimpse of him on earth.
Deities, you decreed the Roman race   870
Would be too mighty if it kept this gift.
What loud groans from our citizens will Mars' Field   *God of War*
Send up to Mars' great city! What processions
Will Tiber see when gliding by the new tomb!
No boy of Trojan blood will raise more hope   875
In Latin forebears. Never will the land
Of Romulus be more proud of any nursling.
Righteousness, old-time honor, strength unbeaten
In war! Nobody meeting him in battle
Could have escaped, whether he came on foot   880
Or gored a foam-flecked horse's side with spurs.
Poor boy—if you could only break this cruel fate!
You'll be Marcellus. Let me give the gifts
I can: armloads of lilies, purple flowers,
Scattered in empty ritual for the soul   885
Of my descendant." Through the airy broad fields
They wandered now, surveying everything.
Anchises showed his son each point of interest   *Aenaes' father*
And fired his lust for glory in the future,
Then told him of the wars he soon must fight,   890
The Laurentian tribes, the city of Latinus,
How to endure or else avoid each hardship.

There are two gates of sleep. The one, they say,
Is horn: true shades go out there easily;
The other—shining, white, well-crafted ivory—   895
Lets spirits send false dreams up toward the sky.
His speeches done, Anchises brought his son here,
And the Sibyl too, and sent them through the ivory.
Aeneas went straight back, to ships and comrades,
Then coasted to the harbor of Caieta.   900
The prows dropped anchors; sterns stood on the shore.

7

Caieta, you as well, Aeneas' nurse,
Gave lasting fame, in dying, to our shores.
The great West keeps your resting place today
In glory—if there's glory in the grave.
Loyal Aeneas rendered her due ritual,   5
Heaping a mound up. When the deep sea calmed,
He spread his sails and left the port behind.
The breezes blew past nightfall, and the white moon
Lit up their course—the gleaming surface trembled.
They sailed close by the shore of Circe's country.   10
The Sun's rich daughter makes secluded groves there
Resound with constant singing, and in high halls
At nighttime, by the fragrant cedar's light,
Runs her shrill shuttle through the filmy weave.
Groans can be heard, and roars of angry lions   15
Fighting against their chains in the late hours,
And savage cries of bristly hogs and bears
In pens, and howls from images of huge wolves,

Once human: potent herbs from the fierce goddess
Give them the faces and the fur of beasts.   20
Saving the blameless Trojans from those grim spells,
From landing in that port on deadly shores,
Neptune now filled their sails with following winds,
And they escaped beyond the foaming shallows.
Sunbeams reddened the sea. Yellow Aurora   25
Shone in her rosy chariot from on high.
The wind abated. Instantly the breezes
All calmed, and oars toiled in the sluggish smoothness.
Now from this watery plain Aeneas saw
A broad grove. There the pleasant Tiber burst through,   30
Darting with whirlpools, yellow with its sand load,
To the sea. All kinds of river birds and shore birds
Fluttered from branch to branch, around and over
The channel, and their songs caressed the sky.
He told his men to turn the prows toward land,   35
And gladly started up the shady river.
Erato, come, let me explain the times,
The rulers, and what ancient Latium was   *Latinus' Kingdom in Italy*
When the foreign army first brought ships to land
In Italy, and how the quarrels started.   40
Goddess, direct your poet. Savage warfare
I'll sing, and kings whose courage brought their death;
The Tuscan army; all Hesperia rallied   *Italy*
To arms. This is a higher story starting,
A greater work for me.

                          Latinus, old now,   45
Had reigned in long peace over towns and farmland.
Faunus and a Laurentian nymph, Marica—
We hear—begot him; Picus, father of Faunus,
Claimed Saturn as his father, the line's founder.
By the gods' will, Latinus had no male child;   50
Sons born to him were taken in their first youth.

An only daughter, sole hope of that great house,
Was now grown up and ready for a husband.
Many from spacious Latium, from the whole
Of Italy sought her. Handsomest was Turnus,   55
Of a powerful dynasty. Latinus' consort
Was ardent, wild to have this son-in-law.
But holy signs, each with its terrors, blocked her.
A laurel, sacred-leaved, revered for ages,
Stood in the central high-roofed palace shrine.   60
They say that when he built the town, the patriarch
Latinus found it, offered it to Phoebus,
And named its settlers, after it, Laurentians.
Now a swarm of loud-buzzing bees—amazing
To speak of—crossed the clear air, occupied   65
The treetop, quickly intertwined their feet,
And in a mass hung from a leafy branch.
An augur said at once, "I see a column
Of foreigners coming, making for the same place,
And from the same place, new lords in your tower."   70
And when pure torches smoked above the altar,
And chaste Lavinia stood by her father, (LAƭiᴡᴜᴧ)
A fire—shocking—seemed to seize her long hair,
And all her rich clothes crackled in the flame.
Her regally bound hair, her crown with bright gems   75
Kindled. She was wrapped up in tawny light
And smoke, and sparks were scattered through the palace—
A frightening, marvelous sight, it was reported.
Prophets foretold a glorious destiny
For her, but for the people a great war.   80
The anxious king approached the oracle
Of his father, the seer Faunus, in the grove
Albunea pours down through—that king of woods,
Loud with its sacred spring, dark, breathing sulfur.
Here all the tribes of Italy, when perplexed,   85
Seek answers. When a priest has brought his gifts,

He lies on sheepskins from the sacrifices
And goes to sleep beneath the still night sky.
There he sees many eerie fluttering forms,
Hears voices of all kinds, consults with gods,   90
And speaks to Acheron in Avernus' depths.
Father Latinus sought advice in person.
He sacrificed a hundred woolly sheep,
Then lay there resting on their spread-out fleeces.
Suddenly, from within the grove, a voice: 95
"My child, don't seek alliance with the Latins
For your daughter—though a wedding is at hand.
Foreigners will arrive, and intermarriage
Will raise our name to heaven. The descendants
Will fling the earth beneath their feet and rule it   100
Clear to both oceans that the Sun rides over."
Latinus didn't keep concealed the warning
His father, Faunus, gave him in the still night.
Rumor had winged it into all the far towns
Of Italy when the Trojan army moored   105
Their ships off Tiber's grassy, swollen bank.
Aeneas, his lieutenants, and his fine son
Sprawled on the ground beneath a high tree's branches,
Prepared a meal, and, at Jove's prompting, set
Spelt wafers on the grass to hold their food,   110
A cereal base to pile with woodland forage.
All this was eaten; hunger drove them further,
To gnawing at the sheets of bread. Their hands,
Their bold jaws now assaulted the baked disks,
Broad surfaces that fate had sent to them.   115
Iulus said, "Look at us, eating our tables!"—
A mere joke, but those words were the first portent
Of hardships' end. His father seized on them
And silenced him, stunned by the miracle,
And cried at once, "Hail, country, pledged by fate!   120
Hail, faithful guardian gods of Troy as well!

This is your home, your country. Father Anchises *Aeneas' father*
(Now I recall) bequeathed this fateful secret:
'My child, when you reach strange shores, and your food
Is gone, and hunger makes you eat your tables,   125
Then trust that home and rest are there. Be mindful,
Lay buildings out and raise defensive walls.'
This is that hunger, waiting till the end
To put a limit to our exile.
So at first light let's fan out eagerly   130
From where we've landed and explore the country—
What people live here? Where is their walled city?
Now pour Jove a libation, send my father
Anchises prayers, and bring more wine for feasting."
Putting a verdant garland on, he prayed   135
To the place's spirit and the firstborn goddess,
Earth, and the nymphs and rivers still unknown;
Then Night, her rising constellations, Jove
On Mount Ida, the Phrygian Mother in her turn;
And his parents, one in heaven, one in Erebus. *God of Darkness* 140
The almighty father, from the clear high heaven,
Thundered three times now, and his own hand struck
To show a cloud that blazed with rays of gold.
The word spread quickly through the Trojan ranks:
The time had come to build their promised walls.   145
Ecstatic at that great sign, they renewed
The feasting, placing garlands on the wine bowls.

The new day rose, the great lamp spread its light.
They split up to explore the shore and borders
And the city's site: here was the Tiber, here   150
Numicius' pooling spring; here lived brave Latins.
Anchises' son now chose a hundred legates *Aeneas*
Of various ranks and sent them to the proud walls *Latinus*
Of the king. They were to put on olive crowns
And take him gifts, peace offerings from the Trojans.   155

They hurried to obey and strode there quickly.
Where walls would rise, Aeneas dug a low ditch
On the shore and started their first settlement,
With battlements and ramparts, like a camp.
The group arrived and saw the Latins' high homes 160
And towers, and came beneath the city wall.
There boys and flourishing young men rode horses
In drill, trained chariot teams on dusty tracks,
Pulled tight-strung bows, hurled pliant javelins,
Or boxed and raced on foot in competition. 165
A messenger rode ahead to the old king:
Some towering men had come; their clothes were foreign.
He ordered them invited in, and sat
On his ancestral throne in the hall's center.
Laurentian Picus' huge, majestic palace 170
Soared on its hundred columns at the town's crest,
Revered with awe from old times, in its forest.
For the good omen kings took up their scepters
And rods of office there. It housed the senate
And sacred banquets; there the elders slaughtered 175
A ram and sat at tables in a long row.
Ancestral busts were in the vestibule,
Old cedar faces, Italus and Sabinus,
Planter of vines—his sickle hung beneath him—
The old man Saturn, Janus' double face, 180
And all the other kings from the beginning,
With heroes wounded in their country's wars.
On the sacred doorposts many spoils of war hung,
Curved axes, chariots in captivity
With plumes from helmets, giant bolts from gates, 185
Spearheads and shields, and rams torn out of ships' hulls.
The famous Picus sat there, tamer of horses,
Shown in a short cloak, with his Quirinal staff *Romulus?*
In his right hand, in his left the sacred shield.
Circe, his lust-crazed wife, armed with her gold staff *Sorceress turned* 190
men to animals

And potions, changed him to a dappled bird.
On his ancestral seat inside this temple,
Latinus called the Trojans in to meet him
And spoke to them serenely when they came:
"Trojans (we know your city and your race;   195
We heard about you as you sailed this way),
What do you seek? What need has brought your ships here
Through endless blue sea to Italian shores?
If it's because you're lost or driven by storms—
Which many sailors on the deep endure—   200
That you've broached our river, camped beside our port:
Make us your refuge. Understand that Latins,
Saturn's race, don't do right through mere compulsion
Of law but choose to keep the old god's ways.
I do remember, though time dims the story,   205
What old Auruncan men said: Dardanus,
Born here, sailed through to Phrygian Ida's cities
And Thracian Samos, now called Samothrace,
Starting from Corythus, his Etruscan town.
The starry sky's gold palace now enthrones him;   210
He ranks among the gods, and has his altars."
When he had finished, Ilioneus answered,
"King, glorious child of Faunus, no black storms,
No roiling waves have driven us to your land;
The stars, the coastlines gave us no false guidance.   215
We all came to your city readily,
On purpose, exiles from the greatest kingdom—
Once—that the sun saw, voyaging from the sky's edge.
Jove first begot our race; in this our people
Delight. From Jove's high kin our king was born: 220
Trojan Aeneas sent us to your doorstep.
How great a storm from pitiless Mycenae
Poured over Trojan fields, when fate brought two worlds,
Europe and Asia, battering together—
The farthest people know this, who are cut off   225

By the Ocean with its tides, or isolated
In the harsh tropics, center of the five zones.
Out of that deluge, through vast seas we've come,
To beg a tiny home here for our gods,
A harmless beach. Water and air cost nothing!   230
We will not shame your kingdom—no, your good deed
Will bring you lasting gratitude and glory;
Italians won't regret embracing Trojans.
By Aeneas' fate I swear, by his strong right hand,
Proven in all his friendships and his battles: 235
Many tribes, many nations have sought union
Or alliance with us. We approach you first
With suppliant words and fillets, but don't scorn us.
On the gods' prophetic orders we have sought
Your country, which was Dardanus'. Apollo   240
Ringingly orders us back to the Tiber
In Tuscany, to Numicius' sacred spring.
Our leader sends you gifts, his poor remains
Of wealth, saved from the flames of Troy. His father
Poured wine out on the altars with this gold bowl.   245
Priam, proclaiming laws to gathered nations,
Held this rod, wore this holy crown, these clothes,
The work of Trojan women."
Ilioneus' words amazed Latinus.
He sat unmoving, gazing at the floor,   250
But his eyes moved in thought. Purple embroidery
And Priam's scepter touched him less. He dwelt
More on his daughter's wedding and her marriage.
In his heart he turned old Faunus' forecast over:
This was the foreign voyager fate pledged him   255
As son-in-law, to join him as an equal
In ruling; his descendants would be heroes,
And all the world would come beneath their power.
At last he spoke in joy: "Gods bless our project,
And their own prophecy. Take what you ask for;   260

And I accept your gifts. While I am reigning,
You'll have a rich land, you'll have wealth like Troy's.
But if Aeneas has such eager longing
To be my guest-friend and be called my ally,
Then let him come—a friend's face holds no terror.   265
I'll clasp your king's hand, making good this treaty.
But you must take this message back to him:
I have a daughter whom an oracle
And many heavenly signs forbid me giving
To a man of our race: foreigners come to Latium   270
Will be our sons through marriage, and the new clan
Will reach the stars. I think—I hope—it's this man
That Fate requires—if my foreboding's right."
The lord chose from the sleek three hundred horses
Housed in his high-roofed barn. He had one led   275
To every Trojan there, down through their ranking—
Swift mounts, and they had saddlecloths embroidered
With purple, and gold collars hanging down.
Their trappings were of gold; they chewed gold bits.
Aeneas was sent a chariot and team,   280
A fire-breathing pair, from heaven's stock,
From mixed breeds cunning Circe had created
By mating stallions stolen from her father
With mortal mares. Aeneas' men rode back
With Latinus' gifts and words and terms for peace.   285

Now Jove's fierce wife was flying back from Argos,
The home of Inachus, in her chariot.
From Pachynus in far Sicily, from the high air,
She saw Aeneas happy, with his fleet:
They worked at building, settled trustingly,   290
Forgot their ships. She halted, pierced by grief,
Then shook her head, and this poured from her heart:
"That hated Phrygian race, their fate opposed
To mine! They couldn't die on Sigeum's plain,

Couldn't stay conquered? Trojans couldn't burn   295
When Troy burned? Through the fire and the onslaughts
They found a way. At last, I guess, my power
Lies slack and weary with its load of hatred.
I even stooped to persecute their exile,
Harrying refugees across the ocean.   300
The sea and sky have no strength left to fight them.
What good were the Syrtes, Scylla, vast Charybdis?
Trojans nest in the longed-for Tiber, fearing
Neither the deep nor me. Mars' strength destroyed
The monstrous Lapiths. Jove himself surrendered   305
Calydon, ancient town, to Diana's rage.
What great crimes merited such punishments?
But I, Jove's mighty wife, have shrunk from nothing,
Made every useless try and now am beaten—
By Aeneas! But if my own power falls short,   310
I'll find help anywhere I can—no scruples!
If heaven resists me, I'll rouse Acheron. *River in Hades*
Fate grants them entrance to the Latin kingdom;
Lavinia must be Aeneas' wife.
But I can put off these great happenings,   315
And crush the subjects of this pair of kings:
Marriage, allying them, will have this price;
Blood from both sides will be your dowry, child;
Bellona will escort you. A fire-bridegroom
Hasn't been born from Hecuba alone.   320
No, Venus' child will be another Paris,
A funeral torch to burn a reborn Troy."
Terrible now, she sped to earth, to summon
Allecto the grief-bringer from her dark home
In hell, among the Furies. In her heart   325
Are treachery, rage, grim war, atrocities.
Her father, Pluto, and her hellish sisters
Loathe her themselves, the monster: all her dire forms
And faces, all the black snakes sprouting from her.

Now Juno made this speech, inciting her: 330
"Daughter of Night, lend me your special service
And safeguard my prestige. Keep it from yielding,
And Aeneas' crew from buying off Latinus
Through marriage, or besieging Italy.
You can set brothers, who were friends, at war,   335
Destroying homes with hate, invading them
With your whip, your flames of death. A thousand names
Are yours, a thousand torments. Rouse your genius,
Shatter their treaties, sow the seeds of war—
War! Wished, demanded, started all at once!"   340
Allecto, steeped in Gorgon poisons, rushed
To the Laurentian king's high halls in Latium
And lurked there, at the threshold of Amata,   *Queen of Latium*
Who smoldered with a woman's anxious anger:
Trojans had come—would they steal Turnus' wedding?   345
Dark snakes made up the Fury's hair—she tossed one.
Into the bodice and the heart it glided,
Monstrous and maddening, to shake the whole house.
Beneath her clothes it coiled, around her smooth breasts.
She couldn't feel it as it breathed its poison—   350
Her frenzy. As a gold chain, the huge serpent
Twined her neck, hung as ribbon from her headband,
Wove through her hair and slid around her body.
The venom oozed in, and the sickness started
To storm her senses, wrap her bones in fire.   355
Before the flames engulfed her heart and mind,
She spoke quite gently, in a motherly way,
And wept: her daughter married to a Phrygian!
"You'll give Lavinia to Trojan exiles,
Not pitying your daughter or yourself   360
Or me? At the first wind, he'll make for high seas
With our girl, the lying pirate. This is how
The Phrygian shepherd penetrated Sparta,
And hauled off Helen, Leda's child, to Troy.

And your oath? The love you had once for your people?   365
Your promises to Turnus, who is family?
If the Latins need a foreign son-in-law,
And it is fixed and ordered by your father,
Then every land that's free, outside our power,
Is foreign, I think—can't the gods mean that?   370
And trace the house of Turnus from its start:
Acrisius, Inachus—Mycenae's heartsblood."
She found these words were useless, for Latinus
Was firm. And now the maddening venom slipped
Into her entrails, seeped all through her body.   375
Now monstrous visions haunted the poor woman.
Frenzied, she ran amok all through the city,
Like a top flitting under coiling whip blows.
Boys in intent play, in an empty courtyard,
Send it in spacious circles. At the lash,   380
It rushes on its curving course. The young group
Watches in wonder as their blows inspire
The flying boxwood. No less fiercely driven,
Amata ran straight through the haughty city.
Pretending Bacchus goaded her, she dashed   385
Into the woods, a greater, wilder outrage,
And hid her daughter in the leafy mountains,
To thwart, to steal her marriage to a Trojan.
She roared, "O, Bacchus, only you deserve her!
She takes in hand your pliant thyrsis, dances   390
Around you, grows a lock of hair to give you."
Word flew; the other mothers caught her passion,
Which drove them from their homes out into new ones,
Hearts flaming, heads and necks bare to the wind,
While others filled the sky with shivering howls,   395
Wore skins, and carried spear shafts wound with vine leaves.
Fevered Amata held a torch among them
And sang her child's and Turnus' wedding song,
Rolling red eyes. She gave a sudden shriek:

"Oh, listen, mothers everywhere in Latium,   400
If your good hearts still cherish poor Amata,
If the flouting of my mother rights disturbs you,
Unbind your hair, take up these secret rites."
Allecto used such Bacchic goads to harry *a Fury*
The queen all through the grim, beast-haunted forest.   405
Satisfied with the force of this first frenzy,
Wreck of Latinus' plans and all his household,
The deathly goddess rushed on her dark wings
To the brave Rutulian's town. (They say that Danae,
Forced there by headlong south winds, founded it   410
For Argive settlers: Ardea, it was called
By the ancients—which is still a glorious name.
Its wealth is gone, though.) There, in his high palace,
Turnus was sleeping through the black of midnight.
Allecto stripped off her ferocious form   415
And changed to an old woman—plowed her forehead
With ugly lines, put on white hair, and bound it
With a fillet and an olive twig, to look
Like Calybe, priestess of the shrine of Juno.
She came before the young man's eyes and spoke: 420
"Turnus, you let your efforts go for nothing?
You watch your scepter pass to Trojan settlers?
The king denies the bride your blood has paid for.
He wants a foreigner to have his kingdom.
They laugh at you! Take risks for nothing, scatter   425
Etruscan lines, and end poor Latium's wars.
Almighty Juno ordered me to say this
Plainly, as you were resting in the still night.
Up, then, and get the young men armed and moving
From the gates to battle. Burn the painted ships   430
And Phrygian lords who squat by your fine river.
The gods' great power demands that King Latinus,
Unless he does your will and grants your wedding,
Should find at last what you are like in battle."

The young man answered, sneering at the prophet: 435
"The news has not escaped me, as you think:
The fleet has traveled into Tiber's waters.
I don't need made-up panic. Royal Juno
Hasn't forgotten me.
Your failing and oblivious old age   440
Torments you uselessly with these false fears
And prophecies about the clash of kings.
Your task is guarding the gods' effigies.
Men, who fight wars, will deal with war and peace."
The speech inflamed Allecto. While still speaking,   445
The young man felt a sudden terror seize him
And gaped: so many snakes hissed on the Fury,
So monstrous was the sight. He stopped and stammered.
She shoved him back, her flaming eyes assailed him.
Two snakes reared from her head. She made the sound   450
Of whips, and with her frothing mouth she spoke:
"Just look at how oblivious I am,
With these false fears about the clash of kings.
See! From the deadly sisters' home I come,
With death and war in hand."   455
She spoke, and threw a smoking torch at him,
To lodge its black light in his youthful breast.
Terror crashed through his sleep, and sweat broke out
To cover him and soak him to the bones.
He roared for arms and searched his bed and rooms   460
In savage lust for iron, depraved war madness,
And, most of all, rage; as a heap of twigs
Is lit to roar beneath a frothing cauldron;
The water leaps and burns. Inside there storms
A smoky river, and foam overflows   465
Beyond its confines, shooting black steam skyward.
Peace was profaned: he sent his young lieutenants
To King Latinus, ordered arms prepared,
Italy guarded, enemies thrust out.

Latins and Trojans—he could face them both.   470
He told the gods what he would give for victory.
Rutulians egged each other on to fight.
His fine and graceful youth moved some, and some
His royal bloodline or his glorious warcraft.
While Turnus filled his soldiers' hearts with fire,   475
Hell-winged Allecto, with a new ploy, hurried
To the Trojans. Scouting out the shore where Iulus,
A handsome boy, stalked animals and chased them,
The infernal virgin struck the dogs with madness.
She tossed a scent they knew before their noses,   480
To goad them on a deer's trail. This began
The disaster, kindling rustic hearts for war.
There was a splendid stag, with wide-spread antlers.
Together with his young sons, Tyrrhus—master
Of the king's herds and keeper of his broad plains—   485
Had taken it from its mother's teats and reared it.
Silvia, the boys' sister, lavished care
On the tame thing, wove its antlers with soft garlands,
Combed it and bathed it in a crystal spring.
It ate its owners' food, put up with petting,   490
And though it roamed the woods, it made its own way
Back to their door, however late at night.
Iulus' ferocious dogs now started it—
It had strayed far from home and swum downstream,
And rested from the heat beneath a green bank.   495
Ascanius was fired by ambition
And aimed an arrow out of his bent bow.
A god directed his uncertain hand.
The dart twanged out and sang through flanks and belly.
The wounded beast took refuge at its home.   500
Moaning and bleeding, limping to the barn,
It filled the buildings with beseeching wails.
Silvia heard. She struck her arms in horror
And called the hardy countrymen to help.

[158] BOOK SEVEN

The vicious Fury hid in the still forest: 505
Instantly they were there, one with a charred torch,
The next, a club with swelling knots. What each found,
Rage made a weapon. Tyrrhus called these forces:
From quartering a log of oak with wedges,
He'd turned and seized his ax in panting fury.   510
On her lookout, the cruel goddess saw her chance
For more harm. Moving to a barn's high rooftop,
She sent her hellish voice out through a curved horn
In the shepherds' call, which set the whole deep forest
Immediately echoing and trembling   515
Clear to Diana's lake and the Nar River,   Huntress
White with its sulfur, and Velinus' spring.
Mothers in fear pressed children to their breasts.
The sturdy farmers swarmed from everywhere,
Answering that grim trumpet's call and seizing   520
Whatever weapons were at hand. The Trojans
Poured from their gate as well, to help Ascanius.
Both sides lined up. It was no yokel brawl now
With burnt stakes and hard cudgels, but a contest
Of two-edged blades; a blackly bristling crop   525
Of swords stretched far away. Bronze armor flashed,
Struck by the sun; the light shot to the clouds:
As when the surface of the sea begins
To whiten, slowly rising, shooting waves
Higher, until its lowest depths heave skyward.   530
Now at the front, the eldest son of Tyrrhus,
Young Almo, fell: a hissing arrow struck him
And lodged below his throat, to choke with blood
The thin, soft passage of his voice and life breath.
Around him many dead lay; old Galaesus   535
Had stepped between to plead for peace—most righteous
And wealthiest Italian of those days:
Five bleating and five lowing herds were driven
Over his soil; a hundred plowshares turned it.

Equally matched, men filled the plain with fighting.   540
The goddess' pledge was kept, war's first blood spilled;
The first deaths were accomplished. Leaving Italy,
She made her journey through the airy heavens
And spoke to Juno haughtily, in triumph:
"Here is your conflict, sealed by dismal war.   545
Invite them to be friends now, with a treaty.
I've spattered Trojans with Italian blood.
I'll do more if you sanction it. With rumors,
I'll spread the war to nearby towns and kindle
The lust for frenzied Mars. They'll come to help   550
From everywhere. I'll strew the land with arms."
"Enough deceit and fear for now," said Juno
"They're fighting hand to hand, with solid motives.
Chance offered weapons; fresh blood sullies them.
Venus' superior son and King Latinus   *of Italy*   555
Can have this as a wedding and a marriage.
But the father, high Olympus' king, would surely   *Home of Gods*
Not want you wandering at will in heaven.
Get out, then. I'll direct whatever action
Is called for now." So Saturn's daughter spoke.   560
The other raised her wings, which hissed with snakes,
And left the steep sky for her home in hell.
In Italy's center, under lofty mountains,
Is the famous valley of Ampsanctus, legend
In many lands. Dark forests crowd both sides   565
With their thick leaves. A torrent in the middle
Crashes through rocks and twists its frothing waters.
They point a fearsome cave out there, where cruel Dis
Breathes from the holes, and Acheron breaks through   *River/Lake in Hell*
A poisonous pit. The Fury, hateful power,   570
Slipped in, unburdening the earth and sky.
Now Saturn's queenly daughter put the last touch
On the war. The shepherds' whole contingent ran
From battle to the town, and brought the dead—

Young Almo and Galaesus with his torn face—   575
Imploring gods, appealing to Latinus.
To raging murder charges Turnus added
New alarms: Trojans asked to share the kingdom,
Easterners breeding in, himself expelled.
The families of the matrons running wild   580
Through trackless woods in Bacchic bands now gathered
(For Amata's name had weight), demanding war,   *Queen of Latium*
Evil war. Everyone was now possessed;
The omens, the decrees of fate meant nothing.
They avidly besieged Latinus' palace.   585
Like a cliff above the sea, he stood unmoving—
A sea cliff, when the crashing of the storm comes;
Firm in its bulk it holds, though waves throng roaring
Around it. Crags and frothing boulders moan—
Unmoving, pouring back the battered seaweed.   590
The old king had no power to defeat
Their blind plans—heartless Juno set things going.
Often he called on gods and empty air:
"Fate wrecks our ship; a whirlwind whips us onward.
Poor things, you'll make atonement with your blood.   595
Turnus, your sin will bring harsh punishment.
Too late, you'll pray and try to buy the gods off.
But I've earned rest. I'm on the haven's edge,
And robbed of nothing but a happy death."
He kept indoors and dropped the reins of state.   600
There was a ritual in Hesperian Latium,   *West Italy*
Which Alban cities afterward kept sacred,   *Pre-Roman settlement*
And lofty Rome performs, when war is launched—   *of Trojans in Italy*
Whether against Hyrcanians or Getans
Or Arabs, or if it's an eastward march   605
To claim our standards from the Parthians.
There stand twin Gates of War (as they are called),
Held sacred in the dread of savage Mars.
Eternal iron and a hundred bronze bars

3/16/19

Seal them, and Janus is their guardian.   610
When the senators resolve to fight, the consul
In person, in the Quirinal robe of state (Romulus
And Gabine belt, throws wide the creaking doors,
And gives the call to war. The fighting men
Follow, and bronze horns blast their harsh assent.   615
Though ordered to declare war on the Trojans
By this custom, opening the deadly gates,
Father Latinus shrank from touching them.
He fled the hateful task and hid in shadows.
But then the queen of heaven, Saturn's daughter,   620
Flew down herself to force the iron war gates
Apart, and pushed until the hinges turned.
Italy, calm and still before, now blazed.
Some looked to march across the plains, some reared
Wildly on dusty mounts. All called for weapons.   625
Some used thick fat to polish shields and lances,
And others ground their axes sharp on whetstones.
The trumpet thrilled them, carrying standards thrilled them.
Five mighty cities made their anvils echo:
Strong Atina, proud Tibur, Ardea,   630
Crustumerium, Antemnae with its towers
Hollowed out sturdy helmets and wove shields
From bending wicker, or shaped cuirasses
From bronze, or glossy greaves from pliant silver.
Forgetting their devotion to the plowshare   635
And sickle, men reforged their fathers' blades.
Horns blared, the watchword spread—the war had come.
One snatched his helmet, on the run from home.
One strained to yoke his neighing team, put on
His shield, gold-woven breastplate, trusted sword.   640
Muses, throw open Helicon, stir my song. Mountain in Central Greece
What kings were roused to war, what armies followed   Home to Muses
To fill the plains, what heroes bloomed already
In that propitious soil, what arms grew hot there?

You know it and can tell it, goddesses;   645
Barely a breath can reach me of the story.
From Etruria wild Mezentius, who scorned
The gods, first armed his troops and came to war;
Lausus his son came with him—there was no one
Handsomer, save for Turnus of Laurentum—   650
Lausus, horse tamer, conqueror of wild things,
Who led a thousand men (what good to him?)
From Caere and deserved more in obeying
His father—he deserved a better father.
Next Aventinus, splendid child of Hercules   655
The splendid, strutted his prize chariot team
On the grass. His shield displayed his father's emblem,
The Hydra girdled with a hundred snakes.
On the wooded Aventine, the priestess Rhea
Secretly brought him to the shores of light.   660
She'd mated with the god, who came as victor
From slaughtered Geryon to Laurentian fields
And bathed his Spanish cows in a Tuscan river.
His son's men now were armed with spears and fierce pikes
And polished swords and Sabine javelins.   665
He went on foot himself, a lion's huge skin
On his head and swept around him: fearsome, matted,
Bristling, white-toothed. He came into the palace
Dauntingly, in this cloak of Hercules.
Next, from the walls of Tibur came twin brothers   670
(Their clan's named for their elder brother, Tibur):
Catillus and keen Coras, youthful Argives,
Ran at the front, where spears and arrows swarmed—
As a pair of cloud-born centaurs leave some high peak,
Dashing down Homole or snowy Othrys   675
At great speed; towering forest yields a path;
Crashing, the underbrush gives way to them.
Caeculus too, Praeneste's founder, legend
Since then, was there: born among herds to Vulcan *God of Fire*

To be a king, and found beside the hearth.   680
An army came with him, from far-flung farms,
At high Praeneste, Juno's rural Gabii,
The frigid Anio's banks, the stream-sprayed boulders
Of the Hernici; some rich Anagnia nurtured,
Some Father Amasenus' river. Not all   685
Had armor or loud chariots or shields.
Most of the men were slingers of pale lead;
Some brandished two spears; tawny caps of wolf fur
Covered their heads. With nothing on their left feet,
And crudely made right boots, they strode along.   690
Messapus, son of Neptune, tamer of horses—
Guarded by heaven's will from sword and fire—
Abruptly called to arms tribes long inactive,
Armies unused to war, and drew his own sword.
From Fescennia's heights, Falisci-on-the-Plain,   695
Soractes' pinnacles, Flavinian fields,
Mount Ciminus, its lake, and Capena's groves,
They marched in equal ranks and sang their king,
Like snowy swans among the liquid clouds
On their way back from feeding, pouring sweet songs   700
From their long necks to make the Asian marsh
And river ring far off.
No one would think bronze battle lines were massing
From the great throng, but that a soaring, hoarse cloud
Of birds swarmed from the ocean to the shore.   705
Clausus, of ancient Sabine stock, led forward
A huge force—he was such a force, alone.
It was his Claudian clan that spread in Latium
After the Sabines gained a share in Rome.
He led old Quirites, Amiternans, men   710
From olive-rich Mutusca and Eretum;
Troops out of Velinus country, walled Nomentum,
Tetrica's rough cliffs and Severus mountain,
Casperia, Foruli, Himella's stream, cold Nursia;

Some drank out of the Tiber and Fabaris;   715
Ortinian horsemen and whole Latin towns came,
And those whose homes the Allia—cursed name—passes:
As many as the glittering Libyan waves,
When fierce Orion dips in winter seas;
As many as the wheat ears scorched by spring sun   720
On Lycia's fields of gold, or the plains of Hermus.
Shields sounded, and the earth was stunned with tramping.
Halaesus, Agamemnon's crony, enemy
Of Troy, now yoked his chariot team and hastened
To Turnus' side a thousand fierce troops: tillers   725
Of fertile Massican vineyards; men dispatched
From high hills by Auruncan lords; from flatlands
Of the Sidicini; from Cales; from the banks
Of Volturnus with its shallows. Rough Saticulans
And an Oscan force were there. As was their custom,   730
They had smooth throwing spears with pliant leashes,
Left-handed shields, and curved swords for close fighting.
Nor will my poem pass over Oebalus
In silence. Telon in old age begat him
On the nymph Sebethis, when the Teleboae   735
In Capreae were his subjects. The son fretted
In his father's realm and now had spread his power
To Sarrastians and the plains the Sarnus waters;
To Rufrae, Batulum, and Celemnae's farmers;
And the apple land beneath Abella's walls.   740
Like Germans, they had spears with barbs as weapons;
Their heads were covered with the bark of cork trees.
Their small shields flashed with bronze, their swords with gold.
Ufens was sent to war from highland Nersae.
He was illustrious, known for luck in battle.   745
His wild Aequiculan people were addicted
To hunting in the woods. They lived on hard soil,
Plowed in their armor, constantly collected
Fresh loot, and liked to live on what they'd taken.

From the Marruvian people valiant Umbro   750
The priest came also, sent by King Archippus.
Lush olive leaves festooned the warrior's helmet.
There was no breed of poison-breathing viper
He couldn't put to sleep with chants and stroking.
He soothed their rage and remedied their bites.   755
And yet he couldn't cure a Trojan spear strike.
Sleep-bringing spells and herbs plucked in the mountains
Of the Marsians were useless for the wound.
Glassy-waved Fucinus, the Angitian forest,
The clear pools wept for him.   760
Virbius, splendid offspring of Hippolytus,
Marched there. Aricia sent her noble son,
Raised in Egeria's grove, around the moist shores
Where sumptuous gifts can win Diana's favor.
When bolting horses tore apart Hippolytus   *Killed by Phaedra*   765
Through the cunning of his father's wife, and paid *through a plot*
In blood the price his father claimed, the legend   *of her stepson*
Holds that Diana's love and the Healer's herbs   *after he refused*
Raised him again, up to the stars in heaven.   *her advances*
Then the almighty father, in his anger   770
At a mortal brought from hell to light and life,
Struck Phoebus' son and blasted to the Styx   *Apollo*
The inventor of a remedy so strong.
But kind Diana hid Hippolytus
In a home apart, in the nymph Egeria's woods,   775
To spend his life obscurely in the forests
Of Italy, with a new name, Virbius. *(Hippolytus)*
And so the goddess's sacred grove and temple
Bars horses with their hard feet: horses panicked
By monsters from the sea depths wrecked his chariot.   780
His son, however, drove an eager team
Over the flat plain, hurtling into war.
Turnus moved back and forth along the front,
Beautiful, armed, a head above the others.

From his triple-plumed high helmet reared the emblem   785
Of a Chimera, spewing flames of Etna:
Her ruinous breath grew wilder, her roar louder
As battle grew more brutal and blood flowed.
The golden blazon on his polished shield
Was Io—as a rough-haired, butting cow.   790
Such detail! Argus guarded her. Her father,
Inachus, poured his stream from a silver urn.
A storm of infantry came next. The whole plain
Was thick with shielded ranks: Argives, Auruncans,
Rutulians, and Sicanians long in Italy;   795
Sarcanians, Labicians with painted shields;
And men who plowed the uplands of the Tiber,
Numicus' holy shore, Rutulian hills,
And Circe's ridge—domains of Jove of Anxur
And Feronia, who revels in her green grove;   800
Troops from Satura's black swamp, and the valley
Cold Ufens threads, to duck into the sea.
Last came Camilla of the Volscii,
With a cavalry array that bloomed with bronze.
Her warrior hands were strangers to the distaff,   805
And Minerva's tasks; although she was a girl,
She endured combat and outran the wind.
She could have skimmed the tips of grain that stood
In a field and never hurt the tender heads,
Or glided clear across the swelling ocean   810
And kept her swift feet dry above its surface.
Men from the fields and matrons from their houses
Swarmed to look on in wonder as she rode.
They gaped, astonished at the royal splendor
Of purple on smooth shoulders, the gold hair clasp—   815
The Lycian quiver hanging at her back,
The shepherd's staff of myrtle, tipped with iron.

BOOK 8

The trumpets gave a harsh blare. Turnus raised *Prince of Rutulia*
The war sign from the tower of Laurentum, *in Italy - prevents*
And whipped his horses up, and clashed his weapons. *Betrothed to Lavinia -*
Instantly all of Latium joined in frenzy *prevents Aeneas*
And panic. Its young men grew cruel and savage. *from marrying her.*
The foremost leaders, Ufens and Messapus, *Prevents Trojans* 5
And Mezentius who reviled the gods, raised levies, *from settling*
Stripping broad lands of farmers. Venulus,
Sent to ask help from Diomedes' city,
Reported Trojans building homes in Latium, 10
Aeneas shipping in his conquered gods
And claiming fate had called him to be king;
And many peoples joined the Trojan warrior—
Far over Latium his renown was growing;
But Diomedes could discern more clearly *Greek hero @ Troy* 15
Than either King Latinus or King Turnus
His purpose and what he desired from victory.

Meanwhile, great waves of worries tossed the hero,   *Aeneas!*
The son of Troy, at everything he saw.
His thoughts were darting one way, then another,   20
At every side of his perplexity,
Like shivering light reflected from the water
In bronze urns, from the sun or shining moon;
Flittering everywhere, then shooting upward
To strike the panels of the lofty ceiling.   25
Now it was night. Deep sleep held weary creatures
Throughout the earth, all kinds that walked and flew.
Under the tall, cold sky Father Aeneas,
Troubled at heart by ruinous war, stretched out
On the bank, to finally give his body rest.   30
The old man Tiberinus, who was god there,
Appeared: out of the pleasant stream he rose
Through poplar leaves. A thin gray robe of linen
Covered his body, shady reeds his hair.
He spoke and took away Aeneas' cares: 35
"Child of the gods who bring Troy back to us
From its enemies, to preserve its tower forever:
Laurentum's earth and Latium's fields await you;
They're promised for your house and gods—persist!
Have courage, though war threatens. All the fury   40
Of the gods has drawn back.
But now, as proof this was no empty dream,
You'll find a giant sow with thirty newborn
Lying beneath the holm oaks on the shore:
White on the dark soil, white young at her teats   45
[The city will be there, and your sure rest.]
When thirty years have circled from this time,
Ascanius will found Alba—glorious name.   *Son of Aeneas*
I prophesy the truth. I'll show you briefly
(So listen!) how to triumph in this crisis.   50
Arcadians, Pallas' lineage in this land,
Followed their king Evander and his standards

And chose a hilly site and built their city,
Pallanteum, named for their progenitor.
They are at constant war with Latium's people.   55
Make them your allies, join them in a treaty.
I'll lead you up the stream between my banks;
You'll overcome the current, rowing inland.
Son of the goddess, come! As the first stars set,
Supplicate Juno, thwart her menacing anger   60
With ritual prayers and vows; and pay me honor
When you prevail. I am the brimming river
Grazing these banks and cutting through these rich fields,
The azure Tibur, favorite stream of heaven.
My halls are here, my source among the high towns."   65
The river disappeared to the deep floor
Of his pool, and sleep and darkness left Aeneas.
Standing, he saw the heavenly sunlight rise,
Cupped river water ritually in his hands,
Lifted it, and sent fervent words to heaven: 70
"Nymphs of Laurentum, who give birth to rivers,
And Father Tibur with your holy stream,
Take me and keep me safe—at last—from danger.
Because you pity our distress, wherever
Your wellsprings gush out, filling you with glory,   75
I'll worship you and honor you with gifts,
Horned king of all the waters of the West.
Only stay with me: prove your holy favor."
He spoke, and chose two biremes from the fleet,
Then oarsmen, and supplied his men with weapons.   80
But suddenly he saw the marvelous portent
Through the forest: a white sow with her white offspring,
Stretched on the grassy bank. Devout Aeneas
Placed the beast and her brood both at the altar,
And offered them to you, majestic Juno.   85
The Tiber flowed less swollen that whole night,
Checking its current, silencing its waves,

And smoothed its surface to the gentle peace
Of a marsh, so that the rowers wouldn't struggle,
And so, with cheers, they sped along their way.   90
Greased hulls slid through the shallows; woods and water
Wondered to see these strange things: warriors' shields
Shining far off, and painted, swimming hulls.
The men wore out a day and night in rowing
Up the long bends. Trees of all kind gave shelter,   95
And the keels cut the virid, still reflections.
The burning sun had climbed to its mid-orbit
When they saw distant walls, a citadel,
And roofs of scattered homes—things Roman power
Raised to the sky; Evander's poor domain then.   100
Quickly they turned their prows and neared the town.
By chance that day, the Arcadian king performed
Rites for great Hercules and other gods
In a grove outside the town with his son Pallas,   Evander's son
The leading young men, and the humble senate.   105
Incense burned, blood was steaming on the altars.
They saw tall ships glide through the shady woods
To the shore, as men thrust at the oars in silence.
The sudden sight alarmed the feasting men—
They all stood up. "Don't interrupt the ritual,"   110
Pallas warned, snatched a spear and dashed to meet them.
From a far mound he cried, "Where are you heading
On roads you don't know? Who are you by bloodline?
Where do you come from?—and in peace or war?"
Father Aeneas answered from the high stern,   115
While holding out a branch of peaceful olive,
"We're Trojan-born, and we're at war with Latins,
Who shamelessly attacked us refugees.
Where is Evander? Tell him chosen leaders
From Troy have come to ask for an alliance."   120
"Come ashore," Pallas said, "though I don't know you"—
Troy's great name staggered him. "Speak to my father

Face to face. Be a guest-friend in our household."
He seized Aeneas' hand and pressed it warmly.
They moved off from the bank into the woods.   125
Aeneas cordially addressed the king:
"Best of men born from Greeks! Fortune has sent me
As a suppliant, to offer boughs with fillets—
Not shrinking from a Greek lord, an Arcadian
From the same stock as Atreus' two sons.   130
No, my own rectitude, shared lineage,
The prophecies of gods, and your wide fame
Unite us, and I am fate's willing servant.
Lord Dardanus sailed to the Teucrians and founded
And fostered Troy. Greeks say he was the son   135
Of Electra, Atlas' daughter—massive Atlas,
Who holds the globe in heaven on his shoulder.
Mercury was your forebear: snow-white Maia
On Cyllene's chilly peak gave birth to him.
If we can trust tradition, that same Atlas   140
Who hoists the constellations fathered Maia.
Your family and mine come from the same blood.
This I relied on, and I used no legates
To test you cannily. No, I came myself
And risked my life, a suppliant at your threshold.   145
The Daunian race hounds both of us with cruel war.
They think they cannot fail, if they defeat us,
To place a tight yoke over all the West
And hold the seas that wash the north and south coasts.
Give me your pledge and take mine. Warlike spirits   150
Are ours, and soldiers proven sound by action."
The whole time that Aeneas spoke, the king
Surveyed his eyes, his face, and all his body,
Then briefly answered: "Bravest of the Trojans,
I welcome you with joy, remembering   155
The words and voice and face of great Anchises.
Yes, Laomedon's son Priam went to visit

Hesione his sister's kingdom, Salamis,
Then went on to Arcadia's cold district.
The down of youth first flowered on my cheeks then.   160
The Trojan chieftains awed me, the prince Priam
Awed me; yet striding higher than the rest
Was Anchises, and I burned with boyish longing
Till I could greet the hero with a handclasp
And lead him to the town of Pheneus.   165
Lycian arrows and a handsome quiver
And a cloak with gold threads were his parting gifts—
And a pair of gold bits that my son has now.
My right hand makes the pledge that you desire,
And when the dawn returns to earth tomorrow,   170
You'll go back cheered and helped by my resources.
Oblige us, meanwhile, since you come as friends,
And join our annual rite—delay is sinful.
Feast with your allies: start the habit now."
The meal was past, but he had food and wine   175
Brought back, and led the men to seats of turf.
A cushioned maple throne and shaggy lion pelt
Welcomed Aeneas, who was guest of honor.
The altar's priest and chosen keen young men
Served roasted bull, heaped baskets with the gifts   180
That Ceres grants to work, and poured the wine.
Aeneas and the other Trojans savored
A whole ox chine and sacrificial entrails.
When they had got the better of their hunger,
Royal Evander said, "No superstition   185
About old gods imposed this ritual,
This feast, this altar for a powerful being.
No, Trojan guest: saved from a savage peril,
We owe a deity this yearly rite.
First, see that cliff with overhanging rocks,   190
The desolation of that mountain house,
And the far-flung boulders of a giant crag-fall.

A cave was there, reaching immensely far back,
Half-human hideous Cacus' home, cut off
From the sun's rays; the ground was always wet   195
With fresh gore. Hanging on barbaric doors
Were pallid heads of men, decayed and grisly.
Vulcan had sired the monster. It was his flames
Cacus belched blackly, moving in his vast bulk. *Vulcan's son*
At last, we had—as people do—an answer   *Killed by*   200
To long prayers, and a god arrived to help us: *Hercules*
Hercules, great avenger, proud of killing
Three-bodied Geryon, and of the spoils:
Huge cattle grazed and waded in this valley.
Cacus' depraved and Fury-haunted mind   205
Could leave no treachery or crime untried.
He took four splendid bulls out of their pasture,
And four resplendent heifers. To prevent them
From making hoofprints in the right direction,
He dragged them by their tails, reversed their tracks,   210
And hid the stolen creatures in his dark cave.
No evidence would lead you to the place.
Meanwhile, Amphitryon's son prepared to drive
His cattle on—they'd grazed their full—and go.
But their complaining lowing filled the forest;   215
With a great noise, they moved off from the hills.
One of the captive cows in the vast cave
Lowed back, and thwarted Cacus' plan to keep her.
At this, black fury blazed up in Alcides.
He snatched the heavy knotted club he fought with   220
And ran up on the steep and lofty mountain.
Then we saw Cacus fearful and tormented
For the first time as, faster than the East Wind,
He sought his cave. His feet were winged with terror.
He shut himself inside and broke the chain   225
His father'd forged for holding up the boulder,
Which toppled now, to barricade the door.

But now the furious Tirynthian
Was there. He gnashed his teeth and peered all over
For a way in. He raged three times around   230
The Aventine; three times he tried the stone door
And each time fell back, winded, in the valley.
A flint spire, with the rocks cut off on all sides,
Rose from the cave's roof, dizzying to see:
A fitting place for ghastly birds to nest.   235
It slanted from the ridge above the river
On the left. By wrenching from the right he freed it,
And tore it from its roots and shoved it over.
The heights of heaven thundered with the impact.
The stream fled backward, terrified; the banks burst.   240
Now Cacus' cavernous palace was laid open,
Its shadowy depths exposed—as if some power
Should split the earth clear to the habitations
Of Hades and uncover that pale kingdom
The gods hate. From above, the huge abyss   245
Would show, and spirits tremble at the light.
The monster, then, caught in the sudden daylight
In the rocky hole, had never howled like this,
As Hercules harassed him from above
With everything at hand—with boughs, with boulders.   250
Cacus in turn—since there was no escape—
Belched out a flood of smoke (amazing sight),
And wrapped his quarters in its blinding darkness,
Tearing away our view of him and heaping
A smoky, fire-flecked midnight in the cavern.   255
Fierce Hercules would not stand for this. He plunged
Straight to the center, where the smoke surged highest,
A black cloud seething from that giant cave.
There he caught Cacus, spewing useless flames
In the dark, and pinned and throttled him until   260
His eyes popped and his throat was dry and bloodless.
Now with the doors torn off, the black lair open,

The sky saw looted cows he'd tried to hide.
The hideous corpse was pulled out by the feet.
Men could not satisfy their hearts with gazing   265
At the half-human creature's fearsome eyes,
His bristling chest, his face, his mouth—its fires dead.
Since then, each generation celebrates
This day, led by Potitius, the cult's founder,
And the clan of the Pinarii, its keepers.   270
And in this grove he set the Greatest Altar—
As we call it: it will always be the Greatest.
Come then, young men, honor such heroism:
Garland your hair, hold cups out in your right hands,
Invoke the god we share with glad libations."   275
Hercules' dappled, dangling poplar leaves
Covered the king's head now, and he had taken
The holy cup in hand. Keenly, all present
Prayed to the gods and poured wine on the table.

The sky moved down, and evening drew in closer.   280
Potitius led a file of priests, who wore
The ritual belted furs and carried torches.
Again they feasted, bringing pleasant gifts
For the next course. Their heaped trays piled the altars.
Around the altar fires came the Salii   285
To sing, with poplar garlands on their heads.
A young choir and an old one sang the valor
Of Hercules, how he throttled his first monsters,
The twin snakes that his father's wife had sent;
Then overthrew Oechalia and Troy,   290
Towns great in war, and finished countless labors
For King Eurystheus—Juno had ordained it
In spite. "You triumphed everywhere: you slaughtered
The cloud-born centaurs Pholus and Hylaeus,
The Cretan beasts, and the giant Nemean lion.   295
You panicked Hades' guard, the pools of Styx,

Sprawled over gnawed bones in his bloody cave.
You even faced Typhoeus with his weapons
Raised high. You found a way to kill the Hydra
Of Lerna, with its crowd of heads that ringed you.   300
Greetings, true son of Jove, heaven's fresh glory.
Come to your ritual with happy omens."
Such were the exploits that they sang—above all
The cave and fire-breathing Cacus in it.
The whole woods echoed, and the hills resounded.   305
The rites were over. Everyone returned
To the city. Hampered by old age, the king
Kept his son and Aeneas close beside him
And spoke of various things to ease the walk.
Aeneas gazed all over, much impressed.   310
For everything he had an eager question,
And learned of what the men of old had left there.
Royal Evander, founder of Rome's fortress,
Said, "Native fauns and nymphs once shared this forest
With a race of men born out of flinty oak trees—   315
Primitive, ignorant of yoking oxen,
And how to gather goods and how to keep them.
Their food came from the trees and savage hunting.
Saturn was first to come, a kingly exile
Running from high Olympus and Jove's violence.   320
This race, untaught and scattered in high mountains,
He brought together under law and called it
'Latin,' since he 'hid' safely in this country.
Under this king, the age that they call Golden
Took place, and in great peace he ruled the people,   325
Till slowly a degenerate age came on
With its war frenzy and its ardent greed;
Then came Ausonians, and Sicanian tribes—
The land of Saturn often changed its name—
Then there were kings, and giant, cruel King Thybris,   330
After whom we Italians called this river;

The Albula has lost its ancient name. *Tiber*
All-ruling Fortune, fate with no escape,
Apollo's mandate, and the nymph Carmentis
My mother's fearsome warnings set me here,   335
An exile to the ocean's farthest edge."
Instantly, he went on and showed the altar
And gate the Romans gave the name Carmental,
An early honor for the nymph Carmentis,
The first to prophesy the coming glory   340
Of Pallanteum and Aeneas' sons. A large grove
Came next: fierce Romulus would one day make it
The Asylum; next, a chill cliff roofed the Lupercal,
Named for Arcadia's Lycaean Pan. *Semi-wild place in*
He showed the sacred grove, the Argiletum, *Peloponesia*   345
And told how Argus, though a guest, was killed there. *Monastery /*
Tarpeia's Rock was next, and the Capitol— *100 eyes*
Gold now, then overgrown with forest brambles.
That cliff and woods made rustics quake already:
They felt a deadly power in the place.   350
"A god (we don't know which) lives in this forest,
This leafy hill," the king said. "The Arcadians
Think they see Jove himself here often, shaking
His dusky aegis, summoning the storm clouds.
But these two towns with ruined walls you see   355
Are a record left of men who came before.
Old Janus built this fort, and Saturn this one: *2 faces*
Janiculum and Saturnia were their names." *beginning of teg?*
They then moved toward Evander's simple home;
His lowing cattle ranged on what is now   360
The Roman Forum and the posh Carinae.
They reached the house. "Hercules stooped inside
And found this palace big enough," the king said.
"Friend, snub wealth bravely; you too must be ready
For godhead—come, don't sneer at my poor home."   365
Beneath the narrow roof he led Aeneas,

A towering man, and placed him on a couch
Of leaves on which a Libyan bearskin lay.
Night fell, embracing earth in her dark wings.

Venus' maternal terror had its reasons: 370
Laurentum threatened, shameless tumult spread.
She spoke to her spouse Vulcan in their bedroom
Of gold, and breathed divine love in her words.
"While the Greek kings were struggling to sack Troy,
With its citadel that had to fall in flames,   375
I asked no help, no weapons from your art,
For the poor things, dear husband, having no wish
To see your work and trouble go for nothing—
Though I owed much to Priam's sons and often
Cried for the bitter hardships of Aeneas.   380
Now Jove's will sets him on Rutulian shores.
I plead for arms, a mother for her son,
From your godhead—which I honor. Nereus' daughter
And Tithonus' wife could win you with their tears.
I see tribes massing, gates shut, iron sharpened   385
Against me, to eradicate my people."
He wavered. Tenderly the goddess wrapped him
In her white arms and fondled him. In no time
He took in the familiar flame, the old heat
Ran through his bones and shook him to the marrow,   390
As when a streak of flame, ripped loose by thunder,
Flashes and shoots through clouds with its intense light.
His wife was glad—her tricks and beauty worked.
Bound in eternal love, the great god spoke,
"Why give these far-fetched reasons? You had faith   395
In me once, goddess. Had you wanted it
Back then, I would have—rightly—armed the Trojans,
Since neither fate nor the almighty father
Had outlawed ten more years for Troy and Priam.
But if you're now preparing for a war,   400

Whatever help my skill and care can promise,
Anything that the force of fire and bellows
Can make from melted iron and electrum
Is yours. Don't plead for it and doubt your powers."
He then made tender love to her, and melted   405
Into sweet slumber in his wife's embrace.
But when he woke from his first sleep, and Night
Had finished half her course—the hour a woman
Who makes a tenuous living from her craft
Of spinning wakes the sleeping ashes, adding   410
Night hours to work, with slaves kept at their long tasks
By firelight, to bring up her little children
And guard her marriage bed from any shame:
At that hour, and as tirelessly, the fire god
Rose from his soft bed to his craftsman's labor.   415
By Sicily and Aeolian Lipari,
An island rears up high, with smoking cliffs.
Dug underneath it are the caves of Etna
For the loud forges of the Cyclops clan.
The anvils boom and echo with strong blows,   420
Dipped iron squeals, and forges roar with fire
In Vulcan's workshop in the land Vulcania.
From the sky's heights the fire god came, to find
His workers beating iron in that vast cave:
Brontes, Steropes, Pyracmon with his bare chest.   425
They had in hand a new-forged thunderbolt,
Part perfect, part unfinished, such as Zeus
The father hurls to earth in lavish numbers.
On it they put three shafts of twisted rain,
Three each of wet cloud, red flame, winged South Wind,   430
And then mixed lightning in, and noise, and terror,
And added wrath with its pursuing fires.
Others worked hard at Mars' winged chariot
For stirring soldiers, for inciting cities;
Others were busy at the ghastly aegis,   435

Armor of Pallas in her rage. They polished (Minerva)
The gold scales and the snake-twined, wild-eyed head
Of the Gorgon that adorned the goddess' breastplate.
"Get rid of all this, Cyclops race of Etna,
And start this new work," Vulcan told them now.   440
"A spirited man needs weapons. You need strength
And quick hands and your craft's full mastery.
Hurry!" He said no more. All swiftly bent
To work, dividing it in equal shares.
Soon rivulets of bronze and gold were flowing.   445
Wound-making steel was melting in the huge forge.
They formed a giant shield, with seven disks
Bound into layers, to meet all the weapons
Of the Latins. While some pump the windy bellows,
Others dip hissing bronze into the basin.   450
The cavern groans with blows on steady anvils.
Alternately they raise their powerful arms
In rhythm; with tight tongs they turn the ingots.

While Vulcan in Aeolia rushed this work on,
Nurturing light and birdsong from the eaves   455
Wakened Evander in his simple home.
The old man rose, tied on Etruscan sandals,
Draped himself in a tunic, hung one shoulder
With a dangling swordbelt and Arcadian sword,
And swirled a panther skin at his left side.   460
Two guard dogs came down with him from his doorstep
And closely paced before their master's steps.
He sought his guest Aeneas' quarters, thinking—
The good man—of their talk and what he'd promised.
Aeneas too rose early; with Achates   Aeneas' reta...   465
He went to meet Evander and his son.
The men clasped hands and sat down in the courtyard;
Now, at last, was a chance for a discussion.
The king began:

"Great Trojan chief, as long as you are living,   470
I would not call the power of Troy defeated.
We can give little help to match your glory.
The Tiber blocks us on one side. The other
Clangs with Rutulian weapons at our walls.
But I propose to join to you vast nations,   475
And armed camps rich with empire; chance has given
Relief unlooked-for; fate has called you here.
Not far off, on its ancient stone foundation,
Is Argylla. Lydians, renowned for warfare,
Settled there long ago on Tuscan mountains.   480
For many years they prospered. Then Mezentius,
A brazen tyrant, came to rule by violence.
Unspeakable his butcheries, his frenzies.
Gods, bring the same to him—and to his children.
He even tied dead bodies onto live ones,   485
Hands against hands and faces against faces—
His special torture. In this grim embrace,
His victims slowly died, in liquid rot.
At last his people, worn down by the horror
Of his rampages, besieged him and his household,   490
Killed his supporters, hurled flame to his rooftop.
Mezentius escaped, though, and took refuge
With armed Rutulians, as Turnus' guest-friend.
All of Etruria rose in righteous anger,
Calling for his return and threatening war.   495
I'll give you to these thousands as a leader.
Their ships now pack the shore, the soldiers clamor
To attack, but an old augur's prophecies
Prevent them. 'Chosen youth of Lydia,
Brave flower of an ancient warrior race   500
Driven by just rage at Mezentius' crimes!
This great race may not serve a man of Italy.
Wait for a foreigner.' The Tuscan army
Has not marched on, in fear of heaven's warning.

Tarchon himself sent legates to deliver   505
The crown and rod of kingship and a summons
To camp, where I could take up Tuscan rule.
But weary old age, slow and cold, denies me
Command; my strength for daring now lies sluggish.
I'd urge my son, but he is part of this land   510
Through his Sabine mother. Fate approves your age
And lineage. Heaven calls you. Come, begin,
Heroic Trojan and Italian leader. *Aeneas*
I'll even lend my only joy and comfort,
Pallas—you'll be his guide. He must grow used   *Evander's*   515 *s r*
To enduring Mars' rough work, from your example.
Let him, from early youth, hold you in awe.
Two hundred chosen knights, rock of my army,
I'll give to him; he'll give to you as many
In his own name." Anchises' son Aeneas   520
And staunch Achates kept their gazes lowered.
Sad-hearted, they turned over many harsh thoughts—
But Venus gave a sign in the clear sky.
Lightning flashed without warning from the heavens,
And thunder boomed—as if the sky were falling;   525
And like a Tuscan horn the high air sounded.
They looked up, and the blaring blasts continued.
In calm, clear sky, between the clouds they saw
Weapons glow red; they clashed like claps of thunder.
It stunned them all—except the Trojan hero,   530
Who knew the sound, pledge of his goddess mother.
"Guest-friend," he said, "these signs allow no doubt:
Olympus calls me. My immortal mother
Promised this sign, a covenant for wartime,
And said she'd bring me weapons made by Vulcan   535
Down through the air.
The slaughter waiting for the poor Laurentians!
The punishment for Turnus! All the helmets,
Shields, brave men's bodies rolling in old Tiber!

Let them break treaties, let them have their war." 540
He rose from the high throne. Hercules' altar
Was smoldering; he stirred its ashes up,
Then cheerfully approached the humble home gods
He knew from yesterday. Evander slaughtered
Chosen sheep; Troy's young men performed the same rite. 545
Aeneas walked back to his ships and comrades
And chose the ablest men to follow him
To war; the others glided with the fleet
Slackly downriver to Ascanius
With news of how things stood, and of his father. 550
The Trojans headed for the Tuscan plains
Were given mounts; a special one was draped
With a tawny, gold-clawed lionskin for Aeneas.
Suddenly Rumor flew all through the small town:
Horsemen were speeding to the Tuscan camp. 555
Over and over mothers prayed: their terror
Grew with the danger, and Mars' specter grew.
Father Evander now took Pallas' hand
In parting, and he couldn't stop his tears.
"If only Jove restored my youth and made me 560
Again the victor at Praeneste, throwing
The front ranks down and burning heaps of shields—!
That day, I sent King Erulus to Hades.
Feronia, his mother, gave him three lives—
Monstrous—and triple weapons for attack. 565
He had to be cut down three times; I took
Each soul from him, three times I stripped his weapons.
My former self would not be torn from you,
My child; Mezentius would not insult me,
His neighbor, with so much barbaric slaughter 570
And a town widowed of so many townsmen.
You, gods above, and your great governor
Jupiter, pity an Arcadian king,
And hear a father's prayer. If your divine power

And fate will keep my Pallas safe for me,   575
And if I live to see him face to face,
I beg to live, no matter what I suffer.
But if you threaten, Fortune, what I can't say,
Let me break off my wretched life already,
While fears are unconfirmed, hope arguable,   580
While you, dear son, sole pleasure of my old age,
Are in my arms, and no hard news is wounding
My ears." The father, at the last farewell,
Poured out these words, and swooned. Slaves took him home.

The cavalry had now passed through the gates,   585
Aeneas and staunch Achates in the first rank,
Then other Trojan nobles; in the middle
Went Pallas, in a vivid cloak and armor;
As, wet with Ocean's waters, Lucifer
Whom Venus loves above all other stars,   590
Raises his sacred face and melts the darkness.
On the walls stood frightened mothers, gazing after
The dusty cloud, the troops that glowed with bronze.
They marched off in their armor through the brush,
The closest way. A shout rose from the column.   595
Horses' hooves rumbled on the fertile plain.
There is a forest near cool Caere's stream,
Widely held sacred, by an old tradition.
Hills covered in black firs encircle it.
They say the old Greeks, first to live in Latium,   600
Made this a shrine, with its own festival,
For Silvanus, who is god of fields and herds.
Tarchon and his Etruscans pitched their tents
In a safe site nearby. A hilltop view
Showed the whole army camped across the plain.   605
Here Father Aeneas and his picked troops came
Tired, cared for their mounts, and ate and rested.
Snowy white, holy Venus brought her presents

Through heaven's clouds. Far off, she saw her son
In a secluded valley, by a cold stream.   610
She went straight up to him and spoke these words:
"My husband's gifts are finished, with the skill
He pledged. So don't hang back from challenging
The arrogant Laurentians or fierce Turnus."
The Cytherean embraced her son, then set   615
The arms beneath an oak, in all their splendor.
The goddess' gift—the honor of it—thrilled him.
He couldn't gaze enough at every piece.
With awe he picked them up and turned them over:
The fearsome helmet with its flaming crest,   620
The deadly sword, the blood-red corselet rigid
With bronze: enormous, like a cloud, blue-shaded
But kindling with the sun's far-stretching rays;
Then the smooth greaves of forged gold and electrum,
And the spear and shield—work beyond telling of.   625
There the god of fire had etched Italian history
And Roman triumphs, from the prophecies
He knew: all of Ascanius' line to come,
And every war the clan would fight, in sequence.
There lay a mother wolf, in Mars' green grotto.   630
Playful twin boys were hanging at her teats,
Fearlessly suckling on their foster-mother.
She arched her neck above the pair and licked
Either in turn, to shape them with her tongue.
Beside this he'd put Rome, and Sabine women   635
Snatched—such a lawless act—from crowded stands
At the Great Games. Old Tatius, with his stern folk
Of Cures, went to war again with Romulus
And his settlers. It was over then: the two kings
Stood before armed Jove's altar, holding bowls,   640
Their treaty hallowed by a slaughtered sow.
Next, chariot teams tore Mettus limb from limb
(You should have kept your promise, man of Alba);

The liar's guts were scattered through the woods
By Tullus—blood dew spattered bramble bushes.   645
Porsena ordered Rome to take back Tarquin,
And with a massive force besieged the city.
Aeneas' people dashed to arms, for freedom.
You saw the threat and anger on his face
When Cocles dared to tear the bridge apart   650
And Cloelia broke her chains and swam the river.
Near the shield's top was Manlius, the guard
Of Tarpeia's heights, the Capitol and temple.
On Romulus' palace there, the new thatch bristled.
In the gold portico a silver goose,   655
Flapping and calling, warned that Gauls had come.
Stealing up through the brush, they'd reached the stronghold,
Protected by the favor of dark Night.
Their hair was shaggy gold, their clothes were gold,
Their striped cloaks shone, around their milky necks   660
Were twists of gold; each rattled in his hand
Two Alpine pikes; long shields were their protection.
The god had hammered out the leaping Salii,
Naked Luperci, wool caps, and shields fallen
From the sky. In dainty carriages, chaste matrons   665
Brought holy objects through the town. Far off
Were Dis' high gates, the settlement of Hades
Where crimes are punished; Catiline hangs there
From a looming cliff and quivers at the Furies.
The good live elsewhere; Cato makes their laws.   670
A picture of a swollen sea, in gold,
Wound through these scenes, and billowed with white foam.
Bright silver dolphins circled in the spume
Of the rim, and swept the surface with their tails.
The bronze-braced fleets at Actium, in the middle,   *Greece/* 675 *Apollo's temple*
Were lined up there to see. All of Leucate
Was seething with them. Gold shone on the waves.
Caesar Augustus led the Roman forces—

Senate and people, hearth gods, mighty sky gods.
High on the stern he stood; from his glad forehead   680
Poured two flames. From his head his father's star rose.
Near him Agrippa—gods and winds both helped him— *General*
Led the line from on high, his head ennobled *1st cent. R...*
With the bright ship beaks of a naval crown. *friend of*
Antony, victor of the East, the Red Sea, *Augustus Caesar*   685
Brought foreign wealth and jumbled troops against them.
He hauled in Egypt, Oriental powers,
And farthest Bactra. His Egyptian wife
Followed him—outrage! Now the navies clashed.
Beaks, backed oars, triple spikes churned sea to foam.   690
To the open! You'd imagine Delos torn loose
And floating, or high mountains smashed together:
Men moved to battle on such towering sterns.
Oakum in flames and iron weapons soared.
Neptune's fields reddened. Rallying her ships   695
To the center, the queen shook her country's sistrum—
Not seeing yet the two snakes etched behind her.
The dog Anubis and all sorts of beast gods
Faced off with Venus, Neptune, and Minerva;
And Mars raged in the middle of the battle,   700
Engraved in iron; grisly Furies hovered,
Discord stalked in a tattered robe, contented.
Bellona followed with her bloody whip.
From his shrine up on the cliff, Apollo saw them
And aimed his bow. Egyptians, Indians,   705
Arabs, Sabaeans turned and fled in terror.
The queen was pictured calling on the winds
And just then loosening ropes to let the sails out.
The smith god made her pale among the slaughter.
She faced her death; the waves and the northwester   710
Swept her along. The mighty Nile, in mourning,
Opened his arms and giant cloak and beckoned
The conquered to retreat to his blue delta.

Caesar rode into Rome in triple triumph
And gave our gods their holy, lasting payment: 715
Three hundred towering shrines throughout the city.
Streets roared with celebration and applause.
Offerings filled the temples, mothers danced,
And slaughtered calves were sprawled before the altars.
Sitting at shining Phoebus' snowy threshold, *Apol&*   720
He viewed the nations' gifts and had them mounted
On the proud doors. All kinds of clothing, weapons,
And languages filed by in captive order:
Leleges, loose-robed Africans, Carians,
Nomads, Gelonian archers. The Euphrates   725
Walked with meek waves; the two-horned Rhine walked by,
The remote Morini, the Dahae now first conquered,
And the Araxes, angry at his new bridge.
Aeneas loved these scenes on Vulcan's shield,
His mother's gift—but didn't know the stories. *Venus*   730
He shouldered his descendants' glorious fate.

9

While, far away, all this was happening,
Iris came earthward, sent by Saturn's daughter   *Goddess*
To a wooded glen where fearless Turnus sat,   *of Rainbow/*
The sanctum of his ancestor Pilumnus.   *Messenger*
Thaumas' child spoke to him from rosy lips: 5
"Turnus, time in its circle, on its own,   *Prince of Rutulian*
Grants what no god would dare to promise you:
Aeneas has left his fort, his fleet, his comrades
For Palatine Evander's kingly home.
He's ventured on to Corythus' distant cities   10
To gather Lydian farmers and equip them.
Why waver? Call for chariots and horses.
Don't hold back: overrun their camp and take it."
On poised wings she rose skyward, and a great arc
Was cut beneath the clouds as she retreated.   15
The young man knew her, and he raised both hands
To heaven, calling these words after her:
"Iris, great splendor of the sky, who sent you

Betothd
to Lavinia
Enemy
of Aeneas
to mean
marrying
Lavinia

Through the clouds? Why has the air grown suddenly
So clear? I see the sky split in the middle—   20
Stars wander at its height. Whoever calls me
To arms, I follow these great signs." Descending
To the stream, he took up water from the surface
And overwhelmed the gods in heaven with prayers.

Now the whole army crossed the open plains,   25
Wealthy in horses, gold, embroidery.
Messapus marshaled the front ranks, the sons
Of Tyrrhus had the rear, the center Turnus,
Wheeling with weapons, taller by a head;
As the tranquil Ganges swells from the infusions   30
Of seven calm streams; as the Nile's rich floods
Ebb from the plains and hide between his banks.
The Trojans suddenly saw black dust massing
In the distance—darkness welled up on the flatlands.
From a high mound, Caïcus raised the alarm: 35
"Citizens, what's that murky, rolling, round thing?
Quick—bring your swords and spears, climb to the walls.
They're here!" The Trojans hollered and sought shelter
Through every gate and crowded on the ramparts;
Such were the parting orders of Aeneas,   40
The able general: that if something happened,
They must not take the field and risk a battle,
But shelter in defensive mounds and walls.
Though shame and anger counseled them to fight,
They shut the gates, as ordered, armed themselves,   45
And braced for the attack, in hollow towers.
Turnus, with twenty chosen horsemen trailing,
Flew past his slow front line and reached the wall
Without warning, on his dappled horse from Thrace,
And wearing a gold helmet with a red crest.   50
"Young men, who wants to join me in the first charge?
Look—" And he whirled his spear up through the air

To start the fight; looming, he plunged ahead.
His men took up the shout—they followed him
With a chilling roar, contemptuous of the Trojans.   55
Why not fight in the open, man to man?
Why sit inside? The agitated general
Rode back and forth but could not find a gap,
As a wolf prowls outside a crowded sheepfold
And growls at every chink. The wind and rain   60
Of midnight lash him. Lambs beneath their mothers
Huddle and bleat and bleat. Though he can't reach them,
He lunges in wild rage, lashed on by hunger
Grown into frenzy, by his blood-starved throat.
So the Rutulian scanned the camp's defenses,   65
Seared to the bone by anger and frustration.
How could he break in? What assault would scatter
The Trojans out across the level ground?
Their fleet lay snug, moored right beside the camp,
Closed in by earthworks and the flowing river.   70
There he struck, calling to his cheering comrades,
"Torches!"—and hectically snatched burning pine.
They set to work, with Turnus there to goad them.
Soon all the troops laid hold of sooty weapons,
Looting the fires. A pitchy, smoky light spread,   75
And Vulcan sent the sparks clear up to heaven.
Muse, say what god it was who saved the Trojans,
Beating the fierce flames from their ships. The ancients
Vouched for the story, and it still endures.
When Aeneas first began, on Phrygian Ida,   80
To build a fleet for voyaging on deep seas,
The Berecynthian mother of the gods,
They say, told great Jove: "You subdued Olympus;
Grant your dear mother this, since I have helped you.
I had for many years a cherished pine woods   85
Up in the heights, a place of offerings,
Shadowed with black pitch pines and maple trees.

I gave it happily to the young Trojan
Who has to have a fleet, but now I'm anxious.
Free me from fear: grant what your mother pleads for,　　　90
That whirlwinds will not shatter and submerge them
On any voyage. Please—they are from my mountains."
Her son, who guides creation's stars, replied,
"Mother, what favor have you asked of fate?
Could it be right for ships a mortal made　　　95
To last forever? Should Aeneas' perils
Be without risk? What god has so much power?
But when they've done their work and reached a harbor
In Italy, each that has survived the sea
To bring the Trojan chieftain to Laurentum　　　100
I'll strip of earthly form and make a goddess
Of the great ocean, like the Nereids Doto
And Galatea breasting through the sea foam."
By the Styx, his brother's stream with its black whirlpools
And banks that seethe with pitch, he swore to this　　　105
With a nod, at which Olympus shook. The Fates
Had now fulfilled the time; the promised day
Had come. The torches flung by Turnus roused
The Mother to defend her sacred ships.
A strange light flashed; a great cloud from the east　　　110
Appeared to dart across the sky, with bands
Of her worshipers. A fearsome voice fell earthward
And filled the Trojan and Rutulian ranks:
"Don't take up arms or anxiously defend
My ships. It will be sooner granted Turnus　　　115
To burn the sea than holy pines. Be free,
Sea goddesses, my daughters: I command it."
Right away, on their own, they broke their moorings
And headed for the bottom, dolphinlike.
All of the bronze-prowed ships that had been standing　　　120
At the shore emerged again as young girls' forms—
It was a miracle!—and skimmed the sea.

The Rutulians were amazed. Even Messapus
Took fright behind his rearing team. The Tiber
Roared as it pulled its current back upriver.   125
But even then, Turnus remained cocksure
And stung his friends to action with this speech:
"These signs are for the Trojans. Jove himself
Arrived before our fire and spears and tore
Their old support from them. The sea is closed now.   130
They can't get out, with that part of creation
Taken away, the land ours, and so many
Thousand Italians armed. The holy oracles
These easterners allege don't frighten me.
The fates and Venus have their due. The Trojans   135
Landed in fertile Italy. *My* fate
Is rooting out this evil. They have stolen   ✝ lavinia
My wife. Not only Atreus' sons were outraged;
Not just Mycenae rightly took up arms.
'Troy fell once—that's enough.' Their crime before this   140
Should be enough; by now they ought to loathe
All women. For their courage they rely
On their palisade and those delaying ditches,
Small gaps before death. But they saw Troy's walls
Collapse in flames, though Neptune was the builder.   145
Which of you picked troops is prepared to splinter
The walls and swarm the quaking camp with me?
I don't need Vulcan's arms to fight the Trojans,
Or a thousand ships. Let the Etruscans join them
As allies. Let them fear no cowardly tricks   150
At night [Athena's slaughtered temple guards]:
We won't be lurking in a horse's belly!
I'll ring their walls with fire—in open daylight.
They won't mistake us for the Greeks, whom Hector
Held back for ten years—no, I'll set them straight.   155
But now the day is past the time for battle.
In what is left, be cheerful—you've done well.

Eat, rest, since there's a fight to come, believe me."
Messapus' duty was to block the gates
With sentries and surround the walls with watch fires.   160
For the patrol, fourteen Rutulian captains
Were chosen, each to lead a hundred men
Arrayed in purple crests and glittering armor.
They scattered to their various tasks or sprawled
On the grass, and drank their wine from cups of bronze.   165
Fires formed a single glow. The watchmen gambled
Through the sleepless night.
Armed Trojans watched them from their walls above.
They anxiously checked gates and—still in armor—
Built gangways and defenses in a network,   170
Urged on by keen Serestus and Mnestheus:
Father Aeneas had appointed them
Leaders and generals in case of crisis.
The whole force on the battlements took risks
In turns to guard the posts assigned by lot.   175
Nisus, Hyrtacus' war-keen son, watched one gate.
Nimble with arrows and a spear, he'd come
From Ida's hunting grounds, to serve Aeneas.
His friend Euryalus was the handsomest
Of all the warriors in Aeneas' band.   180
On his unshaven cheeks were manhood's first signs.
Love bound these two; they dashed to war together,
And now they shared a picket at the gate.
Nisus asked, "Is it gods who make me want this,
Or do we make our deadly urges gods?   185
A long time now I've thought of taking on
Some fight or other great thing—I'm so restless!
You see these overconfident Rutulians
At scattered, flickering fires. Dissolved in wine,
They're sprawling. Everywhere, it's still. So listen   190
To what I might do—no, I've now decided.
Leaders and all, the whole camp wants Aeneas

To know what's happened and come back to help us.
For a promised prize (to go to you—for me,
The glory's plenty), I might find a way   195
Around that hillside to Pallanteum's fortress."
Euryalus, though overwhelmed by passion
For praise, was prompt in answering his fierce friend:
"You mean to bar me from this crucial mission,
And face the risk alone? That's not the way   200
Opheltes, my battle-hardened father, raised me
In the horrors of the Greek siege, in our struggles
At Troy. And at your side have I been like that
In following Aeneas to fate's edge?
I have contempt for daylight, and I count   205
The honor that you aim at worth my life."
Nisus replied, "It would be wrong to doubt you.
So may great Jupiter, or some other fair judge
Of courage, bring me back to you in triumph.
But if a god or mishap steals my life—   210
A thing you often see in such great dangers—
I'd want you living, since your youth deserves it.
And if my corpse is rescued, or else ransomed,
You'd bury it; if fate denies those death rites,
An empty tomb and gifts could honor me.   215
I wouldn't bring such sorrow to your mother,
Since she, of all our mothers, followed you,
Indifferent to the walls of great Acestes."
His friend rebutted this: "Empty excuses!
My mind is made up, nothing's going to change it.   220
Let's hurry"—and he woke the other sentries
To take the watch in turn. They left their post
And side by side strode off to find their king.
All other creatures on the earth were sleeping,
Their cares eased, their hearts free of suffering.   225
The Trojan leaders, picked men in their prime,
Were meeting about vital strategy.

What should they do? Who'd take news to Aeneas?
They leaned on their long spears and gripped their shields
In the yard at the camp's center. Then Euryalus   230
And Nisus pleaded for an urgent hearing:
This would be worth it. Iulus took the lead,
Welcomed the fervent youths, had Nisus speak.
Hyrtacus' son began: "Friends of Aeneas,
Give fair consideration and don't judge this   235
By our age. Our enemies are sunk in silence
And wine and sleep. We've seen a gap to sneak through,
Where the road forks at the gate beside the sea.
There the black smoke from scattered campfires rises
To the stars. If you will let us use this chance   240
To reach Aeneas at Pallanteum's fort,
You'll see us here again soon with the spoils
Of a great slaughter. No, we won't get lost:
From hidden valleys where we hunt, we've seen
The outskirts. The whole river is familiar."   245
Aletes spoke, age-burdened, ripe in judgment:
"Our fathers' gods, forever ruling Troy,
You cannot mean completely to destroy us,
When you have given our young men such strong spirits."
Speaking, he turned to each and clasped their hands   250
And shoulders. Tears were gushing down his face.
"What prizes, warriors, could I think worthy
Of your heroics? Here's the first and finest:
Your soundness in the gods' sight; promptly, too,
Good Aeneas and Ascanius will reward you—   255
The youngster won't forget such vital service."
The prince concurred: "Father's return alone
Can save me. By our city's great gods, Nisus,
By Assaracus' god, and white-haired Vesta's shrine:
I'm trusting all my fortune, all my hopes   260
To you. Bring back my father, let me see him.
What can we fear when he's with us? I'll give you

Two well-made silver cups, deeply embossed—
My father's spoil from capturing Arisba—
Two tripods and two standard bars of gold, 265
And an ancient wine bowl from Sidonian Dido.
If Aeneas wins and conquers Italy,
Claims kingship and distributes all the spoils—
You saw the horse gold-armored Turnus rode?
Nisus, I'll set that beast aside for you, 270
And the shield and red crest: these are yours already.
My father will give twelve choice captive mothers
As well, and twelve men, each one with his armor,
And finally King Latinus' own estates.
You, honored boy, who're closer to my own age, 275
With all my soul I'll hold you as a friend
In everything I have to face, pursuing
No glory on my own account, without you.
In peace and war, you'll be my foremost comrade
And confidant." Euryalus responded: 280
"No day will come that shows me less courageous
Than in this enterprise. If only luck
Won't turn against me—but I ask one favor
Besides these. My poor mother, of the old race
Of Priam, would not stay behind in Troy 285
Or King Acestes' fort but left with me.
I've kept from her my plans, however risky,
And my good-byes (your right hand and the night
Witness this)—I could not endure her tears.
But you, comfort her loss, relieve her need. 290
If I believe you will, I'll take my chances
More boldly." These words left the Trojans heart-struck.
They wept—and handsome Iulus most of all,
Wrung by the thought of how he loved his father.
He spoke: 295
"Be sure of everything this great task earns you:
She'll be my mother, lacking just the name

Creusa—and get no small thanks for having
A son like you. However this turns out,
I swear it by this life my father swore on.   300
My pledges—if you don't return successful—
Are for your mother and your family."
Weeping, he took the gold sword from his shoulders:
Knossian Lycaon, with amazing skill,
Had shaped the blade to fit an ivory scabbard.   305
A lion's rough pelt, spoil of Mnestheus' hunting,   *Remus' lieutenant*
Went to Nisus. Staunch Aletes traded helmets
With him. The armed youths set out; all the leaders,
Both old and young, stood at the gates with kind prayers:
Among them handsome Iulus, with the forethought   310
And duty of a man, before his time,
Sent many messages, but might as well
Have given them to the misty wind to scatter.
In shadowy night, they crossed the ditches, making
For the deadly camp: many would die before them.   315
Randomly on the grass men sprawled in wine's sleep,
And chariots stood upright on the shore.
Among the reins and weapons, wheels and wine jars
Soldiers were lying. Nisus broke the silence:
"This is our chance to strike, Euryalus.   320
Follow this way, and look around and guard me;
Keep anyone from coming from behind.
I'll lead you on a broad path—which I'll empty."
He checked his voice and made his way to Rhamnes
The proud, who happened to be snoring loudly   325
As he slumbered, propped up on a pile of blankets:
A prophet, Turnus' friend, a king himself;
But prophecy would not prevent his death.
Three slaves were slumped among the weapons; Nisus
Stifled them; also Remus' page and driver   330
Under the team, whose drooping necks he cut,
Then lopped their owner's head and left the body

Sobbing out blood: warm, black, it soaked the bed
And ground. He then killed Lamyrus and Lamus
And handsome young Serranus, who'd stayed up   335
To gamble, and lay beaten by the wine god—
Too much for him. It would have been more lucky
For him to go on playing until dawn.
He was like a famished lion bringing chaos
To crowded sheep pens, gnashing, dragging soft beasts   340
In their mute terror, roaring with his red mouth.
Nor did Euryalus' slaughter blaze less fiercely.
Rank-and-file soldiers never saw him coming—
Fadus, Herbesus, Abaris, and Rhoetus—
No, Rhoetus was awake through all of it,   345
And shrank in fear behind a giant wine jar.
He rose to fight; a sword was thrust clear through him
From close quarters and then pulled out, dripping death.
He spewed his soul in wine-stained purple blood.
His killer carried on, in eager stealth.   350
Now he was making toward Messapus' camp,
With its dying outer fires, its horses tethered,
Cropping the grass. But Nisus sensed how greedy
The boy had grown for killing, and spoke briefly:
"We need to stop: light's coming and could catch us.   355
We've hit them hard and made our way beyond them."
They left behind them many splendid weapons
Of silver, mixing bowls, and lovely bedspreads.
But Euryalus took Rhamnes' gold-bossed swordbelt,
And badges. Wealthy Caedicus had sent them   360
To Remulus of Tibur, to befriend him
At a distance. This man left them to his grandson,
After whose time Rutulians plundered them.
Euryalus put them on his strong, doomed shoulders;
Messapus' helmet, with its striking plumes,   365
Fitted him well. They left the camp for safe ground.
At the same time, Volcens led three hundred horsemen

From the Latin city, all with shields, to take
An answer to King Turnus. (The whole army,
Except for these, stayed drawn up on the plain.)   370
Nearing the walls, they saw, off in the distance,
The young men take the path that headed left.
In the dim-glimmering light the radiant helmet
Betrayed Euryalus—he'd forgotten it.
Alertly, Volcens called, "Halt, men! Who are you?   375
Where do you think you're going, and for what?
Why are you armed?" They did not try to answer
But rushed for refuge to the night-black woods.
The horsemen knew the byroads; splitting up,
They blocked all exits with a ring of guards.   380
The place was large, and full of dusky holm oaks
And rough brush; briars choked it everywhere.
Only some sparse trails showed, vague cattle tracks.
Euryalus stumbled through the branching shadows
With his heavy plunder. Fear befuddled him.   385
But Nisus didn't notice; he escaped
And passed the place now called—from Alba—Alban.
(The lofty pens for King Latinus' herds
Were there.) He stopped, looked back: his friend was gone.
"Where did I leave you, poor Euryalus?   390
Where should I look?" Back through the knotted path,
The maze of woods he went, tracing his footprints
Where he could see, and wandered the still thickets.
Horses' tread, clanging, signals—the pursuers!
Before much longer shouting reached his ears.   395
He saw the whole force rush Euryalus
And overwhelm him, though he struggled hard.
He was helpless in that dark and treacherous spot.
But what should Nisus do? How should he strike
To free the boy? Perhaps he ought to plunge   400
Into their swords—a quick and noble death.
He'd hurl his spear. He swiftly drew it back

And gazed up at the lofty moon and prayed:
"Be with me now, Diana, help my struggle,
Keeper of forests, glory of the stars.   405
If for my sake my father brought your altar
His gifts, and if I hung your temple roof
With beasts killed in my hunts, to honor you,
Then guide my spear and let me rout this band."
All of his body strained to throw the weapon   410
Of iron, which flew off, sliced through the shadows
Of night, went into Sulmo's back and shattered,
Thrusting its splinters through his diaphragm.
He writhed, warm blood was spewing from his chest,
Long gasps convulsed his sides as chill death took him.   415
They looked to all sides. Nisus, now grown fiercer,
Poised a fresh weapon high up, by his ear.
As they stood shocked, the spear sang through the temples
Of Tagus and stuck fast in his warm brain.
Volcens, beside himself, still couldn't see   420
The spear's source and attack it in his fury.
He told Euryalus, "Then you can pay
For both with your hot blood." He drew his sword
And strode up. Nisus shouted, wild with terror.
He couldn't hide in darkness any longer,   425
He couldn't stand such agony. "It's me!
I'm here! I did it. Turn your swords on me!
It's all my fault. He didn't dare, he couldn't.
The sky and the all-knowing stars can witness:
He only loved his luckless friend too much."   430
He spoke, but couldn't stop a spear from ramming
Through Euryalus' ribs and splitting his white chest.
Dying, he thrashed. His lovely limbs and shoulders
Poured streams of blood; his neck sank limply down,
Like a purple flower severed by the plow;   435
He fainted into death, like a poppy bending
Its weary neck when rain weighs down its head.

Nisus ran in among them, but he aimed
For Volcens only—that was all he wanted.
Enemies mobbed in close from either side   440
To drive him back. He fought on, thunderous sword
Whirling, and thrust it through the shouting face
Of the Rutulian; and this cost his own life.
He was stabbed through and through and hurled himself
On his dead friend, to find his rest and peace.   445
Lucky pair! If my song has any power,
You'll never be forgotten, while the children
Of Aeneas live below the steadfast rock
Of the Capitol, and a Roman father reigns.
The Rutulian cohort took the spoils of victory   450
And carried Volcens' body back with tears.
As great a grief awaited them, with Rhamnes
Found lifeless, with the massacre of leaders—
Numa, Serranus. Crowds rushed to the corpses
And dying men; the ground was warm with fresh gore,   455
And there were rivulets of foaming blood.
A murmur rose: those were Messapus' badges
And helmet—so much work to win them back!
Already Dawn rose from the saffron bed
Of Tithonus, strewing fresh light on the world.   460
Now in the sun-soaked and revealing day,
Turnus first armed himself, then called his men
To arms. Each leader urged his bronze ranks on,
Inflaming them with news of what had happened.
And—piteous sight—they even raised the heads   465
Of Nisus and Euryalus on spear ends,
And marched behind them, shouting.
Aeneas' hard men stretched opposing ranks
At the left wall (the river hugged the right one),
Guarded their moats, or grimly manned their towers.   470
With a shock of grief, they recognized the heads
Too well. Black gore was oozing down the spears.

Rumor came swooping through the frightened town
And whispered to Euryalus' mother. All warmth,
Down to her bones, went out of that poor lady.   475
She dropped her shuttle, and the thread unwound.
She dashed outdoors with piteous female keening,
Tore at her hair, ran for the walls and front lines,
Oblivious of the men there and the danger
Their spears held. Soon her wailing filled the sky: 480
"Euryalus, is that you, my only solace
As my life closes? How could you desert me
So cruelly, without letting your poor mother
Tell you good-bye before that dangerous mission?
The dogs and birds of alien Latium tear you.   485
I couldn't walk you to the pyre—my own child—
When I had closed your eyes and washed your wounds
And wrapped you in the robe that, night and day,
I busily wove—it soothed the cares of old age.
Where will I look for you? What region holds   490
Your torn corpse? Is this all you bring me back
Of yourself? I came with you on land and sea!
If you have any heart, Rutulians, throw
Your spears at me, and put me to the sword first.
But you, great father of the gods, have pity,   495
Strike me, hurl my unwanted life to Hades
With your lightning: only that would end my pain."
A moan ran through the ranks. They all were heart-struck.
Their strength went numb, their will to fight was broken,
Their grief enflamed—so Actor and Idaeus   500
Obeyed Ilioneus and sobbing Iulus
And hurried her inside, holding her up.
The bronze horn blared its fearful melody
Far off. Men shouted, and the sky roared back.
The Volscians, under overlapping shields,   505
Rushed in to fill the moats and drag the fence down.
One group was set to climb the walls with ladders,

And looked to get in where the ring of guards
Was gapped or thin. The Trojans poured down weapons
Of all kinds and shoved back with sturdy pikes.   510
Their past long war had taught them siege defense.
They spun down massive boulders from the walls
To break the covered column, but the men there
Could smirk at every blow beneath their thick roof—
Until the Trojans rolled a monstrous rock   515
To where the largest cohort threatened them;
This wrecked a stretch of the Rutulians' shelter
And struck its bearers down; the rest, though hearty,
Had no more taste for fighting blind, but struggled
To pelt the Trojans off their wall.   520
Elsewhere Mezentius—chilling sight—was shaking
A fiery, smoking pine trunk in attack,
And Neptune's son Messapus, tamer of horses,
Broke through the palisade and called for ladders
For the walls. Calliope and all your sisters,   525
Inspire me to sing of Turnus' slaughter,
And the men that every soldier sent to Orcus.
Open with me the book of that great war,
Goddesses: help me to recite the story.
There was a looming tower with lofty gangplanks   530
In a strategic spot. With all their strength,
All their resources, the Italians tried
To storm or topple it. Massed at the windows,
Trojans hurled stones and spears in their defense.
Now Turnus took the lead and threw a torch;   535
Its flames clung to the wall, spread with the wind,
Seized planks and ate away the doors they stuck to.
Inside was useless panic to escape.
When the defenders backed away to huddle
In a safe place, their weight collapsed the tower,   540
And the sky echoed with the sudden crash.
Dying, they fell, impaled on their own spears

And the hard splinters—then the huge mass followed.
Only two crawled out, Lycus and Helenor.
This last, a youth, sired by a Lydian king 545
On the slave Licymnia, was born in secret
And sent by her to Troy, though banned from war.
His arms were light: an unheroic shield
With no device, a bare sword. Latin columns
Flanked him now. He saw Turnus' men in thousands, 550
And as a wild thing ringed in tight by hunters
Lashes against their spears and leaps on purpose
To perish on their weapons, so the young man
Rushed in to die among his enemies,
Making for where he saw the spears were densest. 555
Lycus, a better runner, dodged opponents
And missiles till he reached the wall. He struggled
Up it to grip the top edge or his friends' hands.
Turnus ran after him and launched a spear
With a triumphant taunt: "You fool, you thought 560
You could escape me?" And he tore the man down
From where he hung—a stretch of wall came with him;
As when the bird who keeps Jove's lightning soars
Skyward, a hare or swan in his hooked claws,
Or a warrior wolf has snatched a lamb its mother 565
Searches for, bleating. From all sides a shout rose.
Soldiers ran in to filled the moat with dirt
And hurl their torches to the roof. Lucretius
Had brought his to the gate when Ilioneus
Laid him out with a cliff shard. A skilled lancer, 570
Liger, struck down Emathion; Asilas,
Whose arrow stole from far off, Corynaeus.
Turnus killed Dioxippus, Itys, Clonius,
Promolus, Caeneus (who'd just killed Ortygius),
Sagaris, and, on the towered bastion, Idas. 575
Capys dispatched Privernus, who had dropped
His shield, the idiot, to clutch a slight wound

From Themillas' spear. An arrow winged its way
To lodge deep in his left side, splitting open
His hidden breathways with a fatal wound.   580
The son of Arcens was a glorious sight
With his superb arms and embroidered cloak
Bright with red Spanish dye. His father'd sent him
From the grove of Mars along Symaethus' banks,
By the offering-rich altar of Palicus: 585
Mezentius put his spears aside and whipped   *Deposed King*
His hissing sling three times around his head.   *+ ally of Taurus*
The searing lead chunk hit the brow straight on,
Split it, and stretched the tall form on the ground.
They say Ascanius aimed his first war arrow   *Aeneas' son* 590
That day—he'd only used to hunt wild creatures—
And with his own skill brought Numanus down,
Remulus by clan name. He had joined in marriage
Not long before with Turnus' younger sister.
Pride-swollen as a sharer of the kingdom,   595
He came up past the vanguard now to flaunt
His bulk and shout the hit and miss of insults:
"Twice-beaten Phrygians, don't you feel embarrassed
At how we keep you penned behind your fence?
You fight with *us,* to take away *our* wives?   600
What god, what madness drove you to this country?
No glib Ulysses here, no sons of Atreus!
Our stock is tough; we make our infants tougher,
Dipping them in the savagely cold river.
Our boys stay up and wear the woods out hunting.   605
Their games are archery and taming horses.
Our young men, used to scarcity and hard work,
Subdue the soil and batter towns with war.
We live our lives with weapons, drive our oxen
With butts of spears. Not even slow old age   610
Cripples our courage or our heartiness.
Helmets press down white hair, since we prefer

To make our living from habitual plunder.
Embroidery glows on you, saffron and purple.
You love to laze and treat yourself to dancing.   615
Your hats have ribbons and your tunics sleeves.
You're Phrygian women! Climb up Dindymus:
The double flute there plays the songs you're used to.
The Idaean Mother's drums and boxwood pipe
From Berecynthus call. Leave arms for men."   620
Ascanius could not endure these boasts
And ugly taunts. He turned and aimed an arrow
From his horse-gut bowstring, drew his arms apart
And paused to send a suppliant prayer to Jove.
"Almighty Jupiter, bless my daring effort.   625
I'll bring your temple ritual gifts myself
And set before your altar a white bullock
With gilded horns, the same height as his mother,
Who butts and kicks up sand already." Hearing,
The heavenly father thundered from a clear sky   630
On the left, the moment that the deadly bow twanged.
With a grim hiss, the drawn-back arrow fled.
Its iron point transfixed the curving temples
Of Remulus. "Go bait brave soldiers now!
This is your answer from twice-beaten Phrygians."   635
Jubilant Trojans followed up these words
With a roaring shout; their hearts soared to the stars.
In the sky's zone, on a cloud, long-haired Apollo
Watched the Italian army and the town,
And now he spoke to Iulus in his triumph: 640
"Bless your first brave act: that's the way to heaven.
Godborn, you'll father gods. Troy cannot hold you.
All destined wars will one day cease, in justice,
When the nation of Assaracus is ruling."
From the ether he soared down through gusty air   645
To Ascanius, and assumed old Butes' features.
This was the faithful house guard and retainer

Of Dardanian Anchises, in his time,
Whose son then made him tutor to Ascanius.
Just like this ancient man in voice and coloring   650
And armor with its brutal clang, Apollo
Strode up and spoke to Iulus in his fervor:
"Enough, Aeneas' son! You've killed Numanus
With your arrow and survived it. Great Apollo
Granted this first success, with his own weapon.   655
But you must stop now." Halfway through these words,
Apollo put aside the mortal form,
And faded into far-off, filmy air.
The Trojan leaders heard his quiver clatter
As he vanished, and they recognized the armed god.   660
So though Ascanius burned for war, they stopped him,
At Phoebus' holy orders. They themselves
Returned to fight, and risked death in the open.
A shout went all along the walls and ramparts.
With tense bows and the snapping slings of spears,   665
They strewed the ground with weapons. Hollow helmets
And shields were clanging in the bitter fight,
Thick as ground-lashing rain out of the west
When the stormy Kids rise, thick as hail that storm clouds
Plunge in the sea—the soaking storm that Jove hurls,   670
Bristling with southern blasts, splitting the cloud vault.
Bitias and Pandarus, sons of Alcanor
From Ida by the nymph Iaera, raised
In Jove's woods—massive as their native firs
And mountains—opened up the gate assigned them   675
And called the enemy in. Trusting their weapons,
They flanked the entranceway, as strong as towers,
Iron-clothed, their plumes ruffling at a great height,
As when two oak trees rear their bushy heads
To heaven with exalted, nodding crests   680
Beside the flowing water, on the banks
Of the Po, or by the lovely Athesis.

The Rutulians saw the opening and swarmed it:
But soon Aquiculus—fine sight in armor—
Reckless Tmarus, Quercens, and Mars' son Haemon   685
Had either turned and run with all their troops
Or laid their lives down on that very threshold.
The clashing hatred and the fury grew.
The Trojans, massed at one point, dared to fight
Hand to hand, and to sally out ahead.   690
Elsewhere the chieftain Turnus, on a rampage,
Received a message of the raging slaughter:
The enemy even flaunted open gates!
A boundless fury made him storm away
To the Dardanian gate and the proud brothers.   695
Antiphates led the attack, a bastard
Of Prince Sarpedon by a Theban mother.
Turnus hurled an Italian cornel spear
That sliced the soft air, pierced the gut, and thrust
Through the chest. The wound's black hollow pulsed out froth, 700
And the iron point grew warm, lodged in the lung.
He struck down Merops, Erymas, Aphidnus,
And flame-eyed Bitias, with his roaring pride—
Not with a spear (he wouldn't have surrendered
His life to one) but with a shrieking pike   705
Propelled like lightning through his shield's two ox-hides
And the double gold scales of his trusted breastplate.
His massive body crumpled and collapsed.
The earth groaned, and his great shield clanged above him,
Just as, on the Euboean coast at Baiae,   710
A pier built in the sea on massive rock heaps
Collapses, with a steep, fast drag of wreckage,
And bursts on the shallow seafloor before settling;
The water is in chaos; black sand rises.
Islands boom back: high Prochyta, Inarime—   715
Typhoeus' prison bed, placed by Jove's orders.
Now the war master Mars gave strength and spirit

To the Latins, twisting sharp goads in their hearts,
While siccing Rout and black Fear on the Trojans.
The Latin troops swarmed in—the fight was here;   720
The warrior god inspired them.
Pandarus saw his brother's sprawled-out body,
And knew the course that destiny was taking.
With all his strength, heaving with his broad shoulders,
He turned the gate in on its hinge, though many   725
Of his friends were shut out in the brutal battle.
Others rushed through in time—the idiot
Missed the Rutulian prince, who got inside
Deep in the crowd—invited to the fortress!—
A giant tiger penned with helpless cattle.   730
From Turnus' eyes a fresh light flashed, his weapons
Rang fearsomely, his blood-red crest convulsed,
His shield flared lightning. Instantly the people
Of Aeneas knew the giant, hated form
And panicked. But then towering Pandarus   735
Ran forward, burning to avenge his brother.
"You're in no palace now, no wedding gift
Of Amata, or your native stronghold, Ardea.
This is an enemy fort. You can't get out."
Turnus serenely smiled at him and answered: 740
"Come: hand to hand, if you have nerve. Then go
Tell Priam that you've met Achilles here."
Pandarus put his whole strength into hurling
His crude spear with its knots and green bark. Breezes
Wafted it off, or Saturn's daughter Juno   745
Turned it aside. It hit the gate and stuck.
Turnus spoke: "Here's a weapon and a strong hand
You won't escape: it's me who drives this home."
He reared up with his sword and thrust it midway
Between the young man's temples, monstrously   750
Splitting his forehead and his beardless cheeks.
A crash—the ground was shaken by his huge weight:

He crumpled and sprawled dying there, his armor
Covered with gory brains, and one precise half
Of his head dangling down at either shoulder.   755
The Trojans scattered in their terror, routed.
Had their pursuer had the inspiration
To break the bolts and let his comrades in,
This would have been the war's—and Troy's—last day.
But burning frenzy and demented bloodlust   760
Drove him to fight. He caught
Phaleris and Gyges first—he hamstrung Gyges—
Seized both their spears and thrust them in the backs
Of men he chased—with strength and nerve from Juno—
Halys and shield-pierced Phegeus joined the dead,   765
Then Halius, Prytanis, Noëmon, Alcander,
Incautious on the walls, rallying others.
Lynceus called his friends and made for Turnus,
Who lunged left from the earthworks, stopping him
With a flashing sword. His helmeted head lay far off,   770
Severed by one blow at close quarters. Next
Amycus fell, killer of wild beasts—no one
Was handier at smearing spears with poison—
And Clytius, Aeolus' son, and Cretheus,
Companion of the Muses, whose delight   775
Was setting music to the lyre and singing
Of horses, weapons, warriors and battles.
News of this carnage brought the Trojan leaders,
Fierce Serestus and Mnestheus, there at last—
They saw the enemy inside, their comrades   780
Scattered. Mnestheus yelled, "Where are you running?"
What walls, what fortress have you got but these?
Citizens! Will you let a single man
Trapped in your earthworks pile your town with slaughter
And send your finest soldiers down to Hades?   785
Have pity on your ancient gods, your poor race,
And great Aeneas! Cowards, where's your shame?"

This roused them. They now rallied against Turnus
In a dense column. He dropped back at last
To the piece of land encircled by the river.   790
The Trojans pushed more fiercely on, converging
With loud shouts, as a troop of hunters holds
A savage lion at their spear points: frightened,
Glaring, and storming, he retreats, but fury
And courage will not let him run. He longs   795
To strike back at the men and spears but cannot.
So Turnus slowly and reluctantly
Stepped backward, as his spirit seethed with rage.
He even dashed into the enemy ranks
Twice, and twice scattered them along the walls.   800
The camp soon reunited all its forces,
And Juno, Saturn's daughter, didn't dare
Grant strength to fight them: Jove had sent down Iris
From the ether with some harsh threats for his sister
If Turnus didn't leave the Trojans' walls.   805
His shield and sword were not enough—the young man
Couldn't hold out. The missiles from all sides
Engulfed him. Constantly his helmet rang
Around his head. The stones split solid bronze
And tattered off his plume. His shield was weaker   810
Than the blows. The Trojans—thundering Mnestheus
Among them—heaped their spears on. Turnus' body
Was pouring filthy sweat—he had no time now
To catch his breath. He shook, worn, sore, and panting.
At last he jumped headfirst into the river   815
With all his arms. Its tawny surge received him
Gladly, raised him on soft waves and returned him,
Happy and cleansed of blood, to his companions.

BOOK 10

Supreme Olympus' heavenly palace opened,
When the gods' father and the king of mortals
Called an assembly from his looming lookout,
Which showed the Trojan camp and Latin armies.
The gods sat in the hall, between the twin gates.   5
He spoke: "Sky dwellers, what has made your purpose
Turned backward into vicious rivalry?
I forbade Italy to clash with Troy.
Why this rebellious strife? What terror drives
Each side to swarm for arms and rouse the other?   10
The time will come for battle. Don't invoke it.
Wild Carthage will one day send devastation
Through shattered Alps against the Roman walls.
Then you can have your hateful fight, your pillage.
Leave off—be glad: confirm the pact I sanctioned."   15
Brief words—but golden Venus gave an answer
At length.
"Father, eternal king of men—of all things

(What greater being is there to appeal to?)—
You see how the Rutulians gloat and Turnus   20
Storms through the ranks with his fine horses, scornful
In triumph. Without benefit of walls,
The Teucrians now fight within their gates,
Within their earthworks, filling moats with blood;
Aeneas is far off and unaware.   25
When will you end these sieges? A new army
Looms at Troy's walls and stifles her rebirth.
Diomedes—now from Aetolian Arpi—
Assails them. Once again I will be wounded:
Weapons of mortals wait for me, your child.   30
If Trojans came without your holy sanction
To Italy, punish them and do not help them.
But if a wealth of oracles from the gods
And the dead has brought them, how can anyone
Turn back your orders and reorder fate?   35
Why mention ships burned by the shore at Eryx,
Or the crazed gales the king of storms incited
From Aeolia, or Iris sent through clouds?
Now she stirs up creation's only part
Still left in peace, the demons, and thrusts Allecto   40
Up to the light to rave through Italy's towns.
I do not care about the empire hoped for
In luckier times. Let those your favor win.
If your harsh consort grants no land to Trojans,
I beg you, father, by Troy's smoking ruins: 45
Let me discharge Ascanius from the war   Aeneas' son (Iulus)
Unharmed—please let my grandson live. Aeneas
Can toss on foreign seas, for all I care;
Whatever road fate grants him, let him follow,
But let me take his son from ruthless battle.   50
I own Amathus, Cythera, towering Paphus,
And the Cyprus shrine. Let him grow old with me,
Unarmed, inglorious. Command that Carthage

Trample and tyrannize Ausonia.
Nothing from there will stop it. Has it helped him   55
To live through that cursed war, escape the Greek fires,
Take endless risks at sea and on bleak land,
In search of Latium and a reborn Troy?
They should have settled on their homeland's ashes,
On the site of Troy. Give back the wretched Trojans   60
Xanthus and Simois, and the whole round
Of Ilium's rise and fall." Then queenly Juno
Spoke in her rage: "Why shatter my deep silence
And bring my hidden grief to public words?
Has any god or human forced Aeneas   65
To invade Latinus' kingdom? Granted, fate—
Or else Cassandra's ravings—led him there:
I certainly was not the one to urge him
Out of his camp into the perilous winds,
Leaving the walls and army to a child,   70
To suborn the Tuscans and those peaceful tribes.
What god, what tyranny of mine propelled him?
Did Juno do this? Iris, sent from the clouds?
'How wrong to ring this infant Troy with flames!'
But divine Venilia's son, Pilumnus' grandson   75
Turnus, can't get a foothold in his own land.
And Trojans putting Latium to the torch?
And land usurped and looted? In-laws chosen
At will, and girls torn from fiancés' arms?
Hands clasped in peace—and weapons studding prows?   80
You stole Aeneas from the hands of Greeks
And left them mist and empty wind instead.
Out of his ships you made a fleet of nymphs.
Helping Rutulians is a crime for me?
Aeneas gone and unaware—so be it.   85
Paphus, Idalium, Cythera are yours;
Why meddle with this hard, war-pregnant city?
Did *I* attempt to topple shaky Troy?

I, or the man who threw the wretched people
To the Greeks? What could have made two continents 90
Rise up in arms? Why was their pact betrayed?
Did I dispatch the Trojan lover-boy
On his Spartan raid? Did I supply the weapons?
Feed war with lust? The time to fear was then!
Your petty wrangles and complaints come late." 95
This was the plea of Juno. All the gods
Murmured their different thoughts, as the woods murmur,
Catching the first gusts, whisking hidden rustlings,
Speaking to sailors of the storm to come.
Then the almighty father, ruler of all things, 100
Began. The gods' high hall grew silent for him;
The deep earth shook, the towering sky was still,
The west wind settled, oceans calmed their waves.
"Hear what I say and fix it in your hearts.
A league of the Ausonians and Trojans 105
Was not allowed, nor can your quarrel end.
To no one's luck today, to no one's hope
Will I show favor—Trojan or Rutulian.
It might be Italy's fate or Trojan folly
Or false advice behind this siege: no matter. 110
Everyone—the Rutulians too—must fashion
Hardship or triumph: Jupiter is neutral.
The fates will find their way." He nodded, swearing
By his brother's river Styx—the pitch-seared banks
And dark gulf. At his nod Olympus shook. 115
And that was all. He rose from his gold throne.
Gods drew around and led him to the door.

Meanwhile the slaughtering Rutulians thronged
At every gate and ringed the walls with flames.
The Trojan band could not escape their fort. 120
They stood, pathetic, hopeless, and quite helpless,
On the towers, or thinly topped the ring of ramparts.

Hicetaon's son Thymoetes; Asius, son
Of Imbrasus; both Assaraci; old Thymbris;
And Castor were the front line, then the brothers   125
Of Sarpedon, Clarus and Thaemon from proud Lycia.
Huge as his father, Clytius, or his brother
Menestheus, Acmon of Lyrnesus strained
Hugely to haul no small part of a mountain.
They fought with spears and rocks in their defense.   130
Fire was thrown and arrows set to bowstrings.
And in the midst was Venus' rightful darling,
The Trojan boy, who'd left his lovely head bare.
He gleamed like gems in tawny gold, which make
A neck or head resplendent, or like ivory   135
Set skillfully in Orician terebinth
Or boxwood. On his milky neck cascaded
Long hair beneath a band of pliant gold.
The spirited clans saw Ismarus there also,
Poisoning shafts and guiding them to bloodshed—   140
Son of a noble Lydian house whose rich fields
Strong men worked and the Pactolus soaked in gold.
Mnestheus was there too, still exulting
From driving Turnus from the earthwork walls;
And Capys, source of the Campanian town's name.   145
Such was the bitter struggle of the armies.
That night Aeneas cut the channel's water.
Leaving Evander, he approached the king
In the Etruscan camp, told who he was,
His strengths, his needs, the savage heart of Turnus,   150
The allies that Mezentius was gaining.
He warned how risky human projects are,
But mingled pleas with all this; straight off, Tarchon
Joined with him in a pact. The Lydian race
Embarked beneath a foreign captain, paying   155
Their debt to fate and the gods' will. Aeneas
Led with his ship. Its beak showed Phrygian lions

Below Mount Ida—dear to Trojan exiles.
There the great hero sat, considering
The ways the war might end. Close at his left side   160
Pallas asked about the stars, guides of that dim voyage,
And Aeneas' sufferings on land and sea.

Goddesses, open Helicon, recite
What forces came from the Etruscan shore
With Aeneas in those vessels on the sea.   165
King Massicus' armored *Tigress* sliced the waves.
He led a thousand young men out of Cosae
And fortressed Clusium, with deadly bows
And arrows in light quivers on their shoulders.
Fierce Abas' whole force wore resplendent arms.   170
A gold Apollo glittered on his prow.
Populonia, his native land, had yielded
Six hundred battle-hardened youths; from Ilva
(With its endless iron mines) three hundred more marched.
Next came Asilas, who brought prophecy   175
From gods to men. The stars, the guts of beasts,
The tongues of birds, the prescient lightning served him.
He swept with him a thousand bristling spears.
Pisa, Alphean town on Tuscan land,
Had placed them at his service. Lovely Astyr   180
Followed, trusting his horse and rainbow armor.
The Caeretans and the farmers by the Minio,
Old Pyrgi and Graviscae, which breeds sickness,
Sent three more hundred, equally devoted.
I can't pass over Cunarus, valiant leader   185
Of Ligurians, or Cupavo with his small force.
Swan feathers rising from his helmet's crest
Showed Love's guilt in his father's transformation.
Cycnus, they say, mourned his beloved Phaethon
In the leafy shade of poplars, the boy's sisters.   190
He sang because it soothed his bitter longing,
And grew soft feathers, white like old men's hair,

And left the ground, calling and chasing stars.
His son now led the fleet, with troops his own age.
Oars heaved his massive ship the *Centaur* forward.   195
The figurehead held up a boulder, threatening
The waves; the long keel furrowed the deep waters.
His father's banks gave troops to Ocnus, offspring
Of the seer Manto and the Tuscan river.
He founded Mantua, named for his mother—   200
Mantua rich in different lineages:
Three races and four clans in each, but this
Is the capital, with strength from Tuscan stock.
Mezentius drew five hundred enemies more:
The river Mincius, veiled in blue reeds, brought them   205
In a warship to the sea from Lake Benacus.
Stalwart Aulestes' hundred oarsmen surged
To beat the water, turning calm to froth
Round the huge Triton figurehead that blasted
On a blue conch and terrified the straits;   210
His shaggy torso human to the waist,
Below, a whale. Waves roared and foamed beneath him.
These chosen princes sailed in thirty ships
To Troy's aid. Bronze prows cut the briny plain.

Day had retreated from the sky. Kind Phoebe   215
Drove her night horses tramping through high heaven.
Aeneas (wakeful in anxiety)
Trimmed the sails and sat down to guide the tiller.
Suddenly in midcourse a band of comrades
Appeared: the ships that kindly Cybele   220
Had changed to nymphs, goddesses of the sea—
One for each bronze beak that had stood on shore.
They swam along with him and sliced the waves.
Far off, they'd known their king; they danced around him.
And Cymodocea, the most eloquent,   225
Came up behind, her right hand on the stern,

Her left hand softly paddling, breasts emerging.
He didn't know her. "Child of gods, Aeneas,
Are you awake? Then let the sails' ropes go.
We are your fleet, pines from the holy heights   230
Of Ida—sea nymphs now. With sword and flame
The treacherous Rutulian hounded us.
We had to break your chains and seek you here.
The Mother pitied us, transformed us, sent us
To live a blessèd life beneath the waters.   235
The walls and moat imprison your young son
Among fierce Latins and their bristling spears.
Arcadian horsemen hold their posts, brave Tuscans
As well. But Turnus is resolved to block them
With his squadrons so they cannot join your camp.   240
Rise up! Call your confederates to arms
At first dawn. Take the shield the god of fire
Has ringed with gold and made invincible.
Tomorrow's light—if you will trust my words—
Will see great heaps of the Rutulian dead."   245
She spoke and dove away, but first pushed deftly
At the high hull, which ran on through the waves
More swiftly than a spear or wind-quick arrow.
And the rest sped behind. Anchises' son,   *Aeneas*
The Trojan, was dumbfounded, then exultant.   250
He gazed up at the arching sky and prayed:
"Idaean mother of gods, who love Mount Dindymus,
Tower-crowned towns, and chariot-yoked lions:
Lead me in war, achieve your prophecy,
March with the Phrygians, bringing them good fortune." 255
While he spoke, the day returned in its swift circle,
And the Sun in its ripeness routed Night.
He told his troops to arm themselves for action
On his signal and prepare their hearts for war.
Now he could see the Trojans and his camp   260
From the high stern. He raised the flaring shield

On his left arm. His people on the walls
Shouted up to the sky—hope spurred their rage—
And threw their spears with force, like cranes from Strymon
Who skim the upper air beneath black clouds,   265
Fleeing the south wind with their loud, glad calls.
The king and lords of Italy were stunned
To see the vessels turning toward the shore.
The sea became a fleet that flooded in.
A flame poured from Aeneas' feathered crest;   270
The gold boss of his shield was spewing fire,
As when a clear night brings the deathly glow
Of bleeding comets, or the Dog Star rises,
Burning with drought and sickness for weak mortals,
And spreads malignant light across the sky.   275
But Turnus didn't lose his nerve—he'd do it:
Get to the shore in time, beat back the landing.
He issued this harsh challenge to his troops:
"Now you can smash them, as you've yearned to do.
Courage controls the god of war. Remember   280
Your wives and homes. Remake your fathers' fame
And heroism. Hurry to the surf
And catch the sailors staggering and fearful.
Fortune helps daring men."
Still speaking, he considered which to lead   285
On this attack, and which should keep the siege.
Aeneas sent his comrades down the gangplanks
From the high sterns. Most watched the ebbing sea
And made a cautious leap into the shallows.
Some climbed down oars. Tarchon spied out a place   290
Where no waves broke and boomed to mark the shallows,
But untouched sea washed with a gentle swell.
He turned his prow there and implored his troops:
"My chosen company, drive on your oars,
Hurl your ships forward, split this hostile land   295
With their beaks. Let each hull plow itself a furrow.

I wouldn't shrink from breaking on that berth
The moment I seize land." His comrades heard
And surged against the oars and brought the boats
Through frothing water onto Latin soil.   300
Now every hull had settled without harm,
Gripping the dry sand—all except for Tarchon's.
On a projecting sandbank in the shallows
It hung and teetered—and withstood the waves—
Then shattered, pouring men into the surf   305
To fight the benches and the splintered oars
And the hard undertow that caught their feet.
Quickly and keenly, Turnus took his whole force
To stand and face the Trojans on the shore.
The signals blared. Aeneas charged first, cutting   310
The rustic ranks of Latins down—an omen
Of the battle's end. He killed the giant Theron,
Who first came at him. Bronze joints, gold scales yielded,
And the sword pierced his side and drank his blood.
He wounded Lichas, sacred to Apollo: 315
Cut from his lifeless mother yet surviving
The knife himself. Aeneas soon hurled down
In death huge Gyas and hard Cisseus
As they reaped the lines. No use their clubs from Hercules,
No use their strong hands or their sire, Melampus,   320
Hercules' friend in all his stringent tasks
On earth. The hero hurled a javelin
Through Pharus' shouting, boasting, cowardly mouth.
And you, poor Cydon, following Clytius,
Your latest love, with blond down on his cheeks,   325
Would have been brought down by a Trojan hand
That turned all passion for young men to nothing,
Had Phorcus' seven sons, your troop of brothers,
Not hedged you closely, throwing seven spears.
Some fell back from Aeneas' shield and helmet.   330
Others kind Venus turned—they merely grazed.

But now Aeneas spoke to staunch Achates: (retain)
"Give me the weapons planted in Greek bodies
At Troy. Not one I hurl at the Rutulians
Will go to waste." He snatched a giant spear   335
And threw it. Maeon's bronze shield was transfixed—
His breastplate and the breast behind it shattered:
Alcanor caught his brother as he fell,
With his right arm—through which the hero's lance
Continued unimpeded, soaked in blood.   340
His own dead hand now hung by scanty sinews.
Numitor snatched the spear that killed his brother
And aimed it at Aeneas, but to lodge it
Was not his fate. He grazed Achates' thigh.
Clausus from Cures, young and strong and bold,   345
Launched a stiff spear at Dryops, who was speaking.
It drove beneath his chin and pierced his throat:
His words and life both ended in one moment.
His forehead hit the earth. He spewed thick gore.
Three youths from Boreas' lofty clan in Thrace   350
And the three sons Ismaran Idas sent
Fell under various wounds. Halaesus charged
With Auruncan troops. Messapus, son of Neptune,
Followed with his fine horses. All these blocked
The landing, struggling on the very threshold   355
Of Italy. As winds in the vast sky
Battle with equal bravery and strength:
A stalemate of themselves, the clouds, the seas—
The world a standoff, and the end unknown;
So the Trojan and the Latin forces clashed,   360
Foot locked with foot, hands grappling man to man.
Elsewhere a rushing stream had rolled down boulders
And scattered them with trees ripped from its banks.
The Arcadians on this rough and torn-up ground
Had left their horses, but they weren't accustomed   365
To charging as a line of infantry.

When Pallas saw the Latins routing them,
He pleaded and harangued in desperation:
"Where are you running, friends? By your brave acts
And selves, by King Evander and his triumphs,   370
And by my hope of winning fame like his:
Your swords must cut a path through your opponents.
Your feet are useless! Our great country calls
Both you and me to meet the thickest onslaught.
These are not gods but men attacking men,   375
An equal count of mortal hands and souls.
Shall we go back—or to the Trojan camp?"
He pierced the center of the densest ranks.
Lagus was in his way first—evil luck
Brought him there; while he pulled at a huge boulder,   380
A hurtling spear struck where the ribs branched out
From the spine. As Pallas was bent over him
To tug the shaft out, Hispo made a lunge,
In reckless fury at his friend's cruel death.
Pallas was quick to put a stop to him,   385
Driving a sword deep in his panting lung.
He attacked Sthenius, then Anchemolus
Of Rhoetus' ancient race, who'd violated—
Bold crime!—the bedroom of his father's wife.
Twins also fell in those Rutilian fields,   390
Larides and Thymber, who were sons of Daucus—
Their likeness baffled and amused their parents.
Evander's offspring gave them a crude difference
By slicing Thymber's head off with a sword.
Larides' severed right hand kept on twitching,   395
The dying fingers clutching at the sword.
The Arcadians drew strength against the enemy
From angry shame at Pallas' taunts and triumphs. _Evander's sn_
As Rhoeteus drove past, making himself scarce,
The youth impaled him—Ilus was reprieved _Aeneas' sn_ 400 _Ascani_
(For a short time): the spear was aimed at him,

_3/30/19_

But Rhoeteus took it, while the noble brothers
Teuthras and Tyres chased him. Out he rolled
And beat Rutulian ground with numbing feet.
When summer winds he's prayed for start to rise,   405
A shepherd scatters fires in the woods;
The gaps catch suddenly: a battle line
Of fierce, unbroken burning spans the country.
The conqueror sits and watches conquering flames.
Likewise the courage of uniting troops   410
Seconded Pallas. But war-keen Halaesus
Went forward in the cover of his shield.
He slaughtered Ladon, Pheres, and Demodocus.
The bright blade lopped Strymonius' hand, which reached
For his throat. He smashed a rock into the face   415
Of Thoas. Gory brains and skull chips flew.
His seer father hid the child Halaesus
In the woods, but when death closed the old man's eyes,
The Fates could claim the son, a sacrifice
To Evander's weapons. Pallas made this prayer: *Evander's Son* 420
"Come, make this spear throw lucky, Father Tiber,
And let me pierce Halaesus' sturdy breast.
Your sacred oak will have his arms and armor."
The god heard. Poor Halaesus, shielding Imaon,
Had bared his chest to the Arcadian spear.   425
Lausus, a great force here, did not desert
The slaughter-panicked ranks. He first killed Abas,
The mainstay of the fight, who came at him.
Arcadia's children fell, Etruscans fell,
And Trojans whom the Greeks had left alive;   430
Leaders and brawn were equal in the clash.
The rearguard pushed the front line to a mass
Of hampered weapons. Pallas drove his own men,
And Lausus his—the youths were beautiful
And close in age. Homecoming was denied   435
To both by fate. But high Olympus' king

Would not consent for them to face each other.
Their doom would come from greater enemies.
Meanwhile the kind nymph sent her brother Turnus
To Lausus' aid. He sped his chariot   440
Through the line and told his comrades, "Now stand down.
Pallas belongs to me. I'll go for him.
I only wish his father could look on."
He spoke. His comrades quit the field as ordered.
With the Rutulians gone, the youth, transfixed   445
By the haughty orders, let his hard gaze rove
From a distance over Turnus' massive form.
He gave this answer to the tyrant's words:
"Either's a glorious prize: a general's armor
Or death. It makes no difference to my father.   450
So stop your threats." He stepped into the open,
Freezing the blood in the Arcadians' hearts.
Turnus jumped down and closed in on his prey
On foot. A lion on his lofty post
Sees a bull lunging on a distant plain   455
And hurtles toward him: Turnus looked like this.
Pallas first gauged his spear's range, then stepped forward,
Calling on the huge sky in hope that chance
Would bless his bravery against the odds.
"Hercules, come—my father took you in,   460
A stranger—help in this great enterprise.
Let dying Turnus see his bloody weapons
Taken from him by my victorious hands."
The god heard, but he stifled heavy groans
In his heart; the tears were futile that he shed.   465
To comfort him, his father, Jupiter,
Said this: "An end is set for everyone,
For life is brief and cannot be recovered.
But brave men, through their exploits, strive for fame
That lasts. Beneath Troy's high walls many sons   470
Of gods died. My own child Sarpedon died there.

Fate calls: for Turnus too the race is ending."
He turned his eyes away from Italy's fields.
Pallas with all his great strength cast his spear
And snatched his bright sword from the hollow sheath.   475
The spear flew, pierced the layers of the shield,
And struck the breastplate at the shoulder's rim,
Finally grazing Turnus' massive form.
But he in turn deliberately aimed
His iron-pointed pike and launched it, saying,   480
"See if my weapon is the one to stick."
The spearhead, striking, shaking, pounded through
The shield—all of the bronze and iron sheets,
All of the bull-hide layers wrapping it—
Into the breastplate, into that strong chest.   485
Out of the wound he tore the heated shaft,
But with it came his lifeblood and his soul.
Collapsing forward with a crash of arms,
He touched the enemy earth with gory lips.
Turnus stood over him: 490
"Go tell Evander this, Arcadians:
I send him back the Pallas he deserves.
The soothing tribute of a burial
I grant him. But he had a costly guest—
Aeneas." With his foot he held the corpse down   495
And stripped the giant swordbelt with its story
Of crime etched in—a wedding night that left
The bedrooms smeared with gore of slaughtered youths—
That Clonus, son of Eurytus, had embossed
In gold, and Turnus now was thrilled to loot.   500
People know nothing of their fated future.
Their exaltation cannot stay in bounds.
The time would come when he'd give anything
Not to have touched the boy. He'd hate his plunder,
And hate this day. Pallas' friends pressed in, wailing.   505
They laid him on his shield to haul away.

What grief, what glory you will take your father!
A single day brought war and death to you.
But see the heaps of enemy dead you leave.
Not a mere rumor of disaster came   510
To Aeneas, but a trusty runner, pleading
For him to pull his comrades from death's edge.
He reaped his furious way and made a broad path
To Turnus as he triumphed in fresh slaughter.
Aeneas as he ran kept seeing Pallas,   515
Evander, and their banquet for the stranger,
And their hands' clasp. He seized the four young sons
Of Sulmo, then the four brought up by Ufens;
They were reprieved to serve as sacrifices
To the shades: their captive blood would soak the pyre.   520
Ferociously, he cast a spear at Magus,
Who deftly ducked—trembling, it passed above.
He grasped Aeneas' knees, entreating him,
"By your ancestral spirits and your hopes
For Iulus, spare me for my child and father.   525
Fine embossed silver by the hundredweight
Lies buried in my high house—pounds of gold too,
Worked and unworked. The Trojans still can win:
What difference is there in a single life?"
Aeneas gave this answer to his pleas: 530
"So many pounds of gold and silver—keep it
For your sons, since Turnus did away with bargains
In war the moment that he slaughtered Pallas.
My father's ghost agrees, and so does Iulus."
He seized the helmet, wrenching back the neck,   535
And stabbed him as he begged, up to the hilt.
Not far off was Haemonides the priest
Of Apollo and Diana, in a headband
And fillets, radiant white robes, and emblems.
Aeneas chased him down and stood above him,   540
Huge shadow and death. Serestus hauled the weapons

Away, a trophy for King Mars the strider.
Caeculus, born of Vulcan's line, and Umbro
From the Marsian mountains rallied the Italians.
Aeneas stormed against them. With his sword   545
He lopped off Anxur's hand—the round shield fell.
He'd shouted out some self-deceiving boast.
Perhaps he dreamed about immortal fame,
Or reassured himself of gray old age.
Tarquitus, son of Dryope the nymph   550
And sylvan Faunus, strode with his bright weapons
Into Aeneas' rage. He drew his spear back
And made that massive shield and breastplate useless.
The head was slung to earth before it finished
Its pleading, the warm body was kicked over,   555
And from his hardened heart Aeneas spoke:
"Lie there, you menace, so your excellent mother
Can't hide your corpse beneath your father's tomb.
The crows will find you, or the sea will take you
In its waves, where hungry fish will suck your wounds."   560
He turned to chasing Turnus' vanguard: Lucas,
Antaeus, hearty Numa, and blond Camers—
Son of brave Volscens, richest of Italians
In land, and lord of quiet Amyclae.
Just like Aegaeon's hundred hands and arms,   565
His fifty fire-belching chests and mouths,
When—in the story—fifty clattering shields
And fifty drawn swords fought Jove's thunderbolts:
So Aeneas' savage triumph swept the plain
Once blood was on his sword. He made a charge   570
Straight toward the breasts of Niphaeus' four-horse team.
They saw his long strides, heard his gruesome roaring,
And in their panic wheeled and tore away
Their chariot to the shore. Its driver toppled.
The brothers Lucagus and Liger entered   575
The fight, drawn by white horses, Liger driving,

Lucagus fiercely whirling his bare sword.
Galled by their fervent rage, Aeneas dashed
To loom before them, holding up his spear.
And Liger said: 580
"This is no Trojan plain—there is no chariot
Of Diomedes or Achilles. Your life
And the war end here." From Liger in his folly
These words flew. And the Trojan hero offered
Nothing in answer but to hurl his spear.   585
Lucagus had leaned down to prod the team
With his spear butt, and had thrust his left foot forward
For the fight. Aeneas' pike pierced all the layers
Of his shining shield and lodged in his left thigh.
He tumbled, and rolled dying on the ground.   590
Righteous Aeneas spitefully addressed him:
"A cowardly team did not betray your chariot.
False visions didn't turn them from opponents.
No, you yourself jumped and abandoned them."
He seized the horses. Liger, also fallen,   595
Futilely stretched his hands out toward the victor:
"By your great self, by your proud parents too,
Leave me my breath, have pity—I am pleading."
Aeneas stopped him. "You spoke differently
Not long ago. Die—don't desert your brother."   600
He slashed his chest, the hiding place of breath.
The Trojan chief went slaughtering down the field
Rampantly, like a black storm or a whirlpool.
At last Ascanius and the other troops
Broke from the brief blockade around their fortress.   605

Jupiter, meanwhile, turned and spoke to Juno:
"Sister—and darling spouse—you must be right:
Venus alone upholds the strength of Troy,
Just as you thought, and not their vigorous hands,
And not their savage and unflinching hearts."   610

Juno spoke pliantly: "My splendid husband,
Why do you taunt your weak, browbeaten wife?
If you still loved me as you did—and should—
You'd surely do what lies in your great power,
And let me rescue Turnus from the fight   615
To send unharmed back to his father, Daunus.
No, let them put to death an innocent man,
Although he shares divine descent with us—
Pilumnus was his ancestor—although
He piled your shrine freehandedly with gifts."   620
Briefly the king of high Olympus spoke:
"If what you beg is only a reprieve
For the doomed youth, if you accept my terms,
Send Turnus running from his looming fate:
So far I can concede. But if your pleas   625
Hide hopes of greater mercy, and you think
That the war's end can change, you are mistaken."
Juno wept. "If your thoughts grant what your words
Deny, if it's ordained that he can live—!
But no, he'll die a hard, unmerited death,   630
Or I miss the truth. I wish my fears deceived me—
Or you'd divert these plans—it's in your power!"
But then she ringed herself in clouds and shot
Down from the sky, driving a storm before her,
To the Laurentian camp and Trojan line.   635
From empty mist and thin and strengthless shadow
She fashioned an Aeneas—eerie marvel.
She copied Trojan arms—the shield, the crest
Of the goddess' son—and furnished vacant speech,
Sounds without thoughts. She made it stride like him—   640
The thing was like the fluttering ghosts in legends;
It looked like dreams that trick our sleeping senses.
The arrogant image danced before the lines,
Taunting proud Turnus, teasing with its weapons.
Turnus closed in and hurled a hissing pike   645

And saw a back turned, saw withdrawing steps,
As if Aeneas were in straight retreat.
His heart was full of wild, deluded hope.
"Your wedding's promised and you run away?
You sailed here seeking land: I'll lay you on it."   650
Shouting, he chased the thing and shook his sword,
But on the wind his triumph slid away.
Moored at a towering outcrop's base, the ship
That brought Osinius from Clusium
Stood with its ladders out and gangplanks down.   655
The frightened, bolting image of Aeneas
Dove in to hide there, never losing Turnus.
Nothing could slow him—up the plank he vaulted.
He reached the prow, and Juno broke the rope
And wrenched the ship out on retreating waves.   660
On land Aeneas yelled in pointless challenge,
With crowds of soldiers dying in his way.
The fragile phantom left off seeking cover
And soared high up and blended with black cloud.
A whirlwind carried Turnus far from shore.   665
Bewildered, and ungrateful to be safe,
He looked back, raised his hands and shouted starward,
"Almighty father, have I earned this shame,
This punishment? Where am I being swept to?
From where? And how? And how can I get back?   670
When will I see the town and camp again?
And that brave company that followed me,
Left now—the outrage!—ringed by grisly death?
I'll see them scattered, hear them fall and groan?
What will I do? What pit gapes deep enough   675
For me? No, pity me instead, you winds.
I beg you with my whole heart, drive this ship
Into the rocks or cliffs or deadly shallows,
Away from the Rutulians and my shame."
And now two options wavered in his judgment: 680

Fall on his sword, demented from disgrace,
And drive the heartless blade between his ribs?
Dive in mid-ocean, try to reach the curved shore,
And face the Trojan weapons once again?
Three times he tried each course, three times great Juno   685
In heartfelt pity held the young man back.
Current and sea swell made a wafting path
To the ancient city of his father, Daunus.

Prodded by Jove, blazing Mezentius
Joined the fight, charging at the gleeful Trojans.   690
The Tuscan ranks closed in on that brave man—
All of their hatred, all their crowding weapons.
He stood there like a rock in desolate waters,
Bare to the savagery of wind and waves,
To the sea and sky's unending, pounding threats—   695
Unmoved. He felled the son of Dolichaon,
Hebrus, then Latagus and timid Palmus.
Mezentius threw a giant mountain shard
Straight in the face of Latagus, to halt him.
Palmus rolled helpless, tendons cut, and Lausus   700
Was given his corselet and his crest to wear.
Phrygian Euanthes died, and Mimas, agemate
And friend of Paris. One night gave both life
Through Amycus and Theano, and the queen,
Torch-pregnant Hecuba. In his own city   705
One died. The Laurentian shore holds one, a stranger.
Like a boar driven down by nipping dogs
From sheltered years in high, pine-covered Vesulus
Or the nurturing Laurentian lake, a forest
Of reeds—but now the net encloses him;   710
Snarling, he takes a stand with bristling shoulders.
Who's brave enough to bring his anger near?
They leave a space, throw spears, shout cautiously;
Fearless, he faces one way, then another,   717

Gnashing his teeth and shaking off the spears;   718
So righteous rage against Mezentius   714
Never found spirit for a charge with swords.   715
They harried him with long-range spears and yells.   716
Acron, a Greek, had come from ancient Corythus—   719
Banished from both his wedding and his country.   720
Mezentius spotted him, a force of havoc
In a purple cloak and plumes, betrothal gifts.
Like a lion, maddened by his hunger, searching
Deep coverts—now he sees a fleeing goat
Or stag with towering horns, and spreads his jaws   725
Joyfully wide, bristles his mane, then crouches
Engrossed in entrails; on voracious lips
The grim gore oozes—
So keen Mezentius charged his teeming enemies.
Unlucky Acron fell and kicked the black earth   730
And stained the broken spear with dying blood.
The hero would not stoop to kill Orodes
With a spear throw to the back while he was running.
He dashed in front and met him man to man—
Superior in warcraft, not in stealth—   735
Felled him, and stepped on him to pull the spear out.
"Here great Orodes lies—one of their best men."
His troops yelled, echoing his victory song.
Orodes gasped in death, "I'll have revenge soon.
You, stranger, won't be gloating long in triumph.   740
The same fate, in this same field, waits for you."
Mezentius gave a smile infused with anger:
"Die now. The father of gods and king of mortals
Will see to me." He yanked the weapon free.
Hard rest and iron sleep pressed down his eyes.   745
He closed them, entering eternal night.
Caedicus cut Alcathoüs down, Sacrator killed Hydaspes;
Rapo: Parthenius and iron Orses;
Messapus: Clonius and Lycaon's son Erichaetes.

Clonius' horses bolted; he went sprawling.   750
Erichaetes died on foot, like Lycian Agis,
Whom Valerus, heir to courage from his grandsire,
Laid low. Salius killed Thronius, then fell
To Nealces—famous lancer, cunning archer.
Now heavy fighting balanced grief and slaughter   755
Between the sides. On both they won and lost
And killed and fell, and neither would retreat.
The gods assembled in Jove's palace pitied
Such futile rage, such dreadful human hurt.
Venus looked on, across from Saturn's daughter,   760
As pale Tisiphone raved through all those thousands.
Mezentius was incensed and shook a huge spear.
He strode on, massive as Orion walking
Across the sea floor, in the deepest waters,
But towering above them from his shoulders;   765
Or bringing an old ash tree from a summit,
Feet on the earth, head hidden in the clouds.
So Mezentius advanced, in his vast armor.
Aeneas saw him in the long front line
And went to meet him. He stood unperturbed,   770
A rooted bulk awaiting his brave enemy,
And gauged how far he had to throw his spear.
"Hand that I worship, weapon that I launch,
Help me! My son will be the monument—
My Lausus, draped in armor from that bandit   775
Aeneas." And he whipped a whistling spear
At long range. From the shield it glanced—flew—hit
Lovely Antores, just above the groin:
Hercules' comrade, Argive exile, follower
Of Evander, settler in a local town;   780
A hapless proxy victim now, he gazed
Up at the sky and thought of his dear Argos.
Then dutiful Aeneas' spear went slamming
Through Mezentius' domed shield of three bronze layers,

Three hides and linen padding. In the groin   785
It stuck, but not with force. It thrilled Aeneas
To draw Etruscan blood. He drew his sword
Eagerly, charging at his trembling victim.
Lausus saw, and for love of his dear father,
He moaned. The tears were rolling down his face.   790
I won't be silent here about your exploit
Or the hard death it brought—you've earned the telling,
Heroic boy—if we believe tradition.
Mezentius fell back helpless, hampered, dragging
The shield in which the enemy spear was lodged.   795
His youthful son ran straight into the clash.
Aeneas reared and raised his sword to strike.
Lausus ducked in with a defensive stroke
That stopped him. The youth's comrades came up nearer
With a shout and threw harassing spears to let   800
The father get away beneath his son's shield.
Aeneas held out, furious in his shelter.
Just as when storm clouds hurtle down in hail,
And any farmer plowing in the fields
Takes refuge, and the traveler finds some stronghold—   805
A jutting riverbank, an arch of high rock—
Till at the rain's end they resume their day
In sunlight: so, beneath a pelting war cloud
Aeneas held up till its thunder died,
And only shot insulting threats at Lausus.   810
"Why do you rush to die here? You're outmatched,
Dupe of your loyal love!" The boy paraded
In senseless triumph. In the Trojan leader
Rage mounted, and the Fates prepared to cut
The threads of Lausus' life. Aeneas sank   815
His strong sword to the hilt in the youth's belly,
First through the shield—flimsy to brag behind—
And the soft gold coat of mail his mother'd woven.
Blood filled his breast. The soul slipped from his body

And through the air, and made off for the shades.   820
But when Anchises' son saw that pale face— *Aeneas*
The uncanny paleness of the dying youth—
He moaned in pity, stretching out his hand.
He saw in him his own love for Anchises. *Aeneas' father*
"Poor boy! They call me 'good.' What will I give you   825
Worthy of what you dared in your devotion?
You loved your weapons—keep them. And I'll send you
To your fathers' tomb and spirits—will you know it?
Yet this should solace your pathetic death:
It came from great Aeneas." He berated   830
The boy's troops, who were hanging back, and lifted
The corpse with its well-combed and bloodstained hair.
Meanwhile the father staunched his wound with water
At the Tiber's banks, and leaned against a tree trunk,
Exhausted. A branch dangled his bronze helmet;   835
His heavy weapons rested on the ground.
Among his chosen troops, he gasped in pain,
Head down, his combed beard trailing on his chest.
Often he asked where Lausus was and ordered
Runners to bring him to his grieving father.   840
His weeping friends brought Lausus' massive body—
Massively wounded—lying on his shield.
Mezentius knew those groans and sensed disaster.
He dirtied his white hair with dust and raised
Both hands to heaven, then embraced the corpse.   845
"Did I have such delight in life, my child—
My own son—that I let you take my place
Against the enemy? This wound saved your father,
And by your death I live. How miserable
My exile is at last, how deep my wound.   850
And it was me who smeared your name with guilt—
Me, hounded from the kingship of our fathers.
By any means they chose, I should have given
My guilty life to soothe my country's hatred.

But I have not yet left this world, this daylight—   855
Not yet." He got up on his ruined thigh,
Unbeaten. Though the deep stab crippled him,
He had them fetch his horse—his pride and comfort,
Who brought him out of every fight a victor—
And to this grieving animal he spoke: 860
"Rhoebus, if anything lasts long for mortals,
Our life has. Triumphing with me today,
You'll fetch that gory plunder, and the head
Of Aeneas, as revenge for Lausus' pain.
Or if our strength cannot accomplish it,   865
You'll fall with me. Brave thing, I don't believe
You'd take your orders from a Trojan master."
He settled in his old place, with a sharp pike
Hefted in either hand, and his bronze helmet
Flashing beneath a bristling horsehair plume.   870
He dashed into the battle lines, his heart
Seething with shame and grief that drove him wild.
Three times Mezentius shouted for Aeneas,
Who knew his voice and spoke this joyful prayer:
"Father of gods, and high Apollo, grant it!   875
You, come and grapple with me."
He stepped before him, leveling a spear.
"I don't care, savage—since my son is gone.
That was the only way you could destroy me.
I don't fear death. To me, the gods are nothing.   880
Quiet, then. Take these gifts before I die."
He sped in an extensive circle, launching
One weapon, then another, then one more,
And lodged them in the shield. The gold boss held,
The hero stood. Mezentius circled left   885
Three times and hurled more spears. Three times the Trojan
Pivoted with his shield—a ghastly forest.
Impatiently he pulled out all the barbs
And felt the pressure of unequal combat.

He chose to charge straight out and fling a spear,   890
Which struck between the horse's curving temples.
The creature reared up, battering the air.
The rider toppled, and the horse fell headlong,
Pinning him to the ground, his shoulder broken.
Trojan and Latin shouts lit up the sky.   895
Up ran Aeneas, wrenching free his sword.
"Where is the fierce Mezentius now, the wild force
Of his spirit?" He lay coming to himself,
Gasping the sky in, gazing at the air.
"Cruel enemy—why these sneering threats of death?   900
Killing's no crime—I came here knowing that.
My Lausus made no pact with you to save me.
I ask one thing, though, if the beaten can:
Let the earth cover me. I am surrounded
By my people's hatred. Guard me from it, please,   905
And let me share a burial with my son."
He gave his throat on purpose to the sword
And poured his life out—waves of blood on armor.

II

Dawn rose away from Ocean. Though Aeneas
Chafed to inter his friends, though he was tortured
By grief, he took the time, as morning broke,
To make his promised victory offerings.
He lopped the branches from a huge oak, set it   5
On a mound and decked it with the shining armor
Of Mezentius the chieftain, as a trophy
For the war god; he attached the broken spear,
The blood-soaked crest, the pierced and battered breastplate;
At its left side, the figure held the shield;   10
From the neck the ivory-hilted sword was hung.
Aeneas spoke to stir the Trojan leaders
(All cheering in a close-packed crowd around him):
"We've achieved something great, men. Don't be anxious
For the future. These first fruits are from a proud king.   15
This is Mezentius, work of my hands.
Now we'll attack the Latin king and town.
Prepare for war with bold anticipation,

So ignorance, fear, and second thoughts don't slow you,
So you are ready when the gods consent   20
To standards hoisted, troops led from the camp.
Now we must give the earth our comrades' bodies:
That is the only honor down in Acheron.   *river/Hades*
Go, grant this final tribute to the great souls
Who won this country for us with their blood.   25
But first send Pallas to Evander's city—   *Evander's son*
How it will mourn! An early death, a black day *Most important*
Engulfed this warrior, who was no coward."   *ally of Aeneas*
He spoke in tears, then walked back to his doorway,
Where Pallas' corpse was laid out. It was guarded   30
By old Acoetes, squire to Evander
In Arcadia, but ill-fatedly deputed
To go with his dear foster-child—around whom
His entourage now stood, with Trojan soldiers
And Trojan women with their hair loose, mourning.   35
And when Aeneas came beneath the high gates,
The people beat their breasts and raised a moan
To the stars, and heavy grief rang through the king's house.
When he saw Pallas' ivory face, his propped head,
And the gaping wound from the Italian spear point   40
In his smooth chest, Aeneas sobbed and spoke:
"My poor boy, were you all that changing Fortune
Begrudged me? You will never see my kingdom
Or ride back to your father's home in triumph.
This isn't how I pledged to care for you   45
When Evander sent me off with his embraces
To win a great realm—warning that I'd fight
A rugged nation and ferocious soldiers.
Perhaps right now the king, a dupe of hope,
Heaps altars with his gifts, prays for your safety,   50
While—empty honor—we in grief escort
This youth, who now owes nothing to the gods.
How cruel, how pitiful to see his son dead!

Is this the glorious return we hoped for?
Is my great trust fulfilled? Yet you, his father,   55
Will see no wounds of cowardice in his back,
Or pray for death yourself because he's living.
Italy, Iulus, what a shield you've lost!"   Aeneas' Sr
He ordered that the piteous corpse be lifted.
Choosing a thousand men from all his forces,   60
He sent them to attend the final honors
And share the father's tears—for such a great loss
Small comfort, yet it was that poor man's due.
Others worked hard to weave a wicker bier
Out of soft oak twigs and arbutus branches,   65
Build up the couch and make a leafy canopy.
High on this rustic bed they laid the boy out,
Like a blossom that a young girl's hand has reaped,
A drooping hyacinth or tender violet—
Its beauty and its brightness lingering,   70
But without food or strength from Mother Earth.
Then Aeneas brought two robes out, stiff with gold
And purple dye, made long ago by Dido
Of Sidon, happy in the task. Her own hands
Had worked the fine gold threads into the weave.   75
He chose one—sad last gift—and drew it up
Over the young man's hair, which soon would burn.
He heaped up spoils from the Laurentian battle
And had them taken in a long procession,
Along with spears and mounts the boy had plundered.   80
He'd bound the hands of captives—offerings
To the dead, for blood to sprinkle on the flames.
He made his captains carry tree trunks labeled
With enemy names and hung with enemy arms.
Men led along Acoetes, wrecked by old age.   85
He clawed his face and bruised his chest with pounding
And then fell forward, sprawling, on the earth.
Rutulian chariots filed by, soaked in blood,

And then came Pallas' warhorse Aethon, stripped *Evander's S—* 90
Of insignia, his face wet with his great tears;
Then the youth's spear and helmet—Turnus claimed
The rest. Trojans, Arcadians, and Tuscans,
Their arms reversed, came in a sad array.
When this whole file had traveled out a long way,
Aeneas stopped and gave a heavy sigh: 95
"War's same grim fates call me to other tears.
Farewell forever now, my glorious Pallas—
Bless you for all time." Now the man fell silent
And strode back to the high walls of his fort.
Ambassadors in olive wreaths were there 100
From the Latin city, asking for a favor:
That he give back the slaughtered bodies scattered
On the plain, for burial in a mound of earth.
Lightless, defeated, they were not at war now;
He ought to show past hosts and in-laws mercy. 105
Aeneas the good could not rebuff this plea.
Graciously he assented, and continued:
"How have you been caught up in this cruel war
You don't deserve? Why do you run from friends?
Now for the sake of those who died in battle 110
You plead for peace. I'd give it to the living!
I only claim the home fate grants me here.
It's not your people but your king I'm fighting,
Who broke our guest bond, trusting Turnus' weapons—
And he's the one who should have faced his death. 115
If he had to fight this out and drive the Trojans
From the country, why not meet me hand to hand,
And let swords—or a god—decide who lived?
Go now, and light the pyres of your poor people."
The men were stricken by his words; their eyes 120
Turned to each other, and they held their peace.
Old Drances, always hostile and accusing
Toward the young Turnus, spoke up in reply:

"Hero of Troy, great in your fame, but greater
In battle, how could I extol you more—   125
First marveling at your warfare or your justice?
We'll gladly take your message to our city
And join you to our king Latinus—Fortune
Allowing. Turnus needs to make his own pacts.
We're happy to haul stones on our own shoulders   130
And raise the destined walls of your new Troy."
They all roared their assent when he had finished.
They made a twelve-day truce, and in its calm
Trojans and Latins roamed the woods and mountains
Unharmed together. Double axes rang   135
On high ash trees, and soaring pines were toppled.
Steadily, they split oak and fragrant cedar
With wedges; wagons groaned with mountain ash.

Now Rumor, who'd just told of Pallas' triumph
In Latium, flew with early news of anguish   140
To blight Evander's heart and house and city.
Snatching up torches for their ancient death rites,
The Arcadians swarmed the gate. A row of flames
Stretched down the road; light split the land in two.
The retinue of Trojans joined their ranks   145
Of mourning. Matrons saw them reach the houses,
And set the town alight with shouts of grief.
No one was strong enough to hold Evander.
He pushed into the crowd, where the bier rested,
And fell on Pallas, crying, clinging, groaning.   150
At last his anguish let a few words through:
"Pallas, this isn't what you promised me,
Caution in trusting wild Mars with your life.
But I knew how a first campaign can be—
The sweet allure of glory when it's new.   155
Oh, pitiful first offering, hard first lesson
In war so close at hand. Not one god heard

My prayers and pledges. You, the blessèd spirit
Of my wife, how lucky not to feel this pain.
I've triumphed over fate—outlived my son.   160
If only I had gone along and buried
My own life in the spears of the Rutulians,
And this procession brought me home—not Pallas!
Trojans, you're not to blame, and not our friendship
Or treaty. This was fated for my old age.   165
Though he was bound to die, there will be comfort:
He killed so many thousands of the Volscians
And fell while leading Trojans into Latium.
And Pallas, I could wish no worthier rites
Than good Aeneas and the Trojan lords,   170
The Tuscan captains, and their whole force give you.
They bring huge trophies of the men you slaughtered.
Turnus would stand here too, a log with weapons,
Were he as young as you, with your years' strength.
But my grief mustn't hinder Trojan warfare.   175
Go, tell your king that, with my Pallas gone,
I keep my hated life because he knows
His sword owes Turnus to this son and father.
His luck, his heroism are for this.
My fate forbids me joy in life—but let me   180
Bring my son word, among the dead below."

Meanwhile, Dawn raised her nurturing light and summoned
Wretched mankind back to its work and hardship.
On the curved shore, Tarchon and the lord Aeneas
Built pyres where everyone might bring his dead,   185
According to tradition. Kindling black flames,
They hid the towering sky in foggy darkness.
In their bright armor, soldiers marched three times
Around the lighted pyres. Three times the horsemen
Circled the dismal fires and raised their wails.   190
Their tears rained on the weapons and the earth,

And warriors' cries and horn blasts struck the sky.
Some threw in plunder torn from slaughtered Latins:
Helmets and fine swords, bridles, wheels that once seethed
Against their axles. Other men gave gifts 195
The dead knew: their own shields and losing weapons.
Oxen were sacrificed to Death on all sides.
Bristled wild boars and loot from every pasture
Bled from their throats into the fire. The beach
Was full of friends who watched friends burn and nursed 200
The half-dead pyres and clung there till damp night
Wheeled round a sky bejeweled with burning stars.
Elsewhere the Latins too, in desolation,
Built countless pyres. Out of the throng of bodies,
Some were interred, some carried to the country 205
Nearby, and others sent back to the city.
The rest they burned, a heap of muddled carnage,
Uncounted and unhonored. Ravaged fields
Were glowing with an avid crowd of fires.
A third dawn swept away the chill of darkness. 210
The mourners leveled jumbled bones and ash piles
And heaped the warm earth on them in a mound.

But in the homes of rich Latinus' city
The long-drawn shrieks of mourning were the greatest.
Here mothers and their sons' poor wives and sisters, 215
Tenderly sorrowing, and orphaned children
Cursed the disastrous war for Turnus' wedding:
He ought to fight it out—since he demanded
Italy's kingship and the highest honors.
Drances was there to goad them on, attesting 220
That Turnus had been challenged—no one else.
Yet Turnus had his various supporters;
He sheltered in the glory of the great queen—
And could rely on fame from his own trophies.
And now, amid the flames of this contention, 225

Came this: from Diomedes' famous city
The envoys brought an answer: the huge effort
Had failed; the fervid pleas, the gifts of gold
Did nothing—"They must find another ally,
Or ask the Trojan ruler for a truce."   230
The massive blow crushed even King Latinus.
The anger of the gods and these fresh tombs
Left no doubt: it was fate that brought Aeneas.
Therefore he summoned all his people's leaders,
His council, for a meeting in his halls.   235
They streamed together to the palace, filling
The streets, and as the eldest and the king,
Grim-faced Latinus took the central seat.
He asked to hear what answer had come back
From the Aetolian city, every detail   240
From start to finish. Then a call for silence,
And Venulus obediently began:
"Citizens, we came safely through our journey
To Diomedes in his Argive camp   *Greek hero @Troy*
And clasped the hand that brought Troy's kingdom down.   245
Where he'd conquered, he was laying out Argyripa
(Named for his clan), near Iapygian Garganus.
They showed us in and gave us leave to speak.
We proffered gifts and told our names and country,
And who made war on us, and why we'd come   250
To Arpi. With a tranquil face, he answered:
'O ancient, fortunate Italian races,
Kingdoms of Saturn. After your long peace,
What lures you, what incites you into war?
All of us who laid waste to Troy have paid   255
Horribly for our crimes throughout the world.
(And what of warriors under Simois' waters,
And our sufferings beneath those lofty walls?)
Priam would weep for us! Witness the storm
Minerva sent, and the vengeful cliff Caphereus.   260

We're scattered to the world's ends—Menelaus Husband (cuckholded) of Helen of Troy
Clear out to Proteus' columns, and Ulysses
To the Cyclopes at Etna. And the short reign
Of Neoptolemus? The shattered household
Of Idomeneus? The Locrians in Libya?   265
The Mycenean, leader of all the Greeks,
Arrived home for his evil wife to butcher:
He'd conquered Asia, but her lover lurked.
The gods begrudged me my ancestral altars—
The wife I yearn for—Calydon in its beauty.   270
I'm hounded even now by grisly visions
Of my friends changed into birds, roaming the streams
And winging skyward—monstrous punishment:
The cliffs re-echo with their sobbing calls—
But what was I expecting since the moment   275
I lost my mind and stabbed at a divine form,
Profaning Venus' right hand with a wound?
No, don't urge more such battles—not on me.
Since Troy was overthrown, I have no quarrel
With Trojans. I did not enjoy those struggles.   280
These gifts you bring me from your country—take them
To Aeneas. I have fought him hand to hand,
Faced his cruel weapons. I know—so believe me—
How high he rears behind his shield, how fiercely
His spear whirls. Had Mount Ida's country bred   285
Two more like him, Troy could have visited
On the Greek towns the mourning meant for Troy.
All that long siege of stubborn Ilium,
Ten years of victory stalling and retreating,
We owed to Hector and Aeneas only—   290
Both known for bravery and skill in war,
But one more pious. Clasp hands, make a treaty:
You have the chance. Avoid a clash of arms.'
Sovereign, that sovereign sends you this reply,
And gives his view of this momentous war."   295

Immediately, conflicting, anxious words
Raced among the Italians, like the roar
Of torrents choked by boulders, like the banks
Echoing back the clatter of the current.
But when the nervous crowd again grew silent,   300
The high-throned king called on the gods, then spoke.
"Latins, an early plan to meet this crisis
Would have been better than to call a meeting
Now, when the enemy blockades our walls.
How can we fight with children of the gods,   305
With these unwearying, unconquered heroes?
They're beaten, but they never put their swords down!
Aetolian allies? Give that hope up now.
We all have hopes—you see what this one's worth.
Everything else that's ruined in our cause   310
You have before your own eyes—you can touch it.
I don't blame anyone. You've reached the limits
Of courage, fought with all our nation's strength.
Now listen while I tell you in a few words
The judgment that, through all my doubts, I've come to.   315
I have an old tract by the Tuscan river.
It stretches west, past the Sicanian border.
Auruncans and Rutulians plow and sow
Its hard hills; on the roughest heights their herds graze.
I'll give this and a strip of piny summit   320
To the Trojans for their friendship. We must make
Fair terms with them and let them share the kingdom.
If they're so eager, they can raise their walls
And settle. If it's other lands they want,
And they're allowed to leave our soil, we'll build them   325
Twenty ships from our own Italian oak.
If they can man more, wood is on the coast.
How many boats, and what kind, they must say.
We will supply the labor, bronze, and dockyards.
I'll also send the hundred noblest Latins   330

To take the news and finalize the treaty.
These will present the olive boughs of peace,
And gold and ivory in hundredweights,
And the robe and throne that signify this kingship.
Confer together, save us from disaster."   335
Drances, still hostile, rose; half-hidden envy
Of Turnus' stature galled him; he was lavish
With his goods, and in his eloquence a hero—
But not in war—a well-regarded counselor,
And a rabble-rouser (gloriously descended   340
From his mother's side, obscurely from his father's).
He now spoke, stoking up the fire of hatred:
"Good king, to all of us your plan makes sense.
What can I add? Everyone should acknowledge
Our town's way forward, but they're all too frightened.   345
He needs to stop his rants and let me speak.
This man is evil, a disastrous leader.
(I'll say it, though he threatens me with death.)
All those fine captains died, we sank in grief,
When he attacked the Trojan fortress, shaking   350
His sword at heaven—though prepared to run.
Add one gift to the many that you send
And promise to the Trojans, peerless king:
You are a father—get a splendid son
Through your daughter's marriage. Don't let any threats   355
Deter you. Make the bond of peace eternal.
And if we're terrified, let's make our pleas
To Turnus here, and ask him, as a favor,
To let this king and country have their rights.
You are a curse on Latium! Why keep throwing   360
Your hapless people into open danger?
Turnus, the war can't save us. We all beg you
For peace—which has one guarantee, so give it.
You say I hate you (shouldn't I?)—but see
I am the first to kneel. Pity your country.   365

Lay down your pride. You're beaten—you should go.
We're routed, slaughtered, so much land is razed—
If you want fame, and if your will's so hard,
And if you need a palace as a dowry,
Then dare to meet the enemy face to face.   370
But no: to get a royal wife for Turnus,
We'll scatter our cheap lives across the plain,
Unwept, unburied. If you have the strength
Or the courage that your fathers had, go face
Your challenger."   375
This kindled the ferocity of Turnus.
He growled, and these words broke from deep within him:
"Drances, your eloquence just overflows
Whenever war needs fighters. You arrive first
At every senate. Your majestic words   380
Fill it while you stay safe, while earthworks bar
The enemy, and the moats don't brim with blood.
Thunder on in your usual way—accuse me
Of cowardice when as many heaps of Trojans
Have died by *your* hand, when *your* splendid trophies   385
Litter the plain. Try for yourself what courage
And energy can do. We needn't look far:
The enemies are all around our walls.
Shall we go face them now? Or will your fighting
Stay limited to feet that run away   390
And a gusty tongue? You worm—
I'm beaten? Who could say that if he saw
The Tiber swelling with the blood of Trojans,
The armor stripped from the Arcadians,
And Evander's house brought down, without an heir.   395
Beaten? To giant Bitias, to Pandarus
And the thousands I subdued and sent to Hades,
Though I was penned up in the enemies' walls?
The war can't save us? Idiot, give that warning
To the Trojan and yourself. Go on, keep muddling   400

Our plans with terror: a twice-beaten nation
So powerful, our Latin arms so frail!
Myrmidon chiefs, Achilles from Larissa,
And Diomedes quake at Trojan warfare?
The Aufidus bolts uphill, from the Adriatic?   405
There's more—this cunning bastard, when I taunt him,
Shams fear; it gives his allegations force.
My hand won't take a soul like yours—don't worry.
Keep it there, living in your worthless self.
Now to your grave deliberations, Father.   410
If you can place no further hope in fighting,
If we're abandoned, if from one retreat
Ruin prevails, and Fortune can't turn back,
Let's hold our weak hands out and beg for peace.
I long for any trace of our past bravery,   415
And I prefer the man who won't surrender,
Who'd rather bite the dust, once and for all:
He has the most heart, he's most blessed in hardship.
But we still have supplies, and men to call on,
And allied towns and tribes in Italy;   420
And the Trojans got their glory with a bloodbath
(The same storm fell on them, they have their losses).
Why pitifully give in already, quaking
Down to our toes before the trumpet sounds?
Often the changing work of shifting time   425
Brings good again. Commonly, Fortune alters,
And sets her victims back on steady ground.
Arpi and its Aetolian king won't help us;
Lucky Tolumnius, Messapus, leaders
From many towns will. The picked men of Latium   430
And Laurentum's farms will get no petty fame.
And there's Camilla of the glorious Volscians,
Leading her mounted squadrons, bright with bronze.
If the Trojans challenge me to single combat,
And you say yes, since I'm our stumbling block,   435

I'm willing. Victory hasn't yet rebuffed me:
Any risk that I have to take is worth it.
He's greater than Achilles, and wears armor
Like his that Vulcan made? I still will face him.
I'm Turnus, I'm the equal of my fathers.   440
To you all and my father-in-law, Latinus,
I've vowed my life. I beg for single combat!
I don't want Drances paying with his death
For the gods' rage—or getting any glory."
And so they wrangled in this time of danger.   445

Meanwhile, Aeneas moved his camp and forces.
The news sped through the palace, spreading uproar;
The city soon was overwhelmed with terror:
The Trojans and the Tuscans had deployed
At the Tiber and come sweeping down the plain.   450
The common people were appalled and stricken—
And stung into an even greater anger
And feverish calls for arms—youths roared for arms,
And fathers wept in fear. A racket rose
To the sky from everywhere, a storm of discord;   455
As a flock clatters, settling in some tall grove,
Or swans call hoarsely over sounding shallows
Of the Padusa river, filled with fish.
Turnus then seized his chance, "Yes, citizens!
Let's call a meeting and sit praising peace   460
While they invade our land." He said no more,
But rushed away, out of the towering building.
"Volusus, call the Volscian bands to arms!
Bring the Rutulians! Coras, with your brother
And Messapus, spread your horsemen on the plain.   465
Block the approaches too, and man the towers.
The rest can follow me in the attack."
Immediately, the town rushed to the walls,
And even Lord Latinus fled the meeting

In the crisis, and put off his great endeavors—   470
Contrite that he'd not taken in Aeneas
Straight off, as son-in-law and city sharer.
They dug moats at the gates and hauled in boulders
And spikes. The trumpet hoarsely called for blood.
Everyone came out: mothers and their children   475
Stood on the walls in an uneven line.
To Pallas' temple on the heights the queen drove   *Minerva*
With offerings, and matrons thronged around her.
Beside her was the girl Lavinia
(Cause of the crisis), looking down with fine eyes.   480
Women climbed to the shrine with gifts of incense,
And their grief echoed from the lofty door:
"Strong-weaponed ruler of war, Tritonian virgin,
Shatter the Phrygian pirate's spear and stretch him
On the earth, face down before our city's gates."   485
Fierce and impatient, Turnus dressed for battle.
Already he had on a ruddy breastplate
Bristling with scales, and gold greaves—though his head
Was still bare—and a sword hung at his side.
Gleaming with gold, he raced from the high stronghold   490
In thrilled anticipation of the fight,
As a stallion breaks his rope, bolts from the barn,
And gains the open flatlands, finally free,
And gallops to the mares that crowd the pastures,
Or to the river that he used to bathe in,   495
Arching his neck exuberantly high,
While his mane plays across his neck and withers.
Royal Camilla with her Volscian force
Hurried to meet him, Right outside the gates
She now dismounted; her battalion likewise   500
Slid down onto their feet before she spoke:
"If bravery brings the confidence it should,
I'll undertake to face Aeneas' horsemen,
And ride alone against the mounted Tuscans:

I'll go to meet the hazards of this war.   505
You take a stand on foot and guard the walls."
Turnus stared at the formidable girl:
"You're Italy's glory! Could I ever thank you
Or decently repay you? But we know
Your matchless spirit: let me share your efforts.   510
Rumors, backed up by scouts, tell us Aeneas
Has insolently sent ahead light horsemen
To scour the plains, and he himself is coming
To the city by a steep unguarded ridge.
I plan an ambush at a covered path   515
Of the forest, with armed troops at both ways out.
Draw up your troops to meet the Tuscan horse charge,
With keen Messapus, Latin cavalry,
And Tiburtus' band. You take command as well."
He roused Messapus and the allied captains   520
Likewise, and then set off to meet his enemy.
There is a twisting valley, a good trap,
Darkly and thickly overgrown; two cliffs
Crowd from its sides; a wispy path leads in,
And at both ends the jaws are grim and narrow.   525
Above, among the towering lookout places,
There is a hidden clearing, a good refuge
To attack from, swooping from the left and right,
And boulders can be rolled down from the slopes.
Swiftly, by a familiar route, the young man   530
Arrived and took his lurking woodland post.

Where the gods live above, Latona's child
Now spoke these words of sorrow to swift Opis,
One of her sacred retinue of virgins.
"For all the good they'll do her, my Camilla   535
Puts on my arms and marches to cruel war.
She is my favorite, and my love for her
Is no new charm or impulse in my soul.

Deposed through hatred of his tyranny,
Metabus left Privernum's ancient city.   540
Escaping from rebellion into exile,
He took his baby, who was called Camilla,
A small change from her mother's name, Casmilla.
He made for the bleak woods along the mountains
With the infant in his arms. Volscian troops swarmed,   545
Savagely sniping at him from all sides.
The Amasenus foamed beyond its banks
And trapped him—so much rain had burst the clouds.
He was prepared to swim but hesitated
In fear for his dear burden. He was forced   550
To make a rapid choice among his options:
In his strong hand the warrior had a huge spear
Of seasoned hard oak with a mass of knots.
He wrapped his child in woodland cork-tree bark
And deftly tied her halfway down the shaft,   555
Poised it in his great fist, and called to heaven:
'Latona's pure, kind daughter, forest dweller,
A father vows his child to you. It's your spear
She first holds; at your mercy, she's escaping.
I trust her to the hazardous air, so claim her!'   560
His arm drew back; he sent the weapon hurtling.
The water roared. Above the rapid river
Flew poor Camilla on the hissing spear.
And Metabus, as the enemy band drew close,
Dove in and—triumph!—plucked Diana's gift,   565
His daughter, from the other grassy bank.
No walls, no homes of cities took him in
(But such a savage wouldn't have submitted).
In lonely heights, where shepherds live, his life passed.
And there, among the thickets and the beasts' lairs,   570
He milked a half-wild brood mare from the herd
Into his daughter's tender lips to nurse her.
And when the baby's first steps pressed the ground,

He placed a sharp spear in her hand and hung
A bow and quiver from her tiny shoulder.   575
Instead of a gold headband and a long robe,
A tiger skin was on her head and back.
Already her soft hand flung childish weapons,
And she could whirl a sling on its smooth leash
To bring down a Strymonian crane or swan.   580
Throughout the Tuscan cities many mothers
Wanted her for their sons. She was content
With me, and longed to stay a virgin huntress,
Untouched. If only she were not caught up
In warfare and in challenging the Trojans—   585
She would be with me still, a cherished comrade.
Go, since a bitter fate is tracking her,
Glide from these heights, visit the Latin country,
Where the pitiful, ill-omened fight is starting,
And take this quiver: an avenging arrow   590
Must claim as much blood from the soldier wounding
Her sacred body—Trojan or Italian.
I'll take her poor corpse in a cloud, its armor
Unplundered, and entomb it in her country."
Opis sailed lightly down through airy heaven,   595
Veiled in a storm cloud—but her weapons rang.
The Trojan company now approached the walls,
With Tuscan chiefs and all the cavalry
Counted into their units. Horses pranced
And neighed and swerved and yanked resisting reins   600
Everywhere on the plain. Bristles of iron,
A burning haze of spear points, hid the broad plain.
The Latins and Messapus hurried forward;
Camilla's wing and Coras with his brother
Appeared among them, charging, thrusting spears   605
Forward and back, and shaking javelins.
The men and neighing horses blazed ahead,
But stopped within a spear's throw of each other;

Then raised a shout and urged their stormy horses
Into the center. Weapons poured from all sides   610
As thick as snow, and wove the sky in shadow.
Aconteus and Tyrrhenus sped together
With a shove of spears, and were the first to fall.
Their horses' breasts collided with a loud crack
Of broken bones, and like a thunderbolt   615
Or catapulted rock, Aconteus
Was hurled away. His soul seeped through the air.
The Latin army turned in sudden panic,
Shields on their backs, and galloped to the walls.
Asilas led the Trojan squads that chased them.   620
Nearing the gates, the Latins gave the war cry
Again, and turned their horses' pliant necks.
The Trojans now gave rein and fell far back—
As the surf swells back and forth in its assault,
Rushes to land, with foamy waves on high rocks,   625
Arches to flood the beach to its far edge,
And then retreats, but pulls the spinning stones
In its froth; the water thins, the shore is bare.
Twice, Tuscans drove Rutulians toward the city;
Twice they were sent back, with their shields behind them.   630
But the third encounter saw their whole front lines
Embroiled, as every man fixed on another.
Truly the dying groaned then. In blood marshes
Rolled bodies, arms, and half-dead horses mottled
With human gore, as bitter fighting surged.   635
Orsilochus shrank from Remulus but launched
At his horse. The spear point lodged below its ear.
The beast, in rage and agony, reared high,
Lashing its forelegs while its fallen master
Writhed on the ground. Catillus took down Iollas,   640
Then Herminius, great in weapons, bulk, and spirit.
His torso and his tawny head were naked—
Fearless, he left his giant body open

4/6/19

To attack. The spear transfixed his massive shoulders,
Quivering; he was doubled up in pain.   645
Black gore flowed everywhere. They fought, they stabbed,
They killed, and in their wounds sought glorious death.
Like an Amazon, Camilla with her quiver,   *Ally of Turnus*
And one breast bared, reveled amid the slaughter,
Now showering a hail of pliant spears,   650
Now with a strong ax in her tireless fist.
On her shoulder clanged the gold bow of Diana.
Even when forced to give ground and pursued,
She turned around and aimed her arrows backward.
Her retinue was choice: the girls Larina,   655
Tarpeia, and Tulla shaking her bronze ax—
Italians bright Camilla picked to serve her
Staunchly, her ornaments in peace and war:
Like Amazons who gallop in the shallows
Of Thermodon and fight in painted armor   660
With Hippolyta; or like the ranks of women
With crescent shields who wildly whoop the praises
Of Penthesilea as she comes from battle.
Hard girl, who did you first unhorse, who last?
How many lay there dying from your blows?   665
Clytius' son Eunaeus was the first:
Her long fir shaft impaled his naked chest.
He spewed blood, falling, gnawed the gory earth,
And writhed and curled around his wound in death.
Then she killed two, when Liris' horse collapsed   670
And threw him as he grappled for the reins,
And Pagasus stretched a bare right hand to catch him.
Both plummeted together; then Amastrus
And Hippotas' son. She chased Harpalycus, Chromis,
Tereus, and Demophoön with hard-flung missiles.   675
For every spear hurled from the virgin's hand,
A Phrygian warrior died. Ornytus, far off,
Had an Apulian mount and curious armor.

To go to war he covered his broad shoulders
With skin ripped from a bull and kept his head safe   680
In a wolf's enormous, gaping mouth and white teeth.
His weapon was a country pike. He shifted
Through the middle of the throng, a head above it.
She caught him easily, amid the rout,
And spoke in hate above his skewered body.   685
"Tuscan, you thought that you were in the woods,
Hunting? This day, a woman's weapons prove
Your boasts wrong. Yet Camilla's spear has killed you:
You'll take this glory to your fathers' ghosts."
Straight off, she killed the giant Trojans Butes   690
And Orsilochus, spearing Butes from behind
On the gleaming white defenseless strip of neck
As he rode, dangling his spear from his left shoulder.
Chased by Orsilochus in a great circle,
She doubled back inside it—now she chased him—   695
Then rose to hammer with her sturdy ax
Through his armor and his bones, though he kept begging
For his life. His warm brains splattered on his face.
The warrior son of Aunus, from the Apennines—
A great Ligurian, while fate kept him lying—   700
Stood frozen when he found himself before her.
He knew he couldn't turn aside the princess
Or get away, however fast his mount.
Quickly he plotted what to do and spoke:
"What's so remarkable? A woman trusting   705
Her strong horse for escape? Send him away.
Arm for a fair fight, hand to hand, on foot.
You'll soon find out how emptily you boasted."
Stung with the taunt, she handed off her horse
In rage, and took a bold stance, armed like him   710
With a foot soldier's naked sword and plain shield.
The young man thought his trickery had worked.
Without a moment's pause, he wheeled his horse

And sped it in retreat with iron spurs.
"Ligurian, full of nothing but yourself,   715
The slick ploys of your country won't succeed here
And take you home safe to the swindler Aunus."
The young girl spoke. On foot, as swift as fire,
She ran his horse down. Facing it, she seized
The reins and took his hated blood in vengeance,   720
As easily as a sacred falcon soars
From its cliff, pursues a dove in lofty clouds,
Catches it tight and guts it with hooked talons,
Till blood and torn-out feathers fall from heaven.
The father of gods and mortals, sitting throned   725
On Olympus' peak, observed the scene with keen eyes.
The patriarch sharply spurred Etruscan Tarchon
To fury and the savagery of battle.
Through slaughter and collapsing lines the man rode,
With varied shouts to goad the squads. He called   730
Each man by name, regrouping them for battle.
"Etruscans, will your cowardice ever shame you?
What terror grips your cringing hearts today?
A woman drives our ranks in rout and chaos.
Don't you know what to do with swords and spears?   735
For love and your campaigns at night, you're eager,
For dances Bacchus' curving flute announces.
The tables will be rich with food and wine
(Your guiding passion)—when an augur sanctions
Our victory rites, and a fat offering calls you   740
To the tall groves." He wheeled, spurred toward the center,
Prepared to die. He wildly charged at Venulus
And tore him from his horse. He clasped his enemy
With all his strength and sped away. A shout
Rose to the sky, and all the Latins watched: 745
Tarchon blazed down the broad field with his captive,
Arms and all; and he snapped the spearhead off
And groped for some unguarded place to thrust it

Lethally. Venulus fought back and blocked
Stabs to his throat. Strength against strength, they grappled: 750
Like a tawny eagle soaring with a snake
Snatched from the ground and fastened in its claws—
The wounded thing flails with its twisting coils,
Raises its spiky scales and rears its head,
Hissing—its captor gouges at these struggles   755
With a hooked beak, while beating through the high air:
So Tarchon fetched his prize from Tibur's front lines,
Elated. When his Tuscans saw this exploit,
They charged. Fate's hand had come to rest on Arruns.
Craftily he kept circling swift Camilla,   760
Clutching his spear and looking for his best chance.
Wherever the girl raged through heavy fighting,
Arruns came after, softly tracking her.
Where she beat down the enemy and withdrew,
The young man slyly turned his horse to follow.   765
He tested this and that way, all around,
Shaking his deadly spear, unstoppable.
Chloreus, Cybele's votary, once her priest,
Happened to stand out, in bright Phrygian armor.
He spurred a foam-mouthed horse whose leather trappings   770
Had bronze scales linked by gold, in feather patterns.
He wore exotic red and splendid purple
And shouldered a gold Lycian bow, with arrows
From Sicily. The helmet of the priest
Was gold, a gold brooch caught the rustling folds   775
Of his saffron linen cloak. Embroidery
Covered his tunic and barbarian leggings.
The huntress, longing to nail Trojan weapons
On a temple door, or wear proud captive gold,
Picked the man out of all that strife and tracked him   780
Blindly and recklessly across the phalanx—
On fire with a woman's love of plunder.
This was when Arruns saw his chance to trap her

At last. He raised his spear and prayed to heaven:
"Holy Soracte's keeper, great Apollo,   785
Tuscans revere you most; we feed your fire
From the pine heap, and go barefoot through the flames
And deep coals, trusting in our piety.
All-powerful father, let my weapon wipe out
Our army's shame. I want no arms, no trophy—   790
No spoils at all. I'll get my glory elsewhere.
If I can strike this bitch down, I'll return
Gladly obscure to the cities of my homeland."
Apollo heard. Part of the prayer he granted;
The rest he scattered to the fluttering breeze.   795
He let him kill Camilla in an ambush,
But not return again to his proud nation.
That plea went gusting to the southern gales.
So when the spear he launched snapped through the air,
All of the Volscians, avidly alerted,   800
Looked toward their princess. But she didn't notice
The air, the sound, the spear out of the sky,
Till it reached its target under her bared breast,
Drove deep, and lodged, and drank her virgin blood.
Dismayed, her escort ran in as she fell,   805
To hold her up. Arruns' alarm was greatest:
Fear marred his joy. He fled, no longer willing
To trust his spear or meet the young girl's weapons—
As, far ahead of hateful armed pursuers,
A wolf slinks quickly off to trackless heights;   810
He knows how rash he was to kill a shepherd
Or large ox; his tail shakes between his legs
And strokes his belly as he seeks the woods:
So Arruns, in his terror, slunk from view
And merged with the armed crowd, content with safety.   815
Dying, she yanked the spear, but in the deep wound
Between her ribs the iron point was stuck.
She bled, she slumped down, and her eyes were closing

In death's chill. From her face the blush was gone.
Breathing her last, she singled Acca out   820
And spoke to her—this was the most devoted
Of her comrades, and her only confidante.
"Sister, my strength is gone. This bitter wound
Has finished me. It's darkening all around.
Make your escape—take Turnus one last message: 825
'Step in, and keep the Trojans from the city.'
And now good-bye." The reins had dropped. She tumbled
To earth and was released from her cold body
Slowly. She bent her head and laid it down,
Conquered by death, and let her weapons go.   830
With an angry groan, her life fled to the shades.
Then an immense shout rose and struck the gold stars.
When Camilla fell, the fight grew raw. The whole force
Of Trojans, Tuscan chiefs, and Evander's horsemen
From Arcadia stormed massively together.   835
Opis, Diana's spy, had sat a long time
On the mountaintop and calmly watched the battle.
But when, among the far-off shouting frenzy
Of troops, a ruthless death struck down Camilla,
She groaned and spoke from deep within her heart: 840
"This is too hard a punishment—poor girl—
For your attempt to hound the Teucrians!
Useless, your lonely worship of Diana
In the thickets and our quiver on your shoulder.
But even at the end, your queen won't leave you   845
Unhonored. The whole world will praise your death
And know you didn't shamefully lack vengeance.
Whoever gave you that outrageous wound
Should die—and will." Below the mountain, shadowed
By holm oaks, was the massive burial mound   850
Of Dercennus, who once ruled in old Laurentum.
Swiftly and gracefully, the goddess leapt there,
And stood and gazed at Arruns from on high.

His armor glittered, and he swelled with rash pride.
"Why do you turn and go? Come over here,   855
And get the prize Camilla's death has earned you.
But are you worth an arrow of Diana?"
The Thracian goddess took a speedy shaft
From her gold quiver. Full of rage, she drew
The bow out till its curving ends converged.   860
Her right hand on the string against her breast
Was level with the left, at the iron point.
In the same short moment Arruns heard the sizzle
Of the arrow's flight and felt its metal lodge.
His comrades didn't notice, and they left him   865
Groaning his last breaths on the dusty plain.
Opis flew off to heavenly Olympus.
Camilla's light-armed squadron fell back first,
The Rutulians next, with keen Atinas, routed.
The leaders scattered from their regiments;   870
Everyone galloped toward the walls and safety.
Nobody could hold out against the onrush
Of deadly Trojan arms, no one could fight them,
But threw their unstrung bows on weary shoulders;
The speeding hoofbeats shook that soft-earthed plain.   875
Black dust rolled toward the walls, a murky tumult,
And mothers on the watchtowers beat their breasts
And raised a female cry clear to the stars.
The enemy swarmed in, where they could hound
The first who thundered through the open gates.   880
Trapped in their sorry deaths right at the threshold,
Their snug homes and their nation's walls around them,
They choked out life, impaled. Men closed the portals,
And didn't dare let in their pleading comrades.
Now there was butchery, as some defended   885
The gates, and others ran against their weapons.
Their weeping parents watched the locked-out soldiers,
Shoved by the rout, roll headlong into ditches,

Or spur and slack their reins to batter blindly
At the unyielding barriers of the gates.   890
The very mothers on the walls, who'd witnessed
Camilla's love of country, tried to match her.
In their alarm, they hurled down posts of oak wood
And stakes singed hard in place of iron weapons.
They longed to die first in the town's defense.   895
Acca found Turnus in the woods and gave him
The brutal news of that tremendous havoc:
The Volscian lines were smashed, Camilla fallen;
The enemy swept along in pitiless triumph,
Unhindered, and the rout had reached the walls.   900
In rage (and by Jove's hard will), he deserted
His station in the overgrown hill forest.
He'd scarcely left his lookout for the plains,
When Father Aeneas reached the unwatched pass,
Emerged from the dark woods and crossed the ridge.   905
Both hurried toward the town with all their forces—
And no long measure of a gap between them.
Aeneas spotted the Laurentian columns
Down the dust-smoking plain, and just then Turnus,
Hearing the tramp of feet and snort of horses,
Recognized fierce Aeneas under arms.   910
They would have made an instant trial of battle,
But rosy Phoebus plunged his weary team
In the Spanish sea, and day slipped into night.
They camped before the town and built stockades.

BOOK 12

As soon as Turnus saw the Latins shattered,
And felt their stares demand he keep his pledge,
His spirit filled with unrelenting flame—
As on the plains of Punic Africa
A lion wounded in the breast by hunters   5
Relishes going into war at last,
Tosses his mane and snaps the planted spear,
Unflinching, roaring with his bloody mouth.
So Turnus' savagery was set alight.
Disordered, uncontrolled, he told the king: 10
"I'm ready now. Why should Aeneas' cowards
Go back on their agreement? I'll go face him.
Bring offerings, Father, and lay down the terms.
I'll send the Trojan (on the run from Asia)
To hell, before a Latin audience,   15
One sword refuting all our shame, or else
We'll be his slaves, Lavinia his bride."
Latinus kept his manner calm and answered: Lavinia's
                                                          father

"Indomitable young man, your fierce courage
Must weigh against my heavy obligation   20
To take great care in looking to the future.
You have your father Daunus' realm. You've captured
Many towns. I have gold and open hands.
Other unmarried girls, of quite fine families,
Live throughout Latium. Let me be straightforward.   25
I'll use harsh words, but you must take them in.
My child was not for any former suitor: *Lavinia*
Divine and human prophets made this clear.
Our common blood, my love for you, the tears
Of my poor wife prevailed: I broke all bonds,   30
Seized my new son's bride, started godless war.
Since then you see how fights and crises dog me—
And much of this great hardship falls on you.
We lost two battles—Italy's hopes are dangling
From this city; but our blood still warms the Tiber;   35
Our bones have turned these miles of grassland white.
What madness keeps me changing and retreating?
If you were killed, I would adopt these allies.
Shouldn't I end the conflict now and spare you?
Your Rutulian clan, the rest of Italy—   40
What would they say if (fate forbid!) I lured you
To death, while you were chasing this alliance?
Think of war's risks and pity your old father
Far off and grieving in his native Ardea."
These words did nothing to allay his passion;   45
The treatment only made the sickness worse.
As soon as he could speak, he said: "Kind father,
It would be kinder not to be concerned
And let me make my bargain: life for glory.
And yet the spears I throw are not so feeble.   50
The wounds that I inflict don't fail to bleed.
He'll have no goddess-mother there to veil
His flight in womanly clouds and empty shadows."

The queen burst into tears, in deadly panic,
And held her child's fierce suitor in her arms.   55
"If you regard me—and these tears—at all,
Turnus (my only hope now, my one solace
In old age; and Latinus' rule and honor—
And our whole tottering house—are on your shoulders),
Tell me you won't fight hand to hand with Trojans.   60
I have a stake in how this combat ends.
Along with you, I'll leave this hateful daylight,
No captive of my son-in-law Aeneas."
Lavinia was there and heard her mother.
The tears came pouring down her flaming cheeks,   65
Dashing across the heat of crimson blushes;
As a blood-purple dye stains Indian ivory,
Or roses bunched with lilies lend their shadow
Of red—these were the colors on the girl's face.
He stared, distressed by love, which stoked his passion   70
To fight, and spoke a few words to Amata:
"Mother, I beg you, do not let your tears
Be the omen sending me to this grim contest
Of Mars. I am not free to put off death.
Idmon, go and displease the Phrygian tyrant   75
With this message: when tomorrow's dawn first rises,
Blushing and driving her red chariot,
He must not lead his forces out: both armies
Can down their arms and let his blood or mine
End this. That's how we'll court Lavinia."   80
He hurried back inside. Where were his horses?
He smiled to see their whinnying impatience.
Orithyia's splendid presents to Pilumnus
Were swifter than the wind, whiter than snow.
Their drivers fussed around them busily,   85
Slapping their chests and combing their long manes.
Turnus himself strapped on a golden corselet
With pale bronze scales, angled his shield for action,

Took up his helmet with its horns and red crest—
And the sword the god of fire had forged for Daunus,   90
His father, and tempered in the stream of Styx.
On a huge column in the central hall
Leaned a strong spear, won from Auruncan Actor.
He seized and clenched it, brandished it, and shook it,
And cried, "My faithful servant, never shirking,   95
The time has come. Great Actor carried you,
And now it's Turnus. Let me throw him down,
Rip off his corselet with my powerful hand,
And smear dust on his Phrygian eunuch hair,
That drips with myrrh, that's crimped with iron tongs."   100
While he was raving, fire flashed from his eyes;
His face was all aflame and throwing sparks;
As an enraged bull bellows fearsomely,
And tries to vent his fury with his horns—
Charging against a tree trunk, jabbing wind—   105
And kicks up sand in prelude to the battle.
Equally fierce, in armor from his mother,
Aeneas roused his soul to martial rage,
Glad that the proffered pact would solve the conflict.
Now he assured his men and anxious Iulus   Aeneas' son   110
Of their destiny, and sent to King Latinus
A firm reply that set the terms for peace.

The dawn's first glow spread on the mountaintops
As the Sun's chariot rose from the ocean,
His horses' nostrils flaring, pouring light.   115
Beneath the splendid city's walls, the Trojans
And Rutulians measured out the fighting ground
And in the center piled up sod for altars
To their common gods. Some men, in sacred garlands,
And hooded with their cloaks, brought fire and water.   120
The Ausonian army flooded from the gate
In massive columns. Trojans and Etruscans

Streamed from their camp, with all their varied weapons,
As if grim Mars himself had summoned them.
Among them, captains galloped back and forth,   125
In the proud magnificence of gold and purple:
Mnestheus of Assaracus' line, Asilas
And Messapus, tamer of horses, Neptune's brave son.
At the signal, each withdrew to his assigned place,
Planted his spear and leaned his shield against it.   130
Eager to see, mothers, the unarmed plebs,
And weak old men came pouring out to fill
The towers and roofs, or stood in the high gateways.
But Juno looked out from the Alban hilltop
(Not famous yet—it wasn't even named)   135
And saw the field and both the armies, Trojan
And Laurentian, and the city of Latinus.
Now she addressed a fellow deity,
The sister of Turnus, who ruled sounding rivers
And lakes (the honor that the king of heaven   140
Had given for deflowering her by force).
"Cherished nymph, glory of the streams, you know
I favor you above all girls in Latium
Who've been with willful Jove and not enjoyed it.
I've gladly let you have your place in heaven.   145
Learn of the grief in store—but don't blame me.
With Fortune yielding and the Fates indulgent,
I shielded Turnus and your city walls.
But now I see the youth outmatched by fate.
An angry force draws near and brings his ending.   150
I cannot watch them make a pact or fight.
Would you dare help your brother at close quarters?
You should. Poor things, it still might turn out better."
At once, Juturna's face was streaming tears.
Repeatedly she struck her handsome breast.   155
"This is no time to cry," said Saturn's daughter.
"Run to your brother, save him, find a way,

Or stir up war and break the truce they've made.
I will support you." But this goading speech
Left the girl still in doubt, confused and stricken.   160
Meanwhile, the kings came out. Latinus' chariot
Was four-horsed, massive; and around his temples
Shone twelve gold rays, the emblem of the Sun,
His ancestor; while Turnus brandished two spears
With broad heads, as he drove his two white horses.   165
Aeneas, father of the Roman race,
His shield a star, his armor from divine hands,
Marched from his camp beside Ascanius,   *Aeneas'sn*
Rome's second hope. A priest in pure white robes
Brought out a piglet and an unshorn sheep   170
And made them stand before the flaming altar.
The leaders faced the rising sun. They scattered
Grain and salt, notched the foreheads of the victims
And poured out their libations on the altars.
Faithful Aeneas drew his sword and swore: 175
"I call the Sun to witness, and this land
For which I have endured so many hardships;
And the almighty father and his consort—
May she be kinder now, I pray—and great Mars,
Lord who twists every war beneath his power;   180
Rivers and trees, and everything we worship
In the sky's height, and in the blue of ocean:
If Turnus the Italian wins, we losers
Must migrate to the city of Evander.
Iulus will cede this land, Aeneas' people   185
Won't bring another war against this city.
If in this combat Victory sides with me
(I think it will; may the gods' power confirm this),
I will not make the Trojans overlords
Or claim the throne. With neither race the loser,   190
We'll forge a lasting bond, on equal terms.
I'll introduce our rites and gods. Latinus,

My father-in-law, can reign and keep his army,
While the Trojans build my town, Lavinium."
Aeneas had been first. Latinus followed,   195
His eyes on heaven, right hand to the stars.
"Aeneas, I too swear by earth, sea, stars,
Latona's twins, and Janus with two faces,
The power of gods below, and cruel Dis' temples.
Hear, Father, whose lightning bolt makes treaties binding: 200
I touch the altars; by the fire between us,
By the gods, our race will never break this treaty,
Whatever the result. No force will turn me
From my will, though land may flood into the sea
In chaos, heaven melt its way to hell;   205
As surely as this scepter"—in his right hand—
"Won't send out shoots with tender, shadowing leaves,
Once it's been severed from its mother earth
And had its boughs and foliage stripped away—
It was a tree: a craftsman now has wrapped it   210
In handsome bronze, for Latin kings to carry."
So they affirmed the pact before the nobles.
And now they cut the consecrated beasts' throats
Above the flame, pulled out the throbbing guts,
And piled the altars with the laden platters.   215
The Rutulians had long since thought the fight
Unfair; a welter of emotions filled them—
Worse now that they could see they were outmatched—
Still worse when Turnus silently stepped forward,
With downcast eyes, to pray before the altar—   220
His face so young, his youthful form so pale.
When Juturna, Turnus' sister, sensed the murmurs
Were growing, and the crowd confused and shaken,
She disguised herself as Carmers (this man's lineage
Was splendid, and his father known for courage,   225
And he himself tempestuous in battle)
And sowed all sorts of rumors through the army—

She knew what she was doing—and harangued it:
"Rutulians, what's this shameful sacrifice
Of a single man? Aren't we a match for them?   230
Look at how few there are—Arcadians, Trojans,
And Tuscans, Turnus' fated enemies.
Would half of us have one opponent each?
Turnus will have the same immortal glory
As the gods themselves, to whom he's vowed his life.   235
We'll lose our native land, we'll be enslaved,
Since we sat dawdling on the battlefield."
The flame these words set in the soldiers' hearts
Grew and grew. Mutters snaked across the ranks.
Latins, Laurentians changed, and even those   240
Who just before had hoped for peace and safety
Now longed for arms, prayed for the truce to break,
And sympathized with all of Turnus' wrongs.
More forcefully, Juturna gave a sign
In the sky's heights, of just the character   245
To be misread and muddle the Italians:
Jove's tawny eagle chased a shrieking mob
Of shore birds in the ruddy sky—a winged rout—
And then went swooping to the waves and captured
The leader of the swans in his cruel talons.   250
The Italians were transfixed. The other birds
Now rallied with a cry—amazing sight.
The sky was darkened by their cloud of wings
As they pursued their enemy. The eagle,
Harried and weighed down, let his plunder fall   255
To the river, and fled deep into the clouds.
The Rutulians hailed this omen with a shout
And stirred to fight. Tolumnius the augur
Spoke first: "This is the thing I often prayed for,
The gods' sign—welcome! Follow me to battle—   260
Poor people, terrorized by this invader,
Like weak birds, as he sacks your coasts—the outrage!

He'll hoist his sails to get away—a long voyage.
With a united purpose, close your ranks
And fight to save the prince who's taken from you."   265
He spoke, and ran ahead to fling his spear
At his enemies. The well-aimed cornel shaft
Hissed through the air. A shout rose instantly
From every part of the excited crowd.
The spear flew toward the nine magnificent sons   270
A single virtuous Etruscan wife
Had given to Arcadian Gylippus.
It struck one in the waist (right at the pin
That held the chafing sword belt on the belly)—
A very handsome youth with shining armor—   275
Passed through his ribs and pitched him on the sand.
The brave line of his brothers, fired with grief,
Drew swords and took up spears, attacking blindly.
The ranks of the Laurentians dashed against them;
Then came an answering flood of Agyllines,   280
Trojans, Arcadians in painted armor,
All with one passion: settling this with war.
They tore apart the altars—while a wild storm,
A ruthless rain of iron filled the sky—
And stole the bowls and braziers. King Latinus   285
Fled with his routed gods. The truce was broken.
Men seized the reins of chariots, or vaulted
Onto their mounts and drew their threatening swords.
Messapus, keen to spoil the truce, rode headlong
At Aulestes the Etruscan, who wore emblems   290
Of kingship. As the poor man backed away,
He hit an altar, which he tumbled over
Onto his head. Excitedly, Messapus
Galloped up with his spear. While the king pleaded,
The rider loomed and struck and jeered, "He's finished—   295
A better offering for the gods above."
The Italians ran to strip the still-warm body.

Corynaeus snatched a firebrand from the altar
And as Ebysus lunged for him, he thrust
The flame into his face. His giant beard   300
Blazed, with a stinging stench, and the attacker
Laid hold of his befuddled enemy's hair,
Forced him down, kneeling hard, and pierced his side
With the unyielding sword. The shepherd Alsus
Dashed through the flying spears, but Podalirius   305
Pursued him with a sword; now his opponent
Lifted an ax in turn and split his brow
And chin, and spattered gore across his armor.
A sleep of iron pressed his eyelids down,
And left them closed for an eternal night.   310
Good Aeneas stood bareheaded, stretching out
An unarmed hand and shouting to his troops:
"Why are you racing to a brawl again?
Hold in your rage: we've ratified our terms.
Allow me to obey and fight alone.   315
Don't be afraid—my sword will seal this treaty.
Those rituals pledge that Turnus is for me."
The warrior was still yelling this harangue
When a winged arrow hissed its way to him—
But which hand sent it flying is a mystery.   320
Did chance bring the Rutulians so much glory,
Or a god? The fame for this great act was stifled:
Nobody boasted that he'd shot Aeneas.
Hope flared up hot in Turnus when he saw
Aeneas falling back, his captains panicked.   325
He called for arms and horses, proudly vaulted
Into the chariot and grabbed the reins.
Many strong men died in his flying path;
Others he rolled away half-dead; he trampled
Whole ranks, he poured their own spears on the routed.   330
As, by the chilly Hebrus, bloody Mars
Is stirred to clash his shield and storm to war;

He gives his team free rein to skim the flatlands
Faster than south and west winds; farthest Thrace
Groans with their hoofbeats, and the god's retainers—   335
Treachery, Rage, and black Fear—pound beside them:
So wildly Turnus drove his steaming horses.
They cantered on the pitiable carnage,
Spattering blood dew with their tearing hooves;
The sand they stamped across was mixed with gore.   340
Hand to hand he killed Thamyrus and Pholus,
And Sthenelus with a distant shot—as Glaucus
And Lades, raised by Imbrasus, their father,
In Lycia and given matching armor
For sparring or out-galloping the wind.   345
Elsewhere, Eumedes plunged into the fighting:
His name went back two steps; his famous valor
Recalled his father, Dolon, who at Troy
Had dared to name the chariot of Achilles
As payment for his spying expedition.   350
Diomedes offered him a different prize,   *Greek hero @ Troy*
Which kept him from aspiring to those horses.
Now Turnus saw the son far off, exposed,
And let a javelin chase him all that way,
Then leapt down from his chariot to straddle   355
The fallen, dying man. He placed a foot
On his neck and wrenched his shining sword away.
Sinking it in his throat, he taunted him:
"Trojan, here's Western ground for you to conquer:
Measure it with your body, get the prize   360
For daring to attack me. Look, your walls rise!"
He threw a spear to send Asbytes with him,
And Chloreus, Sybaris, Dares, and Thersilochus,
And Thymoetes, whom his bucking horse had thrown.
As when the north wind of Edonia howls   365
On the deep Aegean, driving waves to shore;
And winds swoop down and drive the clouds from heaven,

4/9/19

So from the path that Turnus cut, the columns
And battle lines were turning in a flood.
His soaring plume was quaking in the wind.   370
Phegeus, keen to stop his roaring onrush,
Dove straight into the way and yanked aside
The foam-soaked bridles of his whipped-up horses.
While he hung dragging from the yoke, a spear
Struck him—his shield had slipped. It penetrated   375
The breastplate with its double mesh and grazed him.
And yet he faced his enemy, heaved his shield up,
And tried to make some headway with his sword—
But the hurtling, whirling wheel propelled him headlong,
And he went sprawling. Turnus followed him.   380
The helmet left the neck exposed: he took
The head, and left the body on the sand.
Turnus' success spread death across the plain,
As Mnestheus, staunch Achates, and Ascanius
Took Aeneas, caked with gore, back to the camp,   385
His long spear propping every other step.
The arrow had snapped off. He gouged the wound,
Raging, and called to have the point cut out
With a broadsword reaching deep to where it hid:
Then he'd be able to go back and fight.   390
Iasus' son Iapyx came, the favorite
Of Apollo, who was once in love with him,
And gladly offered all his skills and powers:
The lyre and prophecy and his swift arrows.
But to prolong his dying father's life,   395
He chose to learn the properties of herbs
And the obscure, inglorious arts of healing.
Aeneas seethed in pain, propped on his huge spear
Among the warrior crowd, with grieving Iulus— *Ascanius / Aeneas's son*
But their tears didn't move him. Old Iapyx,   400
His robe hitched up in the physicians' manner,
Made many anxious trials with herbs of Phoebus—

Applied with no result, as when he prodded
The point or took it in his gripping forceps.
But no approach was lucky; no help came   405
From his patron god. Across the plain, cruel horror
Swelled, and disaster neared. Dust filled the sky.
Horsemen came swooping in, and swarms of arrows
Reached the camp's heart. Grim shouts went heavenward,
As young men fought and died in pitiless battle.   410
Now, shaken by her child's unmerited pain, *Aeneas'*
Venus picked dittany in Cretan Ida.
This is a healing herb with downy leaves
And trailing purple flowers. Wild goats know
To eat it when they're wounded by an arrow.   415
Venus, veiled in a dark cloud, brought it down
And steeped the secret remedy in water
A bright bowl held. She sprinkled in ambrosia
And panacea with its pleasant fragrance.
The moment old Iapyx bathed the wound,   420
The pain was gone—though he did not know why;
The blood dried from the bottom of the lesion;
The arrow yielded to his hand—unforced,
It dropped out, and the body's weakness vanished.
Iapyx took the lead and goaded them: • 425
"Why are you standing there? Quick, get his weapons!
It was no human power, no skill of mine
That saved your life, Aeneas. A greater being
Than me is sending you to greater exploits."
Hungry to fight, he'd strapped on both gold greaves   430
Already. Restively, he shook his spear.
With the shield adjusted at his side, the cuirass
Around his back, he gave Ascanius   *Aeneas's*
A steel embrace and kissed him through his visor.
"Learn courage and true work from me, my boy—   435
And Fortune's ways from others. I'll protect you
This time, and lead you where the great rewards are.

Take care to keep in mind, as you grow up,
Examples in your family to inspire you:
Hector your uncle, and your father, Aeneas."   440
Looming and shaking his huge spear, he rushed
From the gates, with Antheus and Mnestheus,
Who led a dense rank. Men poured out and emptied
The crowded camp, and soon the field was muddled
With blinding dust, and shaken and shocked with tramping.   445
From the earthwork, Turnus saw them coming at him;
The Italians saw them, and their blood ran cold.
Juturna was the first among the Latins
To recognize the sound, and she retreated.
Aeneas swept the deadly line with him   450
Across the plain. As storm clouds cross the sea
And block the sun (terror of wretched farmers,
Who, long before the start, foretell the downfall
Of trees, carnage of crops—the whole land ruined),
Winds soar ahead and bring the sound to land.   455
So the Rhoeteian leader led his army
At his opponents, all formations joining
In one mass. Thymbraeus killed huge Osiris;
Mnestheus, Arcetius; Achates, Epulo;
Then Gyas, Ufens; then the first to launch   460
At the Trojans died—Tolumnius the augur.
A shout rose skyward. Now it was Rutulians
In dust-choked flight across the battlefield.
Aeneas didn't stoop to bring them down
In death with duels on foot or with pursuit   465
Of threatening spearmen. He was chasing Turnus
Through the murk, and yelling challenges at Turnus.
The warrior girl Juturna, in alarm,
Toppled Metiscus, who was Turnus' driver,
Over the shaft and left him far behind,   470
Taking his place to steer with rippling reins—
Disguised as him, down to his voice and weapons.

Like a black swallow flying through the mansion
Of a rich man, across his lofty halls,
Gathering scraps to feed her chattering nestlings,   475
Calling in empty porticoes and circling
The cisterns: so Juturna sped her chariot
Through her enemies, and everywhere she went,
She made a show of her exultant brother—
But swept him far away from any fighting.   480
Aeneas tracked him on this winding path
Toward a confrontation, calling through the remnants
Of the ranks. When he could glimpse his enemy,
And fought to catch up with the fleeing team,
Juturna merely turned the chariot.   485
What should he do? As on chaotic currents,
His purposes were pulled conflicting ways.
Messapus happened to be carrying
Two pliant, iron-pointed spears. He ran up,
Aimed one and hurled it for a certain strike.   490
Behind his shield, Aeneas dropped to one knee,
But when the speeding spear passed over him,
It grazed the helmet, ripping off the plume.
His anger flared up at the sneak attack.
When he saw Turnus' chariot receding,   495
He called on Jove, the broken truce's altars,
Then plunged straight in, with Mars now favoring him.
He launched a slaughter—horrifying, cruel,
And random—that gave full rein to his anger.
What god will sing for me such suffering—   500
Deaths of all kinds, the deaths of chiefs, whom Turnus
And the Trojan hero harried back and forth
Across the plain? Jove, did you will this clash
Of nations that would live as friends from then on?
Where the Trojan onrush met its first resistance,   505
Aeneas deftly killed Rutulian Sucro,
Driving his cruel sword through the fence of ribs

At his side—the wound that brings on death the fastest.
Turnus threw brothers, Amycus and Diores,
From their horses, then he dealt with them on foot,   510
One with a javelin, one with a sword,
And hung his chariot with their bleeding heads.
Aeneas sent Talos, Tanaïs, and Cethegus
To death in one charge—then forlorn Onites,
Peridia's son, a Theban; Turnus killed   515
Two brothers from Apollo's Lycia;
And Menoetes, futile in detesting war:
A poor Arcadian, he'd fished rich streams
At Lerna, knowing nothing about service
To the powerful; his father sowed hired ground.   520
Like fires launched into a withered forest
From either side, to set its bay trees crackling;
Or like two frothy rivers crashing down
From mountain heights and dashing to the sea,
Each ravaging its path: with so much force   525
Aeneas and Turnus swept the battlefield.
Their rage swelled as it never had; their hearts burst,
Unconquered. They attacked with all their strength.
Murranus boasted of his ancient family
And claimed a pure descent from Latin kings.   530
Aeneas' whirling giant boulder dashed him
Onto the ground. The wheels propelled him forward
Beneath the reins and yoke. Swift, battering hooves
Trampled him down—his horses didn't know him.
Hyllus charged in untrammeled fury; Turnus   535
Answered him with a spear to his gold helmet.
It pierced the forehead, lodging in the brain.
Cretheus, bravest of the Greeks, was no match
For Turnus. When Aeneas came, Cupencus
Could find no safety in his gods. The poor man   540
Gained just a short delay from his bronze shield.
The Laurentian fields saw your death too, Aeolus—

Stretched on your back, you covered no small space—
Though the Greek phalanx couldn't bring you down,
Nor Achilles, who was toppling Priam's kingdom.   545
Your halls were at Lyrnesus, under Ida:
Your finish line was here, your tomb this ground.
All the lines turned to fight now—all the Latins,
And Trojans, Mnestheus and keen Serestus,
Horse-tamer Messapus, brave Asilas, Tuscans   550
In a wedge, the Arcadian horsemen of Evander,
Each struggling on his own, with all his power—
No rest, no pause in that tremendous fight.
Aeneas' lovely mother prompted him
To make a quick deployment to the walls   555
And stun the Latins with a new disaster.
While tracking Turnus through the hostile lines,
And looking all around, he saw the city
Peaceful—untouched by all the strife. The vision
Of a wider battle roused him instantly.   560
He called his captains, Serestus, Sergestus,
And Mnestheus, and climbed a mound to speak.
His army hurried in to crowd around him,
And listened with their shields and spears still hoisted:
"Obey, and don't waste time. Jove's on our side.   565
It's a quick change of plans, but don't hang back.
Unless the guilty town Latinus rules
Accepts our terms and comes beneath our yoke,
I'll raze its smoking rooftops to the ground.
No, maybe I should wait till Turnus chooses   570
To fight with me and lose a second time.
Trojans, this evil war is his creation.
Bring torches, quick! Enforce our pact with fire."
Now all his forces raced to the attack:
And in a massive wedge made for the walls.   575
Ladders and fire suddenly appeared.
Men scattered to the gates and cut the guards down,

Or made the sky dark with their hurtling weapons.
Aeneas at the front, below the ramparts,
Shouted, stretched out his hand, accused Latinus,   580
And called the gods to witness: he was forced
To war again—a second pact was broken.
The frightened people of the town were wrangling:
Some called for the front gates to be flung open
To the Trojans, and the king forced to the ramparts.   585
Others brought arms, persisting with defense—
As when a shepherd tracks bees to the crannies
Of a pumice cliff and fills it with sharp smoke,
Making them swarm in their wax citadel,
In terror and loud-buzzing, sharpening anger;   590
A black reek billows through their home; inside,
It's whirring shrilly as the smoke pours out.
Another blow to the tormented Latins
Shook the whole town with grief to its foundations.
From her rooms, the queen saw enemies encroaching,   595
The walls attacked, fire flying to the rooftops—
But no Turnus, no Rutulian counterforce.
The wretched woman thought the youth had died,
And maddened by the sudden agony,
She cried she was to blame for these disasters,   600
And babbled in the wildness of her grief.
Prepared to die, she ripped her purple robe
And hung a cruel noose from a lofty beam.
News of this great loss reached the Latin women.
Lavinia tore her hair and scratched her cheeks—   605
And all those with her raved, hysterical.
The sounds of mourning echoed from the palace.
The tragic story traveled through the city,
Spreading despair. Latinus' clothes were tattered,
His white hair smeared with dust. The suicide   610
And the city's downfall stunned him. He kept blaming
Himself: he hadn't readily accepted

Trojan Aeneas as his son-in-law.
The warrior Turnus, at the field's far side,
Was chasing a few stragglers, slowing down,   615
His pleasure in his horses' onslaughts fading,
When the wind carried him the sound of shouting,
Signal of some new horror. The grim roar
Of a town in turmoil struck his vigilant ears.
"What is the terrible loss that shakes the walls?   620
Why is this uproar flooding from the city?"
He pulled the reins and stopped, dazed with alarm.
His sister, though—she steered the chariot,
Looking just like Metiscus, Turnus' driver—
Came back with this: "Let's chase the sons of Troy here.   625
We've started with success—there's more to come.
Others are able to defend their homes.
Aeneas is assailing the Italians.
Let's hurl death at the Trojans, and you'll leave
With no less honor, and no fewer killed."   630
Turnus replied: "My sister,
I recognized you ever since you ruined
The truce, and threw yourself into this war.
Why bother now to hide your holy presence?
Who sent you from Olympus on this mission—   635
To see your hapless brother's brutal death?
What can I do? What stroke of luck could save me?
Murranus died—I saw, he called to me;
No one still living is a dearer friend—
When a massive wound brought down his massive body.   640
Poor Ufens fell but cannot see my shame now.
The Trojans have his weapons and his body.
Should I let them raze the town (that's all that's missing)?
And not put Drances' insults to the sword?
And will this country see me run away?   645
Is death so terrible? Spirits below,
Bless me! The gods above have turned away.

My soul descends untouched by cowardice.
I'm worthy of my glorious ancestors."
A horse came dashing, foaming at the mouth,   650
Through the ranks of enemies and brought him Saces,
Who had been wounded in the face. He pleaded,
"Have mercy on your people—you're our last hope.
Aeneas, in the thunder of his onslaught,
Brings ruin for the towers of Italy.   655
Torches fly to the roofs already. Latium
Now looks to you. The king himself, Latinus,
Doesn't know who his son is, or what treaty
Should bind him, and the queen, your faithful friend,
Has killed herself, fled from the light in terror.   660
Only Messapus and Atinas' zeal
Holds the line at the gates—though hemmed by close ranks
Of swords that bristle like an iron wheat field.
And here you drive around on empty grass."
Turnus was stunned to hear of these reversals.   665
He stood and stared in silence. In one heart
Surged endless shame, madness infused with grief,
Love spurred by fury, and the pride of courage.
The moment the clouds scattered from his mind,
He turned his burning wide eyes to the walls,   670
Looked wildly from his chariot at the city.
The flames were rolling up through every story,
A skyward stretch of waves that seized the tower—
Which he himself had raised, with a dense network
Of beams, wheels underneath, and lofty gangways.   675
"Sister, now fate has won. Don't hold me back.
Let's go where god and brutal Fortune call us:
I am resolved to fight Aeneas, suffer
Anything, die. You'll see no more dishonor
In me. Grant me my final frenzy now."   680
He vaulted from the chariot and burst
Straight through the enemy ranks and clouds of spears

At a tearing run, deserting his sad sister,
Like a boulder plunging from a mountaintop,
Torn loose by wind, or by a scouring rainstorm   685
Or the loosening and undermining years;
Headlong, unstoppable, it speeds along,
Bouncing, and rolling with it trees and herds
And men. So through the scattered forces Turnus
Rushed to the city walls, where blood had soddened   690
The earth deep down, and the air sang with spears.
He waved his arm and shouted out his protests:
"Rutilians, stop! Put down your weapons, Latins!
Whatever fortune brings is mine. I'll pay
For the broken truce and settle this—it's fairer."   695
They all stepped back and made a space between them.
Father Aeneas heard the name of Turnus
And left the ramparts, left the city's towers,
Broke off all action, threw off all delay
In joy, and clashed his arms with nightmare noise,   700
Towering like a mountain—Athos, Eryx,
Or Father Apennine, who relishes
Rattling his oaks and rearing his white head.
The Rutulians, all the Latins, and the Trojans
Turned avidly to look: those on the high walls,   705
And those who worked their battering rams below.
Even Latinus was amazed to witness
The pair of giant heroes strip their armor
And fight it out—though born a world apart.
When they reached open ground, they started forward,   710
Launched their spears at each other from a distance,
And rushed to battle, with their bronze shields ringing.
The earth groaned. Now their swords struck, and the blows
Multiplied, in the thick of chance and courage.
As on Taburnus' heights or massive Sila,   715
Two bulls meet in a savage clash of horns;
The herdsmen back away from them, the herd

Stands mute in fear; the heifers wonder which
Will rule this woods—which will the herds all follow?
Brutally, they converge, exchanging wounds,   720
Straining their horns home; on their necks and shoulders
Blood gushes; the whole glade resounds with groans:
Trojan Aeneas met the Daunian hero
With that much force. The clang of shields filled heaven.
Now Jove himself held up a pair of scales,   725
Evenly balanced, for the pair of fates:
Who was condemned? Which side would Death weigh down?
Seeing a safe chance, Turnus darted forward,
Lifted his sword, and struck with all his strength.
The Trojans and the frightened Latins shouted.   730
The lines both held their breath. The treacherous sword broke,
Deserting its fierce master as it hit.
He saw the strange bare hilt: he was unarmed
And ran—he had to—faster than the east wind.
In his frantic rush to war, they say, he'd mounted   735
His chariot without his father's sword,
And grabbed his charioteer Metiscus' weapon.
This served him well in scattering the Trojans,
But when it fell on Vulcan's holy weapons,
The mortal blade, brittle as ice, was shattered.   740
Its pieces glittered on the tawny sand.
Turnus sought desperately for some way out
Across the plain, and wove erratic circles,
Since Trojans pressed around him, and a swamp
Blocked one side, and the looming walls the other.   745
Aeneas played his part, though sometimes slowed
By his wounded knee. Fervently, step by step,
He kept right at his panicked enemy's back;
As a hunting dog keeps baying at, keeps charging
A stag that's driven back against a river   750
Or a terrifying pen of bright red feathers;
In panic at the ambush and the high bank,

The prey runs back and forth in countless dodges.
The gaping jaws of the keen Umbrian hound
Have got him—almost—now—but snap on air.   755
Then a real outcry rose. The pools around them
Echoed. The whole sky thundered with the uproar.
On the run, Turnus screamed at the Rutulians—
Each one by name, and shouted for his own sword.
But Aeneas threatened instant death for any   760
Who came near, and to terrify them more,
He vowed he'd raze their town. He hobbled on,
Chased Turnus clear around five times, and five
The other way. They fought for no small prize
In a sporting match, but Turnus' life and blood.   765
An olive tree, with bitter leaves, had stood there,
Sacred to Faunus. Sailors saved from shipwrecks
Revered it: it was there they nailed their gifts
To Laurentum's god, and hung the clothes they'd promised.
The Trojans cut it down—though it was holy—   770
With other trees, to clear a space to fight on.
The spear Aeneas threw sped to the stump
And stuck there, anchored by the clinging root.
The heir of Dardanus crouched to yank it out:
The weapon might run down the man he couldn't.   775
A raving terror now took hold of Turnus:
"Faunus, and queenly Earth, I ask your pity.
Hold the spear—if I'm faithful in your rites,
Which Aeneas' mob, by making war, has spoiled."
This was his prayer, which didn't go to waste.   780
Aeneas struggled on at the tough stump,
But all his strength did not suffice to loosen
Its biting hardwood. While he stood there straining,
The Daunian goddess—in Metiscus' form—
Rushed up and gave her bother back his sword.   785
Venus, in rage—why was the nymph allowed this?—
Came near and tore the spear up from the ground.

The confident swordsman, the fierce, looming spearman,
Both tall, with their old weapons and new courage,
Took panting stands as Mars' competitors.   790
As Juno watched the battle from a gold cloud,
The all-powerful Olympian king addressed her:
"My wife, what's left to do? Is it not finished?
You do admit that destiny must raise
Aeneas to the stars, a god of Italy.   795
What hopes can keep you in these chilly clouds?
How could a mortal weapon strike a god?
What of the sword Juturna (you control her!)
Returned to Turnus, new strength for the conquered?
Give way at last, I beg you. Don't let grief   800
Gnaw you in silence—but I want an end
To brooding grievances from your dear mouth.
It's time now. You were free to hound the Trojans
On land and sea, ignite this evil war,
Destroy a house, bring mourning to a wedding.   805
I won't allow you more." The child of Saturn,
The goddess, answered, with her head bent humbly:
"Father Jove, god of power, I knew your will,
And left the earth and Turnus—otherwise
You wouldn't see me here, meek and accepting.   810
I'd be down on the front lines, ringed with flames,
Dragging the Trojans to the bitter fight.
I urged Juturna, yes, to help her brother—
Poor man—and sanctioned bolder acts to save him—
But never meant for her to draw her bow: 815
By the relentless spring of Styx, I swear it,
The only oath that binds the gods in heaven.
But I concede and leave the field, disgusted—
Begging one thing for Latium, for the greatness
Of your children, and no law of fate forbids it.   820
When they make peace with a propitious marriage—
Let them—and treaties and shared laws unite them,

Don't make the native Latin warriors change
Their ancient name to Teucrians. Don't impose
The clothes and speech of Troy. Let Latium be,   825
And grant it centuries of Alban kings,
And Roman stock strong with Italian courage.
Troy fell. Now let her name lie fallen with her."
The god, the earth's creator, smiled at her:
"Truly, you're Saturn's child too, my own sister: 830
You hold such waves of anger in your heart.
What good, though, has it done you? So be calm:
I grant your wish, you've won, I give up gladly.
The Ausonians will keep their speech and customs
And name unchanged. The Trojans will fade out   835
As they breed in. I'll introduce their rites,
But make one Latin people, with one language.
You'll see the new race, with Italian blood,
Surpass the world—and gods—in piety.
Nobody else will bring you greater worship."   840
Juno agreed and changed her mind, contented,
And at that moment left the cloud in heaven.
The father of gods now had a plan in mind
To force Juturna from her brother's side.
The twin fiends named for horror are the Dirae.   845
The Dead of Night gave birth to them together
With Megaera, hellish thing. She wound all three
With coiling snakes and gave them windy wings.
They serve before the throne of ruthless Jove
As goads of terror for poor humankind   850
When the ruler of the gods sows deadly plagues
Or menaces a guilty town with war.
One of this pair of demons Jove dispatched
From heaven to Juturna as an omen.
Fast as a whirlwind, she flew down to the earth.   855
Like an arrow that a Parthian or Cydonian
Sends spinning through the clouds—it's smeared with poison

(A fiendish gall that has no remedy)
And speeds unnoticed, whirring through the shadows:
So the child of Night made swiftly for the ground. 860
She saw the Trojan lines and Turnus' columns,
And in a moment changed into a small bird,
Which perches on deserted roofs, or tombs,
And sings—an evil omen—in the dark night.
The demon screeched and harried back and forth 865
In Turnus' face; her wings beat on his shield.
A strange, numb panic made his body helpless.
His hair stood up; his voice clung in his throat.
When Juturna, his poor sister, heard the far hiss
Of the Fury's wings, she tore her loosened hair, 870
Scratched her face bloody, pounded her breasts livid.
"Turnus, my brother, how can I help now?
What else must I endure? I have no skill
To keep you living. Can I fight this omen?
At last I'll leave the field. No need to threaten, 875
Hideous birds: I know your deadly wingbeats;
I know the will of Jupiter, high-minded—
And high-handed. But can this be how he pays
For my virginity? He made me deathless,
And yet if I could die, I'd end my anguish 880
And go with my poor brother through the shadows.
What is the good of my unending life
Without you? Can the earth gape deep enough
To drop me to the shades, though I'm immortal?"
With many sighs, the goddess draped her head 885
In a gray veil and plunged into the river.
Aeneas pushed ahead and shook his spear—
Big as a tree—and spoke from his fierce heart:
"What's the delay now, Turnus? Why back off?
It's not a race, but combat, hand to hand. 890
Change into every form. See what your courage
Or skill can do. Soar up into the sky,

Or find a hole down in the ground to hide in."
But Turnus shook his head. "I'm not afraid
Of *your* words, when the gods—and Jove—attack me."   895
He looked around: by chance, a massive boulder,
An ancient bulk, was lying on the plain,
A marker to solve conflicts over fields.
Twelve chosen men could scarcely shoulder it—
Men of the strength that earth brings forth today.   900
The hero grappled, grasped it, made a run
And rose and heaved it whirling at his rival.
But the familiar speed was not in Turnus,
Or the strength to lift and throw that giant stone.
His knees gave way, his blood was frozen hard.   905
The stone went rolling through the empty air,
But not so far that it could strike its target.
As, when at night our eyes are sealed with slumber,
We dream we can't run on by any effort,
And finally sink exhausted as we struggle;   910
The tongue is powerless, the body loses
The strength it knew, the voice and words are gone;
So the grim goddess blocked off every path
For Turnus' valor. Baffled and distracted,
He gazed at the Rutulians and the city—   915
And froze in dread: the spear was coming close.
Where could he run—or else attack?—and where
Was his chariot, and his sister driving it?
He paused. Aeneas shook the fatal spear,
Saw a good chance, and flung it from a distance   920
With all his might. No catapulted stones
Smash against walls like this. No thunderbolts
Strike with such noise. Strong as a hurricane,
It carried grim death through all seven layers
Of the shield, and through the breastplate's lower edge;   925
It hissed straight through his thigh. And at the impact
Huge Turnus toppled forward on one knee.

The Rutulians sprang up, groaning. All around,
The hills groaned back, the upland groves re-echoed.
The humbled man looked up and stretched a hand out: 930
"I deserve it—I won't grovel for my life.
Use your good luck. But if an anguished parent
(As Anchises was, who gave you life) can move you,   *Aeneas' father*
Then pity Daunus—please—in his old age.
Send me, or else my corpse, back to my family.   935
You've triumphed: the Italians see me asking
For mercy, and Lavinia is your wife.
Lay down your hatred." There Aeneas stood,
Fierce, armed—but now his eyes had grown unsteady,
His hand still; and his halting change of heart   940
Grew stronger. Then he saw, on that tall body,
The belt with shining studs his young friend Pallas
Had once worn. Turnus, who had cut him down,
Displayed the hateful token on his shoulder.
Aeneas stared—the spoils commemorated   945
His wild grief, and he burned with hideous rage.
"Will you escape, in loot from one of mine?
It's Pallas who's now stabbing you, to offer
Your vicious blood in payment for your crime."
Incensed, he thrust the sword through Turnus' chest.   950
His enemy's body soon grew cold and helpless,
While the indignant soul flew down to Hades.

This is a list of only the most important characters and places, to fill in some background where it seemed necessary and otherwise to summarize their roles in the Aeneid.

Abas	The name of two friends of Aeneas, one Trojan and one Etruscan; possibly also the name of a Greek warrior from whom Aeneas wins armor in a skirmish during the sack of Troy
Acestes	A Trojan hero who hosted Aeneas and his followers in Sicily and founded Acesta there
Achaea	A region in the northern Peloponnese; *Achaeans* is often used to refer to the Greeks generally, especially those who besieged Troy
Achaemenides	A Greek who was stranded on the island of the Cyclopes by Ulysses and later rescued by the Trojans
Achates	Aeneas' retainer
Acheron	A river (or a lake) in Hades
Achilles	Son of the hero Peleus and the sea nymph Thetis; the greatest Greek warrior at Troy; slayer of the Trojan champion Hector
Actium	A headland in Acarnania in Greece with a temple of

	Apollo, near which Octavian, later called Augustus Caesar, defeated the Roman general Antony and the Egyptian ruler Cleopatra in a naval battle in 31 B.C. to become the uncontested ruler of Rome
Adriatic	The sea between Italy and the Balkan peninsula (where modern Serbia and Croatia are located)
Aegean	The sea between Greece and Asia Minor (where modern Turkey is located)
Aeneas	The son of the Trojan prince Anchises by the goddess Venus; he established in Italy the dynasty that would found and rule Rome
Aeolia	An island ruled by Aeolus, master of the winds; in the *Aeneid,* it is probably equivalent to Lipari, north of Sicily
Aeolus	A god, master of the winds
Agamemnon	King of Mycenae and head of the Greeks besieging Troy; he was murdered by his wife, Clytemnestra, and her lover Aegisthus on his return from Troy
Agenor	The founder of Dido's dynasty in Tyre
Agrippa	A politician and general of first-century B.C. Rome and a close associate of Augustus Caesar
Ajax	Two warriors by this name fought for the Greeks at Troy: Telamonian Ajas, or Ajax the Great, of Salamis; and Ajax the Lesser, of Locris, who raped Cassandra and was killed by Minerva, from whose temple he had dragged her along with the Palladium (sacred image of the goddess)
Alba or Alba Longa	The pre-Roman settlement of the Trojans in Italy
Albula	A pre-Roman name for the Tiber
Albunea	Both a grove and a fountain in Latium
Alcides	"Descended from Alcaeus," indicating Hercules
Allecto	One of the Furies
Alpheus	A Greek river that was believed to flow underground to Sicily
Amata	The queen of Latium, wife of Latinus and mother of Lavinia
Amazons	Woman warriors and allies of the Trojans
Anchises	The father of Aeneas
Andromache	Wife of the Trojan champion Hector

Anna	Sister of Dido
Antony	A Roman general who, along with the Egyptian ruler Cleopatra, was defeated by Octavian (later called Augustus Caesar) at the Battle of Actium in 31 B.C.
Apollo	Also Phoebus; the god of music, medicine, light, prophecy, and archery; twin brother of Diana and son of Jupiter and Latona; father of the healer Asclepius
Arcadia	A semi-wild district in the central Peloponnesus, the original home of Evander, king of Pallanteum in Italy
Ardea	City of the Rutulians and home of Turnus
Arethusa	The fountain in Sicily through which the Greek river Alpheus emerges
Argos	A kingdom in the Greek Peloponnesus; Greeks are often referred to as Argives
Argus	A monster with a hundred eyes, assigned by Juno to guard Jupiter's lover Io after he changed her into a cow to hide her from Juno; he was killed by Mercury
Argyripa	Another name for Arpi
Arpi	Also called Argyripa; an Italian city founded by Diomedes
Ascanius	Another name for Iulus
Assaracus	A Trojan king and ancestor of Aeneas
Astyanax	The infant son of Hector and Andromache who was killed by Neoptolemus after the fall of Troy
Atlas	The Titan who holds up the sky
Atreus	The father of Agamemnon and Menelaus
Augustus Caesar	The title adopted by Octavian when he became the first Roman emperor; the *Aeneid* was written under his auspices
Aurora	The goddess of dawn
Ausonia	Another name for Italy; the allies of Turnus and Latinus are sometimes called Ausonians
Aventine	One of the seven hills of Rome
Avernus	A lake in Italy that was said to be located near an entrance to Hades; the Cumaean Sybil had her cave there
Bacchus	The god of wine and ecstatic celebration; his followers were wild women known as Bacchantes
Baiae	A Roman resort town on the Bay of Naples
Bellona	A goddess of warfare

Nero

Berecynthian mother	Another name for Cybele
Brutus	The legendary Roman who overthrew the monarchy, which under Tarquin the Proud had become a tyranny, and established the Republic
Cacus	Vulcan's son, a ravaging giant in the city of Pallanteum, who was killed by Hercules
Camilla	A woman warrior and leader of the Volscians; ally of Turnus
Capitol	The summit of the Capitoline Hill in Rome, with an important temple of Jupiter
Carthage	Dido's city on the coast of North Africa
Cassandra	A Trojan princess who was given the gift of prophecy but also the curse that no one would believe her predictions; she was murdered along with Agamemnon
Castor	Twin brother of Pollux, with whom he spent alternate days in the upper and lower worlds; they were brothers of Helen of Troy
Catiline	A first-century B.C. Roman politician who conspired to overthrow the state but was defeated
Cato	A quintessentially stern Roman statesman and an opponent of the power of Carthage
Centaurs	Creatures that were half-human, half-horse
Cerberus	A monstrous three-headed dog that guarded the entrance to Hades
Ceres	The goddess of agriculture and mother of Proserpina, wife of Pluto
Charon	The ferryman who transported dead souls across the river Styx in Hades
Charybdis	A whirlpool in the straits of Messina located across from the cave of the monster Scylla
Circe	A sorceress who enchanted men, turning them into animals; she plays a prominent role in the *Odyssey*
Cloelia	A young hostage during the Estruscan siege of Rome in the late sixth century B.C., she escaped by dodging arrows and swimming the Tiber
Cocles	A Roman soldier who kept the army of Lars Porsena from Rome in the late sixth century B.C. by holding off the enemy until the bridge on which he was standing could be destroyed behind him
Cocytus	A river in Hades

Corinth	An important Greek city on the isthmus between mainland Greece and the Peloponnesus
Crete	A large Aegean island; it was the home of King Minos and his wife, Pasiphae, who mated with a bull and gave birth to the monstrous Minotaur
Creusa	A Trojan princess and the first wife of Aeneas; the mother of Iulus
Cumae	A colony near Naples and the home of the Sibyl, a priestess and prophetess of Apollo
Cumaean Sibyl	Prophetess and keeper of the entrance to Hades at Cumae, and in Book 6 Aeneas' guide in the underworld
Cupid	"Desire," the god of erotic love and son of Venus
Curetes	The indigenous people of Crete, who cared for the infant Jupiter
Cybele	A name for the Great Mother goddess of Asia Minor; the "Berecynthian mother" of Book 9
Cyclades	A group of Aegean islands
Cyclopes	One-eyed giants of Sicily; one of them, Polyphemus, was tricked and blinded by Ulysses
Cyprus	An Aegean island, important cult center for Venus
Cythera	An Aegean island in the waters off which Venus was born
Daedalus	"The Cunning One," the builder of the labyrinth on Crete in which the Minotaur was hidden; he invented wings to enable him to escape to Italy after he was imprisoned by King Minos
Danae	An Argive princess who was set adrift in a chest by her father after becoming pregnant by Jupiter; the mother of Perseus
Dardanus	The founder of Troy; Trojans are sometimes called Dardanians
Deiphobe	Another name for the Sibyl of Cumae
Deiphobus	A Trojan prince, the son of Priam and Hecuba, who married Helen after the death of his brother Paris
Delos	The Aegean island where Apollo and Diana were born and a chief site of their cult
Diana	The goddess of hunting, the moon, and childbirth; sister of Apollo; she was often joined with Hecate, a goddess of the underworld, and Selene, goddess of the moon, as a tripartite deity

Dido	Also called Elissa; the ruler of Carthage, which she founded after fleeing Tyre, where her husband had been murdered; the tragic lover of Aeneas who killed herself when he deserted her
Diomedes	A Greek hero at Troy who afterward founded the town of Arpi in Italy
Dis	Another name for Hades
Dodona	A famous oracular shrine of Jupiter
Egeria	A nymph who taught the Roman king Numa religious practices
Elissa	Another name for Dido
Elysium	The place in the underworld reserved for those who had led virtuous lives
Erebus	The god of darkness, and another name for the underworld
Eryx	1) A mountain in Sicily; 2) A Sicilian hero, son of Venus and Neptune
Etna	A volcano in Sicily and the legendary workshop of Vulcan and the Cyclopes
Etruria	A nation in Italy; the Etruscans, also called Tuscans, were allies of Aeneas against Turnus and Latinus
Euryalus	The friend of Nisus and his partner on an ill-fated Trojan mission during the war in Italy
Evander	The king of Pallanteum in Italy and the most important ally of Aeneas
Fabii	An important family of Roman statesmen over several centuries
Fates	The three goddesses who spun and cut the threads of mortal lives
Faunus	A king of ancient Italy, later a forest deity
Furies	Demons of female anger, especially active in avenging the murder of blood relatives
Ganymede	A Trojan prince who was raped by Jupiter but then given the honor of being cupbearer to the gods
Gaul	The region that is now France; the Gauls attacked Rome in the fourth century B.C. and were repulsed; the region became part of the Roman Empire in the first century B.C.
Geryon	A three-bodied giant killed by Hercules
Gorgon	A monster in the shape of a woman with hair of snakes;

	she had the power to turn onlookers to stone and was killed by Perseus; her head was then placed on Minerva's aegis
Gracchi	The brothers Tiberius and Gaius, who attempted to reform the Roman state in the late second century B.C.
Hades	Also called Dis, Orcus, and Pluto; the god of the underworld and husband of Proserpina; the terms can also refer to the underworld itself
Harpies	"Snatchers," the daughters of the sea nymph Electra and the sea god Thaumas; monstrous birds with the features of girls
Hecate	A goddess of the underworld and of witchcraft; she is often linked with Diana and Selene
Hector	A prince of Troy and its chief defender until he was killed by Achilles
Hecuba	The wife of Priam and queen of Troy
Helen	The most beautiful woman in the world and the wife of Menelaus of Sparta; her abduction by Paris at the instigation of Venus caused the Trojan War
Helenus	A Trojan prince who married the widowed Andromache and founded Little Troy in Epirus, a region that today comprises northwestern Greece and southern Albania
Helicon	A mountain in central Greece, home to the Muses
Hercules	A hero and son of Jupiter who achieved divinity after completing twelve superhuman labors
Hermione	The daughter of Helen and Menelaus
Hesperia	"The West," or Italy
Hippolytus	Also called Virbius, the name of his son as well; the son of Theseus who was killed through a plot of his stepmother, Phaedra, after he refused her advances
Hydra	A many-headed monster killed by Hercules
Icarus	The son of Daedalus, who fell to his death when his pair of wings that Daedalus invented for their escape from Crete melted in the heat of the sun
Ilia	The mother of Romulus and Remus by Mars
Ilium	Another name for Troy
Io	A love interest of Jupiter, who changed her into a cow to conceal her from Juno's jealousy
Iris	The goddess of the rainbow and a divine messenger

Iulus	Also called Ascanius, the son of Aeneas and Creusa and the founder of the Julian line that included Julius Caesar
Janus	A god with two faces who presides over entryways and beginnings and endings in general
Jove	Another name for Jupiter
Julius Caesar	Brilliant Roman general, murdered in 44 B.C. for his pretensions to autocracy; Octavian, also called Augustus, was his adoptive heir
Juno	The queen of the gods, daughter of Saturn, and wife and sister of Jupiter
Jupiter	Also called Jove, Greek name Zeus; the son of Saturn, he became ruler of the gods after he defeated his father and the other Titans
Juturna	The sister of Turnus, deified after her rape by Jupiter
Laocoön	A Trojan priest of Neptune
Laomedon	A king of Troy who brought on Neptune's curse by refusing to pay him after he built the walls of the city
Latinus	The king of Latium, husband of Amata and father of Lavinia, who refuses to give his daughter in marriage to Aeneas and allies himself with Turnus
Latium	Latinus' kingdom in Italy
Latona	A nymph, the mother of Apollo and Diana by Jupiter
Lausus	The son of Mezentius
Lavinia	A princess of Latium who is betrothed to Turnus but destined for marriage with Aeneas; her father's refusal to give her to Aeneas starts the war between the Italians and Trojans
Leda	The mother of Helen of Troy, who was raped by Jupiter in the form of a swan
Lethe	The river in Hades that the dead must cross, which makes them forget their previous lives
Libya	A region on the coast of North Africa
Lupercal	The grotto where the she-wolf nursed the twins Romulus and Remus, who had been exposed to die
Luperci	Priests who conducted the fertility ritual, the Lupercalia
Manlius	A Roman general who defended the Capitol from an attack by the Gauls in the fourth century B.C.
Marcellus	1) a Roman general during the Second Punic War (218–201 B.C.); 2) Augustus' nephew, who died young

Mars	The god of war
Megaera	One of the three Furies
Memnon	An Ethiopian king and ally of Priam at Troy
Menelaus	The king of Sparta and cuckolded husband of Helen of Troy
Mercury	The messenger god and conductor of souls to the underworld
Messapus	A son of Neptune and ally of Turnus
Metabus	The expelled king of Privernum and father of Camilla
Mettus	A legendary early ally of Rome from Alba Longa who was torn to pieces by horses for hanging back from a crucial battle
Mezentius	The deposed king of Etruscan Caere and an ally of Turnus
Minerva	Also called Pallas; in Greek, Athena; the goddess of wisdom, warfare, and women's handicrafts
Minos	A king of Crete who built the labyrinth and later became a judge of souls of the dead in Hades
Mnestheus	A lieutenant of Aeneas'
Mummius	The Roman general who captured Corinth in 146 B.C.
Musaeus	A legendary singer
Mycenae	The kingdom in the Peloponnesus ruled by Agamemnon, leader of the Greeks at Troy
Myrmidons	Achilles' Thessalian warriors at Troy
Neoptolemus	Also called Pyrrhus; a Greek hero at Troy, the son of Achilles, who married Hermione, the daughter of Helen and Menelaus
Neptune	The god of the sea, who built the walls of Troy but then turned against the city
Nisus	The friend of Euryalus and his partner on an ill-fated Trojan mission during the war in Italy
Numitor	A king of Alba Longa and the father of Ilia
Olympus	The home of the gods, at the top of Mount Olympus on the border between Macedonia and Thessaly
Orcus	Another name for Hades
Orestes	A Greek prince who killed his mother, Clytemnestra, in revenge for her murder of his father, Agamemnon, and was driven insane by the Furies
Orion	The Hunter constellation; its setting was thought to predict storms

Orpheus	A musician who entered Hades in an attempt to retrieve his dead wife, Eurydice
Palatine	One of the seven hills of Rome
Palinurus	Aeneas' helmsman
Pallas	1) Evander's son; 2) Evander's ancestor; 3) another name for Minerva
Pan	Half-man, half-goat god of the wilderness and herding
Paris	The Trojan prince who caused the Trojan War by his adulterous union with Helen
Pasiphae	A queen of Crete, cursed with love for a bull, who became the mother of the Minotaur by it
Paulus	The Roman general who defeated King Perseus of Macedonia in 168 B.C.
Peleus	The father of Achilles
Pentheus	A king of Thebes, cursed and led to his death by Bacchus for barring Bacchic rites from his city
Phaedra	A queen of Athens and the wife of Theseus who was cursed by Venus with an insane love for her stepson, Hippolytus
Phaeton	The child of the Sun, who attempted to drive his father's chariot and was killed when he could not control the horses
Phlegethon	A river of lava in Hades
Phoebus	"Shining," another name for Apollo
Phrygia	A region in Asia Minor that was subject to Troy; Trojans are sometimes referred to as Phrygians
Pirithous	A friend of Theseus who was condemned to perpetual torture in Tartarus for attempting to kidnap Proserpina, queen of the underworld
Pluto	Another name for Hades
Pollux	The twin brother of Castor, with whom he spent alternate days in the upper and lower worlds
Polyphemus	The Cyclops blinded by Ulysses
Porsenna	A legendary Etruscan king and supporter of the exiled Tarquin
Praeneste	A city in Latium
Priam	The king of Troy at the time of the Trojan War; husband of Hecuba and father of fifty sons, including Hector and Paris
Proserpina	Also called Persephone; the queen of Hades and wife

	of Pluto, who spent the spring and summer with her mother, Ceres, in the upper world
Pygmalion	The brother of Dido and the murderer of her husband Sychaeus
Pyrrhus	Another name for Neoptolemus
Quirinus	A native Italian god and another name for Romulus
Remus	The twin brother of Romulus, murdered by him
Rhoeteum	A promontory near Troy; "Rhoeteian" can be used for Trojans
Romulus	Also called Quirinus; a descendant of Aeneas, the son of Mars and twin brother of Remus, and the founder of Rome
Rutulians	Turnus' tribe in Italy, living near where Rome was to be
Samos	An Aegean island with an important temple of Juno
Sarpedon	A son of Jupiter and an ally of Troy during the Greek siege
Saturn	A Titan, the father of Jupiter and Juno, and the original ruler of Italy; he was driven there after being deposed from kingship of the gods by Jupiter
Scipios	A family of Roman statesmen and generals important in the third and second centuries B.C.
Scylla	A sea monster lurking in the Straits of Messina across from the whirlpool Charybdis
Serestus	A lieutenant of Aeneas'
Sergestus	A lieutenant of Aeneas'
Sibyl	A prophetess; in the *Aeneid* the keeper of the entrance to Hades at Cumae, and Aeneas' guide in the underworld
Simois	A river near Troy
Sparta	A city in the Greek Peloponnesus, home to Helen and Menelaus
Styx	A river in Hades; oaths sworn by the gods on Styx were binding
Sychaeus	The husband of Dido in Tyre, murdered by her brother Pygmalion
Syrtes	Sandbanks off the northern coast of Africa
Tarchon	An Etruscan ally of Aeneas
Tarpeia's Rock	Also called the Tarpeian Rock; the cliff on the Capitoline Hill from which criminals were flung; named after the legendary traitor Tarpeia

Tarquin	The name of the last two legendary kings of Rome
Tartarus	A gulf in the underworld, and also a term for the underworld in general
Tatius	A king of the Sabines at the time of Romulus
Teucer	The original ancestor of the Trojan royal house, so that Trojans are often referred to as Teucrians; also a Greek warrior who fought at Troy and was later an exile from his kingdom, Salamis
Theseus	The killer of the Minotaur (with the help of Ariadne) and later a king of Athens; he joined his friend Pirithous in the attempted kidnapping of Proserpina
Thetis	A sea nymph and the mother of Achilles
Tibur	A city in Latium
Tisiphone	One of the Furies
Tithonus	The husband of Dawn (the goddess Aurora)
Torquatus	A renowned Roman general of the fourth century B.C. who had his own son executed for fighting against orders
Triton	A sea god
Troy	Also called Ilium; the city of Aeneas in Asia Minor, destroyed by the Greeks after the ten-year Trojan War
Turnus	A prince of the Rutulians in Italy, who is betrothed to Lavinia and wages war to prevent the Trojans from settling and Aeneas from marrying her
Tuscans	Another name for Etruscans
Tyre	The Phoenician island city from which Dido fled to found Carthage
Ulysses	The king of Ithaca and an important Greek hero at Troy
Venus	The goddess of love and the mother of Aeneas by Anchises
Vesta	The goddess of the hearth
Virbius	The new name of Hippolytus in Italy; also the name of this hero's son
Vulcan	The god of fire and metalworking and the husband of Venus
Xanthus	A river at Troy